Advance Pra

"Readers will relish the connected Primas of Power storylines in this sensational final installment."

—*Library Journal* (starred review)

"Funny, sexy, and heartwarmingly genuine, *Along Came Amor* is the perfect ending to the Primas of Power series and highlights the very best of Alexis Daria's storytelling prowess. I rooted for these characters from the first page and adored every moment of Roman and Ava's journey to their well-deserved HEA."

—Mia Sosa, *USA Today* bestselling author

"Sexy, flirty, and fun, this romance entranced me from the first page. I adored Roman and Ava, and watching two characters with seemingly opposing desires embracing the unexpected—and letting themselves be loved—was pure joy."

—Ashley Herring Blake, *USA Today* bestselling author of *Iris Kelly Doesn't Date*

"I sighed, I swooned, I smiled, I blushed! Ava and Roman are so real, so beautifully flawed, and yet so perfect for each other. I was rooting them from page one!"

—Adib Khorram, *USA Today* bestselling author of *I'll Have What He's Having*

"With the meet-cute of my dreams and the emotional connection that kept me begging for more, Alexis Daria gives us all the delicious tension readers crave. *Along Came Amor* will capture your heart!"

—Julie Soto, *USA Today* bestselling author

"I've always been a huge fan of Alexis Daria's books, and I truly think that *Along Came Amor* is her best book yet. Ava and Roman are complex, fully realized characters, and their chemistry leaps right off the page. I savored every minute of their sweet love story and their HEA is so well deserved. I didn't want the book to end!"

—Kristina Forest, *USA Today* bestselling author of *The Partner Plot*

"For all who shy away from taking up space, who put the wishes of others before their own, Daria has crafted a hero in Roman Vázquez that is the balm your soul needs and the fuckboi fantasy your body desires."

—Tracey Livesay, author of the American Royalty series

"*Along Came Amor* by Alexis Daria is a spicy, hilarious, and oh-so-real romance about love that sneaks up on you when you least expect it. . . . Sexy, smart, and full of heart, this is a love story that's as messy, funny, and unapologetically complicated as real life."

—Nikki Payne, author of *Sense, Lies and Sensibility*

"Only Alexis Daria could create a romance this stunning. The chemistry between Roman and Ava explodes off the page against the backdrop of a loving yet imperfect family. Sexy, vibrant, and electric, *Along Came Amor* will thrill long-time fans and charm new readers."

—Lily Chu, bestselling author of *Drop Dead*

"The most satisfying ending to one of my all-time favorite romance series. Sensual, hilarious, spicy, and full of heart. *Along Came Amor* is an emotional roller-coaster ride that had me hooting and hollering the entire way. Ava and Roman's chemistry sizzles and their HEA is heart-bursting. Alexis Daria does not miss!"

—Susan Lee, author of *Seoulmates* and *The Name Drop*

ALONG CAME AMOR

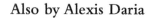

Also by Alexis Daria

A Lot Like Adiós
You Had Me at Hola

What the Hex (novella)
Amor Actually (anthology)

Take the Lead
Dance with Me
Dance All Night (novella)

ALONG CAME AMOR

A NOVEL

ALEXIS DARIA

AVON

An Imprint of HarperCollins*Publishers*

ALONG CAME AMOR. Copyright © 2025 by Alexis Daria. All rights reserved. Printed in the United States of America. No part of this book may be used or reproduced in any manner whatsoever without written permission except in the case of brief quotations embodied in critical articles and reviews. For information, address HarperCollins Publishers, 195 Broadway, New York, NY 10007.

HarperCollins books may be purchased for educational, business, or sales promotional use. For information, please email the Special Markets Department at SPsales@harpercollins.com.

Avon, Avon & logo, and Avon Books & logo are registered trademarks of HarperCollins Publishers in the United States of America and other countries.

FIRST EDITION

Interior text design by Diahann Sturge-Campbell

Title page art © Daiquiri / Shutterstock, Inc.

Library of Congress Cataloging-in-Publication Data has been applied for.

ISBN 978-0-06-296000-9

25 26 27 28 29 LBC 5 4 3 2 1

For my baby.
And for all the recovering perfectionists out there.

In loving memory of:
Isabel, Juan, Renee, and Domingo

ALONG CAME AMOR

Chapter 1

October

To: Ava Rodriguez
From: Pam Perez
Subject: Re: Divorce Petition

Good news. It's done. The Court has signed the Judgment of Divorce. I'll handle filing and sending the papers.

If you need anything else, don't hesitate to reach out.

—Pam

Perez & Russo Family Law LLP

As an English teacher, Ava Rodriguez believed a character's backstory provided vital context for their behavior.

Therefore, to understand her reaction to the email that had

just landed in her inbox, anyone looking over her shoulder would need to know three things.

The first was that a year and a half ago, Ava's husband, Hector, had arrived home from work one evening and announced his hitherto unmentioned dream to travel the world as a photojournalist—oh, and by the way, he no longer wanted to be married to Ava.

Two, he'd said, "I'll be back for my stuff" on his way out the door, and then did not, in fact, ever return for his stuff.

And finally, after Hector failed to initiate proceedings for the divorce *he'd* insisted upon, Ava had, as she'd done so many times during their marriage, taken care of everything herself.

Without this context, Ava's response to the email—*good fucking riddance*—might have appeared callous, cynical, or even bitter. And Ava was none of those things.

Well, maybe a little cynical, after everything that had happened. But never callous, and only occasionally bitter within the privacy of her own mind.

The sentiment wasn't toward her lawyer, of course. Pam had been nothing but kind.

But *good fucking riddance* to Hector, to their marriage, and to the process of disentangling herself from a ten-year relationship.

At least the email had arrived while she was alone in a hotel room, and not, god forbid, while she was around her *family*.

From her rolling suitcase, Ava pulled out her main planner—an A5 six-ring binder with a padded leather cover in blush pink, stuffed to the gills with custom inserts. She never went anywhere without it, and that included dinky little education conferences like this one.

Sitting on the bed, she leaned against the headboard and opened the planner on her lap. She flipped to the checklist labeled "Divorce Tasks" and zeroed in on the final unchecked box. Her fingers itched to mark it as "done," already anticipating the hit of dopamine from completing a goal.

Instead, she ripped out the checklist and crumpled it in her fist.

On the next page, another list waited for her. At the top, in big block letters, was a question.

WHO IS NEW AVA?

Below that, hand lettered in the brush script she'd spent hours perfecting, were three statements.

> *New Ava embraces life boldly.*
> *New Ava is confident in her own skin.*
> *New Ava is open to new experiences.*

She'd started The New Ava List while visiting her cousins Jasmine Lin Rodriguez and Michelle Amato in California earlier that week, as a sort of pep talk before getting a Brazilian wax. The list had been Jasmine's idea, the wax had been Michelle's.

After selecting a purple brush pen from her "Teaching is a Work of Heart" zippered pouch, Ava added another item to the page.

> *New Ava is ready to move the fuck on.*

There. Maybe writing it down would make it true.

She set the planner aside and picked up her phone from the nightstand. Her cousins wanted to know the second the divorce was finalized, so she opened the Primas of Power group text and started a video call. As it rang, Ava fixed an easy smile on her face, one she hoped said, *I'm absolutely fine, no need to worry.*

Neither of them answered.

Ava let the smile fade.

A text from Michelle popped up a second later, followed immediately by one from Jasmine.

Michelle: In a meeting. What's up?

Jasmine: I'm on set, can we touch base later?

Oh, right. It was only Friday afternoon in Los Angeles, of course they were still working. She typed back a reply.

Ava: Sure, maybe later.

It was for the best. Commiserating with her cousins wasn't the same since Jasmine had gotten engaged to fellow actor Ashton Suarez, and Michelle had started dating her childhood best friend, Gabriel Aguilar. Jas and Mich would try to cheer her up, but lately, that only made things worse.

Ava was thrilled for her cousins. They both deserved to find their happily-ever-afters. But she had no interest or desire to get so wrapped up in another person ever again.

A group dinner for the conference attendees was due to start in a few minutes. But as she was refreshing her curls in the bathroom mirror, she paused to study her reflection. Her hazel eyes looked dull and distant, as they had for the past year and a half.

Was this really how she was going to celebrate her divorce? With rubbery chicken and small talk about standardized testing?

Fuck that.

She tossed the nude gloss she'd been about to apply back into her makeup bag and swapped it out for a muted red lip stain, painting her mouth with defiant swipes.

So what if she was stuck in a hotel on the Jersey Shore during the off-season? At the very least, she could swing by the lobby bar to enjoy a nice, stiff drink.

Especially since she wasn't enjoying a nice, stiff anything else these days.

Jeez. She was starting to sound like Michelle.

Unfortunately, it was an accurate assessment. Because while Ava wasn't anxious to jump into anything resembling a serious relationship—now or ever again—she *was* ready to jump on a man.

Alas, the prospects from the dating apps she'd tried earlier in the year had left her so depressed, she'd deleted them before messaging anyone.

Grabbing her phone, she texted Damaris Fuentes, her conference roommate and best work friend.

Ava: What time are you getting here?

Damaris: Around 11. How were the workshops?

Ava: You didn't miss anything. How's the astrology class?

Damaris: Surprising amount of math.

Ava: It's a good thing you're a math teacher.

Damaris: Right?

Ava hesitated, then decided to go for it. She had to tell *someone*.

Ava: My lawyer emailed.

Damaris: And?

Ava: The divorce is finalized.

Damaris: I meant, "And how are you doing?" not, "And what did the email say?" So, I ask again: And?

Ava: And . . . I'm going to the bar to get a drink.

Damaris: By yourself?

Ava: Yes.

Damaris: Good! Do NOT order rosé.

Ava: But I like rosé!

Damaris: You ALWAYS drink rosé. Get something else.

Ava: Like what?

Damaris: I don't know. Something new and different. Trust the Universe!

Ava stopped herself from replying with the eye-roll emoji. As far as she could tell, "the Universe," as Damaris described it, was by turns a benevolent dictator or a prankster with a juvenile sense of humor. Sort of like Ava's cousin Sammy.

Either way, not to be trusted.

From the bed, her own purple brush script urged her to *move the fuck on.*

She headed down to the bar, determined to do just that.

Chapter 2

It was early evening and the restaurant in the Dulce Playa Hotel's lobby wasn't full. Only a few people sat in booths scattered around the open space. The dim lighting emphasized the tasteful deep blue and gold color scheme, and a classic rock song played low in the background.

Ava perched her butt on one of the high chairs stationed at the bar. With her long legs, she was practically the same height as when she'd been standing.

Old Ava would've been mortified to drink at a bar by herself, but New Ava had a book in her purse and she would survive this.

Turning over the menu, a lovely piece of textured navy blue cardstock with gold foil lettering, she immediately spotted the rosé option. She was tempted to order it anyway, regardless of Damaris's decree, but one glass cost more than an entire bottle did at Ava's local liquor store. Besides, she was starting a new chapter, right? Might as well let the Universe decide for her.

Closing her eyes, Ava swirled her index finger for three seconds before jabbing it down on the signature cocktails menu. When she opened her eyes, she peered at the drink the Universe had chosen.

A Limón Dulce.

Hmm, maybe that was like lemonade. Could be refreshing. Despite being October, it was a hot, humid day.

Ava made eye contact with the bartender, a fresh-faced young woman with a rosy complexion and dark hair slicked into a low ponytail. She wore the Dulce's uniform of a black vest over a dark blue button-up with a nametag that read "Luz."

"What can I get for you?" Luz asked as she made her way over.

Ava offered a polite smile. "I'll have a Limón Dulce, please."

"You got it." Luz set a square napkin—dark blue, with the Dulce logo stamped in gold—in front of Ava and moved a few feet away to mix the drink in a cocktail shaker. As Luz poured the liquid into a martini glass, she asked, "You're here for the teacher's conference?"

Ava nodded. "How did you know?"

"I didn't think it was the other one." With a grin, Luz set the pale yellow drink on the napkin. "Enjoy."

Other one? Before Ava could ask, Luz moved away to help another customer. Ava murmured her thanks anyway, then discreetly sniffed the drink. The color bore an alarming resemblance to urine, but the crisp citrus scent reminded her of baking lemon bars with her little sister, Willow, in their father's kitchen. Ava lifted the glass to take a sip.

And nearly spit it back out.

Forget lemonade. This was more like furniture polish, strong and sour and nowhere close to the tangy sweetness she'd been expecting.

Ava couldn't control her grimace as she swallowed.

As the stinging in her mouth subsided, she set the glass back on the napkin and tried to school her features, hoping the bartender hadn't seen.

So much for new experiences. She'd just go upstairs, order French fries, and watch *Pride & Prejudice* for the millionth time. Alone.

The enormity of her loneliness hit her like a sledgehammer. She'd bottled things up during her marriage, acted like everything was fine throughout the divorce, but somehow, this disappointing drink was the last straw.

The need to talk to somebody, *anybody*, welled up in her like a tidal wave.

But there was no one.

Jasmine and Michelle were busy with their new lives. Damaris wouldn't be there until later that night. Ava's mother worked the night shift as a NICU nurse, and never mind her dad or stepmom—they tiptoed around the subject of divorce like it was a contagious sickness and Ava's father was in remission.

Eyes hot, she blinked hard and pushed her glass toward the other side of the bar. As she was opening her purse to pay, someone approached on her left.

Wary, Ava glanced at the newcomer. A ton of empty seats stretched along the bar, so why was somebody trying to sit right next to . . .

Holy shit.

Her thoughts stuttered to a halt as her gaze traveled over the man beside her, taking note of every handsome feature. Dark wavy hair with hints of silver at the temples. Strong jaw. Brown eyes, impossibly long lashes, and thick, straight brows. The faint lines at the corners of his eyes only added to his attractiveness, as if they were neon arrows inviting her to drown in their depths.

The word that came to mind was *dreamboat*. Old fashioned,

but it fit him as perfectly as the dark blue silk suit that accentuated his broad chest and shoulders.

On second thought, he could sit next to her *anytime*.

With a friendly smile, he gestured at her glass. "Something wrong with your drink?"

Shit. He must have seen her reaction. Embarrassment warmed her cheeks, but she tried to play it off, like the smooth timbre of his voice wasn't doing dark and delicious things to her. "Oh no, the drink's fine."

His expression turned skeptical. "The face you made when you tasted it says otherwise."

She waved a dismissive hand. "I'm not really thirsty anyway."

Eyes filled with amusement, he picked up the glass and sniffed. Then, to her surprise, he took a sip.

"Wow." With a slight raise of his brows, he set it back down and cleared his throat. "Did you order that on purpose?"

"I left it up to the Universe," she grumbled.

"What was that?"

"Nothing. I just wanted something . . . strong, I guess." She wasn't going to explain the concept of New Ava to him.

"This wasn't what you were expecting?"

"Not exactly."

When he smiled, soft laugh lines bracketed his mouth. "Let's get you something else."

"That's not—wait, what are you doing?"

He rounded the end of the bar as if it were the most normal thing in the world. "I'm going to make you a different drink."

Ava stared at him, aghast, and darted a look at the bartender. Luz was helping someone else down at the other end and paying this attractive stranger no mind.

"You can't just go behind the bar," Ava hissed at him.

Across from her, he leaned his forearms on the polished wood surface. "Why not?"

This man was handsome, but clearly lacking in common sense. Still, instead of walking away, she found herself answering his rhetorical question. "It's not allowed."

"Says who?"

She sputtered, trying to think of a response. "The law."

"What law?"

"I don't know, but I'm sure this violates the hotel's liquor license, at the very least."

His smile became conspiratorial. "I appreciate the concern, but I think they'll make an exception."

She got the distinct impression that she was walking into a trap. "And why's that?"

"Because I'm the owner. Roman Vázquez." He nodded to her purse. "Look me up before you have me arrested for impersonating a bartender."

Some part of her still felt like he was fucking around, but his self-assured expression had her pulling out her phone. She typed the name he'd given her into the search bar.

And there he was.

Roman Alejandro Vázquez, CEO of VQZ Ltd.

Ava did a quick scan of the results. First, a list of Dulce Hotel locations around the country, then a recent *Forbes* article about a real estate acquisition in Japan. Ava tried not to look at the headlines speculating his net worth, but it was impossible to miss the word *million* at the end. She zoomed in on a picture of him in a hotel lobby very much like this one, where he posed casually with one hand in his pants pocket, then she glanced at the man leaning against the bar. Same broad shoulders, same easy smile, same dreamy brown eyes.

What the photo did not capture was the way his brow quirked with amusement, his playful tone of voice, or the simmering heat in her chest caused by his equally obvious perusal of her.

"Well," she said through a throat suddenly gone dry. "That's you, all right."

"That's me." Roman's gaze flickered over her face. "And you are?"

Now that she knew he wasn't some overentitled asshole with no sense of propriety, she stuck her hand out for him to shake. "Ava. I'm here for the education conference."

"Nice to meet you, Ava." He reached across the bar to shake her hand. His grip was firm and dry, but warm. The lobby was well air-conditioned, and her imagination supplied a flash of those warm hands running down her cool arms. She fought off a shiver, then chided herself. Instead of picturing where else this stranger could touch her with those warm hands, she should've brought a sweater.

"Cold?" Mischief glinted in his eyes.

Ava's cheeks warmed. Was he *flirting* with her? She was saved from having to reply when the actual bartender hurried over.

"Do you need help with anything, Mr. Vázquez?"

He gave Luz a pleasant smile. "I'm good. Just getting back to my roots."

Once Luz left to help another guest, Roman picked up the shaker and gave it a spin before setting it down on the bar.

Ava raised her eyebrows. "Are you trying to impress me?"

The look he gave her could melt a popsicle in winter. "Is it working?"

Holy shit, he *was* flirting with her. She couldn't stop the smile that tugged at her lips. "A little."

"Only a little? I better step up my game." He grabbed a dark blue glass bottle out of the fridge behind the bar and rolled it down his arm to land in front of her. "Start with this."

Ava lifted it to look at the label. "What is it?"

"Sparkling water."

"Oh." She gave a little laugh and unscrewed the bottle before taking a sip to wash away the taste of the Limón Dulce.

Roman gave the martini glass in front of her a pointed look. "What were you going to do? Pay for it and not drink it, or drink it and suffer in silence?"

Ava sighed. "Pay for it and not drink it."

"Well, we can't have that." He slipped the offending lemon drink away and dumped it out. "How do you feel about rum?"

She twisted the cap back onto the water. "I only buy it to make coquito."

His eyebrows rose. "¿Tú eres Latina?"

"Puerto Rican on my dad's side. My mom is from Barbados."

"Boricua and Bajan. I bet you make a killer coquito."

She grinned. "Don't tell my grandmother, but I made a few adjustments to her recipe, and all my cousins agree mine is better."

"Don't worry, Ava. Your secret is safe with me."

Something about the way he said her name had goosebumps prickling up her spine.

Her cousins would know exactly what to do in this situation. Jasmine would toy with her hair and lean forward to show off her cleavage. Michelle would make a sarcastic quip, the kind that managed to be equal parts funny and suggestive.

But Ava wasn't like her cousins. She wasn't sensual or bold. She was practical and polite.

So she ignored her pounding heart and warm cheeks and just murmured, "Thank you."

Roman's gaze landed on her lips. She caught the rise and fall of his chest, like he was breathing deep.

"My pleasure," he said in a low voice, and then he turned, breaking the tension that had wrapped thickly around them, to grab a bottle. He flipped it over to his other hand and said, "Let's start with a tasting."

His movements were a blur as he spun a couple of napkins onto the bar and produced two small glasses from out of nowhere. He deftly poured a small amount of liquid into each.

Ava was, indeed, impressed. "How do you know how to do all this?"

"I didn't always own hotels," he said enigmatically, setting the first glass in front of her. "Smell this."

Ava lifted the glass. It contained less than an inch of dark amber liquid.

"Keep your lips parted as you sniff. You know how when something smells really strong, it's like you can taste it?"

When Ava nodded, he continued. "Así mismo. You have olfactory receptors on your tongue. It's part of the tasting experience."

Somehow, he even made "olfactory receptors" sound sexy. Ava parted her lips and brought the glass to her nose.

"What do you smell?" Roman's voice was soft, nearly seductive, but also curious. "There's no wrong answer."

She closed her eyes and inhaled. "It smells sort of sweet. Like caramel apple. Also a bit . . . woodsy?"

"Oak. From the barrels."

She opened her eyes in time to see him smile at her over the rim of his own glass.

"Take a small sip."

She did as he instructed, letting the rum flow over her tongue and paying close attention to the sensation and flavor.

"Now take another and tell me what you taste."

She rubbed her tongue against her palate, analyzing the flavors. "At first it's almost fruity, but then there's a bit of smokiness in there, rounding it out."

"Do you like it?"

"It's different," she said, then met his eyes. Hadn't she come to this bar looking for something new and different?

He watched her intently, a smile teasing the corner of his mouth. "That's a dark rum. It's made of a blend of rums that have been aged up to fifteen years." He held up a stout, sturdy-looking bottle. The black label read "Casa Donato Quince" in fancy gold lettering, with the faint outline of a large house and a number fifteen.

There was something about the way he cradled the bottle, not just like he was at ease behind a bar, but more proprietary.

"Do you own this too?" She gestured toward the logo and was rewarded when his handsome face broke into a wide grin.

"How did you know?"

She just smiled. "Lucky guess."

"What do you think of it?"

"I think if I'd just gulped it down, it would've been too strong, but drinking slowly like this, taking time to smell it and taste it . . ."

"That's how you drink a good sipping rum," he finished for her. "Savoring every drop."

Her heart thumped at the way he said "savor." She got the feeling he was a man who knew how to linger over the things he enjoyed.

"What are you doing?" she asked, when he shrugged his broad shoulders out of his suit jacket.

The look in his eye was playful, but hinted at darker pleasures. "Don't think I forgot about making you a drink."

"This isn't the drink?"

"Not even close." He folded the jacket and handed it to her. As Ava took it, she caught a whiff of his cologne and automatically parted her lips as she inhaled. It wasn't too strong—woodsy, with a hint of sweetness and spice, like his rum—but there was something erotic about the idea of tasting the scent of him.

The thought made her glance at his mouth. If she kissed him right now, would he also taste like all the flavors she'd teased out of the rum?

Ava quickly set the jacket on the seat beside her. They'd just met; she had no business thinking about tasting Roman's scent *or* his mouth.

Or any other part of him, for that matter.

She turned her attention back in time to see him roll up the cuffs of his sleeves, revealing thick forearms taut with muscle.

The sight made her swallow a whimper. This man was far too appealing.

Oblivious to her inappropriate thoughts, Roman launched into a flurry of movement, tossing bar supplies from one hand to the other, flipping them in the air and rolling them down his arm in a remarkable display of coordination and competency. By the end, there were two glasses sitting between them. Each held a large cube of ice, a couple inches of reddish orange liquid, and a swirl of orange peel.

Ava clapped. "Okay, now I'm impressed."

Roman executed a little bow. "Mission accomplished."

"So what is it?"

Roman spread his hands. "This," he said, "is my version of a rum Negroni, or, as my mother calls it"—he winced—"a 'Romy Negroni.'"

Her lips quirked. "Cute."

"Thanks. So are you."

She tilted her head and gave him an admonishing stare, but the effect was ruined by the smile tugging at her mouth. "Are you going to flirt or tell me about this drink?"

His grin was lightning quick and just as exhilarating. "Why not both?" But then he lifted one of the glasses, his agile fingers turning it as if it were a prism catching the light.

"A Negroni is an apéritif, meant to spark the appetite," he explained. "It has equal parts sweet, bitter, and spirit, usually sweet vermouth, Campari, and gin. I make this with a dark rum, dry vermouth, and Chinole—a passion fruit liqueur from the Dominican Republic."

"I don't think I've ever had a Negroni. I'm more of a 'Rosé All Day' kind of girl."

His brows drew together. "Then why not order that?"

She gave a little shrug. "I wanted something different tonight."

He nodded slowly, and she felt the weight of his simmering gaze like an embrace. He held his glass up in a toast. "To something different."

She repeated the words softly, unable to look away from him, but inside, she made another toast.

Here's to New Ava and trusting the Universe.

She lifted the Negroni to her nose to cover the flush rising in her cheeks. She inhaled first, identifying the citrus notes of passion fruit and orange, the caramel and oak of the rum, and a slight floral aroma. Then she took a small sip.

The cool liquid melted over her tongue, sharp but smooth, and she let out a hum of pleasure. Thanks to the tasting, she could recognize the flavors, appreciating the balanced blend of fruity and tart.

"Better?" Roman asked.

Ava lowered her glass. "Much. Thank you."

His grin expanded. "I'm glad."

He opened his mouth to say something else, but his watch buzzed, startling him.

"Excuse me for one moment." He squinted at his wrist as he typed something on the screen.

Ava sipped her drink and readied herself to say goodbye. Roman had turned her night around, but the man was a CEO—he definitely had more important things to do than sit around flirting with her.

But instead of making his excuses, Roman returned to her side of the bar. Moving his jacket, he perched on the stool and angled his body to face her. From all appearances, he seemed to be settling in, making himself comfortable.

"You said you're here for the teacher's conference?" he asked.

She toyed with her name necklace, the one Abuelo Willie had given her as a high school graduation present. "I am."

"So why are you alone at the bar instead of having dinner with your colleagues?"

She started to give her reasons—because Damaris wasn't there yet, or because the thought of the group dinner didn't appeal—but the phrasing of his question, paired with the kindness in his eyes, pulled the truth from her instead.

In a quiet voice, she said, "My divorce was finalized today."

"Ahh." Understanding dawned over his features, and she caught the way his eyes flicked to her bare left ring finger. She couldn't stop herself from touching the pad of her thumb to where her engagement ring and wedding band used to sit, before she'd sold them.

"Is this drink in celebration or lamentation?" Roman asked, his tone mild.

She huffed a humorless laugh and fiddled with the condensation gathering on her napkin. "Definitely celebration. I'm well rid of him."

"Ava."

"Hmm?"

His eyebrows creased with real concern. "Are you all right?"

At that simple question, something inside her snapped.

"No," she whispered. "I'm not."

And then the messy knot of feelings came tumbling out.

"It's over, and I'm glad it's over, but I have no idea what to do next with my life—which somehow feels worse than ending a ten-year relationship. What does that say about me? About my marriage?" Her voice rose as she picked up steam. "Plus my job sucks, my family is mad at me, and I can't even order a fucking drink!"

She gasped and clapped a hand over her mouth, as if to stem the avalanche of oversharing, but the damage had been done. "I'm so sorry. I don't know where all that came from."

There was nothing judgmental in his expression. "I don't mind."

Embarrassment all but dripped from her pores. "You're too easy to talk to."

"So don't stop," he suggested. "I'm a good listener."

"Ay Diós mío," she muttered, and took another sip of the Negroni. "You must have somewhere you need to be."

One corner of his mouth turned down in a half-grimace. "The only thing waiting for me is reheated leftovers at my desk while answering emails that can wait until tomorrow. I'll go if you want me to. But if you don't, take pity on me and join me for dinner."

Her lungs swelled at the implication that *she* would be doing *him* a favor by eating with him. It was laughable. In the end, it was the vulnerability shining in his brown eyes that convinced her.

"I don't," she said, surprised at her own boldness. "Want you to go, that is."

"Then I won't." He said it simply, like it was easy for him to stay, even though she knew it probably wasn't. "Is that a yes for dinner?"

"It's a yes." Then, in a quiet voice, she added, "Thank you. For coming over. Just before you did, I was thinking . . ."

"What?" he asked, when she trailed off.

Channeling New Ava, she said, "I was thinking that I didn't want to be alone tonight."

He studied her face for a moment, not saying anything. Then he glanced down at her left hand on the bar. He covered it with his own, moving slowly, as if giving her time to react. He slid his fingers around hers and gave them the gentlest squeeze. "You don't have to be."

At his touch, desire curled in her belly, sending a thrill

through her system. How long had it been since she'd felt attraction for someone?

Too fucking long.

For just a moment, she allowed herself to imagine what it would be like to be impulsive. To do something entirely out of the norm.

What would it be like to sleep with a stranger?

Hector was the only man she'd ever had sex with, and suddenly, it felt imperative that she change that.

Pulse racing, Ava screwed up every ounce of courage she possessed and stroked her thumb along Roman's palm. But before she could do or say anything else, a commotion at the entrance of the restaurant interrupted. A group of about thirty people in colorful costumes streamed in, filling the booths and taking up the empty seats at the bar.

Whatever tension had been brewing between them broke as the volume inside the lobby ticked up from a three to a ten.

"Did you know there's also an anime convention this weekend?" Roman asked wryly, and Ava laughed.

"I do now." The bartender's "other one" comment suddenly made sense.

He turned to her. "Do you want to go somewhere more . . . private?"

Her heart pounded. "Like where?"

He ran his thumb over her knuckles in a soft, but somehow companionable, caress. "The penthouse suite has a great view. We can have a meal brought up."

She swallowed hard. His eyes on hers were intent as he waited for a response.

Old Ava would've been too nervous to act on the clear invitation. She'd ask for an order of French fries to go, then eat them in her room while watching a movie and working on lesson plans.

New Ava is open to new experiences.

She sucked in a breath. "I'd like that."

The corners of his mouth eased with something like relief before he got to his feet and used their joined hands to help her up. She let him, even though at five feet nine inches she had no trouble with high bar chairs. Once standing, she noted that Roman wasn't much taller than she was, maybe an inch or two, but he had a solid build that made him appear bigger.

Roman turned to leave, but Ava hung back.

"I have to pay for the drink," she said, and he gave a pained sigh.

"Ava. Please."

"Oh. Right." But she didn't miss him passing the bartender a wad of cash as they left.

Old Ava would have worked up worst case scenarios in her mind. But damn it, she *deserved* to live a little. After everything she'd been through, she owed it to herself to see where this night led.

Still, she pulled out her phone on the way to the elevators and opened her texts.

She skipped over the Primas of Power group chat. As much as she loved Jasmine and Michelle, she couldn't risk this getting back to their grandmother, which meant her cousins could never know.

The thought gave her a pang of guilt, but it was like her mother always said: if you wanted to keep a secret from the family, you didn't tell *anyone* in the family.

Instead, she opened her texts with Damaris and typed quickly.

> **Ava:** I trusted the Universe and now
> I'm going to the penthouse at the
> Dulce Playa Hotel in Asbury Park
> with the owner, Roman Vázquez.
> If I turn up dead, tell the police.

After hitting send, Ava shoved the phone back into her purse before her friend could reply. There was a fifty-fifty chance Damaris would urge her on or try to talk her out of it, and either way, Ava was done overthinking things. At least for tonight.

And at the end of it, she'd have a new item to add to her list.

New Ava does whatever the hell she wants.

Chapter 3

Roman hadn't gone to the bar with the intention of picking up a woman. In fact, he'd been on his way out, but decided to check on the recent lobby renovations before heading back to Manhattan.

Then he'd seen Ava.

She'd caught his attention immediately. How could she not? Tall and beautiful, with soft hazel eyes, golden tan skin, spiraling curls, and legs for days. He'd paused for a lingering glance, but definitely hadn't planned on talking to her.

Until he'd seen her poorly disguised grimace when she sipped her drink. After that, nothing in his overpacked calendar could've stopped him from approaching her.

The spontaneity felt good. Tomorrow he'd get back to his meticulously arranged schedule, but for tonight, he'd just enjoy whatever was happening with Ava.

Shitty drink? Lonely night? Crowded restaurant? He could fix all that.

And if helping Ava took his mind off the supremely frustrating conversation he'd had with his mother that morning—well, that was an added bonus.

Across the elevator from him, Ava toyed with her necklace, a thin gold chain with her name in script. Her eyes were glued to the red digital numbers counting their journey toward the top floor.

He got the feeling she was nervous, so he asked, "Hungry?"

Her rigid posture relaxed a fraction. "Starving."

"Any allergies or preferences?"

She opened her mouth, then shut it and shook her head. "Nothing."

"You sure?"

"Yes." She gave a decisive nod that didn't fool him in the least.

"Seemed like you were about to say something."

She shot him a glance. "Well . . . I don't like olives."

He raised his brows. "And you were afraid to tell me that because . . . ?"

She blew out a breath. "My stepmother is Greek. I'm not allowed to dislike olives, so I don't ever voice that opinion."

And yet she'd told him. That meant something, but he didn't know what.

"I promise not to tell her," he said gravely, and she grinned.

Roman shot a quick text to the kitchen manager, asking them to send up the most popular items and a champagne bucket.

The elevator dinged, and the doors opened directly into the most luxurious suite at the Dulce Playa. Taking her hand, Roman led her into the space, watching for her reaction.

The rooms were decorated in the Dulce's signature gold and blue color scheme, but with more emphasis on lighter earth tones than the New York City locations, which skewed more toward the deep, rich blue. To the left, a sectional sofa and matching pair of armchairs created a conversation center, while to the right, a glass-topped dining table boasted seating for eight.

Ava let out a low whistle.

"Do you like it?" He didn't know why, but he cared what she thought.

She granted him a shy grin. "I have to admit, I thought it would be more ostentatious."

That pulled a laugh out of him. "Yeah? Like with a glass bar and big silver unicorn statue?"

"Exactly." She turned her head, taking it all in. "But I'm glad it's not."

It pleased him that she'd noticed. Décor in a lot of hotels went either too elaborate or too minimalist, in his opinion. When someone stayed at a Dulce, he wanted them to feel like they were at home, but better. Beautiful and elegant, but not cluttered. Clean and spacious, but not cold. "Comfortable luxury" was a surprisingly hard balance to strike, and he'd spent many hours poring over furnishings and textile samples before settling on the perfect mix of sharp angles and plush fabrics. He was more hands-on than some hoteliers he knew, but his attention to detail was what made the Dulce Hotel Group a success.

And if his legendary attention was feeling a little strained these days, well, that was the trade-off for the level of financial security he desired.

Roman guided Ava to the glass doors that led out to the deck, which had a private pool and hot tub. Under an overhang, wooden deck chairs with cushions in gold and blue surrounded a round patio table.

"Wow," Ava breathed, as Roman opened the doors to reveal the last moments of a stellar sunset. She drifted over to the railing as if pulled by the sun's gravity. "Now *that* is a view."

His phone buzzed before he could reply. It was his assistant, Camille Price, aka the Keeper of the Schedule, as his younger sister, Mikayla, called her. Camille was responding to the "cancel the car" text he'd sent from the bar.

Camille: What's going on?

> **Roman:** I'm sticking around the hotel a little longer. Having dinner.

Camille: Do you want me to reschedule the driver for a specific time?

> **Roman:** No, I'll do it when I'm ready to go.

Camille: You have an early meeting tomorrow with your editor.

> **Roman:** As if you'd let me forget.

Camille: That's what I'm here for.

> **Roman:** Enjoy your night. I'll check in tomorrow.

When Roman looked up from his phone, Ava was watching him. The sunset silhouetted her curves, gilding her with the sun's final rays. Her hazel eyes nearly glowed, and she was so beautiful, she made his breath catch.

No, he certainly hadn't planned on her. But now that he'd found her, he wasn't ready to say goodbye just yet.

"So you're a teacher?" he asked, standing next to her again as the sun dipped below the horizon.

She nodded. "Sixth grade. I teach English and social studies."

"Where?"

"Spanish Harlem."

"You live in New York?"

"In the Bronx."

Good to know. "Do you enjoy teaching?"

"Mostly, but . . ."

She trailed off, something he noticed she tended to do when she didn't want to say what she was really thinking. He couldn't resist digging further. "But?"

She sighed and turned away from the sky, now painted a vivid orange, pink, and blue. "My students are great, but what I really want to do is teach drama."

"Why can't you?"

"When I was hired, my school's principal promised I could implement a theater program. It's part of why I took the position—to make theater more accessible for New York City kids. They grow up with Broadway in their backyard, but the high ticket prices make my students feel like it's not 'for them.' But it's been five years now, and the principal keeps putting me off."

He noted her passion and her frustration. It piqued his interest, and also made him think of his sister, who could spend hours discussing the ins and outs of Broadway. It was as good a way as any of getting to know Ava better, and he found he wanted that very much.

"Musicals or plays?" he asked, since it was a topic that never failed to get Mikayla going.

"I love musicals, but I'd teach plays too."

"What's your favorite musical?"

"Oh, that's a tough one. It changes all the time, and for different reasons."

"All right, if not your favorite, what was the first show you ever saw?"

"*The Phantom of the Opera*," she replied. "It was a school trip. After that, I was obsessed."

"With the Phantom?" It was a joke, but when she hid her face, he had to know more. "What, did I just guess your secret Broadway crush?"

"Don't laugh," she warned.

He schooled his features. "I won't."

"Keep in mind that I was *twelve*," she said as a caveat. "I loved the show so much, I begged my dad to get me the CD so I could pretend to be Christine."

"Is that . . . ?"

"The female lead, a soprano. I used to belt the soundtrack when no one was home, and—oh god, this is too embarrassing."

"Now you *have* to tell me."

She put a hand over her eyes like she couldn't look him in the face. "I also concocted elaborate fantasies about a teenage Phantom who bore a striking resemblance to Anakin Skywalker."

"Anakin—" He broke off and swallowed a chuckle. "As in, Darth Vader?"

She pointed an accusatory finger at him. "You said you wouldn't laugh!"

"Apologies." He fought valiantly to keep his expression blank and his tone even. "I swear I am taking your prepubescent crushes on the Phantom of the Opera and Darth Vader very seriously."

She sighed. "In hindsight, it was probably the first indication that I have terrible taste in men." She ticked them off on her fingers. "Exhibit A: a man who terrorized an opera house. Exhibit B: the scourge of the galaxy. And Exhibit C: my ex-husband, a mama's boy who never learned how to use a washing machine or write a check."

Roman felt it prudent to set himself apart from these less than sterling examples of heroism. "In case you were wondering," he said, "I don't like opera, I've never built a Death Star, and I can use a washing machine *and* write a check."

Ava's tone was skeptical. "I feel like one of those things is a lie."

"You're right, my Death Star's parked in the garage."

She grinned. "I knew it."

Since she'd brought up her ex, Roman couldn't resist a follow-up question. "How long were you married?" he asked, then winced. Damn his inner chismoso. "Sorry, you don't have to answer that."

She gave a little shrug. "It's fine. We were married for three years, together for ten."

"How did you meet?"

"In college. His mom and my great-aunt live on the same block and he didn't have a car, so I gave him a ride home for Thanksgiving one year."

"Have you . . . ." How the hell did he ask this without sounding insensitive? He cleared his throat. "Have you dated at all since . . ."

"Since my ex and I separated a year and a half ago?" She

shook her head and turned away, resting her elbows on the railing. "No. All I've been able to think about was getting the divorce completed. What about you?"

"Me?"

"Ever been married?"

He leaned on the railing, watching her while she watched the sunset. "No. No time."

She sent him a curious look, her delicate brows drawing together.

"My whole life has been focused on work," he admitted. "Relationships don't usually last longer than whatever event we need to be seen at."

Her forehead crinkled. "What does that mean?"

He sighed. Why had he mentioned that? "My publicist arranges my dates. Like if I'm attending a premiere, or a gala, or whatever, she pairs me with another one of her clients. And yes, I realize how it sounds."

"Sounds like work," she said lightly, and he nodded.

"It is." He didn't want to get into a discussion about his previous relationships, the ones who seemed to be less interested in him as a person than in what he could buy them. Or how he hadn't dated much since his mother and sister moved in with him five years ago.

Yes, he'd had sex with some of the women his publicist had set him up with. Women who understood the "see and be seen" game and were down for a little bedroom companionship, but who were ultimately just as focused on their own careers.

For Roman, work always came first.

Except for right now, apparently.

Right now, he was supposed to be on his way back to the city, *not* hanging out on a roof in New Jersey with a stunning and intriguing woman. But despite his responsibilities and the to-do list nagging at the back of his brain, he found he could ignore them more easily than usual.

Ava toyed with her necklace again. As if she could hear his thoughts, she said, "I'm probably keeping you from something important. I can get myself food, if you need to—"

"No, it's fine." He spoke quickly, before she could talk herself out of eating with him. "I want to have dinner with you."

She twisted her fingers together and looked down at his loafers. "Roman, I'm flattered. Truly. But I don't understand why someone like you is doing all this for . . ."

"For . . . ?"

Tension coiled in his muscles as he guessed what she was trying to say. He should leave it alone, but the part of him that wanted to fix things for people couldn't let it pass.

Her throat rippled as she swallowed, and when her eyes met his, there was a wealth of pain in them. "For someone . . . like me."

"What do you mean by that?" When she raised her hands helplessly, he pressed. "Someone gorgeous? Someone kind? Someone who'd rather be stuck with a godawful Jersey Shore drink than complain or inconvenience anyone? Why do you think you're not worthy of good things?"

Of being taken care of? he wanted to add, but he held back. No need to bring his own baggage into this.

"Roman, I am a newly divorced middle-school teacher, and you . . ." She waved a hand at him. "I mean, look at you. Look at *this.*"

She gestured around them—at the sunset, the pool, the suite—and Roman stepped forward and caught her hands in his. When he spoke, his tone was low and earnest. "Ava, I am more than my bank account, and you're more than your marital status. We are two people who deserve to have a nice, uncomplicated dinner together. That's it."

She surprised him by rolling her eyes. "Tell that to my family. My marital status is all they care about."

Ah, now they were getting to the heart of it. He felt a little flicker of triumph at her admission. "Why? How did they react to the divorce?"

She groaned and slipped her hands out of his to lean her elbows back on the railing. "Like it was the end of the fucking world. You'd think somebody had died, the way they carried on."

"That must have been overwhelming."

"To put it mildly. My grandmother's been pressuring me to 'just get married again' for more than a year."

His brow creased. "Weren't you still legally married until today?"

"Most of them think the divorce was over a while ago—it was easier that way. But it doesn't matter how many times I tell her that I don't want to get married again. She either forgets or says I'm being 'difficult.'" She made air quotes with her fingers.

"Something tells me you've never been difficult a day in your life."

"All I've ever done is try to be perfect." Her shoulders slumped. "For all the good it's done me."

"What would happen if you weren't?" Roman asked softly. "What would you do if you didn't have to be perfect?"

She huffed. "Why does it matter?"

Before he could answer, his watch buzzed. He squinted at the message. "The food is coming up."

"Good. I built up an appetite bombarding you with my drama."

"I asked," he reminded her. "I wanted to know."

"So you say." She gave him a long, speculative look. "I just don't understand why."

He didn't either. Thankfully, he was saved from having to think about it by the ding of the elevator inside the suite. A moment later, one of the kitchen managers rolled in a tray laden with dishes.

"¿Cómo estás, Jesús?" Roman eyed the man unloading food onto the patio table. Jesús wore a simple dark gray suit and fashionable loafers, and it was absolutely not his job to deliver food.

"Jefe." Jesús gave Roman a respectful nod before his gaze cut over to Ava.

Roman sighed. Jesús was here on a fact-finding mission. Within an hour, the entire Dulce Playa staff would know the boss had brought a woman to the penthouse suite, which meant word would reach Camille—or worse, Roman's *mother*—before too long.

Ava's eyes went round as dishes covered the table. "Are we expecting more people?"

Roman laughed. "These are just to tide us over while we wait for the rest."

"*The rest?*"

Once all the appetizers had been set out, Roman thanked Jesús and slipped him some cash, muttering in Spanish, "Don't tell anyone."

Jesús mimed zipping his mouth shut. "My lips are sealed," he whispered, which Roman didn't believe for a second.

When Ava continued to stare at the spread of food, Roman moved closer. "You said downstairs that you don't know what comes next. Start small. Decide what you want to eat and enjoy it. Don't worry about what's left behind, just focus on each bite."

She blew out a breath. "I suppose I could try that."

She surveyed the selections and made herself a plate, opting to sample a little of everything. There was salmon tartare with avocado and nori, warm burrata with walnut pesto and roasted tomatoes, crab cakes topped with chipotle aioli, pulled pork sliders with cilantro lime slaw and jalapeno cornbread, and—Roman's favorite—crispy sesame calamari with Korean red pepper dip. It had been one of his own additions to the menu, a reminder of the few times when, back in his childhood, he and his mom had gone to a real restaurant for a special occasion and he'd been allowed to order an appetizer.

Once Ava sat down, Roman lifted a champagne bottle out of the ice bucket.

She let out a soft gasp when she saw the label. "But we already made a toast downstairs."

"That was before I knew why you were at the bar," he said. "Had I known, I would have dispensed with the theatrics and gone straight to the champagne."

"This feels too extravagant."

"We don't have to open it," he said. "But I thought we should toast the next phase of your life."

"The next phase," she murmured, her voice hoarse with emotion. "You know, I used to be that person who always had a detailed plan for the future. Now? I don't even know how to dream anymore."

Roman's heart broke for her. "Shall I?"

Her eyes were a little misty, but she bit her lower lip and nodded.

Roman popped the bottle, then filled their champagne flutes. As the tiny bubbles fizzed merrily, he raised his glass and said, "To you, Ava. To imperfection. To dreaming. To welcoming whatever comes next, with or without a plan." He paused. "How was that?"

She took a deep breath. "Thank you."

They sat at the table by the pool sipping champagne and nibbling on appetizers while the sky darkened above them. When the main courses arrived, Ava exclaimed over the selection, but took her time considering each dish and making herself a plate. As they ate, Roman noted what she liked and what she felt lukewarm about. For later? He didn't know if there'd be a later. But just in case, he filed the information away.

They talked as they ate—about the food, about their jobs— and avoided heavier topics like family and relationships.

It was . . . easy. Unhurried. For someone who lived and died by his schedule, it was nice to take an evening off.

The air cooled, but it was still warm out. Ava gazed longingly at the pool.

"I wish I could go for a swim," she murmured.

"What's stopping you?"

She shot him a surprised look. "Well, my hair, for one thing."

"What about it? It looks great."

"Exactly. Do you know how long this takes to achieve?" She twirled a perfectly defined curl around her finger. "Too long. Besides, I didn't bring a bathing suit."

Roman spread his hands and gestured around them. "I won't tell anyone."

She stared at him for a long time, a myriad of emotions

crossing her face, too quick to decipher. Maybe he'd pushed her too hard. Maybe she was rethinking this whole evening. Just as he was about to apologize for teasing her, she spoke.

"You asked me earlier what I'd do if I didn't have to worry about being perfect."

"And what's that?"

She got up and slipped off her shoes. "This."

He blinked. "What are you doing?"

"Getting my hair wet."

"You're going in?" he asked, unable to suppress the note of incredulity in his voice.

She nodded but didn't look at him as her hands went to the button at her waistband. "I love swimming. And I can't pass up a private rooftop pool."

She slipped her pants down her legs, and Roman tried not to swallow his tongue.

Muttering something about New Ava, she straightened and pulled her blouse over her head, revealing a light pink bra that matched her panties. She was tall and long-limbed, with generous hips his palms ached to touch.

She folded her clothes carefully and set them on her chair, then tucked her shoes underneath. When she turned to face the pool and Roman got a look at her from behind, he bit back a groan. God, this woman was perfect.

Then, to his surprise, she unhooked her bra and tossed it onto the chair beside her.

He sucked in a breath.

Instead of going to the steps, she sat on the edge and dipped her legs in.

"It's warm." She sent him a delighted smile over her shoulder.

"Heated saltwater pool," he mumbled, heart pounding as his eyes traveled down her back to the curve of her butt, barely covered by pink panties.

"Saltwater? Oh, this is totally worth having to do my hair again." And then she pushed herself off the edge and into the water, submerging herself completely.

Her flickering form moved gracefully beneath the waves. She came up on the other side of the pool with her hair slicked back, looking for all the world like a siren ready to entice him to his doom.

At that moment, he'd gladly follow her into the mouth of a sea monster, all for one last glimpse of her.

She wiped the water from her eyes. When she saw him watching, she called out in a husky voice, "Aren't you going to join me?"

Fuck yeah he was. Roman leaped to his feet, nearly knocking over his chair. He fumbled to undo the buttons on his shirt.

Was it suddenly more humid out here, or was it just the way she was looking at him? Her lips parted, and her eyes were glued to his hands as they revealed his chest. He slowed, giving her time to look her fill, when he really wanted to rip his clothes off and leap into the water after her. He slipped the shirt off his shoulders, taking care to flex as he did, and it was quiet enough that he heard her sharp intake of breath. Inside, he grinned like a fiend. Then he undid his pants and drew them down. He wore dark gray briefs, which did little to hide his growing arousal.

Across the pool, Ava's gaze flickered over his body, and Roman couldn't stay away from her a second longer. He jumped in. Warm water engulfed him, and although the pool was only five feet at its deepest, he sliced through it in an easy breaststroke, keeping his eyes on her. He thought she'd swim away, maybe make it a game, but she just stood there, waiting for him.

When he reached her, she sent him a shy smile. "I've never done anything like this."

He came to a stop in front of her. Water lapped around their bare shoulders as his feet touched down. "Like what?"

She gave a nervous laugh. "Skinny-dip with a man I just met?"

"I hope this is better than watching a movie in your hotel room." Over dinner, she'd admitted that was her backup plan after the cocktail failure.

Her eyes glowed. "Much."

"I'm glad I could help."

"Thank you. I . . . believe you."

He drew closer to her in the water. "Tell me what you want."

Her brows drew together as if troubled. "That's the problem. I don't know anymore."

"Then tell me what you like," he pressed. "Or what you used to like."

Maybe it was weird to ask, but she said she hadn't dated since the breakup. If there was something she wanted, he would give it to her.

"I like . . ." Her eyes dropped to his mouth and darted away, like she was too scared to say it.

"Tell me," he urged, his tone gentle. "I won't judge you."

Her gaze returned to his mouth and lingered.

"Kissing." The admission came in a hushed whisper. "I used to love kissing."

His pulse beat in his throat. "What did you love about it?"

"It used to be so exciting. But then, I don't know why, we just . . . stopped."

"You and your husband stopped kissing?" He kept his tone light. Inside, he wondered what kind of fucking idiot would ever stop kissing this woman.

"It was a gradual thing. We stopped kissing hello and good-bye, good morning and goodnight." She gave a little shrug. "Then we stopped kissing during sex. Maybe we were too comfortable? Too busy? But it was something I really liked, and then we didn't do it anymore. I can't . . . I can't even remember the last time we kissed."

That particular branch of memory lane seemed to be bringing her down. To distract her, he asked, "What kind of kissing do you like?"

He didn't think she'd answer, but then her tongue darted out to touch her lower lip, and he nearly groaned.

"Deep," she whispered. "Slow, wet, consuming kisses, where the entire world falls away and you can't think about anything else but the other person's lips and tongue."

The heat in her eyes, the breathiness in her voice—and also the hesitation—added fuel to the firestorm raging inside him. He shifted closer, and when he spoke, the question came out rough. "Do you want to kiss me, Ava?"

Her eyes had gone heavy-lidded and molten with desire. Her lips parted and the words escaped in a single breath. "More than anything."

He lowered his voice. "Then do it."

As if she'd only been waiting for permission, she propelled herself forward, sliding her hands over his shoulders until the front of their bodies bumped together and her bare breasts pressed to his chest.

Those long legs of hers wrapped around his hips, bringing their pelvises into contact with only two thin layers of wet cotton separating them. Roman clamped a hand on her ass to hold her to him and felt himself harden. Catching his jaw between her wet hands, she tugged his face to her. His mouth landed on lips that were impossibly soft, impossibly full. The taste of her went right to his head, faster and far more potent than the champagne. Remembering what she'd described, he poured himself into the kiss, taking his time and exploring every part of her mouth with every part of his.

Deep. Slow. Wet.

She moaned in the back of her throat, and her hands fisted in his wet hair even as her tongue slid languidly against his. The combination of hard and soft undid him, and he lost himself in her taste, in her touch, in her scent, like orange blossoms floating on the sea.

Fuck, he'd never had a kiss quite like this.

"What else do you like, Ava?" He pressed her to the side of the pool, his hips surging forward to grind his aching cock on her. "This?"

Her head fell back with a gasp. "Do that again."

How could he deny her? Lining them up, he pushed his hardness against her through their underwear, and she whimpered, clutching at his slick shoulders.

"You like that?" he asked, wanting her to say it, wanting her to voice her desires.

"Yes! Don't stop," she choked out.

As if he could. He paid close attention to the noises she made so he knew when he was rubbing the right spot. Then he ground them together, sliding his cock over her clit again and again.

Was it still called dry humping if you were in a swimming pool? Who even cared? Suddenly, nothing in Roman's life mattered more than bringing this woman to orgasm in exactly the way she wanted it.

She dropped her head onto his shoulder, moaning into his ear and pressing desperate kisses to the side of his neck. Her strong legs kept them locked together, and he gripped the edge of the pool, trying not to come. When her cries reached a higher pitch, he quickened his pace.

"Roman." She gasped his name, her nails digging into his back. "Yes. Just like—"

Her voice broke on a hoarse moan, and her pelvis bucked. In that moment, he wanted nothing more than to tear their underwear aside and plunge into her. Imagining the wet heat of her surrounding his cock made him groan along with her, but he held back. By the time she stilled, they were both breathing hard.

His heart pounded, and not just from the relentless arousal coursing through him. She was the one who'd come, yet he felt an immense level of satisfaction that usually only occurred after successful power plays in the boardroom. Hearing her cries, feeling her cling to him like he was her anchor in a storm, made him feel more powerful than all his many bank accounts.

"Oh my god," Ava muttered, her arms limp around his neck. "That was . . . incredible."

"*You're* incredible." He kissed her deeply, wanting more, taking whatever she was willing to give. Her arms tightened, her fingers sliding into his hair as her tongue tangled with his.

Desperation stole his breath, and he pulled back enough to

look into her eyes. "What else do you want, sweetheart? Just tell me and it's yours."

"Everything." She peppered his face with kisses like she couldn't stop. "I want everything. One night. No overthinking. Give me all of you, Roman."

"I'm yours," he said, and meant it. Bracing his feet, he lifted her out of the water. "Now get that beautiful ass inside."

Chapter 4

*W*ho the fuck was New Ava and where the hell had she been hiding?

It was all Ava could think as she climbed out of the pool.

She stood at the edge, dripping water, in nothing but her panties—and she didn't even care. For once, she wasn't thinking about her body, or her hair, or *what people would think of her.*

And it felt *amazing*.

This whole night had been amazing. And it wasn't over yet.

Holy shit. She was about to have *sex* with this man. This sexy, attentive man who'd stepped in when she was feeling low and made her feel better than she had in ages.

Not just the orgasm—although that had been fantastic—but the way he *saw* her. The way he listened. The way he made her feel . . . about herself. It was like his innate confidence had rubbed off on her.

A warm breeze hit her wet skin, and instead of acting like a slap of reality, the humid air whipped her desire up once again, especially as Roman hauled himself out of the pool. Illuminated from below, the pool lights seemed to gild every ridge of his body. He was broad and thick with muscle, but not overly defined like someone who spent all their time in the gym. The water sluiced off his chest and drew her eye down to his groin where . . . *holy hell.*

His wet underwear clung tightly to him, leaving even less to the imagination than when the fabric had been dry. As if that weren't enough, the head of his cock poked up out of the waistband. The teasing sight filled her with the overwhelming urge to lean forward and press a kiss to the tip, right before pulling the fabric aside and filling her mouth with him.

God, who *was* she? She couldn't ever remember fantasizing about giving a blow job before.

Well, it seemed there was a first time for everything. And since she was feeling so bold, she licked her lips and took a step toward him.

As if he'd read her intention, Roman pinned her with a look that was pure electricity.

"Ava." His voice held a little growl that thrilled her. "I am forty, which is at least five years too old to fuck on concrete. But that's what will happen if you take another step closer, and we'll both regret it tomorrow when our knees are torn to shreds. So for the love of god, I beg you—*get inside so we can fuck on the bed.*"

His words made her giggle, but they also lit a fire under her. Ava darted for the doors that led into the suite, only to be brought up short when faced with the prospect of walking indoors soaking wet.

"We're drenched," she pointed out as Roman came up behind her. "Should we—"

"I don't care." Roman scooped her into his arms and carried her inside.

"But what about the bed? Should we dry off first? Take a shower?"

He dropped a kiss onto her nose. "You're overthinking things," he chided gently.

She let out a sigh. "I can't seem to help it."

"Maybe I can be of some assistance." He lay her down on the king-size bed and knelt beside her. "Because I'm dying to taste you, Ava."

"Holy shit," she whispered, his words sending shimmering waves of desire through her. "Are you—"

"Do *not* ask me if I'm sure." Roman gave her a stern look. "I am very, very, *very* sure I want to bury my face in this sweet pussy. And I'll be extremely disappointed if you deny me the pleasure."

His dirty talk had her insides clenching in readiness for him. She was extra glad she'd let Michelle talk her into getting that Brazilian wax. If anyone had asked when she'd have a man's face between her legs again, she would have said *never*.

And yet here she was . . .

Ava tried to keep her tone light. "Well, if you're sure you're sure."

He wrangled her wet panties down her legs and tossed them over the side of the bed. Stretching out on his stomach, Roman grabbed her hips and yanked her toward him. He slid her thighs over his shoulders and parted her folds with his thumbs. "You ready?"

Ava nodded quickly. Anticipation stole her voice and tensed her leg muscles, and when he stroked a finger down her slit, she trembled like a leaf in a storm.

"I'm going to thoroughly enjoy this," Roman murmured.

Before Ava could think of a reply, he dragged his tongue up her vulva and over her clit.

She nearly shot off the bed like a rocket, and only his strong grip kept her in place. His damp hands were cool, but his mouth was hot on her flesh.

He licked and sucked at her, using his lips and tongue in just the right rhythm. How could it be that they'd just met, and he could make her feel this good? Maybe it was *because* they'd just met. There was no baggage between them, no reason to worry about what he thought of her.

All Ava knew was that he was attracted to her, and right now, that was more than enough. To feel desired, to feel wanted and cherished . . . that in and of itself was a gift.

And then he teased her entrance with the tip of his index finger, dipping and sliding as he swirled that agile tongue against her clit.

It was *perfect*.

Despite her climax in the pool, she came apart in his arms all over again. The orgasm was bright and hot, exploding within her like a supernova, and she couldn't hold back the cry of pleasure, or the way her legs trembled. And damn it, she didn't want to hold back. Not tonight, not anymore.

So she let him see her reaction, let him hear the way he made her feel. And from the look in his eyes as he tongued her, he ate it up, just as he did her pussy.

When she was panting and boneless on the bed, Roman pressed a kiss to her inner thigh. "Be right back."

"Okay," she replied, her voice barely a croak. Her mind was blissfully blank.

He returned a moment later holding a condom. "You haven't talked yourself out of this yet, have you?"

Ava shook her head and reached for him. "I want this. No strings, no feelings, just . . . this. You. Tonight."

"I can do that." He peeled his damp underwear off and climbed back onto the bed.

She bit back a whimper at the sight of his cock jutting out, straight and hard.

"Talk to me, Ava," he whispered, his voice gravelly. "Tell me what you want."

For once, there was no hesitation in her breathy response. "Can I touch you?"

"Of course."

At his husky assent, she curled her fingers around his girth and made a noise low in her throat. "God, you're thick."

He let out a chuckle that turned into a moan as she stroked him, her fingertips skimming over the head and the droplet that beaded there. As she learned his shape, she tried not to think about the fact that Roman's cock was only the second one she'd touched in her whole life.

"*Ava.*" With a ragged groan, he withdrew himself from her grip. "Enough teasing, querida."

Because she knew he was about to ask, she blurted out, "Kiss me."

She didn't imagine the flash of pleasure in his eyes as he brought his mouth to hers. He was glad she'd told him what she wanted. She kissed him back hungrily, eager to dispel all thoughts of the past. With Roman, every touch was different, every feeling was new, and all the more thrilling because of it. Heat flared as he trailed kisses down her neck and chest. Her back arched as he sucked one of her nipples into his mouth, and she moaned when he slid two fingers into her and pumped.

"Are you ready for me?" His words were muffled against her breasts.

"So ready," she said on a gasp.

He swirled his wet fingers over her clit one last time, making her shiver. Then he rolled a condom on and hooked his arms under her knees, lining up his cock at her entrance. The head nudged her and she squirmed.

"Now, Roman," she said, panting. "Please, *now*."

"Yes, *now*," he agreed. With his dark eyebrows drawn together in intense concentration, he pressed forward into her.

Ava groaned at the delicious fullness. It had been so long since she'd felt this. Yes, the sensation of being stuffed, but also since she'd felt desired like this, since she'd wanted someone like this. This was *not her husband* fucking her, and while she half-expected the thought to make her clam up, it had the opposite effect. The awareness that Roman, a man she barely knew, had his dick inside her, shot a searing bolt of excitement through her.

For the first time ever, she understood why people hooked up with strangers from bars. This was *hot*.

And then he began to move.

She whimpered when he withdrew, and her eyes rolled back as he surged forward again. She gave herself over to it, trusting him with her pleasure.

At first, Roman kept the pace slow and steady, as if sensing she needed time to adjust. Sensations overwhelmed her—the slide of his wet hair through her fingers, the delicious weight of his body, the drag of their chests pressing together, damp with saltwater and a light sheen of sweat.

With each touch, each kiss, each thrust, he was overwriting the memories on her skin and helping her make new ones.

Then, just as she was thinking she wanted more, he shoved

up onto his arms and looked down at her, a devastating grin illuminating his handsome face. "Ready?" he asked, for the third time that night.

She nodded, not fully understanding what he was asking, but before she could do anything else, he drove deep, pulling a strangled gasp from her lips.

His hips snapped, plowing her into the mattress. This position changed the angle of his thrusts, and he hit that sensitive spot deep inside.

Roman gripped her jaw, gentle but firm. "Look at me, Ava."

She blinked up at him, taking in the fiery intensity in his gaze, the urgency in his tone, the way his breath sawed in and out through parted lips.

"Talk to me."

"I can't," she said on a moan. "I need—"

"Yes," he rasped. "Tell me what you need."

He surged within her, making her clench around him. The words exploded from her throat. "Touch me!"

His grin was quick and fierce. "Gladly."

He pulled out and rolled her onto her side. Settling behind her, he curled around her like they were spooning and lifted her leg over his hip, opening her to him. Ava moaned as he slid into her again from behind, then gasped when he reached around to rub her clit while he thrust.

"Oh yes, that's it," she murmured, her eyes closed and her head thrown back into the curve of his neck. "Just like that."

"Come on, Ava," he ground out, the command hot against her ear. "Come for me, querida."

That decadent feeling inside her swelled, and as if his words were magic, the climax crashed over her, sweeping her away in its current. Her entire body throbbed with aftershocks, and she was only dimly aware of Roman's ragged groan as he clutched her hip and thrust to completion a few seconds later.

Her heart pounded against her ribs as she stared at the bedside lamp and fought to catch her breath.

Three times. Roman had made her come *three times* tonight.

Had that ever happened before? In the early days, Hector had sometimes made her come before they had sex, and then again during. By the end, she was lucky if she came at all.

Roman ran his hand down her side in a lazy caress. "You all right there?"

She twisted to peer at him over her shoulder. With his head cushioned on his bicep and his eyelids drooping sleepily, he looked utterly adorable.

"Thank you," she said softly. "That was everything I could have hoped for."

His lips curved, the look in his eyes warm and friendly. "All I did was give you what you asked for."

Exactly, she thought.

He pressed a kiss to her shoulder. "As much as I'd love to stay like this, I should get you a washcloth."

"I'll get it."

She started to shift, but he held her still with a hand on her hip.

"No, you will not. You stay here and relax." When he withdrew from her body, her core gave a twitch at the loss of him.

Ava rolled onto her back and smiled contentedly at the ceiling. "All right."

While Roman ducked into the private bathroom, her mind picked over all the things she'd shared with him, things she told almost no one, let alone a stranger.

It was part of what made Roman the perfect one-night stand. He was incredibly easy to talk to, and apparently that extended to telling him how she liked to be kissed, touched, and fucked.

Best of all, they were from completely different worlds, and no one in hers—in other words, *her family*—would ever find out.

But this night couldn't last forever, and it was time to get back to her real life.

Roman was still in the bathroom. Even after what they'd just done, there was something too intimate about joining him in there, so she climbed out of the bed and found her sodden panties on the floor. No point putting those on. The rest of her clothing was outside with the food and the champagne they'd abandoned. She felt a pang of guilt at the thought of all the wasted food, which meant Old Ava was rearing her head. Definitely time to make her exit.

Clutching her panties, Ava tiptoed to the bedroom door and peeked out, just in case someone had come to clean up the food while they were occupied. The coast was clear, so Ava made a mad dash for the doors that led outside. It was dark and quiet, but she was too paranoid to feel comfortable waltzing around outdoors in the nude. Grabbing her clothes, she threw everything on as quickly as she could. She'd wash up once she was back in her own room.

That brought up another thought. Did saltwater pools have chlorine? Could you still get a UTI from having sex after swimming in one? Damn, she needed to get downstairs and pee, ASAP.

Roman was calling her name when she reentered the suite. He was still fully naked, and it was an effort to keep her eyes on his face. Then she caught a glimpse of herself in the mirror and froze. Holy shit, her *hair*. Even Roman's sexiness couldn't distract from the mess of frizz. She was going to have to get up at the crack of dawn to wash and dry it if she wanted to be presentable for the conference breakfast the next day.

"You're going?" Roman asked.

Was it her imagination, or did he sound disappointed? Ava glanced over at him, but his expression was neutral. He was holding a wet washcloth in his hand—for her, she realized.

"I should get back to my room," she said. "Early day tomorrow."

He nodded. "All right. Hang on a minute."

She tried to finger-twist her curls into some semblance of order while Roman went out to the deck. Thank goodness Damaris was showing up in a few hours because Ava desperately needed to debrief with someone.

Roman came back with his pants on, still looking sexy and rumpled, his hair mussed. He handed her a business card.

"In case you ever want to do this again," he said.

The elegantly printed cardstock was velvety in texture and showed his name and phone number in block letters, along with the logos for VQZ Ltd, Dulce Hotel Group, and Casa Donato Rum.

Smiling tightly, Ava tucked the card into her purse. "Thank you, but I think it's best that we don't."

"No strings, no feelings?" he asked wryly, repeating her words from earlier. But he didn't sound offended.

"Yes." She snapped her purse shut. "Can I contribute to the cost of the meal?"

He let out an exasperated sigh. "Ava. Come on."

She put her hands up. "Right, right. I get it. You know I had to ask."

"I know." He gestured toward the exit. "Let me at least walk you to the elevator."

They moved through the suite side by side while Ava tried not to think about the wet panties in her purse. She'd wrapped them in a cloth napkin in the hope that she'd be able to remove them before they soaked through, but part of her felt guilty for taking the napkin, even though she planned to leave it behind in her own room.

He pressed the button for the elevator, then leaned in and gave her a kiss on the cheek, leaving her with a lingering whiff of his cologne.

Lips parted, she inhaled, cementing one last sensory memory of him.

"I mean it, Ava," he said, his eyes serious. "Feel free to reach out. Anytime."

She nodded, knowing she wouldn't. "Thank you, Roman. Goodbye."

The elevator pinged and the doors opened. She stepped on, and with a final nod at Roman, pressed the button for her floor. The doors closed, her last glimpse of him shirtless and barefoot, hands in his pockets, with the understated opulence of the hotel suite behind him, and a look she couldn't read on his handsome face.

As the elevator started moving, Ava let out a long breath and slumped against the mirrored wall.

Then, since she was alone, she pumped a fist in the air.

She'd done it! She'd had a one-night stand. Casual sex with a man she didn't know. She'd asked for what she wanted, taken what was given, and maintained clear boundaries. For the first time in probably ever, she'd been reckless, and it had been *fun*.

Tomorrow, she'd go back to being Ms. Rodriguez again,

the unassuming middle-school teacher known for her in-depth lesson plans. But tonight, she was a woman who'd reveled in her desires, who'd lived in the moment and come out on the other side so much better for it.

She had a secret. A good one.

And no one in her family ever had to know.

Chapter 5

After Ava left, Roman showered and dressed. While he waited for his driver, he sat by the pool while the water rippled gently in the warm breeze. He was tempted to pull out his phone and reading glasses to catch up on emails, but he wasn't ready to jump back into hustle mode quite yet. Instead, he replayed the unexpected events of the evening.

With Ava, it was like time had stopped and he'd been able to take a break from his constant thoughts about work. Tonight, he hadn't been Roman Vázquez the CEO, he'd just been . . . himself.

And it had been *fun*. Every time he'd gotten her to clearly state what she wanted and then to let him give that to her, he felt a rush of satisfaction. Seeing her strip down, both literally and figuratively, from the buttoned-up middle-school teacher she'd been downstairs to the sweet, responsive siren writhing in his arms, had blown his mind.

Ava's obvious reluctance to accept *anything* had only made him want to give her even more. Especially since it seemed like the thing she wanted most was for someone to simply *listen*.

After all the years he'd spent as a bartender, he was good at listening. Converting what people said into what they needed, and then figuring out how to meet that need, was why the Dulce Hotel chain was one of the fastest growing in the country and had won multiple hospitality awards.

It was why it was driving him crazy that his mother wouldn't let him help her find a new apartment.

All in all, meeting Ava had been a fantastic diversion, one he wouldn't mind revisiting.

But he didn't have her number. Hell, he didn't even know her full name. If they did meet again, it would be up to her.

A text buzzed, saying that his car had arrived. After one last look at the pool, he headed downstairs.

Back to the grind.

An hour and a half later Roman strolled out of the elevator directly into his apartment on Central Park West. On his way to his side of the apartment, he passed his seventeen-year-old sister, Mikayla Jenkins, at the kitchen counter with her laptop.

Despite having a custom-built workstation in her bedroom, Mikayla preferred to set up shop on any horizontal surface. When she was fourteen, Roman had once awakened to find her sitting cross-legged on his bed studying for a math quiz. After that, they'd had a conversation about respecting personal space, but he still found her doing homework all over the apartment.

He stopped across the counter from her and set down his bag. "What are you still doing up, Mickey?"

She rubbed her eyes behind her glasses—brown eyes, the same as his, the same as their mother's. On Roman, those eyes looked weary whenever he stared at his reflection in the mirror, with more and more lines fanning out from the corners. But on Mikayla, those big brown eyes gave her the appearance of a fawn, all curiosity and innocence, especially with her slim build, light brown skin, and long curly ponytail. Or maybe it was just that when he looked at her, he still saw the baby she'd been, back when he'd made her a silent promise to do everything he could to make her life easier than his own had been.

"College essays," she replied, and followed it up with an exaggerated groan.

"Where's Mami?"

"Asleep."

Roman came around to her side of the counter and kissed her on the cheek. And even though he had an early morning and should probably go to bed too, he slid onto the high chair next to her.

"How's it going?" he asked.

"Not great." She toyed with the spiral binding on her notebook. "Trying not to write about Dad."

"Ah." A pang went through Roman's chest. Keith Jenkins, Mikayla's father, had been a good stepfather and friend. Roman had been in college when Keith came into his life, and the older man had been supportive without trying to parent him. Roman had learned a lot about what it meant to be an adult from Keith.

After Keith passed away, Roman's mother, Dulce, sold her row house in Queens. That had been five years ago, and Dulce and Mikayla had been living with Roman ever since.

It had been an adjustment, sure, but Roman wouldn't have had it any other way. While he wasn't able to spend as much time with them as he wanted, he liked knowing where they were, and that all their needs were being met.

Which was why his mother had knocked him for such a loop that very morning when she'd announced that once Mikayla went off to college, she would be moving out too.

Roman, a forty-year-old bachelor, would soon be an empty-nester.

The thought gave him a sick, panicky feeling in his gut. But that was almost a year away. Plenty of time to convince his mother that there was no need for her to leave, and to encourage Mikayla to apply to colleges in the tri-state area.

He gestured at her notebook. "What are the essay prompts?"

Mikayla pointed to her screen. "This one wants to know about intersections of identity."

"You could easily write about that."

Mikayla's eye-roll told him he was one hundred percent wrong. "If I submit an essay about being Puerto Rican and Black and bisexual, it's going to sound like I'm playing diversity bingo."

Roman stifled a laugh. "Okay, what else is there?"

"Some ask about growth, overcoming an obstacle, or being grateful for something, and all I can think about for those is Dad. It feels too personal to write about him, but maybe I should."

"Only if you want to." He waited a beat, watching her. "Do you?"

She tapped her fingernails, painted in chipped rainbow stripes, on the edge of the laptop. "I think I do. But I can't talk about Dad without talking about you, too."

"Why me?"

"Lots of kids lose a parent, right? Through some way or another."

Roman nodded. He'd grown up without a father, so he knew firsthand.

"But not every kid has a big brother like you," Mikayla went on.

"Rich?" he joked.

"Not just that." She gave him a *don't be stupid* look that was the spitting image of the one their mother used to give him when he was younger. "You could've just paid for everything and left Mami and me to our lives. But you let us move in—"

"Because I *wanted* you here. It wasn't out of obligation, Mickey."

"That's exactly my point. Yeah, I was sad, and you know, grieving, but you made sure we weren't alone. That we had a place to live. That we were still a family."

"We *are* a family. And this will always be your home."

"Stop being cheesy." But she looked like she was trying not to smile.

"Mickey." He waited until she met his eyes. "When you were born, all I had to my name were student loans and a shitty old Toyota. But I made a promise that I would always, *always* take care of you, the best that I could. I meant it then, and I mean it now."

"Hard to imagine you like that," she murmured, glancing at his silk suit. "Driving a shitty old Toyota."

He inclined his head, then spread his arms to encompass the spacious apartment. "You know all this is new to me. Inside, I'm still that kid hustling to make a buck."

Her gaze turned shrewd. "Is that why you work so hard?"

He tried to shrug it off, since he didn't ever want her to feel guilty. "Partly. I wanted you to have an easier life than I did."

"You're a good big brother, Ro." She hugged him, and when she pulled away, she said lightly, "Anyway, you won't have to take care of me much longer. I'll be away at college soon. *If* I manage to finish these stupid essays."

"You'll finish them." And how the hell was she already old enough to be applying to college? "And if you don't, I'll happily donate a gymnasium to your top choice."

Mikayla snickered. "I knew name dropping my rich and famous big brother would be a good idea."

"Hey, it works for the rich white kids. Why have all this money if I can't game the system in your favor now and then?"

"Wish I'd known a gym donation was on the table before I spent the last few years getting a 4.0 GPA the old-fashioned way." She wrote three big dollar signs in her notebook, then shoved it aside. "So, how's *your* book coming along?"

Roman blew out a breath, thinking about the business memoir he'd been approached to write. "Don't ask. I have a meeting with the editor tomorrow morning. I'm supposed to turn in some ideas, but I don't have any."

"All that time you spend working, and you don't even know what you do all day?"

He bit back a sigh. "Meetings. So many meetings. No one wants to hear about that."

She gestured at her laptop. "Do what I'm doing. Write about what's important to you."

"Then I'll just be writing about you and Mami."

"You really need to get out more."

"I get out. Hell, I went to four galas last month. If I never see a tux again, it'll be too soon."

Another exasperated eye-roll. "Yeah, but when was the last time you went on a date that wasn't arranged by your publicist?"

Tonight, he thought, but Roman slapped his hand to his chest. "Ouch, Mickey. Ouch. Also you're not supposed to know that."

She preened. "I know everything."

"You're scaring me."

"I'm just saying, you should have a girlfriend. Or boyfriend. Whatever."

"Girlfriend," he clarified. "And no. I don't have time for one of those right now."

"Why not?"

"I'm busy."

"*Busy.*" She made air quotes with her fingers as she repeated the word, like it was an excuse.

"I *am* busy."

"I know, you work *all* the *time.*"

The pang of guilt was another direct shot.

"You're really interested in boyfriends and girlfriends," he deflected. "Got anything you want to tell me?"

She let out a plaintive groan. "I wish. I kind of have a crush on someone, but I don't think it's real."

"No?"

"Well, we've only met one time. I should probably see someone more than once before I know if I like them, right?"

Roman thought of Ava. Sometimes one time was all it took.

"Probably a good idea," he said, then got to his feet. "How about you worry more about getting into college and less about my love life?"

"Your nonexistent love life," Mikayla muttered under her breath. "Going to bed?"

"Early morning tomorrow. Don't stay up too late."

"I'm a teenager. That's what I do."

He dropped a kiss to the top of her head, then went to retrieve his bags and bring them to his bedroom.

Mikayla would pry again—as she'd said, she was a teenager and that was what she did—but he was absolutely *not* telling his little sister he'd spent the evening with a woman he'd just met in a bar. Even if he owned said bar.

But he had told Mikayla the truth about one thing: he *was* too busy for a relationship. Relationships required time, energy, and effort, and right now, all of those resources went toward expanding his business.

Besides, he liked working. Not everyone could say that, but he liked feeling useful, he liked helping people, and most of all, he liked having money.

Huh. He should write that down for the book he was supposed to be writing, which was yet another reason why he was too busy for love.

The evening he'd shared with Ava, while eminently satisfying, was the extent of what he could afford to fit in right now. And luckily, it seemed like Ava was on the same page.

If she never called him again, it would be fine.

Still . . .

He really hoped she did.

Chapter 6

"Did anything interesting happen at the conference?"

Ava kept her face blank as she answered Jasmine's question. "Not particularly."

Michelle smirked. "No 'teachers gone wild' scenarios?"

You mean like grinding on the hotel owner in a rooftop swimming pool? Ava took a quick sip of champagne to cover her reaction to the memory and kept her voice cool as she replied aloud.

"Only if you mean wild with boredom. Would *you* want to spend two hours in a master class on standardized test prep?"

Michelle wrinkled her nose. "Absolutely not."

From her spot between them, Jasmine shook her head. "Do they at least pay you for the hours you're at the conference?"

On Ava's other side, Jasmine's sister, Jillian, snorted. "You know they don't."

Jillian, a quantitative analyst on Wall Street, was hunched over a laptop balanced on her knees. Aside from the occasional muttered comment, she largely ignored the champagne and conversation flowing around her.

It was Sunday afternoon, two days after Ava's one-night stand with Roman. Ava and her cousins—along with Jasmine's mother, Titi Lisa—were sitting in what had to be the most ostentatious bridal showroom in New York City. The place was huge, decked out with heavily padded purple sofas, gaudy golden chandeliers, and coldly beautiful mannequins modeling every style of wedding dress one could imagine. Ava couldn't help but compare it to the more tasteful ambience of Roman's hotel.

Thanks to Jasmine's celebrity status, their little group had it all to themselves, though not for lack of trying on Titi Lisa's part. When Jasmine's mother had attempted to invite all the other tías and cousins to come along to watch Jasmine try on dresses—and offer their opinions—Jasmine had put her foot down. As a result, only the five of them were present.

Titi Lisa rushed over to them with her phone outstretched. "Smile, girls."

Jillian snapped, "I'm working, Mom!" and leaned out of view. But Ava and Michelle obliged, leaning in on either side of Jasmine and smiling widely.

Titi Lisa was Filipina and Puerto Rican by way of Southern California, and both of her daughters favored her. Jasmine was gorgeous, with golden brown skin and dark hair even curlier and thicker than Ava's. But after getting her photo snapped by paparazzi on wash day with the headline, "Hot Mess: Is Jasmine Lin Okay?" Jasmine now straightened her hair more often than not. Jillian looked a lot like Jasmine, but taller and more serious-looking, with a short haircut and thick-framed glasses. Michelle was short and curvy, with creamy skin and dark wavy hair.

Ava towered over all of them. She often felt like a giant lumbering amongst her more petite Rodriguez relatives. Her height came from her maternal grandfather, who lived in Barbados. Her cousins there were tall, like she was, but she didn't get to see them often.

Sometimes she wondered if she'd only married Hector for his height.

Roman wasn't much taller than she was—she guessed he was five-foot-ten barefoot, which hardly counted as *short*—but he had so much . . . presence, he seemed to take up more space. He commanded attention and was fairly bursting with personality.

His solid physique didn't hurt either. He was muscular without being overwhelming, as she'd told Damaris in their hotel room. Her friend had shown up with a chilled bottle of sparkling rosé—bless her—and demanded all the juicy details of Ava's passionate evening with the handsome hotelier.

Damaris was Dominican and despite being half a foot shorter than Ava, people often mistook them for sisters. They both had big curly hair and a similar facial structure, although Damaris's light brown skin was a few shades darker than Ava's. Damaris also had massive boobs, whereas Ava's own breasts could best be described as modest.

When Ava had finished recounting a loose outline of the events that had taken place, Damaris had stood up and clapped, the tiny jewels on her manicured nails glinting in the lamplight. But then her dark eyes turned serious.

"On the one hand, I'm really proud of you. You deserve to have fun, and this man sounds like a dream."

Ava's brows drew together. "I feel a 'but' coming."

Damaris raised her own expertly tweezed eyebrows. "But on the other hand . . . what would Colleen say?"

Ava had huffed. Colleen had been the only person in Ava's life who felt Ava should hold off on dating. The therapist hadn't said it in so many words, but she'd urged Ava to work on her boundaries in other areas of her life—namely with her family—before entering into another relationship.

"It was a one-night stand. How much more straightforward about boundaries could I be?"

Ava didn't mention that Roman had given her his card and very clearly left the door open for another . . . appointment . . . in the future.

Damaris had raised her hands like *you do you* and said, "If that's how you learn to establish boundaries, don't let me stop you. There are definitely worse ways."

Then they'd gossiped about their school's principal, drank rosé, and watched *Pride & Prejudice*.

Now, Ava glanced over to where Michelle and Jasmine chatted with their heads together and snapped a photo of them. As much as she wanted to tell them about Roman, something held her back.

For one thing, there was always the chance that it would somehow get back to their grandmother. But it was more than that.

In their family, Ava was the perfect one. The good one. She and her cousins had joked about the Ranking, a rating system of who was in their grandmother's good graces versus who was on the viejita's shit list. For as long as Ava could remember, she had strived to be at the top of the Ranking.

And she had been. She'd been on the receiving end of Abuela's praise for everything from her looks and behavior to her cooking skills and life choices. Poor Jasmine had often been subject to passive aggressive remarks, both for her decision to become a professional actor and her many breakups. And after Michelle had quit her corporate marketing job to go freelance, the old woman had berated her endlessly. Ava had sympathized, but it wasn't until Hector had left her that she'd finally known the full force of her grandmother's judgment and disapproval.

Ever since, she'd been trying to claw her way back to the top spot. And that meant being even more helpful, even more hard-working, even more *perfect*, than before.

Ava busied herself taking photos of the showroom until the consultant came over to collect Jasmine. The woman introduced herself as Debbie in a thick Long Island accent. She was short, with olive-toned skin, a dark bob, and heavily applied mascara ringing her blue eyes.

"So, Jasmine, do you know what you're looking for?" Debbie asked.

"I'm not sure." Jasmine's stunning features pinched with uncertainty. "I don't want a typical wedding dress. Something glamorous, but not too extravagant."

Michelle rolled her eyes. "Jas, it's a *wedding dress*. Extravagance is the point."

"Exactly!" Titi Lisa jumped in. "I told her, you only get married once, so this is your chance to look like a queen." Then Lisa glanced at Ava with an apologetic look. "I should say, your first wedding is, um . . ."

"It's okay," Ava murmured. "I know I'm divorced."

Michelle opened her mouth—likely to come to Ava's rescue—but Ava gave a brief shake of her head. Debbie, who probably had lots of experience navigating tense family dynamics, smoothly breached the awkwardness.

"Jasmine, why don't I take you into the fitting room to show you some dresses you might like? While we're doing that, the rest of you can each pick out something for Jasmine to try on."

Following Debbie, Jasmine mouthed "sorry" to Ava, who waved her off.

Despite muttering about the exploitative nature of the wedding industrial complex, Jillian leaped to her feet and ventured into the racks of wedding dresses farthest from where they all sat.

"Jilly's not wrong," Michelle mused as she strolled over to a rack full of white dresses encased in clear plastic. "This whole thing is a capitalist's wet dream."

Ava went over to another rack, but her aunt's offhand comment stayed with her.

You only get married once.

And then, echoing unbidden in her mind, came Hector's voice: *I don't want to be married to you anymore.*

Eyes burning, Ava stared at the wedding dresses in front of her. She let out a shuddering breath and darted a look around.

Michelle was hunting for dresses on the next rack, and if she saw Ava, she'd know something was up. Ava hurried to the restroom and locked herself in one of the private stalls. There, she pressed her hands to her eyes and willed herself not to cry.

No matter how many times Colleen had told her that crying was healthy and natural, Ava hadn't been able to uproot her deeply ingrained beliefs. Crying was bothersome. Crying was "making a scene." Crying was *messy.*

Ava almost never cried, and now would be the worst time to fall apart. The others would worry, Jasmine would feel awful, and Ava would be racked with guilt for bringing down Jasmine's special experience.

Not only that, Titi Lisa would absolutely tell Titi Val, Michelle's mother, who would tell her sister, Titi Nita, who would tell Abuela, and then it would be a *thing.*

Did you hear Ava cried at Jasmine's dress shopping trip?

They'd transition from a pitying *Ay, bendito* to a scornful *What's her problem?* in the blink of an eye.

Ava didn't miss Hector, but knowing she'd failed at the most important thing her family expected of her wore her down like a cliff buffeted not by the sea, but wave after wave of criticism.

Roman's business card was still in her bag. With shaking fingers, she pulled it out and typed his number into her phone. Then she tapped on the message bar.

After a brief hesitation, she wrote, *Are you free?*

And immediately deleted it.

What the hell was she doing? She didn't need Roman. Who was he to her? Some man she'd met at a bar. A one-night stand.

Besides, she was the one who'd laid out the boundaries. It wasn't fair to step over them not even forty-eight hours later, just because she was, what—feeling jealous? Sad? Sure, he was a good listener, great in bed, and looked at her with an intensity that she felt down to her very soul, but that didn't mean she had any right to ask for more. And on top of that, she didn't *want* more. She was done with love, done with relationships, done with romance in general.

Even so, just knowing she *could* message him, if she wanted to, was enough to settle her.

She tucked his card and her phone back into her purse. Then she washed her hands, touched up her lip gloss, and left the bathroom.

The others were still looking at dresses when she returned. Ava joined them at the racks. As hard as it was reliving the memories of her own wedding, she wanted her cousin to have what she hadn't. After everything Jasmine had been through, she deserved the perfect dress, the perfect wedding, the perfect everything. And it was Ava's duty as maid of honor to make that happen.

A moment later, Jasmine came out wearing a strapless mermaid dress with a sparkly bodice and a textured skirt. Clips pinched the fabric in the back to make it fit her form. She looked great, but then, Jasmine always looked great. She had a perfect Hollywood body—not too tall, not too short, taut and lean, but curvy in the right places.

Ava, on the other hand, often felt like she was curvy in all the *wrong* places. She'd inherited her mom's wide, shapely hips, but she didn't have the butt to match. Buying pants was always an exercise in frustration, and she wore a lot of dresses to avoid doing it.

That was one thing she couldn't fault Hector on. He'd adored her body, and even if the sex had been unsatisfying by the end, she'd at least known he'd found her attractive.

Unfortunately, there were times she wondered if that was all he'd loved about her.

Jasmine stepped onto a block in front of a trio of mirrors and turned this way and that, examining her reflection.

The dress looked good on her. But . . .

"It's not right," Jasmine said, and Ava let out a sigh of relief.

"No, it's not the perfect dress for you," she said.

Titi Lisa and Michelle agreed, and Jillian nodded without looking up from her phone.

Jasmine went to try on something else while Michelle filled Ava in on her latest client meetings in LA.

Titi Lisa had selected a ball gown with cap sleeves and a fitted bodice covered in floral lace. The skirt was enormous, the layers of taffeta and organza decked out with pearls and more lace. When Jasmine came out in it, tears gathered in Titi Lisa's eyes.

"You look like a princess!" she gushed.

Jasmine shook fistfuls of the voluminous skirt. "I look like a vanilla cupcake, Mom."

Titi Lisa turned to her other daughter. "Jilly, do you like it?"

Jillian growled something about the egos of patriarchal finance bros and kept her eyes glued to her laptop.

"What do you think, Ava?" Titi Lisa turned imploring eyes on Ava, who patted her arm.

"It's very nice, but I'm not sure it's exactly Jasmine's style," Ava said diplomatically.

As Jasmine passed Ava on her way out, she mouthed, "Very nice?"

Ava shrugged. "You wanted me to tell her it looks like a kaleidoscope of butterflies is attacking your tetas?"

Jasmine cackled all the way back to the fitting room. Minutes later, she stomped out with her hands on her hips, wearing Michelle's pick—a slinky Chantilly lace number with a deep V framed by scalloped edges. Even with the sheer "illusion" panel in the center, the dress was quite revealing.

Jasmine glared at Michelle. "I look like I'm channeling J.Lo at the 2000 Grammy Awards."

Michelle grinned. "Hey, that green Versace was iconic."

"Yes, but not for my wedding!"

Ignoring Jasmine's stormy expression, Michelle snapped a photo on her phone. When she saw Ava looking, she winked. "I told Ashton I'd pick out the sexiest dress I could find and send him a picture."

Ava shook her head as Jasmine sailed away with Titi Lisa hot on her heels. "Why do you tease that man?"

"Because it's so easy." Then Michelle got a speculative look in her eye. "Maybe I should try that one on and send a picture to Gabe. We're never getting married, so this is my only chance."

"With your boobs, it's going to look obscene," Ava warned.

Michelle smirked. "That's the point. Be right back."

After Michelle disappeared into the dressing room, Jillian glanced over at Ava and said, "Thanks again for taking on maid of honor duties."

"Don't mention it," Ava said. "I'm happy to help."

"I mean it. You're saving me a lot of hassle."

Ava shrugged it off. "Between your workload and Michelle's travel schedule, it just makes sense."

Jillian grabbed the half-full bottle of champagne and handed it over.

"Here," she said. "Don't bother with a glass. I won't tell anyone."

Ava huffed out a laugh. "Thanks. But Jas hasn't gone full Bridezilla yet."

"Give it time," Jillian muttered darkly and returned to her work.

If Jillian had noticed Ava's tension, it meant Ava had to be more careful.

Fixing her features into what she thought of as her Resting Pleasant Face—serene smile, smooth brow, eyes slightly unfocused to mask the internal screaming—Ava returned to the racks to find the perfect dress for Jasmine.

Jillian surprised them all by selecting a whimsical off-the-shoulder gown with sheer puffy sleeves, a sparkling corset top, and a long flowing skirt.

When Jasmine came out in it, Jillian looked up and shrugged. "Pretty, but not your style," she said, and went back to her laptop.

Jasmine posed for a few pictures, then returned to the fitting room, this time forbidding her mother from coming with her.

Michelle distracted Titi Lisa with trying on headpieces while

Ava kept looking through the racks. She searched and searched, debating between a lacy mermaid dress and a sequined one-shoulder design. They both screamed "Jasmine," but in different ways.

"It's almost harder because she looks amazing in everything," Ava muttered to herself, not at all bitterly.

Then she saw it. The perfect dress.

She gathered it up and rushed over to the dressing room.

"This one," she told Debbie. "I have a good feeling."

As Ava went back to the seating area, memories of her own wedding dress filled her thoughts. It had featured an asymmetrically draped sweetheart bodice with cap sleeves and a flowing A-line tulle skirt. It hadn't been her first choice, but it had been flattering on her body and she'd managed to find it used for less than half the retail price. She'd splurged on a tiny tiara to attach the simple veil. Her cousin Ronnie had done her hair and Titi Val had done her makeup. Ava had felt beautiful.

A year later, she'd sold the dress to Hector's cousin, who'd added lace sleeves and a rhinestone belt to give it a different look. As much as Ava had wanted to keep it, she was nothing if not practical. The dress took up too much space in her tiny closet, and she'd needed the money for student loans.

Now she was just glad the damn thing was out of her life.

Same with Hector.

She thought of how tightly Roman had held her in the pool, the strength and warmth of his body surrounding her own. It had been so long since she'd been skin to skin with another person, she hadn't even realized how much she'd needed it.

Just then, Jasmine came out wearing Ava's selection, and Titi Lisa burst into tears.

The romantic boho style dress had a subtle V-neck, flutter

sleeves, and an open back. The skirt fell from Jasmine's trim waist with an overlay of delicate floral tulle lace that managed to be both ethereal and chic at the same time. Ivory lace complemented Jasmine's golden complexion and dark hair, making her appear to glow with otherworldly beauty.

As Jasmine stepped onto the block, she wore a hopeful smile on her face.

"I think this is it," she said quietly, her gaze seeking out Ava. "What do you think?"

Ava couldn't speak. She blinked fast and nodded. Titi Lisa sobbed. Michelle gave two thumbs up. Even Jillian glanced up from her laptop and said, "Yes. This."

Jasmine's eyes grew wet. "It's perfect. Ava, what would I do without you?"

"You'll never need to find out," Ava promised, her voice cracking with emotion.

With her Resting Pleasant Face firmly affixed, Ava took photos and dutifully documented the moment while Jasmine spun and posed.

And if underneath the joy of helping her cousin find the perfect wedding dress stirred something that resembled jealousy, well, Ava would just deal with it on her own time.

Chapter 7

January

> **Unknown Number:** Hi, it's Ava. From the Dulce Playa. Any chance you're free tonight?

A jolt of adrenaline burst through Roman as he stared at the text on his phone.

Ava. After three months, she'd finally reached out.

It was a struggle to keep his expression impassive as the quarterly results meeting droned on around him. Inside, he was jumping for joy.

When he'd given Ava his card, he'd hoped to hear from her. But as weeks turned to months with no word from her, he'd categorized their encounter as what it was: a one-night stand, nothing more.

Just because he caught himself thinking of her at odd times didn't mean she was thinking of him too. Sipping rum made him remember the taste of her lips. And when he was lying in bed at night, trying to shut his brain off, he'd recall the look of sheer delight on her face when she'd dipped her feet into the pool.

He'd hoped that she was okay, wherever she was.

And now, a message, out of the blue.

Typing furtively, he added her number to his contacts and wrote back, "Happy New Year. And yes."

But a thought occurred to him, and he paused before hitting send.

Why now?

When they'd parted, Ava seemed sure that they'd never see each other again. So what had changed?

Not only that, he *wasn't* actually free. It was Friday afternoon, and his schedule for the rest of the day was packed with meetings, calls, and appointments. He could cancel or reschedule most, but the GQ interview was key to boosting Casa Donato's summer sales, and the *Shark Tank* dinner had taken months to coordinate. Plus, he'd bailed on his last three PT sessions, and his lower back was extremely unhappy about it.

Roman glanced at his unsent reply.

His body screamed at him to say yes.

His brain was like *what the fuck are you doing*.

His soul begged him to take a night off.

In the end, curiosity won out. He desperately wanted to know what had made Ava reach out after all this time.

Promising his lumbar vertebrae that he'd stretch tomorrow, he pressed send.

"Mr. Vázquez?"

Roman glanced up. A conference room full of people gazed at him expectantly, like . . .

Fuck. Like he was their *boss*.

And as their boss, he was *supposed* to have been paying attention. Not responding to booty calls.

Roman bit back a frustrated sigh. He should've invested in cloning technology back when he was in his twenties instead of a gamified language learning site. Between the hotels, the distillery, and now the book, he was drowning in work.

If he had clones, one could handle the Dulce expansion into Asia, another could take meetings about Casa Donato's distribution channels, and he could lock another one in a room and not let it out until it had a finished manuscript.

And one could be here arguing about the latest DEI statement.

"Publish it as is." Roman got to his feet before the PR manager could argue. "Sorry to cut the meeting short, but an emergency has come up. I'm sure no one's sad about ending a little early on a Friday afternoon."

There was light laughter as everyone started to pack up. To Roman's right, his assistant, Camille Price, collected her things without a word. Roman took his tablet and left the conference room with Camille at his side.

She was a tall Black woman with shoulder-length locs and luminous umber skin. In their many years of working together, Camille had revealed a penchant for pairing brightly colored pantsuits with sensible shoes, and an uncanny knack for sussing out bullshit.

That last trait was about to bite Roman on the ass.

"An emergency?" Camille spoke in a hushed tone as they hurried down the hallway. "Is everyone okay?"

Camille scheduled every second of every day of Roman's life. She knew that any emergency likely involved his mother or sister.

It was on the tip of his tongue to tell her the truth so she wouldn't worry, but he found he didn't want to tell Camille about Ava. Maybe it was because dropping everything to meet with a woman was *not* a normal thing for him. In fact, claiming an assignation counted as an "emergency" was so out of the norm, Camille would probably insist on making an appointment with his doctor.

"Everyone's fine," he assured her. "There's just something I have to do."

Camille raised her eyebrows at his vague excuse. Her expression said, *I'm going to let this drop . . . for now.* She just pulled up his calendar on her phone as they walked. "I assume you've already seen what you have on tap for the rest of the day. Do you want me to cancel or reschedule?"

"Cancel the marketing meeting, reschedule everything else."

"Should I mark anything down in your calendar for tonight?" Her tone was cagey, digging for information.

He could say he was having dinner with a friend, but Camille scheduled those too, so it would be weird if he refused to tell her the supposed friend's name. And if he said he was going on a date, he'd never hear the end of it. "No. Thank you."

"Where are you headed now?" When he eyed her, she sent him a perfectly innocent smile. "So I know where to have the car take you."

"Home," he said. He wouldn't be staying there, but it didn't matter. Camille could trace his phone, and she always knew where he was. When she looked—and he was sure she would—she'd see that he was at one of his hotels overnight, and she'd probably guess what was going on.

They'd cross that bridge when they came to it.

Camille gave him a long look but didn't ask any more questions. She tapped away at her phone, starting the process of rearranging Roman's commitments.

All so he could see Ava.

At the elevators, Roman paused Camille before she could make a call.

"After this, take the rest of the night off," he told her. "Completely. No calls, no texts, no emails. Do something nice with your family and charge it."

Her eyebrows rose. Now she definitely knew he was up to something, but she wasn't going to ask. Not now, anyway. She'd enjoy the time off and drag it out of him later.

Ava had texted him for a reason. And he wanted to know why.

More than that, he wanted to see her again. Immediately.

A black SUV was waiting at the curb when he and Camille got downstairs. Once they climbed inside, Roman texted Ava back.

> **Roman:** Meet me at the Dulce Flor in Times Square tonight.

> **Ava:** The hotel?

> **Roman:** MY hotel. I'll send a car for you.

> **Ava:** You don't have to do that. I can take the train.

Roman made a sound of frustration in the back of his throat and didn't miss Camille's curious look. She was on the phone with GQ, rescheduling his interview and promising them more time with him.

He typed back quickly.

> **Roman:** PLEASE let me send a car for you.

Ava: But there will be traffic!

> **Roman:** Are you overthinking this?

Ava: Yes . . .

> **Roman:** You don't need to. Not with me.

Two full minutes passed, during which Roman quietly freaked out, thinking she was going to tell him to forget it. But then his phone buzzed and her reply appeared.

Ava: Okay.

The relief was intense. He asked where to send the car, and the address she gave was in the Bronx.

Camille did a lot for him, but Roman could at least schedule a car to pick up Ava. He sent a text to the service he used, then got out of the SUV at his building, directing his driver to take Camille to her home in Queens. Then he went upstairs to get ready for his night with Ava.

Text Exchange with Damaris Fuentes

Ava: Remember that guy I met a few months ago?

Damaris: You mean Mr. Dulce, your one and only one night stand?

Ava: That's not his name, but yes.

Damaris: As if I'd forget. Why? What happened?

Ava: I'm seeing him again tonight.

Damaris: You know I'm a fan of manifesting the life you want and all that shit, but what brought this on? You said it was a one time thing, never to be repeated.

Twenty Minutes Later

Ava: I'll explain tomorrow.

Chapter 8

Roman flopped onto his back, his heart hammering against his rib cage. Ava lay naked on her back beside him, her skin shiny from exertion. They were stretched out on a king-size bed in the Dulce Flor's penthouse suite, the blankets tangled all around them.

The second they'd walked in, she'd grabbed him by the tie and kissed him senseless, and his intention to find out why she'd contacted him had flown out of his head. They'd fallen on each other with ravenous hunger, more like long lost lovers reuniting than the virtual strangers they actually were.

Roman hadn't questioned it. Like the first time, he'd simply given her everything she'd asked for and taken everything she'd been willing to give.

And it had been *explosive.*

But now that they'd come—him once, her twice—he wanted to get to the bottom of what had brought her here tonight.

It took him several seconds to find his voice. Clearing his throat, he spoke as nonchalantly as he could. "So, how was your day?"

Ava huffed out a laugh, which had been his goal. But then her mouth pinched tight, and her gaze cut away before she answered in a subdued tone.

"It was fine."

He propped himself up on his elbow to get a better look at her face. "Did something happen?"

Her chest rose and fell as she let out a long sigh. "You could say that."

"Do you want to talk about it?"

She fingered her "Ava" necklace—the only thing she wore—and didn't meet his eyes. "I, um, I saw my ex today."

"Oh." Roman's brows rose and he suddenly understood, although he wished he didn't. "Where?"

"I was getting coffee before I caught the train to work," she said. "I usually make it at home, but I wanted to splurge, you know? Get a fancier drink. Before I could even take a sip, I turned around and there he was, standing right between me and the door."

Roman's heart broke for her. "Did he see you?"

She gave a hollow laugh. "Oh yeah. He was already staring right at me, so I know he recognized me from behind."

Roman's mouth tightened. So the asshole had seen her, and then hadn't said anything *or* left, knowing that she'd turn around and spot him. Probably also knowing how it would affect her and letting it happen anyway. What a dick.

But Roman didn't want to make this about him, so he kept those thoughts to himself and only asked, "Did he say anything?"

Her lips twisted bitterly. "Yeah." She dropped her voice to mimic her ex's tone. "'Hi Ava.' That was it."

"And what did you say?"

She shrugged. "I just said, 'Hi Hector,' and left. Then I threw my drink out."

"I'm surprised you didn't throw it at him."

Her lips curved slightly, but she looked sad. "I'd never make a scene like that."

Roman had the feeling there was more she'd wanted to say to the guy, but she wouldn't do that in public, either. He hesitated, not sure how she'd respond to comforting, but it wasn't in his nature to hold back when someone was hurting. He reached out and twined his fingers with hers. She gave him a squeeze and didn't let go, which he took as a good sign.

"It really threw me off," she admitted after a moment. "I accidentally handed out the wrong quiz and only realized it when three kids started crying because the questions were about material we haven't covered yet."

"I'm sure they were very relieved to hear it was a mistake."

"They were, but I felt terrible for stressing them out. I let them rip the quizzes up and toss the pieces in the air like confetti, which they loved, but it meant I had to sweep the room during lunch. At the end of the day, one of my students even asked if I was okay. I said I was, but . . . I wasn't okay. I'm *not* okay. All because I saw stupid Hector at Starbucks."

The brittle tone of her voice snapped something in Roman and he stopped worrying about comforting her too much. He pulled her into his arms and tucked her head against his chest. To his immense relief, she slipped an arm around his waist and cuddled closer.

"It's ridiculous," she muttered. "It's going on two years, and most of the time, I don't even think about him. But running into him unexpectedly . . . it was like all the old pain and grief came flooding back."

Roman didn't know exactly what had gone down with Ava and her ex-husband, and it didn't seem like his place to ask, but he wanted to make her feel better. "He can't do anything to you anymore."

She sighed, her breath fanning along his pecs. "Except for reminding me how I tried so hard to do everything right and I still failed."

"Trying isn't failing. You only fail when you don't try."

"Whatever you say, Master Yoda."

Before he could commit fully to the *Star Wars* reference, her phone rang. Ava twisted in his grip to reach for it, but when she glanced at the screen, her face fell.

"Do you need to take that?" he asked.

She gave him a miserable look. "It's my ex–mother-in-law, Gloria. Hector must have told her he saw me."

"Are you going to answer?"

She stared at the ringing phone in her hand for a long moment. Then she silenced it and tossed it into a pile of blankets they'd kicked aside during their lovemaking.

"No. There's nothing I need to hear from her."

Roman's chest swelled with pride. It was clear it wasn't easy for her to ignore the call. He wanted to ask more but stopped himself. If she wanted to tell him, she would.

Ava disentangled herself from his embrace and sat up, her dark curls tumbling enticingly over her shoulders.

"Look, Roman," she began. "This is all . . . well, it's amazing. Really."

"But . . . ?" Looked like the sharing portion of the evening was over.

She dipped her chin, as if she were feeling shy. As if they weren't still naked, as if she hadn't just had her gorgeous thighs wrapped around his hips, her mouth around his—

"But I've never done something like this before," she went on. "And I think it's best to be up front."

He sensed her pulling away from him, and he didn't like it. Acting on impulse, he cupped her ankle gently and slid his hand up her leg. "I agree."

"I think you can understand why I don't want more than . . . this."

"Uh-huh." He ran his hand over her knee. "I understand."

"Just one perfect night, then back to my real life." She glanced down to where his fingers caressed her inner thigh. "What are you doing?" ·

"Touching you. Should I stop?"

"No, but I—" Her cheeks reddened, and she lowered her voice. "I have to go clean up."

"Ava." His hand drifted nearer to his goal. "You're not dirty."

"But we just—"

"*Sex* is not dirty."

She sent him a stern look that didn't match the bashful lilt of her voice. "Roman. I'm still wet."

God, she was delightful.

"I know," he said, the words close to a purr. "I was licking you here earlier."

She covered her face with her hands and mumbled, "Oh my god."

"I want to do it again," he said in her ear, just to see her reaction.

As predicted, her eyes went wide and scandalized.

"But you already . . ." She glanced down at his lap, where the condom he still wore was holding on by a hope and a prayer.

"I already came?" He shrugged. "Doesn't mean I'm finished giving you pleasure."

"Even after we . . . ?" She trailed off, like she couldn't even say it. Like she couldn't even contemplate that he'd want anything to do with her after he'd climaxed.

He trailed his fingers to the sensitive crease of her thigh. "Why not?"

While he enjoyed her demure responses—so at odds with her demeanor when in the throes of passion—he couldn't stand her thinking he found any part of her body unappealing.

Uncertainty lurked in the hazel depths of her eyes. Like maybe she didn't believe him, but she wanted to. She looked away again before she spoke.

"I just . . . want to make it clear what we're doing here," she said, but the huskiness in her tone gave her away. "I don't expect anything from you. And as for me—"

Her breath hitched as he brushed his fingertips over her folds. When she didn't continue, he paused. "You were saying?"

Her eyelids fluttered. "I don't remember."

He pressed soft kisses to her shoulder, nuzzling her hair and inhaling the faint scent of orange blossoms. "You want to know what I think?"

She leaned into him and tipped her head back to rest against his chest. "What?"

"I think . . ." He drew his fingers up to swirl them over her clit. ". . . that we are two consenting adults who enjoy each other's company, and if we want to get together occasionally for mind-blowing sex, then we should."

"Exactly." She sounded relieved. "I'm glad you understand."

"There's only two things I want from you."

Her eyes went wary. "And those are?"

He bit back a smile. Had she really thought he would let her set the terms without a little negotiation? Who did she take him for?

"One: you let me make all the arrangements and pamper you."

She sucked in a breath, probably to complain, but at his raised eyebrow, her lips settled into an adorable pout. "Fine. But don't go overboard. What's the second thing?"

"That you believe me when I say I like every part of you." He slipped his middle finger inside her, finding her soft and dewy. "Even the wet bits. *Especially* the wet bits."

She uttered a gentle groan, her body going pliant against him. He worked his finger back and forth in her tight heat, teasing her. "Do you believe me?"

When she nodded, he added a second finger.

"Mmm, I do believe—oh! One more thing."

He nuzzled her neck. "You drive a hard bargain, lady. What's your one more thing?"

"I don't . . ." She let out a little whimper as he began to pump his fingers faster. "I don't think we should communicate. In between our, um, meetings. I'll reach out to you, and if you're free, we'll—"

"Do this?" He picked up the pace, fucking her with his hand.

"*Yesss.*" It was more of a moan than a word. And after that, it was the only word she said for some time.

After round two, she lay against his side with her head on his chest.

"You know," she said softly, "I'm not up front like this with anyone else in my life."

"No?" He tucked her curls behind her ear so he could see

her face. Her eyes were closed, and she was the perfect picture of relaxation.

She shook her head, and the curls sprang free. "With you, I can do the opposite of whatever I'd normally do. It's refreshing."

"Why me? How am I different?"

He tensed, waiting to hear her reasoning. He'd once had a woman he was dating tell him she didn't see him as a real person because he was rich. As if having money—something he'd come to later in life—meant he didn't have feelings.

"You're easy to talk to," Ava mused, idly tracing the outline of one of his nipples with her index finger. "And it's probably *because* you have no connection to anyone else I know. It means I can come to you when . . . when I need to."

"Happy to be of service," he murmured.

So, Ava wasn't using him for his money, or his business, or for fame. But she *was* using him as a coping mechanism.

It rankled a bit, but Roman couldn't really blame her. He didn't know what it was like to be divorced, didn't know how he'd navigate the emotional aftermath if he were in that situation. He'd had business ventures fail, but that wasn't the same thing.

Besides, he'd be lying if he said he wasn't getting something out of this arrangement too. A night's reprieve from the crushing weight of his responsibilities to have incredible sex with a smart, beautiful woman who made no other demands on him or his time? Some would say he was living the dream.

So why did part of him wish she'd make a few demands other than *don't call me?*

The fact was, it didn't matter if she was using him to get over her ex or not. She'd been clear from the beginning where she stood. And it wasn't like he had the time or inclination for anything more either. She was right to clarify the terms between them.

Still, he wasn't ready to let her go just yet.

"Stay tonight," he said, even as he worried he was coming on too strong. "My schedule is clear until morning, and then I can arrange for you to be driven home."

She tilted her chin and gave him a long look. Then she smiled, and it was like the sun breaking through clouds after a heavy rain, filling him with warmth.

"Yes," she murmured. "I'd like that."

There was no reason why that should've made him so happy. But it did.

Chapter 9

It was Ava's thirty-third birthday. The magical night Ava had spent with Roman at the Dulce Flor a week ago seemed light years away. She stood at the sink in her grandmother's kitchen in the Bronx and tried not to scream.

Over the course of her life, she'd managed to accumulate a number of impressive skills. She could manage a classroom of twenty-five sixth graders, navigate Manhattan traffic like a seasoned cabbie, and crochet with her eyes closed.

One thing she could not do?

Stop an eighty-one-year-old woman from harassing her about marriage.

"Abuela," she said, smiling through clenched teeth. "It's been nearly two years. Hector and I are over."

Her grandmother, however, was not to be deterred, and she brandished a wooden spoon for emphasis. With her diminutive stature and red lipstick, Esperanza Rodriguez looked like a Boricua fairy godmother, one who could turn overripe platanos into stretch limos and chancletas into high heels—but instead of glass, the shoes were made of ceramic and had the date of someone's cousin's Sweet Sixteen scrawled along the side in metallic gold marker.

"Yo sé," Esperanza said, despite the fact that she clearly did not seem to know. "Pero I was visiting my sister and we saw Gloria sweeping outside, so we went over and she said—"

At the sound of her ex–mother-in-law's name, Ava squeezed the sponge so hard every drop of soap exploded onto the dishes.

"You don't have to tell me," she said, her voice as tight as her grip. Considering she'd only run into Hector a week before, she could well imagine what Gloria had said. After all, Gloria had said it to Ava herself a number of times.

Por favor, nena. Take him back. He doesn't know what he's doing.

Even now, anger seared through Ava's veins. As if *she* had been the one to leave him instead of the other way around. As if Hector simply *hadn't realized* he was throwing away a ten-year relationship, like he was a child who'd accidentally given away his favorite toy and needed his mommy to retrieve it.

Esperanza scowled and banged the spoon against the side of the pot, startling Ava out of her memories. "Ay muchacha, no seas difícil."

Ava shut her eyes, remembering Roman's words. *Something tells me you've never been difficult a day in your life.*

Not according to Esperanza Rodriguez.

"Déjalo, Espie," Ava's grandfather Willie said from his seat at the counter, where he flipped through the pages of *El Diario* newspaper. The expression on his lined brown face was mild as he raised his cafecito for a sip. "No habalamos de Hector, cariño."

Ava bit back another scream. Damn her cousin Sammy for singing the song from *Encanto* anytime someone brought up her ex. Now "We Don't Talk About Hector" was going to be stuck in her head all freaking day.

Since she didn't trust herself not to break something, Ava

abandoned the dishes and opened the fridge to retrieve a head of lettuce. The door of the refrigerator was covered with photos of Esperanza and Willie's children, grandchildren, and great-grandchildren. Ava's high school yearbook photo had once held the central place of honor under magnets shaped like vejigante masks, but it had been shifted over to make room for the *Buzz Weekly* magazine cover announcing Jasmine and Ashton's engagement.

The oven door squeaked as Esperanza checked on the pernil. The aroma of slow-roasted pork filled the kitchen, comforting and familiar. Alas, Esperanza's criticism was also all too familiar.

"¿Pero tú sabes qué?" her grandmother went on. "These days, you don't need to be married to have children. ¡Soy progresiva!"

Great. Esperanza was moving on to her other favorite topic: Ava's childlessness. Instead of rolling her eyes, Ava slipped on her Resting Pleasant Face.

"I'm fully aware of that," she muttered, smiling as she tore lettuce leaves with more force than necessary.

"And then, when you have a baby, you can move back in here with us and we can take care of it!"

Ava nearly choked at her grandmother's gleeful declaration. Across the room, her grandfather cast his gaze toward the ceiling and sighed.

"That is . . . very sweet of you," Ava began, even as she pictured her grandmother telling a newborn that crying would cause wrinkles.

Setting aside the spoon on a glass dish shaped like a coquí, Esperanza reached up to cup Ava's cheeks in her hands. "I just don't want you to be alone cuando eres una vieja, like me."

"You're not an old lady, Bwela," Ava replied, even as she

tried not to notice how frail her vibrant, larger-than-life grand-mother's wrists had become.

"Está bien, I know I'm old. ¿Pero tú?" Esperanza tapped Ava's chest. "You're already thirty-three. You need to have babies while you can. Then, after your husband dies, your children will take care of you."

"Oye." Willie looked up from the newspaper. "No me mates."

His affronted *Don't kill me* did the trick. When Esperanza scurried over to argue with him, Ava took the opportunity to duck out of the kitchen to collect her thoughts.

In the living room, next to a glass-enclosed cabinet full of porcelain angels, Ava pressed her fingers to her temples, trying to stave off the stress headache that was brewing.

She loved her grandmother. Truly, she did.

But sometimes? The old woman drove her fucking nuts.

Ava wished she could state in no uncertain terms that she was never getting back together with Hector and she didn't want to hear another word about it. She often lay awake at night imagining how that conversation would go, and how it would feel to let loose all the things she wanted to say.

But that would only lead to a fight, and nothing would change. It would only confirm that *she* was the problem. Besides, her grandparents had helped raise her and she simply didn't have it in her to be rude to them.

A knock at the door echoed through her pounding temples.

"I'll get it," Ava called. She straightened her shoulders, gave her curls a shake, and strode to the door. When she opened it, her face broke into a wide smile.

"Mommy," she said with relief.

"Happy birthday, baby." Patricia Griffith stepped over the

threshold, bringing the January cold with her, and caught Ava in a tight, freesia-scented hug. She was a couple inches shorter than Ava, her skin a couple shades darker. Her hair was mostly gray now, and she kept her tight curls cropped short, but she made aging look stylish. Patricia kissed Ava's cheek and whispered, "Is she going on about Hector again?"

"All the greatest hits," Ava mumbled as she straightened.

Patricia shrugged out of her long down coat—even after living in New York for forty years, she still wasn't fond of the winters—and gave Ava a conspiratorial smile. "I'll distract her."

"¿Quién es?" Esperanza yelled.

"It's me, Espie," Patricia called, strolling into the kitchen.

There were a lot of excited exclamations from Esperanza, and through the doorway Ava could see her grandmother embracing Patricia warmly.

Esperanza and Willie were technically Ava's father Miguel's parents, but they loved Patricia as one of their own. Ava knew it drove Olympia crazy, although her stepmother would never admit it. Patricia had been best friends with Michelle's mom, Valentina, since they'd met working at Macy's when they were in college. During those years, Patricia had spent holidays with the Rodriguez family, since her own still lived in Barbados. That was how Patricia had met Ava's dad, the oldest of Esperanza and Willie's six kids. After a whirlwind romance, Patricia and Miguel got married, and along came Ava. While the marriage didn't last, Patricia stayed close with her former in-laws.

After Patricia and Miguel divorced, Ava had spent a few years living with Esperanza and Willie while Patricia finished nursing school. Ava had adored her grandparents, and in their house, she had her own room, something she hadn't had in either of her parents' apartments. But she'd never been able to shake the feeling that she was a guest, and her mom had reminded her constantly that she needed to be on her best behavior for her grandparents.

In the back of Ava's mind, she'd worried that if she was bad, her grandparents would kick her out too. And then where would she go?

But those days were over. She had her own place now. Sometimes she even left a dish in the sink overnight, just because she could.

Logically—and thanks to Colleen, her former therapist—Ava understood that her parents hadn't divorced because of her. She knew that she'd been sent to live with Esperanza and Willie because her parents had been struggling financially and needed help with childcare. Still, deeply rooted beliefs had a way of twining themselves into the foundation of a person's psyche, and no matter how diligently she tried to root them out, they managed to push through the cracks.

Behind her, someone else knocked on the door, and Ava opened it to see Jasmine's smiling face. Jasmine was flanked by her fiancé—the telenovela star Ashton Suárez—and Ashton's ten-year-old son, Yadiel.

"Happy birthday!" Jasmine rushed in and kissed Ava on the cheek. "I'm so glad we're in town to celebrate with you."

"We brought you a present." Yadiel held up a massive silver gift bag stuffed with light pink tissue paper.

"Oh, you didn't have to do that," Ava said in surprise, taking the bag from Yadi.

"Es tu cumple." Ashton kissed Ava's cheek as he passed by, and then Yadi popped up on his tiptoes—and Ava leaned down—so he could do the same.

Ashton was tall, with dark curly hair and chiseled features

that had made him a star in Spanish language television. The older Yadi got, the more he looked like his father. They had the same dark brown eyes and smile, although Yadi's teeth would probably need braces in the next couple of years, and his hair was a lighter wheat blonde.

Everyone hung up their coats and trooped into the kitchen—the heart and soul of Casa Rodriguez. Esperanza hugged and kissed everyone, and made a big deal over Jasmine's engagement ring, even though she'd seen it before. Then she pulled Ashton, her favorite telenovela star, off to the side to get his opinion on the pernil.

Ava and Jasmine sat at the kitchen table, where Yadi bounced on his toes until Ava opened her gift. Ava let out a gasp when she saw the expensive hair dryer.

"It's the kind my stylist uses. The diffuser is *amazing* for drying curly hair," Jasmine said.

Yadi dug deeper into the bag. "There's more."

He filled Ava's lap with office supplies—brightly colored sticky notes, gel pens, fancy highlighters, and more.

"I picked them out," Yadi explained proudly, slinging his skinny arms around Jasmine's neck and leaning his head on her shoulder. "Because you're a teacher, and Mami said you like this stuff."

"I do." Ava smiled through the pain of hearing him call Jasmine "Mami."

Jasmine gave Yadi's arms a squeeze and ruffled his hair fondly. "Go ask Abuelita for something to drink, okay? You said you were thirsty in the car."

When Yadiel bounded away, Jasmine turned her attention back to Ava. "How's it going? You've been quiet in the group chat."

"Just busy with school," Ava said lightly. She couldn't admit that the constant wedding chatter was wearing on her. Or that when she saw Jasmine with Ashton and Yadiel, she couldn't stop the jealousy burning in her gut, the intense feeling of *I want that too.* God, she was a terrible person. Jasmine had gone through hell before meeting Ashton, even having her last breakup splashed across magazine covers. But it didn't matter how much Ava chastised herself for envying her cousin—the feeling was there, and it wasn't going away.

Her phone buzzed with an incoming text, and Ava was grateful for the distraction.

"Is it Michelle?" Jasmine asked.

Ava shook her head as she typed back a quick reply to her sister. "It's Willow. Dad and Olympia are running late with the portokalopita."

"Mmm. Olympia's orange cake." Jasmine's expression turned wistful. "You know, I don't miss the chaos of this place when I'm in Los Angeles, but I do miss the food."

Ava had to agree. While the central point of her family experience revolved around her Puerto Rican grandparents' house, her extended family was a case study in multicultural diversity. Jasmine's mother was half-Filipina, Michelle's father was Italian, Ava's mother was Bajan and her stepmom was Greek, and Ronnie and Sammy's dad was Jamaican. The mix of cultures, customs, and foods present at every birthday party and holiday celebration had imbued the Rodriguez family with flavor and depth.

And a huge gossip network.

Michelle showed up next, with her boyfriend Gabriel Aguilar in tow. Gabe, a physical therapist and personal trainer, carried a large white bakery box in his heavily muscled arms. Michelle often referred to him as her "Latino Superman," and the moniker fit.

"We come bearing cannoli," Michelle announced to the room at large. "And no, that's not a euphemism."

Yadiel scrunched up his face. "What's a—"

"It's a joke," Ashton said quickly. "It means she's not kidding."

"Like when people say 'literally' but they mean 'figuratively'?" the boy asked.

Ashton blinked. "Claro. Just like that."

Shooting Michelle a flinty-eyed look, Ashton ushered Yadiel into the living room. "Time for television."

Michelle grinned. "He's gonna learn what innuendo is at some point."

"In the window?" Yadiel repeated on the way out.

While Abuela fawned over Gabe—and the box full of Italian desserts from Arthur Avenue—Michelle joined Ava and Jasmine at the table.

"Happy birthday, A." Michelle passed Ava a card. "Your gift is in the mail. Didn't think you'd want to open it here."

"Did you send her another vibrator?" Jasmine hissed under her breath.

"I sure did. Which is why I'm her prima favorita."

"Look, I can't argue that it's not a good gift, but wait until you see this blow dryer—"

Ava tuned them out.

January used to feel like a double fresh start—the beginning of a new year, followed closely by her birthday. But with the divorce finalized and the last of her boxes unpacked in her new apartment, she was at a loss for what to do next. Her usual January tradition of making vision boards and journaling about her life goals seemed pointless.

No, not pointless. *Scary.*

She was thirty-three years old, and she had no idea what she wanted from the rest of her life.

The question Roman had asked her that first night still lingered in her mind.

What would you do if you didn't have to be perfect?

She still didn't know the answer. All she'd ever wanted was a big romantic love story. A happily-ever-after. A husband and kids. A steady job. A good life.

She'd given it her all.

And she'd failed.

Her family wanted her to try again. But she couldn't stand the thought of opening her heart, giving herself to another person, only to have them throw her away.

As the conversation flowed around her in a mix of English and Spanish, Ava tried to imagine bringing Roman to one of these gatherings.

Her brain immediately rejected it. They were from different worlds, and his role in her life was specific and defined. Besides, there was no way Roman, in his three-thousand-dollar suits, would fit in here in her grandmother's kitchen.

Although he'd seemed at home behind the bar . . .

It didn't matter. There was a reason she hadn't told him her birthday was coming up. He might have wanted to do something—get her a gift, probably—and she didn't want to invite that level of closeness. Boundaries made her time with him easier to compartmentalize.

Physical intimacy was one thing. Everything else? Been there, done that. No gracias.

She understood, on an intellectual level, that other people managed to fall in love again after heartbreak. But in her soul,

Ava knew the truth: that big, romantic, forever kind of love just wasn't for her.

No strings.

No feelings.

No falling in love, she told herself sternly.

She looked at Jasmine and Michelle, talking and laughing with their men. They'd both hidden their relationships at first. And while everything had worked out for them, Ava had no such delusions about her fling with Roman turning into anything more serious. Eventually, he'd realize he was too busy, or that she was too boring, and he'd stop entertaining her whims. He would likely end up with some socialite who knew how to be a CEO's wife. Which was fine, because she didn't want to be anyone's wife.

Still, she didn't want to face the embarrassment of telling her cousins when it ended—because it *would* end—so it was better not to say anything at all.

Maybe she didn't know what the rest of her life would look like just yet. But New Ava was in charge now, and at the very least, what was coming had to be better than what had come before.

That was what Ava wished for later that night as she blew out the candles on the cake her father and stepmother had finally showed up with.

Please, let it be better.

Chapter 10

It was a Tuesday in late January, just after twelve noon, and Roman's bare feet were soaking in bubbling, lavender-scented water.

It was his mother Dulce's birthday and this was the only time he—well, Camille—had managed to carve out from a day packed with meetings. Camille had scheduled all of them to take place at the Dulce Flor in Times Square, and now he was squeezing in a midday pedicure with his mother at the hotel spa.

He'd gotten the idea for a mother-son spa date from Ava, of all people. Not that she was talking to him—he was abiding by her "no communication" rule, even though he chafed at the limitation. He wasn't sure if he was more frustrated by the boundaries she'd set or the fact that he was tempted to cross them.

Don't text her. Should be a simple enough rule to follow, right? But he found himself wanting to reach out multiple times a day. And not just about sex either.

Like now. While Ava hadn't directly suggested he go with his mom for a pedicure, she'd helped him recognize the value of spontaneous free time with people he cared about. And he wanted to tell her about it.

But he couldn't.

Beside him, the other frustrating woman in his life sat with her feet wrapped in some kind of pink substance. Since she couldn't get away, Roman took the opportunity to broach the topic of her imminent move.

"How's the apartment search coming along?" he asked.

His mother didn't look up from the copy of *Buzz Weekly* she was flipping through. "Bien."

Thanks to her many years working at a nail salon, Dulce had a deep appreciation for gossip magazines. And now that she'd retired, one of her favorite pastimes was to get her nails done by someone else.

"I can put you in contact with my real estate agent," Roman offered.

"That's okay."

"Mami, I—"

She pinned him with a look. "Who do you think found all the apartments we lived in when you were young? Who do you think found the house Keith and I bought in Queens?"

Shit. He'd offended her. "All right, but there's no rush, and you'll still have your rooms in my apartment if you ever want to come back."

She cut him off with a shake of her head. "It's your space, you should use it how you want. Mickey and I have already taken up room in your home for too long."

Roman's gut felt hollow at the reminder. Not only was his sister going to college and his mom moving out, but Mickey wouldn't even be coming back during her breaks from school.

"How is the book coming along?" Dulce asked.

Roman bit back a groan, but gratefully accepted the change in subject. "Not well."

"I don't see why. You wrote all the time when you were a kid."

"That's because my friends were paying me to do their homework for them."

She gave a dismissive shrug and didn't look up from the magazine. "Bueno, we all have to start somewhere. Put it in the book."

Roman wasn't sure "cheating on homework" was the best thing to admit in a book about successful qualities in business, but he did have to start the manuscript somewhere, and he was short on ideas. He jotted down a note in his phone.

Dulce turned a page and let out an exclamation. "¡Mira pa' allá! It's your friend."

Roman peered at the glossy two-page spread. His old buddy Ashton Suárez smiled up at him from a red carpet photo. Ashton wore a slick black suit and at his side, his fiancée Jasmine Lin was decked out in a red strapless gown. They looked stunning, every inch the Puerto Rican power couple who'd taken Hollywood by storm.

"Ay, they look so beautiful," Dulce said wistfully. "Have you heard any updates about the wedding?"

Roman shook his head. "Not since they asked me to be the best man. They've been busy."

"Did they set the date at least?"

"August. At the Bellísima in Condado."

Dulce made a judgmental noise in the back of her throat. "August wedding in Puerto Rico? It's going to be hot."

He shrugged. "It's when their filming schedules allow it."

She turned the page to a tell-all from a former child star. "Well, they still have plenty of time to plan."

A pair of salon aestheticians entered the room and Roman

stopped talking about his notoriously private friend. But when he glanced at his phone, he saw he had a text from Ashton. Speak of el diablo.

Ashton: Boarding our flight. Sorry we missed you. It was Jasmine's cousin's birthday.

Roman: It's cool. I'll be in California in a couple months. We'll meet up then.

Ashton: Oh, and thanks for the signed Jeter jersey. Yadi está que se mea.

Roman grinned at the implication that Ashton's son was so happy, he was pissing himself. A second later, a photo of Yadi wearing a blue and white Yankees jersey and a huge smile popped up on the screen.

Not for the first time, Roman was glad he and Ashton had reconnected. The two of them had met in Miami in their early twenties. Roman had been fresh out of college and working as a bartender while he applied for jobs he wasn't sure he wanted. Dulce had a friend whose cousin was a casting director, and while auditioning for a telenovela, Roman had crossed paths with Ashton, an aspiring actor newly arrived from Puerto Rico.

The second Roman had seen the other man, he'd been sure Ashton would get the part. Ashton was tall and handsome, and Roman had been floored by how quickly Ashton's entire personality and demeanor shifted when he was in character. Witnessing the transformation had given Roman permission to delve more fully into his own role, and by the time they'd left the studio, they'd formed a bond. Fortunately, *Recuerdos Peligrosos* had revolved around two brothers who loved the same woman, so they'd both gotten cast.

The experience of filming together had cemented their friendship, and even after Roman left show business, they'd remained thick as thieves.

Until one day, Ashton had dropped off the face of the planet. He still appeared in telenovelas, but he'd become famously reclusive, not answering phone calls or emails.

Roman couldn't say it hadn't hurt. He'd wondered if he'd done something, but whenever Ashton did reply, he just said he was working a lot, or that he was busy with his family. Eventually, Roman had taken the hint and left him alone.

Then, a year and a half ago, Roman had been buying mints during a layover at Chicago O'Hare when he'd seen Ashton's face on the cover of a magazine. Roman couldn't resist buying it, and from his first-class seat he read about the son Ashton had hidden from the world for eight years.

Most of the article had been speculation, but it had included some blurry photos of Yadiel, along with pictures of Ashton and Jasmine.

Roman had texted Ashton immediately, just a single word: "*Drinks?*"

He'd waited, chest tight, bracing himself for silence, or a refusal, or another "I'm busy," until he saw the indication that Ashton was typing back. A second later, a reply popped up: "*Sí.*"

They met up in New York at a speakeasy, and it was like they'd never been apart. Ashton had explained everything and apologized for shutting Roman out. Roman, happy to have his friend back and to finally know why Ashton had disappeared, forgave him. They laughed over the crow's feet and gray hairs they'd developed since the last time they'd gotten trashed together, and proceeded to drink too many gin and tonics before parting for the night. Shortly after, Roman took a rare day off to meet Yadiel and Jasmine. From then on, he made time for them whenever he could and did his level best to spoil Yadi rotten and earn the "tío" label he'd been given.

The phone rang before Roman could text Ashton again, and the name of Roman's publicist, Nigella Daniels, popped up on the screen.

Roman hesitated. He knew why Nigella was calling, and he didn't want to talk about it, especially not with his mother present.

"Answer it," Dulce said, not looking up from the magazine. "I don't mind."

Biting back a sigh, Roman accepted the call and raised the phone to his ear. "Hi Nigella. And no, I haven't been avoiding you."

"Glad to hear it." Nigella's tone, as always, was a mix of cheerful and hurried. "The HIV/AIDS research fundraiser gala is next week. Did you line up your plus-one?"

Roman sighed, remembering how Ava had erected her boundaries before he could even consider how to issue the invitation. "Not yet."

"Well, there's going to be a lot of Broadway people there, and Anastasia Marquez would love to go, if you want a companion. Do you remember her? She's—"

"I remember her," Roman broke in.

Anastasia was an up-and-coming stage actress, a triple threat of incredible talent. Roman had escorted her to last year's Met Gala and attended the premiere of her current Broadway show, *Light It Up*, over the summer.

The "Dominican Diva," as she called herself—a nod to her opera background—was an excellent plus-one. She was confident and charismatic, had a great sense of humor, and knew how to rock a designer dress.

The only problem was, both times he'd seen Anastasia, they'd ended up going back to her tiny walk-up apartment in Hell's Kitchen to fuck.

Roman thought of Ava. They'd spent only two nights together, three months apart, and he wasn't even allowed to text her unless she initiated contact first. The boundaries were glaringly clear.

So why did the thought of attending an event with another woman, one he'd previously been happy to engage in adult activities with, strike him as wrong?

"Thanks, but I'll go on my own," he told Nigella. "Need to make it an early night."

"Working on the book?"

He latched on to the excuse. "Precisely."

"Excellent. I'm already lining up late night talk shows for when it comes out."

Roman's back prickled with sweat. "You're the best, Ni."

"Don't mention it. Say hi to Camille for me."

"Will do."

He hung up, then put his reading glasses back on, the better to ignore the speculative look his mother was casting in his direction.

"Was that Nigella?" Dulce asked, all innocence, as if she hadn't been sitting right there when he said the publicist's name.

"Yes." He opened his email, although he barely registered the new messages flooding in. He tensed, like a mouse in a field who'd seen the shadow of a predatory bird overhead.

His mother's voice was sly. "Is this about a *date*?"

The raptor's claws clamped around him.

"No."

"*Román.*"

The way she said his name—the way she'd *always* said his name when he was trying to pull a fast one on her—awoke his inner teenager.

He tore off his reading glasses and sent her an exasperated look. "Go ahead and ask. I know you want to."

And he wouldn't have a moment's peace until she did.

A spark of glee lit her eyes, and she dragged it out, likely just to annoy him. "Are . . . you . . . *seeing* someone?"

He huffed out a breath and cast his gaze at the ceiling. "Mami—"

"Because if you are—"

"I'm not—"

"Ay dios mío, you *are*." Delight transfused Dulce's features. "Tell me all about her."

"There's nothing to tell," he mumbled, annoyed at having somehow given something away. "It's not serious."

Her brows snapped together and the corners of her mouth pinched in disapproval. "Mijo, you're too old to be pulling that shit."

He sputtered. "But it's *not*."

"You're forty, Roman. When is it going to *get* serious?"

"She doesn't want it to be," he muttered, irritated at himself for falling into his mother's trap.

"What's her name?"

"I'm not telling you." He realized immediately how immature that sounded, and sighed. "It doesn't matter. I'm probably never going to see her again."

Dulce returned to her magazine. "Well, you let me know when you do."

"I will not."

"Suit yourself. I'll find out anyway."

Knowing her, she probably would. Roman put his reading glasses back on and tried to focus on emails.

But all he could think about was what it would be like to attend the gala with Ava on his arm.

Chapter 11

February

Ava: Are you free tonight?

Roman: For you? Of course.

Ava exhaled in relief when Roman's reply popped up. She was going to start climbing the walls if she stayed in tonight, and if she had to spend it with her family, she would scream.

It wasn't her first wedding anniversary without Hector, but it was the first since the divorce had been made official. To make matters worse, for the past week her grandmother had been texting her old photos of Hector. Ava was on the verge of blocking Esperanza's number.

Yes, she could have reached out to Jasmine or Michelle, or her mom or Damaris. It wasn't like she didn't have people in her life who cared about her. But they'd know what today was— why the hell had she gotten married the day before Valentine's

Day?—and they'd spend the whole night looking at her with worry in their eyes. Or worse, *pity*.

She couldn't take it. Not tonight. Not when her feelings were already so close to the surface. Ava didn't *do* breakdowns. She didn't do dramatic displays of emotion. Not even after Hector told her he was leaving. When she'd called her mother and Michelle to come over, she'd been calm. Okay, she'd probably been closer to catatonic, but she hadn't yelled or cried or cursed. She hadn't made a scene.

Even in the worst moment of her life, she'd behaved well. She'd been *good*.

Be good, Ava.

How many times had she heard that phrase? Every time her mom dropped her off to visit her dad and his new wife. Or for sleepovers with Michelle at Titi Val and Uncle Dom's house. Or when she had moved in with Esperanza and Willie.

Be good for Abuela.

Be good for Daddy and Olympia.

Be good for Titi Val.

Be good for your teachers.

Ava was so fucking tired of being *good*.

Not that being with Roman was about being *bad*, per se. It was more about being *free*. Nothing she said or did with him would get back to her family, thus affecting their perception of her and her role in the Rodriguez dynamic.

Even her apartment, which was brand new and all hers, was a reminder of her divorce. It was a perfectly nice one-bedroom in a prewar elevator building. No, it wasn't renovated, but there were new appliances in the galley kitchen, and Ava had made it cozy with a profusion of plants, a muted pink and cream color scheme, and scented candles on every surface—all things Hector had hated.

But the only reason Ava lived here at all was because Jasmine had accidentally opened the door to the second bedroom in Ava's old apartment and found it crammed with all the things Hector had left behind. Once her cousins had realized Ava was struggling to cover the rent on the two-bedroom she'd shared with Hector, they'd staged an intervention. Michelle had hired a moving company to box up Hector's shit and drop it off on his mother's porch, and Jasmine had enlisted her real estate broker to find a rental Ava could afford on her teaching salary. While Ava was grateful for their help, she also felt horribly guilty about inconveniencing them, not to mention embarrassed.

So no, she didn't want to spend the evening sitting around the apartment that should have felt like home but didn't, reminiscing about all the sad and shameful moments that had landed her here.

A night with Roman, making new, pleasurable memories, was a *much* better alternative.

For security purposes, Ava shot Damaris a text.

Ava: I'm seeing him tonight.

Damaris: Where?

Bless Damaris for not asking why Ava was spending her anniversary with Roman.

Ava: At the Dulce Flor in Times Square.

Damaris: Check in tomorrow morning, please.

Ava: I will.

Damaris: Then meet me for brunch afterward because I want DETAILS.

Ava chuckled, glad she had at least one person to discuss Roman with. Damaris had also sneakily maneuvered plans on Valentine's Day, probably so Ava wouldn't be alone, which was sweet of her.

Ava: I'll make a reservation. Isla Bonita Cafe?

Damaris: You know it. Best deal on bottomless mimosas in the entire borough!

Another text appeared. This one was from the fancy car service Roman used, containing the info for her pick up. While Ava still felt a little guilty about Roman paying for things like food, transportation, and the hotel, she couldn't deny it was a turn on. For someone who'd spent her whole life counting pennies, and who was the "responsible one" when it came to organizing any sort of outing, it was nice to have someone else handle all the details.

One of Hector's stated reasons for leaving her was that he wanted to get out of the Bronx and travel the world. Considering he had never once purchased a plane ticket on his own, Ava couldn't imagine how he was managing that goal. But Hector and his inability to navigate an airline's website weren't her problem anymore.

Right now, her biggest problem was deciding which of her sexy new lingerie to wear for her assignation with Roman.

Opting for the black and red lace demi bra with matching thong, she covered it up with a thick purple sweater, black slacks, and gray ankle boots with a low heel. After packing her overnight bag, she went downstairs to the car.

Roman was waiting for her in the lobby when she arrived.

There was something very *Pretty Woman* about the whole scenario. On one level, Ava didn't like how it felt to arrive at a hotel when every single employee probably knew she was there to have sex with their *boss*. But at the same time, stepping into the luxurious and modern lobby and being greeted by a handsome and successful hotel magnate . . . it definitely gave her a thrill. She couldn't reconcile the two conflicting feelings.

But then wasn't that her whole life? Feeling one thing while doing another? At least this time she was doing what *she* wanted instead of what others wanted of her.

Besides, she was hardly the first person to show up at a hotel for sex. Probably not even the first woman to show up at *this* hotel to have sex with *Roman*. She could be a reasonable adult and stop worrying that everyone was judging her.

Maybe she could even stop judging *herself.*

With Roman, at least, she had an easier time doing that.

He leaned in to kiss her cheek when she approached him. The soft press of his lips and the inviting scent of his cologne sent a thrill racing down her spine and right into her panties.

How are you real? she thought, but all she said was, "Hi."

"I was glad to hear from you," he murmured. His smile was polite, but barely banked fire flickered in his eyes. "Come on."

They entered the elevator with a man and woman who were clearly a couple. The man had his arm wrapped tight around the woman's waist and was whispering in her ear while she giggled. By contrast, Ava stood with her back pressed to the elevator wall, her hands clasped in front of her. Roman was next to her with about two feet of space between them, his hands in the pockets of his designer suit pants, his stance casual.

The couple got off without even sparing Ava or Roman a glance. The doors shut behind them and Ava finally spoke.

"I appreciate you taking the time to—"

"Ava. Please." His brow creased into the pained expression he got whenever she offered to pay for something. Bridging the distance, he took her hand and gave her fingers a squeeze. "Spending time with you is a gift. Stop overthinking."

Her shoulders relaxed a fraction. "All right."

The elevator doors opened and he led her into the suite with a hand on the small of her back. Not possessive, but not *not* possessive either. She kinda liked it.

The penthouse at the Dulce Flor Hotel was the epitome of luxury. This was Ava's second time here, and as before, she was drawn to the view of the quiet, twinkling city through the floor to ceiling glass windows. Despite the Times Square location, none of the noise from below permeated the rarefied air this high up. It was an oasis in the middle of chaos, a sparkling tower rising far above the crowds below.

Ava swallowed hard as she gazed out. Once again, the feeling that *she didn't belong here* washed over her.

"What's going on in there?" Roman asked. She could see

his reflection behind her, a sophisticated and charming phantom with his dark suit and his hair tamed with gel. She knew it would loosen into curls when she ran her fingers through it, and that beneath those designer suits his body was solid and warm, with a scar on his knee from climbing over a chain-link fence when he was a kid.

She turned to look at him, just a flesh and blood man, and yet, at times like these, she felt like they were worlds apart. "In where?"

He tapped his temple.

"Oh." Her cheeks flushed. Her first impulse was to brush it off, but he never ridiculed her questions. "Do you ever feel . . . guilty?"

"Because of all this?" He gestured at the opulence around them, then nodded. "All the time."

Her eyes went wide. "You do?"

"Of course." He stuck his hands in his pockets and moved closer to the glass, looking down at the streets below. "But I work hard on the things that make me the most money in order to funnel it back into the programs that'll help people like . . . well, like who I used to be. People like my mom, who was a single mother for most of my life. The hotels are named for her, you know."

"Dulce?"

He nodded and continued. "I give to the organizations helping people even more vulnerable than we were, in a way I never dreamed would be possible. It's not out of guilt, though, it's out of . . ."

His dark brows dipped in frustration, like he was looking for the right word. She waited without offering a suggestion, giving him space to think.

"Responsibility," he finally said. "Not that it's an obligation, but . . . why have all this if I can't use it to help?"

"You feel a duty to your community?" she clarified, and he looked relieved.

"Yeah. That's it. I grew up in South Williamsburg before it was gentrified. All this? It's still new to me too."

"Do you ever worry about it going away?"

"Constantly. Why do you think I never stop working?"

"What was your first business?" she asked, and was surprised at the cheeky grin he sent her.

"You're not going to like this, profe."

She grinned at the pet name, a shortened version of profesora. "Let's hear it."

"I was in sixth grade."

"A little entrepreneur."

"You know it. By the end of the year, I had a whole homework smuggling ring going on."

"No me digas." She covered her face, muffling the laugh that escaped. "What were you doing, stealing test answers?"

He shook his head. "In hindsight, that would've been easier. Instead, I did other kids' homework for five bucks a pop."

"You scoundrel," she said fondly.

"That was how it started, anyway. Then it became a study circle—five of them paying me three dollars each. I'd read the material out loud and help them organize and write their papers."

"Roman, that's basically tutoring."

"I see that now. I think some of them had undiagnosed learning disabilities."

"If that's the case, I'm sure the smaller group setting helped too."

"Probably. The first time I gave my mom the money I'd made, she asked me if I was selling drugs." He peered around at the suite, as if seeing it for the first time. When he spoke again, his voice was low and distant. "I work hard. Lots of long hours. Most of the time, I don't even get to enjoy what I've built."

Then his gaze flicked to hers, and a smile played at the corner of his mouth. "Until you came along."

"Me?"

"I wouldn't have taken tonight off if you hadn't texted."

Dismay colored her voice. "I knew I was keeping you from something important. You should've told me."

"I deserve a night off every once in a while, too."

"Yes," she said, thinking of the child he'd been, and the man he was now. "You do."

He put his hands on her hips and leaned in. The kiss was short and sweet, and still managed to take her breath away.

"Come on," he said, stepping back and taking her hand. "Let's eat."

Her heart pounded, but she couldn't have said why.

Chapter 12

After dinner, they took their wine glasses out to the balcony. Roman turned on the heat lamp, but it was still chilly, so he used the cold as an excuse to put his arms around Ava while she gazed at the view of the city and the Hudson River.

They knew why they were there, and while he adored getting her naked, he also liked these companionable moments. He wasn't working an event, Ava wasn't one of Nigella's clients, and there were no expectations other than enjoying each other's company for the time they were together. Whether that looked like sex or a quiet interlude like this, he was happy to indulge in either.

He was happy to indulge *her*.

Receiving her text after weeks of radio silence had been a balm to his soul after an extremely difficult day at the office. Yes, it had required some finagling to free up his schedule, but after their night together the previous month, when he'd been so worried about taking time off, everything had been . . . fine. Not a single thing had exploded in his absence.

Which made him wonder if all the calls and meetings and business dinners were really as necessary as he thought they were.

So this time, when Ava had reached out, he'd replied immediately, ready to drop everything to see her. It was killing him to stick to her edict of "no communication" aside from what she initiated. He wanted more.

Starting with the reason for her missive tonight.

"Ava?" He waited until she looked at him. "What happened this time?"

Her face scrunched. "What do you mean?"

He raised his brows meaningfully. "You only text me when something's happened."

He saw the moment when she realized what he meant. Biting her lip, she looked away. There was a long pause before she spoke.

"My anniversary."

The blast of sympathy was like a kick to the solar plexus, flooding him with compassion for this woman. Did she have no one else to turn to in these moments?

It didn't matter. He was honored that she was here. Maybe he was just a coping mechanism for her, but he could also understand that she'd want some area of her life where she had control.

"Ava," he began, tenderness in his voice, but she held up a hand.

"Don't," she said, not meeting his gaze. "Don't pity me. I'm fine."

So she said. Still, he set their glasses aside on the low table and folded her into his arms.

She clutched him around the waist and let out a long sigh, deflating against his chest.

"Thank you for being here," she whispered. "I didn't want to be alone."

"You don't have to be."

She rested her head on his shoulder and tucked her face into his collar, then jolted suddenly and pulled back.

"Shoot, I'm probably getting lipstick on your shirt—which is such a cliché, I can't even stand it. I'll pay for dry—"

He cupped the nape of her neck and yanked her back into his embrace. His chest shook as he chuckled softly.

"I'm proud to have your lipstick on my collar," he said solemnly, making her smile.

"Hush," she said. "Don't tease me."

"I'm serious." He dipped his head to look at her. "But I think I deserve a little background information."

Her hazel eyes turned wary. "Like what?"

His jaw worked as he tried to figure out how to ask the question that had haunted him since their first night together. "Ava, did he . . . did he hurt you?"

She sighed and clutched his lapels. "My mother asked the same thing, the night he left me. But no, he never hurt me. Just my heart."

He shut his eyes, holding her tighter. "That's not nothing."

She was quiet for a long moment. "You know how when something big happens, you remember the weirdest details?"

"Mm-hmm."

"Well, the part that always stays with me . . . is that he left his shoes on when he came home."

"Ah." Roman imagined her home was spotless, definitely a no-shoes zone.

"I noticed it, but I was distracted by him throwing his jacket— the one he wore *on the subway*—over the armchair, something I'd repeatedly asked him not to do."

"Disgusting," Roman murmured, thinking about how his mom used to respond when he sat on his bed in "outside clothes."

"So that's what I was thinking about," Ava continued. "I was making a mental note to hang his jacket in the closet, like I always did after he tossed it where it didn't belong."

She released him and paced a few feet away, hugging herself with her arms. Her curls fell around her shoulders in perfect spirals. So pretty, and so remote. Like she was a million miles away. Her voice was hollow when she spoke again. "And then he said he wanted to talk about something."

Roman's eyebrows popped up. "Uh-oh."

"Yeah, uh-oh. It put me on high alert. Had he lost his job? Was someone sick? Had someone *died*?" She shook her head. "But it wasn't any of those things. He just wanted a divorce."

His heart twisted, both at the thought of someone hurting her that way, and at the dispassionate way she recounted the events, like she could have been talking about getting caught without an umbrella during a surprise rain shower. "That must have been devastating."

She didn't answer, just rested her hands on the railing and gazed out at the city. "I asked if there was someone else, because it was the only thing that made sense to me in the moment. And you know what the bastard did?"

He loved the fire that infused her voice when she said "bastard." "What did he do?"

"He said, 'No, babe. There's no one else.'" She made a sound of disgust, her lip curling. "'Babe.' The absolute nerve, to call me 'babe' while ruining my life."

Roman wasn't particularly vengeful, but he was creative. He could think of a few nonviolent ways to ruin *Hector's* life.

Like making political donations with the guy's phone number so he'd be besieged by campaign texts for the rest of his days.

"Note to self," Roman murmured. "Never call Ava 'babe.'"

She shot him an amused look, but he noticed the way her fingers curled into tight fists, like they were cold. Roman shrugged out of his suit jacket and walked up behind her to drop it over her shoulders. Her smile was grateful, and he caught the way she inhaled deeply. Breathing him in? He liked that idea.

When she continued, it came out quieter, like she was running out of steam. "We had a plan. And even when it changed, I never envisioned a future that didn't have him in it."

Roman ached to take her in his arms, but he held back, giving her room to finish. "What did you do?"

"What I always do. I tried to fix it." She shrugged and cast her gaze toward the dark sky. "But he'd already made his decision. A decision that didn't include me, even though it affected me. He looked me dead in the eye and said, 'I don't want to be married to you anymore.' And then he left."

Her voice was bleak, but not fragile. She'd been hurt horribly, but she was strong.

And Roman was humbled that she'd gifted him with this much of herself.

He stepped forward and cupped her face in his hands.

"He was a fool," he said quietly, when what he really meant was, *He was a fucking idiot who never deserved you.*

She sighed and wrapped her cold fingers around his wrists. "I figured that out a little too late."

"Come inside. Let me show you how much of a treasure you are."

"Don't say things like that," she mumbled, but she let him take her hand and lead her back into the suite.

"Why not?"

Her cheeks were red, and he didn't think it was only from the cold. "I'll start to believe you."

"Ah. Can't have that, can we?"

His light tone masked simmering anger. The underlying pain in Ava's words as she recounted the memory had unleashed a torrent of fury inside him toward the man who'd broken her heart and made her think she wasn't perfect exactly as she was.

He hoped Hector never had a good night's sleep for the rest of his life.

When the balcony door shut behind them, Roman tugged Ava in for a kiss. Her lips were cool, but her tongue was hot as it tangled with his.

"I mean it, Ava," he whispered against her mouth as he pushed his jacket off her shoulders. "You're a treasure."

She jolted when his cold hands skimmed under her sweater, then she melted against him. "Convince me."

And for the rest of the night, Roman did everything in his power to do just that.

Chapter 13

The next morning, when Ava went to text Damaris that she was still alive, her phone battery was almost dead.

"Oh shoot," she said. "I forgot my charger."

"You can use mine." Roman pointed at the cord on the nightstand. "It's right there."

"Thanks. The damn thing barely holds a charge anymore."

"You need a new phone?"

Ava tapped out a quick message to Damaris. "I'll buy one soon. They're so expensive these days."

"I'll get you one," he said, not even looking up from his tablet.

Ava stilled. She turned and took in Roman, sitting comfortably at the dining table in the robe provided by the hotel. A robe she wouldn't have even thought to touch, because her mom had always told her there were fees for using anything but the soap and towels.

Except now, she was wearing the accompanying robe. Because Roman owned this hotel. Because part of their arrangement was that he'd take care of everything when they were together.

And now, because she'd made an offhand complaint about her battery, he'd said he'd get her a new phone.

This had to stop.

"Roman," she said in a quiet voice. "You don't have to buy me anything."

"It's nothing," he said, and she sucked in a breath, because for him, it probably was. He hadn't said, "I'll buy you one," he'd said, "I'll get you one." He probably had extras sitting around his house.

House? Did he live in a house? Or did he live in an apartment? She knew he lived near Central Park, but other than that, she didn't know where, or what kind of home. Hell, he probably owned multiple homes!

The thought was a wake-up call. What was she doing? This wasn't her life. It wasn't anywhere close. She was a middle-school teacher who barely managed to pay her rent and student loans every month. She had no business sitting here in a plush hotel robe, luxuriating over an extravagant breakfast spread in a penthouse suite.

And she still couldn't believe she'd told Roman about the night Hector had left her. What on earth had possessed her to do that? Sure, Roman was a good listener, but she barely knew him.

Let me show you how much of a treasure you are.

His response had made her feel warm and mushy inside. And true to his word, the way he'd made love to her all night—she couldn't think of it as just fucking or screwing, it had been too soft and reverent for that—had indeed made her feel treasured.

She was in over her head, and if she didn't reinforce the boundaries, this was going to get messy. For *her.*

"Please don't buy me anything, Roman. That's not what we have going on here."

At her serious tone, he looked up. His sharp gaze traveled

over her face, and he nodded once. "Fine. But I want to be able to text you."

Her pulse fluttered. "Why?"

He shrugged and looked back at his tablet. "We're negotiating, aren't we? You don't want me to get you a phone, so in exchange, I can text you whenever I want."

"That . . . that doesn't make any sense!"

The corner of his mouth ticked. "Those are my terms."

"I—" She snapped her mouth shut before she gave in to the urge to argue. Something told her that if she didn't stay firm, he'd end up wresting some other kind of agreement from her. "I don't think that's a good idea."

He cast an assessing gaze her way, but whatever he saw in her expression seemed to convince him. He gave a short nod and said, "All right."

She worried she'd upset him, but after Roman interrupted her shower to give her not one, but two toe-curling climaxes, Ava was pretty sure they were okay. Still, she was surprised when he came up behind her while she was getting dressed and wrapped his arms around her waist.

"Stay," he said in her ear. "I'll have someone drive you home early tomorrow morning so you're not late for school."

She smiled at his reflection in the mirror and cupped his arms, holding him to her. "I'd love to, but I'm having brunch with a friend this afternoon."

"Ah." He kissed the side of her neck and gave her a little squeeze before releasing her. "Next time, plan on a whole weekend."

"Sure," she murmured. This, she understood, was his negotiation. He'd let her win this time—no phone—but he wanted more.

She didn't say, *There might not be a next time*. What they had was a spur of the moment, no-strings fling. It didn't matter that she'd bought a slew of new underwear and that she had regular waxing appointments scheduled because Roman seemed to love going down on her. The beauty of this arrangement was in the boundaries, and she had to keep them strong.

Maybe someday she'd be ready to take a crack at a relationship again. But not now. And not with Roman.

But as she sat in the backseat of the car he'd arranged to drive her back to the Bronx, what replayed through her mind wasn't the sex or the penthouse view or any of the delicious things they'd eaten for dinner.

It was the way he'd held her close while asking about her past.

He never hurt me. Just my heart.

That's not nothing.

She squeezed her eyes shut and let her head fall back against the exquisitely cushioned leather seat.

God, she was in so much trouble.

Chapter 14

March

Following the GPS instructions, Roman pulled his rental car into the driveway of the Spanish style bungalow in West Hollywood where Ashton was staying while he and Jasmine were filming a movie in Los Angeles. A slew of texts had come through while Roman was driving, so he took a moment to reply before he climbed out of the car and strode up the path to the front door. After a day full of meetings, it was a blessed relief to leave his suit jacket and tie in the car.

The one-story house, with its signature white walls and red tiled roof, was charming, and the small front yard featured a profusion of desert plants. What might have once been a lawn had been replaced by gravel. It was a sunny spring day, not a cloud in the sky, but the cooling breeze marked the evening hour.

Roman had tried to invite them all out for dinner at a restaurant owned by another of Nigella's clients—someone Roman wanted to talk to about stocking Casa Donato rum—but Ashton had said Jasmine and Yadiel needed a quiet night in.

Roman suspected it was Ashton who actually wanted to stay home, but he didn't call his friend out on it. Besides, it would be nice to have a meal that wasn't also *work*.

After ringing the bell, he heard the pounding of running feet before the door swung open, revealing Yadiel's grinning face.

"Tío!" the boy yelled, launching himself into Roman's arms.

"Whoa!" Roman braced his legs as he caught the boy, who at ten was all long limbs held together by rubber bands. It was hard to believe this kid had only been in his life less than two years.

"Yadi, cuidado con tu tío," Jasmine said in mild warning as she joined them in the entranceway. "Hi, Roman."

As Yadi slid back down to the floor, Roman leaned in to kiss Jasmine on the cheek. "Thanks for having me over," he said.

"Thanks for being flexible." She shot him a grimace. "We're both on production diets. I hope you're okay with high protein and low carb. Although of course we have French fries for this little monster."

At the word "monster," Yadiel bared his teeth and emitted an exaggerated growl.

"I'm okay with whatever you've got," Roman said easily. He let Yadi drag him by the hand into the house.

"Ashton's outside at the grill." Jasmine paused in the arched doorway that led into the kitchen. "Yadi, you want to spear the vegetables on the skewers?"

"Yeah! Stabbing vegetables!" The boy bounded into the kitchen ahead of her.

"I'll try to keep him occupied for a bit," she said. "Let you two chat without a shadow."

Roman nodded his thanks and slipped through the sunroom and out the sliding glass door to a covered patio area. There was a low table, outdoor chairs with dark gray cushions, and a grill. Beyond, the surface of a turquoise pool sparkled in the early evening sun.

The sight of it immediately brought to mind the last time Roman had been in a pool.

With Ava.

Whom he hadn't heard hide nor hair from in three weeks.

"Nice pool," he said, coming up behind Ashton.

Ashton turned, breaking into a smile. "I thought you were Yadi," he said, setting down the tongs to give Roman a quick hug. "Thanks for coming by."

"Not a problem."

Fifteen years ago, they'd been tearing it up in South Beach. Now, Ashton was opting to stay home on a Saturday night with his son and soon-to-be wife, grilling chicken cutlets in a guayabera shirt and ratty cargo shorts. Hard to believe this was the same guy who'd once done tequila body shots off a model's bare stomach.

But then, Roman wasn't the same person he'd been back then either.

Roman eyed his friend, noting the differences since the last time they'd seen each other. "You've bulked up."

"Working with a trainer. El novio de la prima de Jasmine."

Roman raised an eyebrow. "Got anything you want to tell me? Maybe a certain superhero franchise came calling?"

Ashton's mouth twisted in a smirk. "No se nada."

"*Riiight.*" Roman crossed his arms and dialed up the sarcasm. "You're training with Jasmine's cousin's boyfriend to put on twenty pounds of muscle, but you don't know anything about it. All right, don't tell your best friend. I see how it is."

Ashton grinned and elbowed him. "You of all people should know how NDAs work."

Roman sighed. "Wish I didn't, sometimes."

Ashton's brow creased. "¿Qué pasó?"

Sometimes Ashton was too perceptive for his own good, but Roman didn't have an easy answer for what was wrong. He just shrugged. "Nothing specific. Just tired of the grind."

"How's Dulce's apartment hunt?"

Roman blew out a breath. "She's looked at a few places but says she hasn't fallen in love with anything yet."

"She's still not letting you help?"

"Nope." Roman ran a hand through his hair. "She won't even give me a list of the specs she's looking for, or what neighborhood she wants. Just keeps saying she'll know it when she sees it."

"¿Y tu hermana?"

"Mickey's fine. I think. Teenagers, am I right?"

Ashton gave a shudder. "I don't want to think about it."

"Aside from spending too much time on her phone, she's focused on finishing high school and prepping for her summer internship."

"College?"

"Still waiting on her acceptance letters." At Ashton's piercing look, Roman narrowed his eyes. "What?"

His friend pointed the tongs at him. "Why is this bothering you so much?"

Roman scowled. "Who says it's bothering me?"

Ashton's famously expressive face said *don't bullshit me.*

"Fine, it's bothering me." Roman shoved his hands in his pockets and wished he were wearing comfortable shorts like Ashton instead of ridiculously expensive trousers. "I don't want them to move out."

"¿Por qué no?"

Restless, Roman began to pace. "What if something happens? And I don't know about it? I can't stand the thought of not being able to protect them."

Ashton was quiet while he checked the grill. In Spanish, he murmured, "I didn't realize they needed you to protect them."

"Don't give me that. You have a family. You know what it's like."

"Yadi's *ten*. I can't even trust him to keep his shoelaces tied. Your sister, on the other hand, is almost eighteen, and your mother has already handled the worst life has to throw at her."

"That's exactly my point. I don't want anything else to happen to them."

"Maybe you're not giving them enough credit."

Before Roman could dispute that, the screen door opened and Yadiel came out in a pair of orange swim trunks.

"I want to go swimming," he announced.

Ashton gestured at the pool. "Dale."

As the boy walked to the steps in the shallow end, Roman opened his mouth to point out that the air was getting cooler, but Ashton shot him a quelling look.

There was a quiet splash as Yadi stepped in, followed by an indignant squawk. "It's cold!"

Roman bit back a laugh at the sight of the kid standing ankle deep in the water, hugging his skinny chest with his arms.

Ashton just shrugged. "Bueno. Use the hot tub."

Shivering dramatically and making *brr* noises, Yadi hurried over to the hot tub, leaving wet footprints on the concrete.

"Wait for it," Ashton whispered to Roman.

Sure enough, a second later, Yadi yelped. "It's hot!"

"Called a hot tub for a reason," Ashton said mildly.

Yadi climbed out and glared at his father. "Are you trying to boil me alive?"

"You know we're on a high protein diet." Ashton tossed the boy a towel. "Don't get the floor wet."

The sliding door slammed, and Ashton sighed. "We go through that exact exchange once a week."

Roman grinned, glad to drop the conversation about his family. "Not your fault your son is Goldilocks."

Ashton snorted. "You have no idea. He only speaks in complaints these days."

"I believe it." Roman's phone had been buzzing in his pocket, so he finally checked his texts. In the ten minutes since he'd arrived, he'd received messages from Camille, Nigella, Mikayla, his accountant, and his estate lawyer, in that order.

No Ava.

"Do you need to use the office?" Ashton jerked a thumb toward the house. "There's a third bedroom with a desk in it."

Roman shook his head and put the phone away. "Just waiting for some news."

Ashton snorted. "Waiting? That doesn't sound like you."

Roman cracked a smile. It was true.

It had been three weeks since he'd seen Ava, and true to her word, there had been no communication in the interim.

And the waiting was killing him.

After what she'd shared about her ex-husband and hinted

about her family, it was easy to see why she needed rules to feel like she was in control of the situation. But it had also become obvious that Ava pulled back after opening up.

He thought about the way she'd refused to let him upgrade her phone, which triggered a memory, or maybe it was the fact that he was standing next to Ashton. "You remember Cassie?" he asked.

Ashton made a face as he turned the chicken over. "Why? Did she call you?"

"No. Just crossed my mind."

After the language app took off, Roman had been flush with cash for the first time in his life, but he'd also been a dumb guy in his mid-twenties. He'd met Cassie, an Italian model, at New York Fashion Week, and she'd been living the kind of glamorous, jet-setting lifestyle he was just starting to taste. They'd gone on vacation, partied at clubs, took lavish shopping trips—until Ashton had told Roman point blank that Cassie was using him for his money. Roman hadn't believed it at first. Sure, he didn't see Cassie often, but they were both busy, and when they were together, they had fun.

Then he started to notice how she'd drop subtle hints when she wanted something, or only came around when she wanted him to take her somewhere. When he stopped buying her things and made himself less available for first class flights to Europe, she disappeared pretty quickly.

It had been a wake-up call, and looking back with the benefit of hindsight, Roman could see that he'd stopped dating seriously after that.

Still, he wanted to help the people he cared about, so when Ava had remarked that her phone didn't hold a charge anymore, he hadn't thought twice about offering to get her a new one. She had a problem, and it was within his power to fix it, so he would. End of story.

Except Ava clearly wasn't used to people spending money on her.

In some perverse way, it only made Roman want to indulge her more.

Jasmine came outside then, her chancletas scuffing the concrete as she carried over a tray of vegetable skewers.

"These are ready," she said.

"I've got it." Roman took the tray and began laying the skewers on the grill.

Ashton moved aside and pulled Jasmine close before dropping a kiss on her forehead. "Is he sulking?" he asked.

She rolled her eyes. "Already forgot about it. He's playing Mario Kart in his underwear."

Ashton sighed. "I'll make him get dressed before dinner."

"Don't stand on ceremony on my account," Roman murmured, watching them from the corner of his eye and noting the way Jasmine slid an arm around Ashton's waist. Her other hand patted his chest, as if offering comfort.

They *fit*, Roman realized. In less than two years, they'd met, fallen in love, and fit the pieces of their lives together to form a cohesive family unit. Jasmine had stepped in as the mother Yadiel had never had, and as the perfect partner to Ashton. And they'd made room for her, expanding their family to absorb her seamlessly.

Maybe not seamlessly. Roman remembered Mikayla at ten, a know-it-all who thought all adults were idiots. As if on cue, Yadiel came out then, wearing only tighty whities and flip-flops.

Ashton and Jasmine sighed in unison.

"When are we eating?" the boy asked.

"Soon." Ashton released Jasmine and hustled Yadiel back into the house. "Get dressed. You don't want Tío to think you were raised in a cave."

Yadiel chortled at that, but he let Ashton bring him inside.

"He talks about you a lot, you know." Smiling, Jasmine joined Roman at the grill.

"Ashton?"

"Yadi."

"Does he?"

"He remembers every gift you've ever given him, and he asks when we're going to see you again."

Warmth suffused Roman's chest, and it wasn't from the grill. "That so?"

Ashton came back out alone. "I promised we'd all play Mario Kart after dinner if he put on pants."

Jasmine groaned. "I always lose."

While Ashton monitored the grill, they sat on the patio, enjoying the cool breeze as they chatted. Roman filled them in on the latest developments with Casa Donato—his ideas for expansion, the connections he was making, and the upgrades in the distillery.

In the back of Roman's mind, he was hoping to bring Ashton on as a celebrity spokesperson, or maybe even as a partner. But he didn't want to come on too strong.

Eventually, they also discussed the wedding.

"Are you going to use an event planner?" Roman asked. "Bellísima has an excellent wedding planner attached to the resort."

Jasmine pursed her lips. "Probably. But I still want to be involved, you know?"

Ashton raised his eyebrows but didn't look up from the grill. "It's a lot of work," he said in a mild tone that made Roman think they'd covered this topic before.

"Turning all the decisions over to a planner makes it impersonal." Jasmine shifted like the idea alone made her uncomfortable. "I want it to feel like an intimate family gathering, not a flashy celebrity wedding."

"An intimate gathering with two hundred and fifty people," Ashton muttered under his breath.

"And that's just my immediate family," she said with a laugh.

When Ashton declared the food was done, Roman was surprised by the way they all leapt into action as a unit, each of them working together and fulfilling their roles without debate. Yadiel set the table with barely any prodding, even going so far as to fold the paper napkins beneath the utensils, and Ashton piled food from the grill onto the serving dishes Jasmine brought him. While she filled a pitcher with filtered water and opened a bottle of seltzer, Ashton and Roman carried the food into the dining room and set it out on trivets.

Seeing the three of them together was fascinating. They didn't have a normal life, by any means. Jasmine and Ashton were famous actors who worked long hours, and Yadi traveled with them, studying with a team of tutors in person or online. But despite the unusual structure, they'd formed a family.

The boy's bond with Jasmine was undeniable. And when Roman looked at Ashton, he didn't see the party guy he'd once known. There was a steadiness about his friend that hadn't been there before, as if Jasmine balanced his ambition with her compassion. From the way Ashton focused all his attention on his fiancée and his son, he looked like a man who had everything he'd ever wanted.

An uneasy feeling spread in Roman's gut as he wondered if maybe, in his quest to have it all, there was something important he'd missed along the way.

Chapter 15

Damaris appeared in the doorway of Ava's classroom. "Ready?"

Ava opened her desk drawer and grabbed her purse, her jacket, and a small yellow and white polka dot umbrella. "Let's go. I'm starving."

The two women left the small brick building that housed Alliance Arts and Science Charter School and hustled to the shawarma place two blocks away, determined to make the most of their lunch break. After collecting the dishes Damaris had ordered in advance, they sat at one of the cafe tables in the small restaurant and dug in.

Damaris finished chewing her first bite and washed it down with iced tea. "Almost spring break. Got any Easter plans?" She waggled her eyebrows. "Maybe with a certain hotel-owning millionaire?"

Ava shot her a look. "Of course not. I'm going to church in the morning with my mom and spending the rest of the day with my dad's family."

Damaris raised an eyebrow. "Cooking a week's worth of food for them?"

"I—" Ava snapped her mouth shut, thinking of the menu her stepmother had requested—lasagna, sancocho, and enough stuffed grape leaves to feed an army. "Maybe. How's the meditation class going?"

Damaris pointed a finger at her. "It's going great, but don't change the subject."

"The subject of my family's Easter dinner?"

"The subject of *Roman*." Damaris gestured with her pita. "You've seen this guy—what, three times now?"

Ava nodded, already sure that she wasn't going to like wherever this conversation was headed.

Damaris spread her hands, and a piece of lamb fell onto the paper plate in front of her. "And?"

Ava swallowed a mouthful of chicken shawarma. "And what?"

Sighing, Damaris used a plastic fork to dab hummus on her falafel.

"*And* you clearly enjoy him enough to go out with him more than once."

Ava took her own scoop. The hummus alone made this place worth coming to on their lunch break.

"We're not *going out*," Ava grumbled. "We're . . . I don't know. Staying in."

Damaris rolled her eyes as she chewed. "Semantics."

"It's not a relationship, Dee."

"But it's *something*."

Ava shrugged and focused on her side salad. "It's just sex."

She hadn't told Damaris that she'd filled Roman in on some of the details of her divorce. Her friend would read too much into it, and it didn't mean anything. He'd asked, Ava had answered, and that was all there was to it.

"Have you even Googled him yet?" Damaris tapped on her phone. "Let's see. Roman Alejandro Vázquez was born in

Brooklyn. He owns almost a dozen hotels around the country, along with a rum distillery, plus—did you know this?—he also starred in—"

"Dee." Ava raised a hand, cutting her off. "It's not that serious. Unless there's something about women mysteriously going missing after being in his presence, I don't want to know anything more about him."

Damaris sighed and put her phone down. "All right then."

Ava's own phone buzzed and she glanced at it. "It's Jasmine," she murmured. "About the engagement party."

"When is that?"

"In June. Right before the end of the school year. You're still coming to the wedding as my plus-one, right?"

"I wouldn't miss it for the world. How are you doing with the maid of honor duties?"

Ava sipped her mint lemonade. "Not much to do yet. Jasmine's been in LA."

"I meant, how are *you* doing? Not how is Jasmine doing."

Damaris was too damn perceptive.

"I'm fine," Ava said lightly.

"Really?" Damaris's eyebrows were so high, they were practically in outer space.

"Of course. Why wouldn't I be?"

Stupid question, especially since Damaris latched on to the opportunity to reply. "Maybe because it would be normal and natural to feel some type of way about watching one of your closest cousins plan her dream wedding to a literal movie star?"

"I'm happy for her," Ava insisted.

"I don't doubt that. But it would be okay if you also felt a little . . ."

"What—jealous?" Ava scoffed. "No. I'm perfectly fine."

"Okay." Damaris's eyebrows flicked upward like she didn't believe it, but she let it drop. "Well, let me tell you what happened in this meditation seminar. You are not going to believe the messy shit these mindfulness people get up to."

For the rest of their lunch break, Ava listened and responded accordingly, while inside, she packed away all the untidy feelings Damaris's words had stirred.

Chapter 16

May

Ava: Are you free tonight??

Roman bit back a smile when Ava's text popped up. Over the past two months, it had taken all his self-control not to call her every time she crossed his mind—which was frequently.

He tapped the reply box, then glanced at the time. It was just after noon on a Wednesday, which meant Ava should be at work. And they'd never met up on a school night before.

"Is it a holiday?" he asked Camille, who sat across from him. They were working in his apartment, and even though they both had desks in his home office, more often than not they used the dining table. The sleek and shiny wooden surface was big enough to seat eight, but his work sessions with Camille were the only times it got any use. Roman, Dulce, and Mikayla all preferred to eat at the kitchen's high granite countertop, and when Roman entertained, he used one of his hotels.

Besides, the dining chairs Dulce had picked out were somehow kinder to his lower back than his outrageously expensive desk chair. And he had once again been skipping PT.

Camille squinted at him. "It's the middle of May. What holiday would it be?"

He didn't have an answer for that. "So your kids are in school today?"

Camille's expression grew suspicious. "Yes . . ."

"Thanks."

Roman looked at his phone again before Camille could ask a follow-up. Then he opened his calendar app. He had numerous meetings and calls scheduled that afternoon, plus tickets for the Mets game that night. He also had an early flight the next day.

And none of it mattered, because Ava wanted to see him, and he was once again about to drop everything to be with her.

He typed back his response.

> **Roman:** Yes. I'll send a car.

> **Ava:** No need. I'll leave right after school and meet you at the Flor.

He was about to say the car could pick her up at her school, but he knew she wouldn't go for that. Still, there was one other thing he could do . . .

> **Roman:** I have an early flight tomorrow. Come to my apartment instead.

There was a long pause, and he could guess why. So far, they'd only arranged to meet at the Dulce Flor—which, granted, he owned—but there was something a lot more intimate about inviting her to his home. And if he knew anything about Ava, it was that she shied away from intimacy.

But now that the idea of her in his apartment had taken root, he couldn't let it go. His mom was in Puerto Rico visiting his aunt, and his sister would be sleeping over with a school friend. It was the perfect night for Ava to come by.

Another minute passed before Ava's reply appeared.

Ava: Okay.

Alight with anticipation, he sent her the address.

Camille was watching him closely, so he set his phone aside and went back to reviewing the redesign for Casa Donato's dark rum label.

"Who was that?" Camille asked, her tone full of feigned nonchalance.

"Don't worry about it," he said mildly, zooming in on the label to make it seem like he was working.

"You're about to make me clear your schedule again, aren't you?"

Sweat prickled on Roman's back, and he refused to look at her. "What makes you say that?"

She snorted. "You want me to reveal your tells?"

Now that got his attention. "My what?"

"Every so often, out of the blue, you get this sappy look on your face, and then you tell me you're going to be 'busy' for the rest of the night." She made air quotes with her fingers.

Roman frowned. "What do you mean, *sappy*?"

"Like this." She picked up her phone screen and mimed reading something. Then her eyebrows dipped and the corners of her mouth pulled down in an exaggerated pout, like she was gazing at an adorable puppy or something. It was an *aww* face. She tossed the phone back on a stack of papers and pinned him with a look that said, *See? Sappy.*

"I do not do that," he scoffed.

"You do. And it's not the face you make when you hear from your mother, your sister, or one of your few friends. I know it's a woman, but I've never seen you make that *particular* look before, which tells me—"

"I don't want to know what it tells you," he cut in grumpily. "And yes, I want you to clear my schedule for the rest of the night."

Camille's lips pressed together like she was holding back a smug smile. As she reached for her laptop, she whispered, "I knew it."

Was he that obvious?

Apparently, yes.

A jolt of panic seared through him. How would Ava react if *she* noticed?

He had to play it cool tonight. Not because he wanted to, but because Ava would go running in the opposite direction if she had any inkling that he wasn't abiding by the "no feelings" part of their agreement. He had to keep her from finding out that he wanted to add some strings, too, at least until he'd determined the best way to proceed. Mulling that over in the back of his mind, he continued working.

An hour later, Mikayla stomped off the elevator and into the apartment.

A seed of unease sprouted as Roman exchanged a look with Camille. His assistant had a twenty-year-old son and two daughters aged fourteen and twelve. She could well spot a teenager in high dudgeon.

When Mikayla saw them, she marched over and flung herself into one of the empty chairs.

Roman slipped off his reading glasses and took in his sister's creased brow and the slight pout. He kept his tone neutral even as his pulse kicked into high gear. "What's up?"

"My museum internship fell through," Mikayla said, her voice wavering. "I'm supposed to start right after graduation, and now it's all gone to shit."

"Why? What happened?"

She dropped her hands into her lap. "The person running the internship program is going on maternity leave, so the museum is canceling it. They're not even going to try to get someone else to cover it, or let us work in other areas. I've been signed up for this since February. How am I going to find something else this good on such short notice?"

And then Mikayla did something that really ratcheted up Roman's blood pressure—she dashed away a tear.

"I'll call them," he said immediately. "They can't leave you in the lurch like that."

"Oh my god, don't you dare!" Her eyes went wide in horror. "That would be *mortifying*."

"Then we'll find you another internship. I'll text Nigella, I'm sure she has lots of contacts—"

"No!" she screeched, covering her face. "I can't have my big brother using his connections to find me a job. Everyone's going to think I'm some rich kid who gets everything handed to her."

Roman opened his mouth to point out that this was exactly

how her classmates from her expensive private school got their internships, but Camille sent him a quelling look and gave a minute shake of her head.

"All right," Roman went on, changing tacks. "I'm sure we have lots of internship opportunities available in VQZ. Just pick the department you want to—"

"That's even worse!" Mikayla pressed her fingers to her temples. "You can't just *give* me a job. It's nepotism."

Feeling helpless, Roman spread his hands. "Tell me how you want me to fix it, Mickey, and I'll do it."

"I don't want you to *do* anything!" Mikayla snatched up her schoolbag from the floor. "Just forget it!"

Then she stormed off to her room.

Roman turned wide eyes on Camille, who started to pack up her belongings.

"I don't understand," he said, bewildered. "What did I do wrong?"

Camille huffed out a laugh. "You don't pay me enough to answer *that.*"

Roman stared in the direction his sister had gone and re-played their conversation. He'd given her three solutions, and she'd shot down all of them. What good was all the wealth and power he'd amassed if he couldn't even help his sister when she was distressed?

"Here, I got something for you," Camille said, breaking into his thoughts.

"You didn't have to—" He started absently, then halted as he stared at the thing Camille had pulled out of her shoulder bag. "Wow. You *really* didn't have to. What am I looking at?"

Camille stifled a laugh. "It's a dog."

"Are you sure?" Roman stared at the furry lump. It was covered in brown fuzz that had certainly seen better days. Black plastic eyes stared at him with a maniacal gleam. The nose was also made of black plastic and scuffed by what might have been teeth marks. Four stumpy legs and a sad little puff of a tail stuck out from the body. A ragged red paisley bandanna was tied around the thing's neck.

"It was Amara's," Camille said, referring to her youngest daughter. "Go ahead, pet it."

Raising an eyebrow, Roman patted the head of the toy dog. Even though he was expecting some kind of response, he still jumped when it barked at him, the sound louder and more gravelly than he would have thought possible.

"Amara played with it kinda hard," Camille admitted. "I think she did something to the voice box. If you scratch under its chin, the tail wags."

"You don't say." Against his better judgment, Roman took his eyes off the dog and narrowed them at Camille. "Why are you giving me this?"

"Don't want you to be lonely," she said, hoisting her bag onto her shoulder. "Since Dulce and Mickey are moving out, and you aren't around enough for a real pet."

The dog barked again.

"Are you sure it's not possessed?" Roman asked, taking it with him as he walked Camille to the elevator. "I feel like I've seen this movie before."

"I make no promises." She pressed the button and gave him a flippant grin. "Enjoy your night off."

Roman only grunted in response as the elevator arrived, but the dog barked again, as if saying goodbye. Camille laughed, and as the doors closed, Roman was left with a glimpse of her features contorted in the sappy expression she'd accused him of making.

Alone, he gazed down at the toy dog in his hand. There was something pleading in its bulging black eyes.

"What the hell am I supposed to do with you?" he mumbled. The dog wagged its tail and let out a whine that sounded like gears grinding.

With a sigh, Roman set the dog on the coffee table and went to try again with Mikayla.

Text Exchange with Damaris Fuentes

Damaris: I'll be in class until 7, but I can come over after that if you need me to.

Ava: Thank you. I'll be okay.

Damaris: You sure? Maybe you shouldn't be alone.

Ava: I won't. I'm . . . actually on my way to Roman's place now.

Damaris: Oh! The Dulce Flor?

Ava: More like . . . his apartment?

Damaris: Okay then! I'm not going to ask for his address but make sure your location tracker is turned on. We'll debrief tomorrow at lunch. This calls for shawarma.

Ava: It's a date. ♥

Chapter 17

An hour later, Roman was in his kitchen uncorking a bottle of wine when the front desk let him know Ava was on her way up.

He let out a sigh of relief. When he'd tried to talk to Mikayla again, she'd snapped at him to "mind his business" before sweeping off for a sleepover with her friend.

In the back of his mind, he'd worried that Ava wouldn't show up. That she'd think coming to his home would be crossing one of the boundaries she seemed so fond of. Or that she'd somehow guessed he was "catching feelings," as his sister would say.

But she was here. *Thank Christ.*

He went to the elevator to greet her, and she stepped out wearing dark pants, simple flats, a cheery yellow blouse, and a navy blue cardigan. With her large shoulder bag, she looked every inch the middle-school teacher. Roman was so fucking happy to see her, he couldn't hold back his grin.

Except Ava didn't smile back. Her pretty face was pinched with distress, and when she rushed into his arms, she seemed to be on the verge of tears.

"¿Qué pasó, mi cielo?" The Spanish term of endearment slipped out as he noted with alarm that she was shaking. Panic tensed his muscles, and it was a struggle to keep his tone even. "Did something happen with Hector?"

Ava shook her head and clung to him. "No, nothing like that."

He held her close, that familiar feeling of helplessness rising up in him. "Ava, *please* tell me what's wrong."

She shoved her curls out of her face and took deep breaths. She blinked fast, like she was trying not to cry. "I'm sorry. I thought I had myself together."

"Hey," he whispered, guiding her over to the living room area and drawing her down to the sofa. "You don't have to have it all together. Just talk to me. Let me help."

She shuddered out a sigh as she leaned into him. "Something happened today to one of my students."

He held her while the whole story came in halting bursts. Apparently, one of her students had gone into anaphylactic shock in the classroom. Ava had caught the child before they fell out of their seat, then upended their bag to find an EpiPen before administering the shot. She'd called an ambulance while one of the other kids ran for the school nurse. The child was taken to the hospital immediately and was okay, but the whole experience had left Ava and the rest of her students on edge.

"Maddie's fine," she said. "I know they're fine, but watching them react like that . . . The trust my students and their parents place in me isn't something I take lightly."

"You did everything right." Roman rocked her and patted her hair, wishing he could do more to reassure her. "You knew the signs, knew the child carried an EpiPen, and knew how to administer it for them. You were prepared, and you reacted immediately. You're a good teacher."

She sniffled. "I know, on a logical level, that all of that is true. But I feel so responsible for these kids. I want to protect all of them from everything. And I couldn't protect poor Maddie from a rogue peanut butter cookie Armando's grandma packed in his lunch."

Ava's words struck a chord, strumming in harmony with Roman's own protective instincts. "You did, though. They're okay."

"But what if . . ." Her voice hitched and the look in her eyes was bleak. "Roman, I don't even want to tell you how often we do school lockdown drills. Most days I try not to think about it, otherwise I can't do my job. But afterward, my thoughts spiraled, thinking of all the ways I might fail, and I barely held it together the rest of the day."

He tried not to picture Ava or her students in the situation she described. It was a concern he had about his own sister, especially since she'd be going off to college in a few short months, moving even farther from his protection. But this wasn't the time to discuss the country's inadequate gun safety laws, so he just rubbed Ava's back and held her.

Moisture gathered in the corners of her big hazel eyes, and Roman used his thumbs to gently wipe it away.

"I'm so sorry." She covered her face with her hands. "I never cry."

"It's okay to cry." He pressed a kiss to her temple. "It's a release of tension."

This was why Ava came to him, he realized. With him, she could let off steam—whether through sex, tears, or even just voicing her frustrations aloud.

He tipped her chin up so she was looking at him. "I'm glad you came here tonight."

Her lashes lowered, shuttering her eyes from him. "You were the only person I could think to turn to."

Her quiet admission left him feeling honored, and a little bit awed. He should've left it alone, but he couldn't. "Why me?"

She exhaled and cast her gaze around, like she was looking for the words. "You listen without worrying about me. Without judging me."

"Who says I don't worry?" He slid his fingers into her hair to cup the back of her head. "But you're right. I'll never judge you."

"I think you're the only person who doesn't," she muttered.

Roman had the feeling she judged herself more harshly than anyone else did, but he kept that thought to himself.

Before he could consider what to say next, her brows drew together and she cocked her head, directing a quizzical glance at the coffee table.

"What . . . is that?"

He swallowed a laugh. "That's my dog."

The corners of her mouth tilted up. "Your dog?"

Roman picked up the toy and patted its head. The dog barked like it was smoking two packs a day.

Ava's eyes were still wet, but she let out a surprised giggle. Roman made a mental note to send Camille a gift card for her favorite restaurant as he handed Ava the dog.

She turned it over in her hands. The shameless animal wagged its stumpy tail and whined. "Does it have a name?"

"We haven't gotten that far. It only arrived this afternoon."

"I see." She gazed down at the silly toy, a smile lingering on her lips. "Thank you."

"For what?"

"For being here and listening. For making time for me."

A vow hovered on the tip of his tongue, something impulsive, like *I'll always make time for you*, but he didn't want to scare her away. All he said was, "You're very welcome."

Then he kissed her fingers before he drew her up from the sofa. "Why don't we go out to dinner? Somewhere nice."

He wasn't sure how she'd react, since she'd been very clear from the beginning that their arrangement was only about sex and nothing more. But she'd come to him when she was in distress and there was nothing sexual about the vibe tonight. Taking her straight to his bedroom felt wrong. Would dinner at a restaurant—instead of room service in a hotel room—seem too much like a date?

But she shook her head. "Maybe I should go. I'm not fit company tonight."

His fingers tightened on her hand. He wasn't ready to say goodbye yet. Who knew how long she'd stay away now that he'd seen her cry?

Mikayla's words from earlier came back to him. *I don't want you to do anything!*

Maybe that was the key here. Not trying to fix it. *Not* trying to do something.

It ran contrary to everything that drove him, but it was worth a shot.

He rested his hands on Ava's hips and watched her expression closely. "What do you need right now, sweetheart?"

She bit her full lower lip and looked away, like she was uncertain of how he'd respond. "Would it be . . . well, could we just stay in and relax?"

"Sure. You want to have a movie night?" He made the suggestion on a whim, but when her eyebrows twitched with interest, he went on. "When I was a kid, whenever my mom or I had a stressful day, we'd splurge on a pizza and watch movies. It helped."

Funny, he hadn't thought about that in ages, but those were some of his fondest childhood memories.

Ava's lips curved slightly. "What kind of movies did you watch together?"

He winced. "Well, we were at the mercy of our local Blockbuster. I don't like to speak ill of the dead, but that store was notoriously out of anything good. We once spent an entire Saturday watching four of the *Land Before Time* movies in a row."

"Oh no. How old were you?"

He groaned. "*Fifteen.*"

She covered a laugh. "Whose idea was it?"

"Mine, I'm sad to say. And let me tell you, nostalgia will only take you so far." He put his arm around her and led her toward the kitchen. "Let's hope we find something a little more engaging than cartoon baby dinosaurs."

The way she smiled up at him did funny things to his insides, and he found he was more excited about the prospect of a movie marathon with her than the fanciest dinner in the world.

On their way into the kitchen, Ava stopped short. Her eyes widened slightly as she took in their surroundings.

"What's wrong?" he teased.

"Nothing's wrong. It's actually more comfortable than I expected."

"Which was what? Some sort of sterile open plan living space with chrome furniture and marble floors?"

"Actually, yes."

He snorted. "As if my Puerto Rican mother would let me get away with that. She thinks minimalism is a dirty word."

She smiled. "To be honest, I thought you would live in one of those hundred-story glass monstrosities."

He shuddered. "Not in a million years."

He tried to see his home as she might. The five-bedroom apartment was located in an unassuming prewar building where Roman was one of the youngest co-op owners—and only one of two with Latin American heritage. Art from around the world mixed with framed family photos on the walls. The furnishings showcased a variety of textures in warm colors, with thick rugs covering cherry hardwood floors. Bits of personal clutter—Mikayla's purple headphones, his extra reading glasses, a pair of his mother's earrings—were scattered about. There wasn't a hint of marble or gilt anywhere in sight.

"How long have you lived here?" Ava asked, examining the picture frames on the bookshelves. He caught her quick smile when she spotted his old Little League photo.

"Five years. I bought it when my mother and sister moved in with me." Before that he'd lived downtown in a fancy new building full of young professionals, and he'd hated it.

"How many . . ."

When she trailed off, he gestured for her to go on. Taking a deep breath, she completed the question. "How many homes do you have?"

He almost didn't want to answer. "A house in the Hamptons, another in Puerto Rico, and I'm looking for a place in Los Angeles. But New York is, and has always been, home to me."

She nodded, then moved to the windows, where the view of Central Park spread out before them.

He wanted to tell her how he'd spent his twenties living in one shitty studio apartment after another, enduring everything from roaches to poor heating to dorm-size kitchen appliances.

But there was no way he could say it that wouldn't sound defensive.

"Is it too much?" he asked quietly, worried that, like the hotels, the lavish environment would put her off. So he was surprised when she turned back to him with a soft smile on her face.

"It's perfect," she said. "It feels like a home."

And just like that, his nerves settled.

In the kitchen, they raided his sister's stash of snacks—Doritos, Reese's Pieces, and gourmet popcorn—and Ava insisted on ordering pizza for them to be delivered. She hadn't brought an overnight bag, so Roman gave her one of his own T-shirts to change into before they climbed into his king-size bed.

It occurred to him that he probably could've found pajamas for her in either his mother's or his sister's closets, but there was something satisfying about seeing Ava in his old University of Miami shirt.

"What's your favorite comfort movie?" he asked, turning on ScreenFlix.

She busied herself opening the Doritos. "We can watch whatever you want," she said, then shot him a grin. "Except *The Land Before Time*."

"Ha. I noticed you didn't answer the question."

"It's really okay—"

"Ava, *please*. Whatever it is, it can't be more embarrassing than what I've already told you."

She searched his face for a moment. "*Pride & Prejudice*. The 2005 film version," she hurried to add. "I mean, I love the 1995 BBC miniseries too, but we'd be up all night and you have a flight tomorrow."

Roman had never seen it, and even though Ava told him at

least a dozen times that he could pick a different movie, he put it on.

It wasn't so much about the movie as it was learning what made her tick, to see her reactions and hear her memories from past viewings.

Snuggled together in bed, they cuddled, joked, ate pizza, and spilled Doritos in the sheets. They didn't touch the wine.

"This Mrs. Bennet is a trip," Roman commented, as the woman on screen had another attack of nerves.

"Mm-hmm. I can relate to having a matriarchal relative with no filter."

At the description of Mr. Darcy, he said, "Are they talking about me?"

Ava squinted at him. "I'd say you're *in*conveniently rich."

He huffed out a laugh. "Only to you. I suppose Darcy's a step up from Darth Vader, at least."

She tossed a piece of popcorn at him, then settled her head against his shoulder and continued to watch.

"My cousins and I used to debate who was who," she murmured. "They argued over who got to be Lizzie."

"Who were you?"

"They always said I was Jane."

He noticed that she'd said "they," not "I." "Is that the blonde one?"

"The perfect one." After a moment, she added, "Deep down, I feared I was Charlotte."

"The one who marries that boiled potatoes pendejo?"

She sighed. "The one who sacrifices her happiness for the sake of her family."

Ah. He gave her a gentle squeeze and stroked her arm in soothing movements. "Who do you want to be now?"

"That depends." She peered up at him from under her lashes. In the dark bedroom, the light from the TV flashed across her face, highlighting the sweet arches of her cheeks, her pretty eyes, her supple mouth. She'd piled her curls into a bun on top of her head and washed the makeup from her face. She looked younger, softer, like the embodiment of vulnerability and quiet strength, like the answer to a question he'd never dared to ask.

She was the most beautiful being he'd ever seen.

"On what?" he asked, nearly breathless at the wealth of affection threatening to swamp him.

A smile quirked the corner of her lips. "Are you Darcy or Bingley?"

He lifted a hand to stroke the curve of her jaw. His answer came out husky and full of honesty. "I'm just Roman," he said. "And you're just Ava. That's all we need to be. Not perfect, not cool, not a martyr. Just us."

The look in her eyes was so wistful it broke his heart. "I like that better."

"Me too."

She fell asleep three-quarters of the way through the movie with her head resting on his chest. He held her and watched until the end, needing to know why this was the movie that had so captivated her when she was young. He could see how the story of a woman finding love despite her wacky and dramatic family would appeal, and why she still turned to it for comfort now.

Tonight, though, she'd turned to *him* for comfort.

A deep sense of fulfillment permeated his soul, and suddenly, their arrangement wasn't enough. He needed *more*.

More of Ava. More time with her, more insight into who she was and what made her tick. He wanted to know what she'd been like when she was younger and understand how she'd become the amazing woman she was today.

He wanted strings, damn it.

He thought about his visit with Ashton and Jasmine, about the indefinable connection he'd witnessed between them. Together, they were more than just the sum of their parts. They were a *family*.

When he pictured coming home and finding Ava here, maybe grading homework at the dining table or reading in the living room, he got a weird sort of thrill he'd never felt before, and he wanted it more than he ever could have imagined.

But he needed to go slow. Ava would need to think about it, to take time to get used to the idea of *more*. He'd have to ease her into it, expanding her boundaries inch by inch until they included him in all aspects of her life, not just when she needed some kind of release.

So he wouldn't bring it up right away. He'd stick to her rules for a while longer. But he needed to talk to *someone*. The good feelings were bubbling up inside him, yearning to be let out.

Heart pounding, he grabbed his phone from the bed and texted Ashton, opening the door to what was sure to be an avalanche of questions.

Roman: I've met someone.

Chapter 18

June

Don't let Mom catch you." Ava's sixteen-year-old sister Willow spoke out of the side of her mouth like they were old-timey movie spies passing along top-secret information, instead of half-sisters hanging out at their cousin's engagement party.

All around the packed ballroom, A-list celebrities mingled with Ava's multitude of aunts, uncles, and cousins. Over by the photo staging area—a floral background emblazoned with the words "Jasmine & Ashton" with an oversize ampersand between them—Ava spotted Michelle's mom, Titi Val, chatting with a recent Tony Award winner, and next to the open bar, her cousin Ronnie laughed with a former popstar-turned-sitcom actress.

Ava narrowed her eyes at that. She was currently holding Ronnie's daughter because her cousin had claimed she needed to run to the restroom.

Ava hoisted the sleepy and overwhelmed three-year-old higher on her hip and turned back to her sister. "Why is Olympia looking for me?"

Willow's tone turned dark. "She's going to ask you to paint more chairs."

"More?" Ava suppressed a groan. "Is she opening a restaurant? How many could she possibly need?"

Willow and Ava had different mothers, so they didn't resemble each other closely, but they had the same heart-shaped face and big, thickly lashed eyes, and when they smiled, the kinship was clear. Her curly hair was looser and a few shades lighter than Ava's, and she had fair skin with a smattering of freckles across her nose.

Willow shrugged and reached out to tickle her little cousin under the chin. "I swear, the patio chairs breed like rabbits while I'm sleeping."

More like Olympia was a compulsive shopper, but Ava kept that to herself. She was careful not to bad-mouth Olympia in front of Willow, for fear of influencing their relationship.

Over the past twenty-five years, Ava had done everything in her power to stay on her stepmother's good side. Which was why she'd spent the previous weekend painting patio chairs in ninety-degree heat and dodging Olympia's passive aggressive remarks about Ava's aunts and uncles. Olympia had picked up more than a dozen beige plastic patio chairs at a clearance sale—despite the fact that she already had twenty scattered around the backyard—and because Olympia had never met a primary color she didn't like, Ava, Willow, and their father had been summoned to paint them red. Willow had sung "We're painting las sillas red" under her breath on and off, to the tune of the song from Disney's *Alice in Wonderland*. And any time Olympia had critiqued the way they were painting, Willow had muttered, "Off with your head!" until Ava had bitten her tongue to keep from laughing.

Ava had only survived the day by texting Roman updates from the chair-painting trenches.

It had been more than a month since they'd last seen each other—he'd been traveling a lot, and she'd been busy preparing for the end of the school year—but they texted almost daily. Despite Ava's initial boundary, something had changed after their movie night.

It started when she sent Roman a meme about Mr. Collins and the boiled potatoes. He'd sent back a Colin Firth gif from the BBC miniseries and admitted he'd been watching it on the plane. From there, they sent each other questions and updates every day, often adding thematically appropriate *Pride & Prejudice* memes in response. The Mrs. Bennett gifs had gotten quite a workout during Ava's adventures in patio chairs.

She should've put a stop to it. Their exchanges had nothing to do with sex, yet somehow felt more intimate than anything they'd done in a bed. But every time Roman's name popped up on her phone, her heart soared, and she jumped to reply. When Willow had caught Ava grinning at her phone, Ava had lied and said she was texting Damaris.

"It's okay to tell them no," Willow said now. "To the chairs. And anything else they ask you to do."

Ava sent her sister a mild smile. "I don't mind. I'm happy to help."

"*I* mind," Willow muttered under her breath, gazing across the dance floor to where their father swayed with Olympia.

Ava tamped down the frustration rising within her. She *hated* that Willow saw their family dynamic so clearly. It meant Ava wasn't hiding her emotions well enough. She'd never wanted Willow to notice what she had long suspected, that their parents took advantage of Ava's helpfulness, of her need to belong.

Before Ava could think of what to say in response to that, she spotted Titi Nereida striding toward them. Their grandmother's older sister leveled Ava with a haughty glare made even more menacing by her heavily painted-on brows.

Willow took one look at their great-aunt and grabbed Ronnie's daughter from Ava's arms. "I'll take her back to Ronnie. See ya!"

Titi Nereida cornered Ava. "¿Y el chocolate fountain?" she demanded.

Ava blinked. The non sequitur was so out of left field, even for Titi Nereida, that Ava couldn't guess what the older woman meant. "Huh?"

Her great-aunt gestured impatiently. "¿Por qué está apagado?"

Ava glanced at the table where the chocolate fountain was supposed to be flowing like something out of Willy Wonka's factory. Sure enough, it was off, and a ring of disappointed children poked halfheartedly at the thickening chocolate.

Turning back to her great-aunt, Ava pressed her lips into a tight smile. As much as she wanted to point out that there was an event planner in attendance, she didn't dare. If Ava was rude to Titi Nereida, she'd never hear the end of it.

"Don't worry," Ava assured her great-aunt. "I'll fix it."

Stepping away, Ava grabbed a crab puff on a toothpick and popped it in her mouth as she navigated the packed ballroom. She skirted the dance floor, looking for the doors she'd seen the catering team slipping in and out of.

At least there was no risk of running into Roman while she was here. The engagement party was being held at the Echo Luxe SoHo, not one of the Dulce hotels. Thank goodness for small favors.

Although if they *were* at a Dulce, she could ask Roman to fix this chocolate fountain business.

Ava was on her way into the kitchen to grab someone from catering when her grandmother pulled her aside.

"Ava, mi amor. ¿Estás bien?" Esperanza asked in a hushed voice.

Ava offered her grandmother a confused smile. "I'm fine, Abuela. ¿Qué pasó?"

Realization dawned on Esperanza's lined face, and her gaze darted to the side. "Nereida didn't tell you?"

"That the chocolate fountain isn't working?" Ava nodded. "I'm on my way to the kitchen now."

Her grandmother's dark brown eyes went wide and she started to back away. "Oh, never mind then. No es nada."

Ava's own eyes narrowed in suspicion and she caught her grandmother's shoulder. "Esperate. What did you think Titi Nereida told me?"

Esperanza waved it away. "It's nothing."

"It's clearly not nothing, Bwela. Díme."

Esperanza sighed, and her eyebrows dipped in resignation. "I thought you already knew, nena. Lo siento."

Now Ava was really worried. Her grandmother almost never apologized—for anything. The old woman was loving and affectionate, but she could also be critical and mean. If she was saying she was sorry, it must be really bad.

Anxiety blossomed as Ava took her grandmother's hands. "Please just tell me. Is everything okay? Is someone sick?"

"No, nothing like that. Pero . . . you know Nereida is neighbors with Gloria, sí?"

Ava froze at the name of her former mother-in-law, then forced herself to nod.

"Well, Nereida told me . . ."

Ava waited silently, gaze glued to her grandmother's face, but inside she was screaming *JUST SAY IT.*

Esperanza let the rest out in a rush. "Hector is getting married."

Ava's lips parted, but nothing came out.

Her first ridiculous thought was to correct what her grandmother had said. Not *married*, but *remarried*. Hector was getting *remarried*. Because he had already been married before. To *her.*

But now . . . Hector was getting married to someone else. Someone who was *not her.*

I don't want to be married to you anymore.

God, when was she going to get those words out of her head?

"Ava? ¿Cómo te sientes?" Esperanza's brow creased, and Ava wondered how long she'd been silent, letting the news sink in.

"Fine, Abuela. Estoy bien."

She was fine. Of course she was fine. She was always fine.

And when she wasn't fine, she knew where to turn.

"I have to fix the chocolate fountain," she told her grandmother, and her voice sounded hollow even to her own ears.

Esperanza pulled her down to kiss her cheek. "Cuídate, nena. I'll pray for you."

"Gracias, Bwela." The reply was robotic, and as Ava headed for the doors to the kitchen, she dimly registered that her legs were numb and the sound in the room was muted. She was in shock. Yes, that's what this was. Shock.

And she didn't fucking have time for it.

The initial shock gave way to anger. It had been more than *two years* since she and Hector had separated. When was she going to be allowed to forget about him and move on? The jerk had been so enmeshed in her family, she couldn't even get away from mentions of him, even after all this time. Why the hell did she need to know he was getting remarried? He wasn't part of her life anymore. She didn't *want* to hear any updates about him.

Especially now—at an engagement party, surrounded by family members, when she was supposed to go stand in front of them in a few minutes to be announced as the maid of honor. Maid, not matron, because *she wasn't married anymore.* Chisme like this would spread like wildfire, and by the time she got to the dais, every Rodriguez relative in the room would be gazing upon her with pity.

She could hear it now. *Pobrecita Ava. Her husband left her and now he's getting married again and she's all alone.*

The thought of it made her sick.

She stared around her, at the photo backdrop and "She Said Yes!" banner—Ronnie's doing—at the famous faces interspersed among her relatives, at the DJ booth where her second cousin Javi played a mix of classic salsa, pop hits, and typical Latin party music, at Michelle and Gabe tearing up the dance floor to "Suavemente."

In Ava's memories, Elvis Crespo would forever be the soundtrack to this moment.

Enough was enough. She needed something to look forward to after this emotional shitstorm. Slipping her phone out of the pocket of her dress, Ava opened her texts with Roman and wrote, *Are you free tonight?* And then, before she could overthink it, she added, *I want to see you.*

She hit send.

Something about the admission felt a little reckless, in a good way. It was more forward than she would typically be, but with Roman, she wasn't afraid to be bold.

Roman. That sexy, attentive, sweetheart of a man. When she was with him, she felt like she was enough, just as she was. Not because she was *helpful*, not because she was *nice*. Just because she was Ava.

She recalled what he'd said while they were watching *Pride & Prejudice* in his bed.

I'm just Roman. And you're just Ava. That's all we need to be.

She wasn't Jane Bennett, or Charlotte Lucas, or Hector's ex-wife.

She was Ava Rodriguez, goddammit. And she was done letting other people's expectations define her.

One of the caterers slipped past her carrying a tray of ropa vieja sliders, and Ava deflated a bit. Okay, she still had some expectations to meet before New Ava could fully take the reins.

Squaring her shoulders, she marched into the kitchen to find the catering manager and demand—politely—that they fix the fucking chocolate fountain before anyone else in her family could nag her about it.

Chapter 19

Five Minutes Earlier

Roman found Ashton at the edge of the crowded dance floor and nudged him with his elbow. "Quite a party."

Ashton let out a relieved sigh. "You made it."

"I told you I would." Roman planted his hands on his hips and surveyed the ballroom, noting that everything seemed to be progressing as it should. "I didn't realize you had so many friends. Remember when you were hiding from the world like a hermit?"

Ashton's mouth was set in a grim line. "I wasn't hiding from the world, I was hiding from the *press*."

"You say tomato, I say *tomate*." Roman kept his tone light, since Ashton looked like he was ready to snap from tension.

"I'm starting to regret making friends again. Jasmine and I could have eloped and avoided all . . . this." Ashton gestured at the mass of people like they were a mess he had to clean up.

"Don't tell me you regret resurrecting *our* friendship," Roman teased.

"I don't." Ashton shot him a quick grin. "Especially since

you're giving us the friends and family discount for your hotels."

"Hey, it's the least I could do for my telenovela hermano."

"Speaking of family . . . tu mama y hermana? Están aquí?"

Roman shook his head. "Mickey's doing something with her school friends, and Mami's on a cruise with her sister."

"Mikayla's going to Yale, sí?"

Roman nodded. It was still hard for him to believe that his baby sister would be a college freshman in just a few short months. He remembered being eighteen and going off to college for the first time, driving down to Florida in the junker he'd bought with the money he'd made working at the pizzeria. He'd felt like a motherfucking grown-up, but when he looked at Mikayla, who was the same age he'd been then . . .

He still saw her as the baby he'd held in the hospital all those years ago.

How had eighteen years passed in the blink of an eye?

He was fulfilling the promise for her now. She wasn't limited by things like scholarships and student loans. She would never know what it was like to live on ramen and peanut butter for weeks at a time, to bartend at night and go to class during the day and work at the school in the afternoons, and still barely have two pennies to rub together.

While the thought of Mickey driving herself between Manhattan and New Haven made his lungs seize with panic, Connecticut wasn't that far. And his mother had not only agreed to let him help her find a place, she'd decided she wanted to stay on the Upper West Side. Roman still wasn't thrilled that they were leaving, but he was at least feeling more settled where they were concerned.

And then there was Ava.

They'd come a long way since that day in February when she'd refused his request to initiate contact with her. It had required more patience than he'd thought he possessed, but giving her time and space had been the right move. After the night she'd spent in his home, her first non-booty call text to him—a *Pride & Prejudice* meme—had given him a surge of absolute triumph. They shared harmless selfies—Ava in her father's backyard with paint on her face, Roman in the University of Miami T-shirt she'd worn at his place—but never veered into sexting territory. She messaged him whenever she had a rough day at work, which happened more often than he suspected she realized, and he'd revealed his conflicted feelings about Mikayla going to college and his mother moving out.

It was a delicate balance, but Roman would take whatever Ava was willing to give, while constantly being on the lookout for more. And in the meantime, he was just happy to get to know her better.

He and Ashton moved to the open bar, and while they were waiting for their drinks, Roman's phone buzzed with a text. He expected it to be Camille with an update from his real estate broker, but a quick glance showed it was from Ava, as if she'd known he was thinking about her.

> **Ava:** Are you free tonight? I want to see you.

His heart flipped over in his chest, and his face stretched into a goofy grin.

This was the first time she'd asked to see him since their movie night—his fault, since he'd been traveling so much—and the first time she'd said something as overt as *I want to see you.*

He'd just returned the night before from two weeks in Japan, and while he was feeling more than a little jetlagged, the prospect of spending time with Ava had the effect of chugging three Red Bulls.

Ashton elbowed Roman. "Texting your mystery mujer?"

Roman nodded, unable to suppress his grin. "Yeah. Looks like I'll get to see her tonight."

"La profe still holding you at arm's length?" Ashton didn't know all the details about Ava, but he knew enough.

"She is, but I'm working on it."

"Does she know you're rich?" Ashton asked wryly.

"She knows. If anything, it's a point against me."

The phone rang before he could respond to Ava's message. This time, it *was* Camille.

"I have to take this," Roman said.

"Almost time for the announcement," Ashton warned.

"Don't worry, I won't miss it."

"Jasmine will hunt you down if you do. She has a whole song and dance planned."

"Wait, literally?"

When Ashton only shrugged, Roman stepped aside and took the call.

While he listened to Camille's updates, he imagined what Ava would say if he asked her to be his plus-one to Ashton's wedding. She'd probably decline and remind him of her rules. But he'd ask anyway, just to test the waters.

All he had to do was get through this party. Then he'd take her in his arms and show her how much he'd missed her.

Chapter 20

After extracting a promise from the catering manager that he would personally fix the chocolate fountain, Ava left the kitchen, only to be drawn up short by Jasmine and Michelle lying in wait outside the door.

Ava gave them the warning look she used on her students when she could tell they were about to act foolish. "Please, don't do this now."

Jasmine did her best impression of sad puppy dog eyes—which, considering her profession, was pretty damned good. "Can we hug you at least?"

Ava swallowed hard. If her cousins hugged her now, she was going to lose her grip on her rapidly fraying self-control. She wasn't sure what she'd do—scream, cry, throw up—but either way, it was bound to be messy, and *she did not do mess.* "I would really prefer that you didn't. I'm *fine.*"

"Whatever you say, prima." Michelle's tone was dubious. "We totally believe you."

"I mean it," Ava said firmly. "Hector is not my problem anymore. And anyway, it's almost time for the announcement. We should get going."

Jasmine tucked her arm through Ava's. "Marry You" by

Bruno Mars played overhead as they wound their way through the crowd.

"Let's get together after the party," Jasmine suggested. "We'll open a few bottles of rosé and talk."

Ava thought about the text she'd just sent Roman. He hadn't replied yet, but she knew he was back from Japan, and she was mentally crossing all her fingers and toes that she'd be with him tonight.

"Maybe," she hedged, instead of saying that Hector was the absolute last person she wanted to discuss.

On their way to the front of the ballroom, they were stopped every two feet, either by celebrities who wanted a selfie with Jasmine or family members who kissed Ava's cheek and murmured, "Lo siento, muchacha."

It was the longest walk of Ava's life.

When they finally reached the stage, Jasmine sent Ava a look full of worry. "Are you *sure* you're okay?"

Ava plastered a serene smile on her face and nodded. "Yes. Totally okay."

She was not even a little bit okay. She was hanging on by her fingernails.

A quick glance at her phone showed there was no response from Roman. Granted, it had only been a few minutes, but if she knew she could see him tonight, that would at least give her the strength to get through the rest of this party.

Jasmine's sister Jillian joined them, and from the corner of her eye, Ava spotted Ashton and his dad, Ignacio.

When Jasmine took the mic and launched into her prepared speech—which included jokes and singing, because Jasmine was nothing if not an entertainer—Ava tucked her phone into her pocket and resorted to her Resting Pleasant Face. She smiled and laughed at the appropriate moments, but she didn't hear a single thing Jasmine said. It must have been good, though, because her cousin had the assembled partygoers eating out of her hand.

Inside, Ava's brain pinballed between images of Hector standing at an altar with some nameless, faceless woman, and thoughts of kissing the hell out of Roman when she next saw him.

She didn't *care* about Hector. She really didn't. It had been two years, for god's sake. But her family didn't know she'd moved on. They thought she was alone. Not that things with Roman were serious, but they had . . . a companionship, of sorts. It didn't feel right to keep him in "booty call" territory now that they were texting about things that had nothing to do with sex. Were they friends with benefits? That sounded too juvenile, considering their ages and Roman's level of success, but she couldn't say they *weren't* friends. Fuck buddies? Ugh, that sounded terrible too. Anyway, it didn't matter what they were called, because the only person who knew about him was Damaris.

If her family knew about Roman, maybe they wouldn't be gazing at her now with undisguised pity. *I'm not alone!* she wanted to scream. *I have an amazing, sexy man in my life, and I never even have to pick up his dirty socks.* But they didn't know, and they never would.

So she stood there, pretending everything was okay. Pretending she was happy to be fixing chocolate fountains and painting patio chairs and watching other people's children. Pretending to be Old Ava.

For how long? a tiny voice whispered in the back of her brain.

Shut the hell up, she told it viciously.

When she heard Jasmine say her name, Ava stepped forward,

smiling and waving. Luckily, she didn't have to say anything. She fixed her gaze into middle distance until all the people in front of her were a big, shapeless blur.

Beside her, Michelle and Jillian also waved when their names were called. Then Ashton took the mic to introduce his groomsmen.

Ava let her mind drift again, but then Ashton said something that pulled her out of her reverie.

"—my best man, Roman Vázquez!"

Ava's Resting Pleasant Face cracked as she craned her neck to peer around her cousins.

No, this couldn't be happening, he couldn't be the same—

Holy shit.

She watched in horror as Roman—*her* Roman—jogged up to the stage. He held a phone to his ear and muttered something quickly before sliding it into his pocket. He gave Ashton a quick hug then turned to wave to everyone, flashing that endearing smile she knew so well.

Ashton continued speaking into the mic, but Ava didn't hear any of it. The music began again, and she guessed that meant the introduction of the wedding party was over, but there was a rushing in her ears, and inside, her carefully constructed image of Roman was falling apart.

Roman, her perfect fling, a man who couldn't possibly have any connection to anyone in her family . . .

Was Ashton's best fucking friend.

Not only that, Roman was in the wedding party! As the best man! And *she* was the maid of honor, which meant . . .

She was going to have to walk down the fucking aisle next to him.

This was it. They were over. Because it anyone found out she and Roman had something going on, she would once again be left to deal with her family's criticism when it ended.

God. She could hear it now. *Ay bendito. Ava can't keep a man, even when it's only about sex.*

Not that any of her relatives would use the word "sex." They'd come up with some kind of inventive euphemism instead. She'd once heard Titi Nita refer to it as "playing hide the plátano."

While Ava was quietly dying inside, Roman turned and spotted her. She knew because of the way his face lit up like a kid at Christmas seeing a pile of toys under the tree. She tried not to let that soften her heart and instead steeled herself for their interaction. He immediately started toward her, but then she saw confusion pass over his features—probably wondering why the hell she was here. Before he could say anything, Ava leaped forward with her hand outstretched.

"Hi there," she said, smiling broadly. "I'm Ava, Jasmine's cousin. Nice to meet you."

Chapter 21

Roman shook Ava's hand, bafflement swirling with elation as her words sank in. *I'm Ava, Jasmine's cousin.* Well, that certainly explained why she was here, but he still had a million other questions.

"Nice to meet you too," he mumbled. But before he could do anything else—like pull her in for a searing kiss or ask why she was pretending not to know him—a shorter woman with long dark hair stuck her hand at him as well.

"Michelle," the newcomer said. "Also Jasmine's cousin. And that over there is Jillian, Jasmine's sister."

As Roman looked between Ava and Michelle, something dawned on him. Ashton had often talked about "Jasmine's cousin" without mentioning a name. But now he had the sneaking suspicion that every time Ashton had said "su prima," he was talking about *two different people.*

Ava wore a slightly panicked expression as she turned away to greet Ashton's father, and Roman stuffed his hands in his pockets, puzzling it out. Ava clearly didn't want anyone to find out they knew each other, but why should it matter? Did it have something to do with her family? He began to mentally file through everything she'd ever said about them.

Ashton clapped him on the back, making Roman jolt to awareness.

"You just made it," Ashton said with a grin. "I thought I was going to have to drag you onto the stage."

"Yeah, sorry, I . . ." Roman trailed off, watching Ava lean down to give Yadiel a big hug.

Ashton followed his gaze. "That's Ava. Jasmine's cousin."

"We've met," Roman murmured, then quickly added, "she just introduced herself."

"The three of them are close." Ashton gestured at Ava, Jasmine, and Michelle. "They call themselves the Primas of Power."

"Cute." Roman wondered if they knew about him. Probably not, if Ava's reaction was anything to go by. He knew there was someone she texted whenever she stayed with him, but who was it, if not her cousins?

It stung a little to realize she was hiding his existence like some dirty little secret, when all of the most important people in his life—his mother, sister, Camille, and Ashton—all knew about Ava, even if they didn't have all the details.

The dance floor was filling up and the entrees would be brought out soon, so everyone trooped off the stage to mingle. Roman was talking to Ashton's father when Ava caught his eye. He excused himself from the older man and stepped aside. Barely a minute passed before Ava sidled up to him.

"We need to talk," she said under her breath, her serious tone at odds with her cheery smile. "Now."

Roman smiled too and waved to the head of catering, who was heading back to the kitchen. "Meet me by the bathrooms in five," he said out of the corner of his mouth.

With a barely perceptible nod, Ava disappeared into the crowd.

A few minutes later, Roman loitered in the hallway outside the entrance to the restrooms. Soon, Ava appeared. Her smile was gone, and her expression was pinched. It reminded him of the way she'd looked when she arrived at his apartment the last time he'd seen her, after a nerve-racking event had shaken her to the core.

"Is there somewhere private we can go?" she asked the second she'd reached him. "I'm assuming you own this hotel too."

He didn't respond to that because it was true. "There's an office nearby."

He wanted to take her hand, but something told him she wouldn't go for it. Instead, he led her through an employees-only hallway and used his master keycard to unlock an office door. He happened to know this one was out of use, since the hotel was undergoing major changes in the lead-up to being remodeled as a Dulce Moderno soon.

The moment the door closed behind them, Ava rounded on him.

"You didn't know?" Her tone was accusatory.

Roman shook his head. "How would I? Did you?"

She began to pace, fiddling with her necklace. "Jasmine only referred to you as 'Ashton's best friend.' I figured you were some famous actor, and maybe your name was supposed to be a secret."

He stuffed his hands into his pockets because all he wanted to do was grab her and kiss her. "Ashton and I starred in a telenovela together almost twenty years ago, but I would hardly call myself a *famous actor.*"

Ava pressed her fingers to her temples. "I can't believe this is happening."

"That *what's* happening?"

"That you're in my cousin's wedding!"

"Why does it matter?"

She dropped her hands and gaped at him. "Why does it matter that the random guy I met at a bar is in my cousin's wedding party? This practically makes you family."

He winced. "Not really. Also, ouch. *Random guy?* Is that all I am?"

Her eyes skittered away from his. He didn't think she'd meant to sound so dismissive, but damn, it had hurt.

"Ava." Roman approached her slowly, gratified when she didn't back away. He took her hands, not sure how she'd react if he tried to hold her right now. "Please talk to me. I don't understand why you're so freaked out by this."

She pulled her hands from his and paced away. "We're going to have to act like we just met and have no history. Can you do that?"

"Why? What's the big deal?"

Her expression was severe. "Why? Because my relatives are the absolute worst when it comes to relationships."

"What do you—?"

"The gossip, the teasing, the judgment. And when it's over, they *never* let you forget about it." She slashed a hand through the air for emphasis.

Ah. He was starting to see what the problem was. They'd barely even begun, yet Ava had already raced down Worst Case Scenario Boulevard to where they were broken up. He needed to bring her back to the present.

"Is that what this is about?" He kept his tone gentle. "You're worried about the aftermath?"

"Of course I am! Do you know what happened after I told them Hector was leaving me?" She plowed on before he could say anything, continuing to pace back and forth in quick, angry strides. "My grandmother reacted like the apocalypse was coming. Like we all had to go into survival mode because I was both husbandless and childless. Hector's mother called me every day crying about how sad *she* was, and my sister-in-law sent me no less than a dozen phone numbers for couples therapists. My great-aunt told me to apologize for whatever I'd done so he'd take me back, while *his* aunt told me cheating is a normal part of marriage and I should stop making a fuss. Like the divorce was *my* idea."

Roman's hands balled into fists as he pictured what she described, but he tamped down his response.

"I hate that you went through that," he said carefully. "And we're going to come back to it later. But what does that have to do with *us*?"

"If they knew about you . . ." She shook her head, cutting the comment short. "No. I can't go through that again. We're done."

She was so beautiful in her cheerful yellow dress, pacing the room like an anxious daffodil, that it took a moment for her words to sink in. When they did, panic flared. "What do you mean, *done*?"

"Whatever we were doing, it's over. I can't see you again. Not . . . not like this."

His first internal gut reaction was *No*. No, they couldn't be over.

But it was true they'd never made any commitments to each other. In fact, this whole thing had been founded on a lack of commitment. *No strings, no feelings.* At the time, that had been an easy promise to make. Now?

He *did* have feelings. Feelings for *her*. And he knew he wasn't the only one who'd gotten attached. She cared more than she was letting on, but fear was getting the better of her, and now she was ready to toss it all away.

Ava turned to leave. "I need to get back to the party."

So Roman played the only card he had left.

"Why did you text me?"

When she paused at the door, he went on.

"You said you wanted to see me. Something happened, didn't it?"

Her shoulders tightened and she didn't answer, but he already knew. Something must have triggered her need for her coping mechanism. If that's all he was to her, well, all relationships had to start somewhere.

"What do you need, Ava?" He lowered his voice to a seductive growl. "Do you need *me*?"

Her back heaved like she was breathing hard, then she spun around to face him. "Yes, damn it. I do."

The words were a fierce whisper, as if she were scared to say them out loud, but they were all Roman needed to hear.

Striding forward, he caught her in his arms. Her eyes were wild as she strained against him, fisting her hands in his lapels and tugging him closer. Propelled by the thick tension surrounding them, he gave them both what they wanted and crushed his mouth down on hers.

It was always passionate when they were together, always hot, but this level of desperation and intensity was new. They'd never kissed like this, like she would consume the very essence of his soul if she could, like the world could end at any moment.

He fucking loved it.

"I need you," Ava panted between kisses. "Now, Roman. I need you now."

"You have me," he growled, spinning her to face the door. "Anytime, anywhere."

He hiked up her dress, grabbing fistfuls of fabric in his haste. Her palms pressed to the door and she arched her hips toward him. He was glad he'd started carrying condoms in his wallet.

Something told him to hurry, that if he took too long, she'd start second guessing the entire situation and run away. Better to make sure her mind was otherwise occupied.

Crouching behind her, he tugged her panties down and helped her step out of them. After tucking them into his pocket, he skimmed his hands up her legs, loving the look of them in her high red sandals. The heels made her a smidge taller than he was, which was sexy as hell. He pressed kisses to the backs of her knees and thighs, and nipped at her ass cheek before parting her so he could see her bare pussy.

"You need this?" he asked, brushing his thumb over her folds. "From me?"

"Yes," she whined. "I need it. Need *you*."

God, he loved to hear her say that.

He pushed her thighs farther apart, then buried his face in her sex. He loved the taste of her, the scent of her, the little noises she made as she unraveled. Every time they were together, he paid close attention to exactly which touches made her sigh, and which ones made her moan. Now, he brought all of that observation and practice to bear, in an effort to drive her wild.

First, he slid his tongue through her slit with one long lick, reacquainting himself with her taste. The strangled groan she made was music to his ears, and he knew that, for now at least, she wasn't thinking about anyone but him. With that victory in mind, he fastened his mouth to her clit and pleasured her like his life depended on it. Hard licks and soft nips, varied by unexpected suction followed by soothing strokes with his fingers. The angle was awkward but he didn't fucking care, he didn't care about anything except this woman, and showing her exactly what she meant to him in the only way she'd allow.

He'd meant to do this later, in his bed. But there was something more raw, more real, about pressing her against the beige slab of a door in an unused office with décor that could best be described as utilitarian. There were no reminders of wealth here. Nothing to distract from who they were.

Just Roman. Just Ava.

Not just sex. This was so much more.

By the time he rose to his feet, she was panting and writhing, begging him for release. He'd kept her on the edge, knowing that if she came, her rational brain would kick in and she'd be back to saying they couldn't be together.

He was determined to show her why they should be. Starting with this.

Opening his pants, he pulled his erection free and rolled a condom on. She was ready for him, wet and stretched by his mouth and fingers. When he positioned himself at her entrance and pushed, he slid right inside. The way she clamped down on him made him groan.

"Fuck, Ava."

"Move in me." She gasped out the words. "I need to feel you."

How could he deny her? Roman grabbed her hips, those

lush curves he loved so much, and pulled her back against him
with each thrust.

Thanks to the heels, she was at the perfect height for them
to go hard and fast. Roman gave it to her with a desperation
borne of his burgeoning feelings, and the fear from when she
told him it was over. From the way she bucked against him and
whined *yes, oh my god, yes*, she was into it too.

He was getting close, so he licked his fingers and reached
around to rub her clit. Already, he knew the pattern, rhythm,
and speed to make her shatter. Sure enough, the second he
touched her, her cries rose in pitch.

"Roman, please . . ."

"Anything you want, Ava. Anything."

They weren't just idle words uttered in the midst of lovemaking. He meant them. Anything that was in his power to
give, he would give her. She only had to ask.

And he knew she never would.

Except for this. If worshiping her body with his was all she'd
take from him, he'd make sure to give her *exactly* what she
wanted.

She gripped his arm, as if to keep his hand between her legs.
Her other hand fisted against the door. She was close.

"Come for me, mi cielo," he whispered in her ear. His own
climax was rapidly approaching, but he grit his teeth and held
back. She came first, always.

Ava chanted a litany of *please please please* and Roman bit his
cheek to suppress a chuckle. Always so polite, even when he
was buried to the hilt inside her. Then she let out a soft cry,
like the orgasm had caught her by surprise. Her inner muscles
clamping down on his cock brought on a climax that caught

him by surprise. He thrust against her hard, her gorgeous ass cushioning his pelvis. With his face tucked into her sweetly scented hair, he came with a guttural groan.

Ava's eyes were closed, her cheek pressed to the flat metal door. Roman's knees felt like they were going to give out, but he marshaled his strength and eased back from her, taking one last reverent look at her butt before he lowered her dress.

"How are you feeling?" he asked, his voice rough and breathless.

"Better, I think." She blinked like a baby owl. Satisfaction rushed through him as he took in her dazed expression.

He found a new box of tissues in the desk drawer and wrapped the condom up before tucking himself back into his pants. "Are you ready to talk about why you want to end this?"

Her dreamy expression hardened and she shook her head. "No. I meant it, Roman. My entire family knows who you are now. We can't—" She huffed out an angry sigh. "This was the last time. I can't do this anymore."

Then she glanced at the door he'd just fucked her against, and her next words were wistful. "But I wish we could."

With that, she yanked open the door and bolted from the room.

He didn't follow her.

After all this time, he knew her patterns. She'd shared something today, so she was going to pull away for a while.

That was okay. He'd give her space, and use it to prepare.

After leaving the office, Roman stopped by the bathroom to clean up. He took his time, figuring Ava would have a fit if he returned to the party right after she did. When he reached into his pocket to check his phone, he was surprised to find a scrap of fabric in there. A wicked grin spread over his face when he pulled out Ava's white lace panties. Oh yeah, he was keeping these.

Before he could question the wisdom of teasing her, he shot her a text.

Roman: Missing something?

He attached a photo of the panties dangling from his finger.

While he didn't expect her to reply, he wanted her to know this wasn't over. He'd respect her wishes, of course, but he wasn't giving up hope. There was something real between them, something more than sex, and they owed it to themselves to see what it was.

He had two months to figure it out.

Back at the party, Roman noted that the food had come out and most people were sitting down eating. He looked around nonchalantly, trying to spot Ava.

"Where have you been?" Ashton hissed, appearing at Roman's side.

"Had to take a call," Roman replied absently.

Ah, there she was. Across the ballroom, Ava bent low to speak to an older woman who was seated at one of the family tables.

Ashton followed Roman's gaze and sucked in a breath. "No lo creo."

Roman shot him a look. "What?"

Ashton's jaw dropped, and he gave Roman a once over. Roman quickly patted his hair, but he knew it was fine, because he'd fixed it in the bathroom mirror. Maybe his pants were a little wrinkled, but—

"*What?*" he repeated, growing irritated.

"You're shitting me." Ashton's voice dropped to a whisper. "You and Ava? ¿En serio?"

Oh shit. This was exactly what Ava *didn't* want. Roman's heart pounded, and he tried to evade. "What are you talking about? I didn't say anything." ·

"You don't have to." Ashton's brows drew together, and he looked angry. "What the hell? Sneaking off with the maid of honor during the engagement party? Right after she finds out her ex is getting remarried? That's a bit cliché, even for you."

"No, we—what the fuck? What do you mean, *even for me?*" Roman quietly noted the ex-getting-remarried part. So *that* was why Ava had texted him. The knowledge deflated him a bit.

But Ashton wasn't done. "How many models have you dated, huh?"

"How many models have *you* dated?" Roman shot back, pissed off at this line of questioning.

Ashton gave him a dark look. "That was a long time ago."

"Same for me. And what the hell do models have to do with anything?"

"They're a metaphor. My point is, you date women who are convenient, who you can show off at an event and kiss goodbye at the end of the night—or the next morning—without a care in the world."

It was eerily similar to what Roman's mother had said. "So?"

"So, your type isn't emotionally vulnerable divorcées. I'm warning you, Ro. Ava's not going to be your wedding party hookup."

Roman scowled. "It's not like that."

"Then qué es eso? Besides, weren't you dating a . . ." Ashton trailed off, and Roman could all but see the gears turning in the other man's head. A second later, Ashton gave a gasp worthy of a telenovela matriarch. "*No me digas.*"

Roman sighed. "Now what?"

"It's her, isn't it?" Ashton's dark eyes went round and he dropped his voice to a whisper. "Ava is your mystery mujer. La profe."

Roman narrowed his eyes, somewhat alarmed at how easily his friend had put the pieces together. "Why do you think that?"

"Because her lipstick is gone, and when she saw you on stage, she looked like she'd seen a ghost. Also, she's a *teacher.*"

It was actually a relief to have the cat out of the bag. "Yeah, it's her."

Ashton smacked his own forehead. "Puñeta. How the hell did you two even meet?"

"Long story. And I don't see why this is such a big deal." Roman hunched his shoulders and stuck his hands in his pockets. His fingers tangled with Ava's lace panties.

"How did she react?"

"To what?"

"To finding out you're in the wedding, obviously."

Roman glared at him. "How do you think?"

Ashton let out a laugh that could only be described as a cackle and clapped a hand on Roman's shoulder. "Ay muchacho. You have no fucking idea what you're in for."

"What's that supposed to mean?" Roman grumbled.

"You'll find out." With a smug expression, Ashton strolled toward the dance floor.

Roman mulled over their conversation, along with what Ava had revealed. She saw their situation as temporary, and her family's outsize reaction to her divorce made her fearful about the fallout from another possible breakup.

It was too soon to convince her he had something more per-manent in mind, especially since he was just starting to figure out for himself what that might mean. If he told her now that he wanted more, she wouldn't believe him. And worse, she'd probably think he was just trying to get in her pants again.

Being with her had brought him some clarity, and the stra-tegic part of his brain kicked in. She'd said they couldn't see each other anymore "like this"—as in, for sex. But they were both part of Ashton and Jasmine's wedding for the next two months. There was plenty of time to develop and execute a plan for winning her over.

Roman slipped on his reading glasses and pulled out his phone.

It was time to make a spreadsheet.

Chapter 22

Ava survived the rest of the school year by drinking too much coffee, grading late into the night, and binge-watching Reese Witherspoon's romantic comedy oeuvre. Her ultimate comfort movie had been ruined—she could no longer look at Mr. Darcy without thinking of Roman—and she was on the hunt for a replacement.

Michelle had suggested *Moulin Rouge*, but Ava didn't want anything that ended in tragedy. Jasmine suggested *The Wedding Planner*, but Ava had enough of wedding planning in her real life, thank you very much. Damaris was the one who brought up *Legally Blonde*, so Ava started there and was working her way through Reese's other greatest hits. Unfortunately, there weren't enough rom-coms in the world to distract Ava from thoughts of Roman.

As far as goodbye sex went, that scene in the empty office had been phenomenal. Which was entirely the problem. If it had been awful, she'd have felt much better about her decision to cut things off with him. But he'd done everything perfectly, from his devastating kisses to the way he'd dropped to his knees and licked her until she'd been ready to scream. And then he had the nerve to follow it up with a fast, grinding fuck and a bone-melting orgasm she wasn't likely to forget anytime soon.

Even now, as she sat across from Damaris at their favorite Bronx brunch spot, Isla Bonita Café, to celebrate the end of a grueling school year with bottomless bellinis, Ava's body longed for his touch.

To make matters worse, she'd gotten so used to texting him, she found herself periodically reaching for her phone throughout the day, only to snatch her hand back like it was a hot stove.

Don't you text him, she told herself. *Stay strong!*

Except he wasn't texting her either. Which was good. Right? She was the one who'd ended things. And he was respecting her decision. So why was she so pissed off about it?

She excused herself to go to the restroom and left her phone at the table so she wouldn't check it approximately 128 times while she was gone.

As she washed her hands, she studied her hollow-eyed reflection in the bathroom mirror and sighed.

Fuck, she wasn't just pissed. She was *sad*.

The honest truth? She missed him. Even when they hadn't been communicating in between their trysts, the knowledge that he was out there, only one text message away, had been a solace. Now she didn't even have that.

Why the hell did he have to be friends with Ashton? Of all the telenovela actors in the world Roman could have for his best friend, it had to be Ashton Fucking Suárez, her soon-to-be cousin-in-law.

Thanks a lot, Universe.

She recalled how bewildered Roman had been by her reaction to seeing him at the engagement party, and she knew she could've explained herself better. But the combination of hearing that Hector was getting married, plus the revelation that Roman was *in* Jasmine and Ashton's wedding with her, had caused some kind of short circuit in her brain, and all she'd been able to do was vent about her family's reaction to her divorce. Not her finest moment, but he seemed to get the picture.

The saving grace was that Ava had managed to end it without anyone in her family finding out. She didn't have to deal with their censure or judgment. She didn't have to deal with letting them down. Again.

Anger gave way to despondency. Ava had tried to put herself out there, but now her special, secret affair was over. She couldn't imagine going through all that with someone else, someone other than Roman. He'd probably ruined her for all other men.

It confirmed what she already knew to be true. Love, romance—even amazing sex—those things just weren't for her. Other people got to have them, but Ava couldn't trust a relationship to last, and at the end of the day, all she had left was her family.

Which was why Jasmine could never know. It would put her in the awkward position of choosing between her cousin and her husband's best friend for the rest of their lives. Ava wouldn't do that to her.

Especially since there was a chance that Jasmine would pick Roman instead.

Back at the table, Damaris was asking the waitress to bring more ketchup, and Ava's phone was lighting up with texts.

Her heart leaped at the thought that it might be Roman, but when she took her seat and glanced at the screen, she saw it was her cousins.

Jasmine: EMERGENCY

Michelle: What's wrong?

Jasmine: Ashton and I have to fly
back to Vancouver to do last minute
reshoots on the Sambrano Studios
Christmas rom-com.

Michelle: My cynical little heart loves
a holiday rom com! But what's the
problem?

Jasmine: It means we're going to miss
our wedding planning appointments
in Puerto Rico! Ashton is saying we
should move the date to next year. I
know he's right but I am SO SAD.

Jasmine's last text was followed by three crying face emojis.
After skimming the exchange, Ava immediately typed a reply.

Ava: I'll go.

Jasmine's response appeared a second later.

Jasmine: Omg Ava, are you sure?

Michelle: I'd join you, but Gabe and I
are stuck in California for the next two
weeks.

> **Ava:** I'm sure. Just send me
> all the details.

> **Jasmine:** Ava, you're the BEST!! What
> would I do without you?

> **Ava:** Happy to help!

Ava added the blushing smiley face and went to put her phone back in her purse, but it buzzed again with another incoming text. She picked it up to see Jasmine's response, but it wasn't from Jasmine.

> **Roman:** I'll charter a plane for us.

Ava sucked in a breath. *Shit.* She'd thought she was replying to the Primas of Power group thread, not the one for the entire wedding party. That's what she got for answering too quickly.

With a sense of dread—and an illicit little thrill—she switched to her private texts with Roman. The last message was the photo of her missing underwear, something she hadn't even noticed until she'd sat down to eat next to her *grandmother.* She'd gone through the rest of the engagement party with no panties, because she'd been too embarrassed to track Roman down and demand he return them. For all she knew, he still had them.

The thought of her panties in his possession made her cheeks hot. She put that mental image aside and typed quickly.

> **Ava:** What do you mean, US?

> **Roman:** You and me. I'm going with you.

Her nostrils flared. Jasmine had already replied in the other thread, and Ava couldn't make a big deal about it to her cousins without explaining exactly why she'd turn down a generous gesture like the one Roman had just made. Huffing out a breath, she replied directly to him.

> **Ava:** I can handle it myself.

> **Roman:** I'm sure you can, but it'll be easier if I'm there.

> **Ava:** And why is that?

> **Roman:** I own Bellísima Resort, where the wedding is being held.

"Of course you do," Ava grumbled. A second later, Damaris's glossy purple fingernail tapped on the table in front of her, and Ava jumped.

"Who are you talking to?" Damaris asked. "Because it sure isn't me."

Ava sighed and dropped the phone into her purse, where it continued to buzz. "Sorry, I didn't mean to be rude."

"It's not rude if you fill me in. Was it *Roman*?" She drew out the first syllable of his name teasingly. "By the way, I *did* try to tell you he had starred in a telenovela. But you told me to stop researching him, so I didn't see that it was with Ashton."

Ava grabbed her bellini and took a big sip. They were approaching the end of the bottomless drinks hour, and she had some catching up to do. "You're right. I should have dug a little deeper. And yes, it's about Roman."

Damaris propped her elbows on the table and rested her chin on her hands, brown eyes wide in a *tell me everything* expression.

"Well," Ava began, "it looks like Jasmine isn't going to be able to fly to Puerto Rico to take care of the rest of the wedding planning."

Damaris raised her eyebrows. "So you volunteered to go in her stead?"

Ava scowled. "How did you know?"

Her friend's eyelids flicked in a barely suppressed eye-roll. "Ava, you *always* volunteer to help."

Ava fiddled with her necklace, not wanting to examine the *why* of that too closely. "Of course. They're my family."

"I know, beba." Damaris's voice was sympathetic, but firm. "But at some point, that helpfulness is going to bury you. Anyway, continue."

Damaris's words troubled her, but Ava went on. She filled Damaris in on the group text mix-up and Roman's high-handed offer to charter a plane.

Damaris gasped. "I've always wanted to fly in a private plane. You have to tell me what it's like."

"You're missing the point."

"Which is?"

"That he's going with me!"

"Good, he can pay for everything."

Ava let out a frustrated groan. "No, he can't. I broke things off with him."

"So don't fuck him. Although if you want my opinion, which I know you do, it'll be a missed opportunity. This is the romantic island getaway you deserve. Remind me where you went on your honeymoon?"

"Niagara Falls," Ava grumbled.

Damaris sipped her bellini. "I rest my case."

"I just don't want Roman to think this means anything."

"He knows you're only going for the wedding stuff. And besides, this is on you for stepping up to help."

"Jasmine needs me."

"Ava, there's helping, and then there's whatever you do, Ms. Katniss Everdeen." Damaris waved a hand in front of Ava as if to indicate her impulsive volunteering behavior. "This is your first summer off in years and you're spending it on Jasmine's wedding stuff."

It was true. Every year, Ava had cobbled together extra jobs—summer school, theater camp, tutoring—first to pay down her student loans faster, and then to cover the rent on her old apartment full of Hector's shit. But she didn't want to talk about that. "Look, I'm aware that when it comes to my family, my boundaries aren't the greatest. But that's why I'm trying to have better boundaries with Roman. Running off to Puerto Rico with him is the opposite of that!"

"If you can keep your distance from that man in PR, you'll know your boundaries are strong as steel."

"You're right." She just had to move Roman out of "hookup" territory and keep him firmly within the bounds of the wedding party. Regardless of how Ava felt, Jasmine deserved the perfect wedding and Ava wouldn't do anything to jeopardize that. "We're the maid of honor and best man, and we're only going on this trip to help the bride and groom. That's it."

Damaris toasted her with a nearly empty glass. "That almost sounded convincing."

Ava groaned. "What will it say about me if I can't keep my hands off him?"

"That you're a grown woman who can do whatever she

wants?" Damaris shrugged. "What does it matter? Who will know?"

"You've met my family. If any of them find out, I will never know a moment's peace."

"Why do you even care what they say?" At Ava's incredulous look, Damaris held up her hands. "Forget I asked. Just get the wedding stuff done and try to enjoy yourself. For my sake, if not your own." She raised her glass. "Trust the Universe!"

Ava clinked her glass to her friend's and didn't point out that the Universe was what had gotten her into this mess in the first place.

It didn't matter. She was in control now. The nature of her relationship with Roman might have changed, but she would handle it, just like she handled everything else that came her way.

And if she got tempted . . . well, that was why God had created travel vibrators.

Chapter 23

July

Roman didn't charter planes often, but a private flight with Ava had been too good to pass up. And watching her pretend not to enjoy it was a fucking delight.

When they'd boarded the midsize jet, she'd gazed around the cabin, slowly taking in the wood paneling, plush leather seats, tables laden with snacks thanks to the cabin attendant—a friendly young man named Enrique—and windows unblocked by other passengers. She'd started out sitting primly, but in less than an hour, she'd reclined and kicked her long legs out in front of her, all while savoring a glass of expensive champagne.

Roman sat diagonally across from her, so he could see her face. He wanted to be closer, but didn't push it. Besides, there were other ways to charm a schoolteacher.

He'd given her space since the engagement party, partly because he wanted to regroup, and also because he figured she needed time to wrap her head around the change in their situation.

Not only that, Ashton had specifically told him *not* to mess this up. They had a job to do, and they'd do it, but Roman hadn't gotten here by squandering opportunities.

The second Ava had volunteered to go to Puerto Rico, Roman had leaped into action. Rearranging his schedule to unexpectedly take three days off was no small task, but now that they were here, Operation Ava was in full swing.

He needed to handle it carefully so Ava didn't feel like she was being maneuvered. And since she wouldn't let him buy her gifts, he'd lined up a series of romantic evenings instead. On the first night, he'd booked them a private sunset cruise. For the second, they'd take an overnight trip to Vieques by helicopter with a tour of the bioluminescent bay. On the last night, he'd arranged for dinner from one of the top chefs on the island. He hoped the gestures would show her that he was serious about their relationship, and that he'd meant it when he said she deserved to be treasured.

Looking up from the reports he'd been reviewing, he took in the office supplies strewn across the table before her. They weren't the kind he was used to. For instance, his paper clips didn't have tiny white bows on them, and he'd never in his life used so many stickers.

He slipped off his reading glasses. "What on earth are you doing over there?"

She blinked like she'd been pulled out of deep focus. "I'm working on the planner for the wedding."

"Planner?"

Ava turned the small three-ring binder around so he could see it. She deftly flipped through the pages, which were sorted by cardboard dividers featuring stylized illustrations of tanned women in bridal attire.

"Each section relates to a wedding event," she explained. "Engagement party, bridal shower, dress fitting, and so on, along with all the tasks we have to complete while we're in Puerto Rico. Cake tasting, ceremony location, florist—"

"But the wedding planner sent us a spreadsheet."

Ava's mouth pinched in what Roman had realized was her version of a fierce scowl. "A spreadsheet isn't tactile. I can't easily take notes in a spreadsheet."

He held up his tablet. "This is tactile and I can take notes on it with a stylus."

"You have your way and I have mine," she replied tightly, pulling her planner back.

Roman hid a smile. On his tablet, he opened a spreadsheet titled "All About Ava" and in the "Likes" column, he added, "Paper planners and fancy office supplies."

While he disagreed with her on the functionality of a well-organized spreadsheet, she was certainly right about keeping track of research in one place. He'd started this document after the engagement party, adding everything he knew about her—likes, dislikes, the names of her family members he'd met at the party, and so on. He had a whole section for the Primas of Power, a moniker he found fascinating.

"About the Primas of Power . . ." he began.

She looked up from her planner. "What about them?"

"Where did the name come from?"

Her gaze softened, as if his question evoked a sweet memory. "The year I was in kindergarten, and Jas and Mich were in pre-K, our dads were in charge of our Halloween costumes. You know the superhero pajamas with the little capes you can stick on your shoulders with Velcro?" When he nodded, she continued. "Jasmine was Wonder Woman, Michelle was Supergirl, and I was Batgirl. Michelle dubbed us the Primas of Power, and the name stuck."

Roman's mouth pulled into a grin at the thought of it. "Are there photos?"

"Of course." She tapped her phone screen a few times before passing it to him. "It's the main photo for our group text."

Roman put his glasses on and took the phone. His heart lurched in his chest as he stared at the picture. All three girls wore leggings, rain boots, and what looked like knee-length nightgowns with little capes attached. The front of each nightgown bore the logo of the superhero they represented. Ava's was purple, with the Batman symbol in yellow and black, and a yellow utility belt printed directly on the fabric.

The photo had been taken on a short set of concrete steps leading up to a house. Jasmine and Michelle were hamming it up for the camera—Jasmine stood on the middle step with her chin held high and her hands fisted on her hips, and Michelle was on the top step, balancing on one leg with a fist thrust into the air like she was flying. Ava, already much taller than both of her cousins, stood on the bottom step. Instead of succumbing to the silliness of the moment and pretending to be punching or kicking a bad guy, she posed with her hands clasped tightly in front of her, a sweet smile on her adorable little face. She was the embodiment of five-year-old decorum, and his heart broke for this child who already felt the need to suppress, to restrain, to hide. What had it cost her to keep still while her cousins played? How many times over the years had she held back in exactly this manner?

He wanted to ask her, but the questions made his heart hurt, and he didn't want her to withdraw further. So he just cleared his throat, said, "Cute," and returned her phone.

The picture made him think of his own childhood, the way he'd started hustling at a young age to help pay the bills. His mother hadn't wanted him to worry about their finances, had begged him to just be a normal kid. But when she hadn't been able to stop him, she'd used some of the money he earned on activities for the two of them, like ordering pizza, going to the movies and buying popcorn, taking trips to Rockaway Beach or the Prospect Park Zoo, or eating in an actual restaurant.

Making money had meant he and his mom could have fun together. Things had been hard, but they were happy.

"I looked for my father once," he murmured, not sure where the thought came from or why he was saying it aloud.

Ava's head lifted, and even though he wasn't looking directly at her, he knew he had her full attention.

"Oh?"

He swallowed. This wasn't something he talked about with a lot of people. "After I opened the first hotel. It occurred to me that he might come crawling out of the woodwork to ask for money. You hear about stories like that all the time."

She nodded but didn't say anything. After a moment, he went on.

"My mom wouldn't give me details, but she talked to the private investigator I hired." He shrugged. "It was a short search. The guy was dead. Car accident when I was nine."

"I'm sorry," Ava said quietly. "That must have been hard to hear."

Roman nodded. It had been hard, in a myriad of different ways.

He'd expected the news to be a sort of relief. His father wasn't going to reappear to hurt his mother or make Roman's life difficult. But it had come as more of a blow than he could have imagined.

All those years, he told himself he didn't think about his father, but it was a lie. The specter of the man who'd sired him had hung over his head, the possibility of him a constant companion, even if the man himself hadn't been. As a child, he'd imagined all kinds of scenarios where the guy came back. Roman had pictured how he'd react—with rage, with cool detachment, with scorn. And in some cases, even with acceptance. As he got older, his responses changed, but he'd never considered that his father would just be . . . gone. All those years, the man was dead, existing only in Roman's thoughts. Roman had invented a life for him that hadn't, and would never, be.

The investigator had put together a document with information he'd managed to dig up, but Roman had deleted the file without opening it.

"He wasn't a villain," his mother had said, when he finally talked to her about it. "He was just young, and he didn't want to be a father yet."

"That doesn't change the fact that he *was* a father."

Dulce had only shrugged. "Honestly, it was a relief when he left. It was easier to be alone than to rely on him and have him constantly let me down."

Roman had no sympathy for men who broke promises and abandoned their responsibilities. It made him think of Ava's ex-husband, the asshole who'd promised to love her forever and then cut and run without even having the decency to try to work things out. Although if he had, Ava would probably still be married to him, and then where would they be?

"I'm sorry your ex hurt you," Roman said to Ava. Her eyebrows leaped in surprise, probably at the abrupt change in subject. "But I'm glad he was an immature asshole."

Her expression turned wary. "Why?"

"Because if he'd been just a tiny bit smarter, you and I might not be here."

Her cheeks reddened. "We would've ended up in this wedding together regardless."

"But you would've still been married to *him*."

She blinked, like that hadn't occurred to her, then shook her head. "It doesn't matter. I already told you, our . . . whatever this was, it's over."

"Is it?" He kept his gaze steady when she looked over at him, willing her to see what he felt for her.

She licked her lips. "Yes," she said, but her voice was shaky, and it almost sounded like a question. She cleared her throat. "Don't . . . ah, don't look at me like that."

"Like what?"

"Like . . . you know what. You're doing it now."

A slow smile spread across his face. "Like I'm thinking about you not wearing any panties at the engagement party? Like I'm remembering the sounds you make when I—"

"That's quite enough," she interrupted, her cheeks flaming. "Speaking of, what did you do with my panties?"

Finally. He thought she'd never ask.

"You mean these?" He reached into the inner pocket of his jacket and drew out the small bundle of white lace.

She winced. "Please tell me you haven't been carrying those around with you."

He hadn't, but he'd brought them along on this trip just in case there was an opportunity to tease her about them. Like now.

"I keep them close to my heart," he murmured, pressing the lacy scrap to his chest. Her eyes widened, in embarrassment or outrage he couldn't tell, and he had to bite his cheek to keep from laughing.

Clearing her throat, she flipped to a new page in her planner. "I think we need to lay some ground rules before we land."

He sent her a mild smile. "I wouldn't have you any other way."

She opened her mouth, closed it, and gave him a stern look. "Rule number one—"

"I thought the first rule was that I can't look at you like I want to spread your—"

"*Right.* That's the first rule. Rule number two is . . ." She waved her hand in a vague gesture. "No . . . hanky-panky."

Roman laughed so hard he started coughing. Enrique brought him a bottle of water, and Ava's face was flushed by the time the attendant left.

Once they were alone again, Roman wiped the corners of his eyes. "I can't believe you said that."

Ava sighed and cast her gaze toward the plane's ceiling. "Honestly, neither can I. I spend too much time censoring myself around twelve-year-olds."

"Have you ever said 'hanky-panky' in front of your students?"

Her mouth twitched. "No. I'd lose their respect forever."

"So what are we calling it then, if not 'hanky-panky'?"

She covered her face. "It gets worse every time you say it."

"Then what should I call it?" God, he loved teasing her like this.

She dropped her hands and cast around for an idea. "I don't know . . . how about 'inappropriate touching'?"

"I think the way I touch you is very appropriate, considering I haven't done anything you haven't asked for."

He could see that she wanted to refute that, but didn't dare. He'd realized early on with Ava that the only way to get her to open up and stay in the moment with him was to make her explicitly say what she wanted and liked. There was no way she was getting away with claiming any of it had been *inappropriate*.

"Fine, no touching at all."

"What if you trip?" he asked innocently. "Should I just let you fall?"

"Oh my god." She rubbed her forehead and it took all of Roman's self-control to keep a straight face. "No sexual touching. Is that clear enough?"

"Crystal." He decided they'd had enough fun with this one and moved on. "Any other rules?"

She scowled. "No more stealing my panties!"

He gave her an affronted look. "I didn't *steal* them."

She held out her palm. "Then give them back."

"No." He placed a hand to his chest, covering the inner pocket where her underwear resided. "You abandoned them. They're mine."

Her lips twitched like she was trying not to laugh. "Fine. You get temporary custody. For now."

He loved that she was being playful with him, but when she turned back to her planner, he narrowed his eyes. "Are you writing all this down?"

"Of course I am."

"Let me see."

She reluctantly passed him the binder. He slipped on his

reading glasses and sure enough, she'd jotted down her rules in neat script, under the heading "Rules for Roman."

No LOOKS.

No sexual touching.

No panty stealing.

He heaved an exasperated sigh. "Ava, this list makes me sound like a pervert."

She snatched the planner back. "No flirting either."

"No."

Her gaze whipped to his in shock. "What do you mean, *no*?"

"Forget it. I'm not going to pretend I haven't seen every inch of you naked and flushed with—"

"No dirty talk!" Her face was red as she scribbled furiously.

He sat back in his seat. "I'm not agreeing to that one either. Besides, I think you like it."

Her voice was prim and she refused to look at him. "That's neither here nor there."

"Is that it for your rules?"

"I'll let you know if I think of any others."

"What about *my* rules?"

She gave him an arch look. "You don't get rules."

"That doesn't seem fair, but fine. What do I get if I play along?"

"Is everything a negotiation with you?"

"Yes."

She blew out a breath. "What do you want?"

He suppressed the urge to grin. "I want to buy you gifts."

She responded exactly as he'd expected her to. "Absolutely not."

He threw out another term he knew she wouldn't accept. "No underwear."

"What do you mean?"

"I'll play by your rules if you don't wear any underwear on this trip." He held out his hand. "Starting now."

Her mouth fell open, and while the look in her eyes was outraged, her cheeks turned pink, and he knew she was thinking about it.

"Only if you don't wear any underwear either," she shot back.

La profe had surprised him with that. "All right." Fighting a smile, he dropped his hands to his belt and began to undo the buckle.

Apparently she hadn't expected him to agree so readily because she gestured wildly for him to stop and looked over her shoulder, as if to make sure Enrique wasn't hovering nearby. "Never mind," she said quickly. "We both keep our underwear on."

"Then I want to spend the evenings with you." This was what he really wanted. "I get to choose the activities. No *hanky-panky*, as you called it, but outside of that, you go along with my plans."

Her eyes sparked and her chest heaved, but she nodded. "Fine. Provided we sort out all the required wedding stuff each day, you can plan how we spend the evenings."

Jackpot.

"Then we have a deal." Roman stretched his hand across the aisle for her to shake. After a moment's pause, where she bit enticingly on that lush bottom lip, she grabbed his hand and gave it two quick pumps. Then she drew back and muttered something like, "What have I gotten myself into?"

She flipped to a new page and began to glue magazine cutouts onto it. Roman thought it would've been easier to do it digitally, but she seemed happy, so who was he to judge? Maybe he could buy her some fancy scissors or something.

If she ever allowed him to give her presents.

"Roman?"

He looked up from his spreadsheet. "¿Sí, mi cielo?"

She blinked, like she was flustered by the term of endearment, but her face was carefully blank. "You and Ashton were on a telenovela together?"

He was a bit surprised she hadn't drilled Jasmine for information about him, but he was happy to tell her. "Almost twenty years ago. *Recuerdos Peligrosos*."

Ava squinted, like she was trying to remember it. "Which one was that?"

"We played brothers on a ranch."

"And one brother was kidnapped by the father and presumed dead, and then the other brother fell in love with the first one's pregnant fiancée?"

Her summary made him smile. "That's the one."

"I missed it when it aired. I must have still been in high school, probably around the time I moved into my dad's house to help take care of my sister."

"That sounds like a lot of responsibility for a teenager," he said mildly. She'd shared enough for him to suspect that her relationship with her father and stepmother bordered on toxic.

Her gaze fell to the planner in front of her and she shrugged. "Olympia was on bedrest during her third trimester, and she had a long recovery after Willow was born. I lived with them through the last two years of high school."

"I bet you still got straight As."

She nodded, but her smile was sad. "I graduated with more

than a 4.0 GPA, along with regular migraines and what I now recognize as anxiety."

He dug his fingers into the armrests to stop from reaching for her. "Where'd you go to college?"

"In Westchester, so it wasn't too far. Dad wanted me to live with them to save money, but I needed to get away, so I took out extra loans and moved into the dorms. The second I was gone, my stepmother packed up my things and put them in the basement, turning my room into the guest room."

The unspoken message couldn't have been clearer—Ava had been a guest in her father's home. He thought about Mikayla, who felt comfortable enough to leave her slippers and hair ties and coffee mugs all over his apartment. He'd bet Ava never even left so much as an earring out of place.

Ava unzipped a pouch that said "Keep Calm and Plan On" in gold script and pulled out a small purple ruler, which she used to draw lines on a blank page.

"Enough about me. How did you get from telenovelas to . . ." She gestured around the plane. "Here?"

"That is a long and boring story."

"I'm not going anywhere."

He shifted in his seat, and his back twinged in protest at sitting for so long. "To make it brief, I was bartending and applying for jobs when I got the role on *Recuerdos Peligrosos*."

"And that's how you met Ashton." She sent him a curious look. "Why didn't you continue acting?"

He shrugged. "The money was nice, but the hours were grueling and my heart wasn't in it. But it led to some voiceover work for a few kids' shows."

"En español?"

He nodded. "Voice acting was easier and put money in my

pocket faster. From there, I did some recording for a language learning app, which took off. Since I was also an early investor, I made more money, along with connections. Those led me into the hospitality business, and then the Dulce Hotel Group was born."

"And the rum distillery?"

"A recent acquisition." And mostly a labor of love, he thought wryly.

She opened her mouth like she wanted to ask more, but all she did was nod and return her attention to her planner.

The rest of the flight passed mostly in silence. Roman surreptitiously added the new information he'd learned about her to his spreadsheet, and since they'd been talking about his work history, he jotted down notes for his book. It was hard to focus, though, when he couldn't stop sneaking glances at Ava.

Three days. He had three full days to devote to winning her over.

Before the plane landed, Roman sent one last text to Camille.

> **Roman:** Landing soon.

> **Camille:** Noted. How's the schoolteacher?

> **Roman:** Ignoring me and playing with her planner.

> **Camille:** Smart woman.

He'd broken down and told Camille about Ava after the engagement party. Camille had immediately whipped out his calendar. After clarifying that all his sudden nights off over the past few months had been spent with Ava, a knowing smile had spread across her face.

Roman had always refused to entertain the notion of *doing less*, but he wondered again if he wasn't as essential to the day-to-day running of VQZ as he believed himself to be. So while he was in Puerto Rico, he'd decided to run an experiment, and had instructed Camille to reach out only in the event of a true emergency.

Ava was quiet as the plane landed, and she said nothing about the luxury SUV that was waiting for them. But when they drove past the gate and into the driveway of Roman's house in Ocean Park, she balked.

"I thought we were staying at the resort."

"Why would we? I have a house, and the resort is in Condado. It's easy to get to from here."

She shot him a stern look. "I am not sharing a room with you."

That strict teacher voice probably shouldn't turn him on so fucking much, but it did.

"Ava." He lowered his eyebrows and tried to mimic her serious tone. "There are six bedrooms. You can sleep in a different one every night if you prefer."

The corner of her mouth twitched, but she shook her head. "Really, it's okay. I can stay at the resort. Didn't Jasmine have a room reserved?"

Roman went around to open Ava's door before the driver could do it. "Ashton and Jasmine were going to stay here. It's my home when I'm visiting, and I let friends and family use it whenever they want."

Ava stared up at the house. Roman glanced at it, taking in

the cream- and sand-colored exterior walls, the terra-cotta roof, the glass balconies jutting out from the second story bedrooms, and the proliferation of surrounding palm trees. It was a far cry from the blocky peach concrete house where he'd spent his childhood in Bayamón.

"You want me to stick to your rules?" he murmured.

Her head whipped around to look at him. "What does that have to do with this?"

"You agreed that I could plan our evenings. I plan for you to stay here."

Her gaze narrowed. "Evenings. Not nights."

They were interrupted by the arrival of Oscar, the man who maintained the house and served as butler when Roman was on the island. Oscar was in his late fifties and medium height, with a trim graying beard, shaved head, and stylish round glasses. His tan skin had yellow undertones, and he had a penchant for brightly patterned shirts. The one he currently wore was teal with orange and pink roses.

Oscar greeted them in Spanish, and Roman made introductions. Ava switched over to Spanish to speak with him, and before long, Oscar left to supervise the unloading of their bags.

Ava made a sound of distress. "I'm not even sure I'm staying here yet."

"Let me show you something." Roman led her through the house, with its pale tiled floors, high white walls, and sleek greige furniture. The décor was kind of blah for his taste, but he hadn't outfitted this place. Besides, the interior wasn't the draw. He slid open the glass doors that led onto the patio.

Ava gasped when she saw the pool, and Roman knew he had her. The turquoise water glittered in the sunlight, a cool and inviting counterpoint to the oppressive humidity in the air. Lounge chairs with marigold yellow cushions sat under striped umbrellas, and the side of the patio where they stood was furnished with a low table, two armchairs, a long sofa, and a round outdoor daybed adorned with a mountain of pillows. At the other end was a grill, bar, and counter with four high chairs. A hammock hung between the arches leading out to the pool. The wicker furniture was dark brown with teal cushions—not as fashionable as what was inside, but in Roman's opinion, more comfortable. Above their heads, a ceiling fan stirred the thick air. The space wasn't huge, but it was lush and private. High walls enclosed the yard, and thick foliage—a combination of hedges, palms, and ferns—made it cozy. It was his favorite part of the whole house.

Roman glanced over at Ava and caught the ripple of her throat as she swallowed.

"All right, I'll stay," she said.

Score! Out loud, he said, "Are you hungry? We have an on-site chef who can make whatever you want."

"It's okay," she murmured, backing away. "I'm going to freshen up."

"Sounds good."

Roman led her to the only bedroom on the first floor. "This one is yours. If it doesn't meet your needs, we can have your bags moved to a different one."

The room was decorated in white with turquoise accents. It held a king-size bed, low dresser, small writing desk, and chaise lounge. The adjoining bathroom had both a large shower stall and a soaking tub, which was why he'd selected this room for her. She'd once let it slip that while she enjoyed baths, the tub in her apartment was too small for her long-legged frame.

She gave the room a cursory glance and nodded. "It's fine. Thank you."

Then she went inside, shutting the door behind her.

Roman stared at the door and sighed. What had he expected, an invitation? At the very least he was hoping she'd join him for a bite to eat before their meetings. Maybe he could have the chef whip something up to entice her out.

But before he could check his spreadsheet for her favorite foods, his watch buzzed with an all-caps text from Camille.

Camille: URGENT. CALL NOW.

Roman groaned. "Already?"

The text was followed by two fire emojis. According to their code, one fire meant customer service issues, two was public relations, three was personnel, four was financial, and five was a family emergency.

With a sigh, Roman pulled out his tablet and got to work putting out fires.

Chapter 24

Inside the room, Ava set her things down. After counting to five, she tiptoed back to the door and peeked out. No sign of Roman. Or Oscar, or the chef, or the driver, or whomever else might be lurking. She was alone.

Shutting the door again, she strode over to the bed and flopped backward with her arms outstretched. She landed in the center of the mattress with a soft bounce. As the padding settled, she closed her eyes and let out a contented sigh.

Bliss.

Now that all was quiet and still, Ava became aware of a dull pounding in her temples. It had started a couple hours earlier, but sparring with Roman and the novelty of her surroundings had made it easier to ignore. She'd hardly slept the night before, second- and third-guessing everything she packed in her suitcase, and she was probably dehydrated from being on the plane. The luxurious bed tempted her to take a nap then and there, but she and Roman were meeting the wedding planner in an hour. If she drank enough water, the budding headache would go away. Still, she gave herself a few minutes to mull over everything they'd discussed on the plane.

The negotiation of rules had veered dangerously into flirting territory, but the whole point of them was to maintain the boundaries of their relationship.

She'd been surprised when he told her about his father, and even more surprised that she'd talked to him about her own family. Roman was just too damned easy to talk to, and she always ended up revealing more than she'd intended.

He's just the best man in my cousin's wedding, she told herself. They were only here to help. No more wondering about his past, and no more opening up about her own.

And her, acting like she'd never seen *Recuerdos Peligrosos. Of course* she'd watched it. Not when it had aired—she hadn't been lying about that—but as soon as she'd gotten home from that ill-fated engagement party, she'd subscribed to the streaming service that had the show and tormented herself by watching all the episodes in one weekend, when she should have been grading.

No one knew about that, not even Damaris.

And no one knew that she'd also done a search for decades-old celebrity gossip to see if Roman had ever been romantically linked with the actress who played the love interest. There wasn't even a whiff of a rumor, which hadn't come as a total surprise. The lead actress had been married at the time, and Roman and Ashton had more on-screen chemistry as brothers than either of them had with her. It made sense that the guys were still close friends after all these years.

Roman had been good in the role, but not amazing. Knowing him as she did, Ava could see that he was too sweet, too earnest to relish playing a resentful and hot-tempered rancher. Ashton, on the other hand, had been entirely believable as the poetic older brother plagued by the demons of their TV father's cruelty. Even then, it had been clear that Ashton had the kind of star power that couldn't be taught.

Watching Roman on screen had made Ava feel close to him, although it had also made her miserable to think of never being with him again.

After giving herself another thirty seconds to enjoy the sensation of being weightless, she hauled herself up. Her fling with Roman might be over, but while she was here, she was determined to enjoy herself.

Her usual vacation MO was to live out of her suitcase as much as possible in an effort not to "mess things up," but Michelle had made her promise to unpack more than just her toiletry bag.

"You're not at your dad's house," Michelle had said with her typical bluntness. "You're allowed to take up space."

While Ava still struggled to internalize that concept, this gorgeous room absolutely begged her to make herself at home. She unzipped her suitcase and got to it.

By the time they had to leave, Ava had hung some of her clothing in the closet and put the rest in the dresser. She'd also lined up her makeup and hair products neatly on the bathroom counter and set a book—a young adult fantasy novel her students had raved about—on the nightstand. There. That looked lived in, right?

She took a photo of the unpacked toiletry bag and sent it to Michelle with the caption, *Happy now?*

While checking her planner one last time, she stifled a laugh. Under "To Do," Roman had written his own name in loose, quick cursive.

"We'll see about that," she murmured, smiling.

Tucking the planner under her arm, she grabbed her purse and left the room. Time to get this show on the road.

But despite all her planning, Ava was entirely unprepared for "Belinda de Bellísima," as the wedding planner introduced herself. Belinda Barrios was a petite woman, probably around Ava's mother's age, with creamy skin, wavy brown hair, and pink lipstick. She wore a bright pink pencil skirt and a white sleeveless blouse with three-inch yellow espadrilles. Belinda looked every bit her role, right down to the tiny wedding cake earrings and the diamond ring appliqué on her fourth fingernails.

She was also an absolute whirlwind, hustling them through the resort at breakneck speed to provide details about the ballroom, the cocktail lounge, and the beach where the ceremony would take place, all the while speaking Spanish a mile a minute and peppering her descriptions with trivia about the island and anecdotes about other weddings she'd managed.

They stood on the beach in the glaring sun, in the exact spot where Jasmine and Ashton would say their vows. Ava's head throbbed as she tried to take notes and visualize the verbal pictures Belinda had painted so she could give Jasmine a full accounting.

"Do we have a time for the ceremony?" Belinda asked, having just rattled off the pros and cons for every hour of the day. She carried a pink umbrella to protect herself from the sun.

Ava scribbled furiously in her planner, but she'd missed a few things, and while she was verbally fluent, listening in Spanish and writing in English was taxing, especially with a headache brewing. Plus she'd forgotten her water bottle. She paused her note-taking to ask for clarification.

"Can you please repeat—"

"Early evening," Roman cut in, tapping on his tablet. "Looking at sunset times and angle of descent in August . . ." He rattled off a time.

Belinda nodded as she typed something on her phone. "And where do you want the arch?"

Roman pointed. "Over here, so everyone isn't blinded by the setting sun."

"First look photoshoot or at the altar?"

"First look. We'll also get the family photos out of the way beforehand."

"Very good."

"Ashton and Jasmine can take more photos at sunset while everyone else is enjoying the cocktail hour. There are also going to be a number of celebrities attending, and we have to assume many of them will also be out here doing their own photoshoots. So we'll bring the couple into the reception a little later."

Belinda looked impressed. "Excellent thinking. We can work backward to figure out exact times for photography, hair and makeup . . ."

Belinda and Roman walked away, leaving Ava to stare after them, open-mouthed.

What the hell? Not only had she not gotten a word in, they'd decided the entire day's schedule without any of her input!

By the time she caught up to them, they were halfway through a discussion about flowers and décor. Ava tried to jump into the conversation, but there was never a lag, never a moment where either of them said, "Ava, what do *you* think?" And Belinda was tossing out so much information, it was a struggle to write it all down.

Belinda showed them photos of centerpiece flower arrangements on her tablet, and Ava was at least able to narrow it down to the two she thought Jasmine would like best. Meanwhile, it seemed like all the decisions Roman made were based on logic—like the sunset timeline, which Ava could admit was a smart thing to take into account—and not on what Jasmine and Ashton would actually *like*.

Besides, Ava had pages and pages of notes about Jasmine's preferences. That was why she was here, to be her cousin's proxy, and Roman was cutting her out of the decision-making process without even giving her the chance to ask follow-up questions.

And so it went through place settings and seating options.

By the time the three of them headed to the tasting, Ava had fucking had it. It was difficult to keep her Resting Pleasant Face intact when she wanted to outright glare daggers at Roman. If this man talked over her one more time, she was going to explode.

And then he had the absolute nerve to ask her what was wrong.

Not wanting to get into it in front of Belinda, Ava kept her dreamy smile in place. "Nothing."

His frown was concerned. "Are you sick?"

"No."

"Then why do you look like that?"

She dropped the serene expression and scowled at him. "It's my Resting Pleasant Face."

He blinked. "Is that like the opposite of . . ."

"Resting Bitch Face? Yes."

"How often do you do that?"

Ava flipped to the tasting section of her planner as they walked. "Do what?"

"Hide what you're feeling."

And because she was tired, hungry, and getting a fucking migraine, she answered honestly. "Always."

As soon as she said it, she realized this was the first time she'd made this face around Roman.

Not only that, he was the first person to ever notice she was doing it.

Unable to confront the implications of those realizations, she ducked her head and pretended to study something in her planner.

He reached for her, his expression troubled, but Ava side-stepped. Before either of them could say anything more, Belinda ushered them inside one of the smaller ballrooms for the tasting.

The resort's head chef and in-house pastry chef had put together a custom menu. Jasmine had provided a series of questions and notes for Ava to bring up, which were all tucked away in Ava's planner. There was no way Roman was cutting her out this time.

They'd been waiting for ten minutes when the chef stuck his head in to apologize and say a few things were running late. As he was on his way out, Ava's phone rang.

A glance at the screen showed that it was her stepmother, Olympia.

Ava sighed. She didn't really feel like talking to Olympia right now, but she couldn't bring herself to decline the call either. What if it was an emergency?

"I'll just be a few minutes," she told Roman and Belinda, who were discussing some of the recent weddings the resort had hosted.

"When I planned Ricky Martin's cousin's best friend's wedding . . ." Belinda was saying, and Ava was actually sorry to miss that story.

Tucking the planner under her arm, Ava accepted the call and ducked into the hallway. "Hi Olympia. What's going on?"

"Ava, oh my god, I'm so glad you answered. I know you're in Puerto Rico, but this child is going to be the death of me."

Ava shut her eyes. There was only one child Olympia could be talking about. "Where is Willow now?"

"She stormed off to your grandmother's house, but Ava, the things she said to me. I never would've dared to talk to my mother like that."

Biting back a sigh, Ava found a low sofa in the hall across from the ballroom doors and sat down. This would be a while. "She's sixteen. It's a tough age."

"All I did was suggest she put on a little makeup and a nice dress for our family photos, and she accused me of 'upholding the patriarchy,' whatever that means!"

Of *course* they were taking family photos while Ava was out of town. Ava ignored the familiar pang of being left out and said, "Do you want me to call her?"

"No, not yet. Just listen to this and tell me if I'm being unreasonable."

At that, Ava rolled her eyes. As if she could ever tell Olympia such a thing.

By the time Ava hung up, forty-five minutes had passed. Every time she'd tried to go, Olympia had said tearfully, "And another thing!" before launching into something else Willow had done. Ava had explained as best she could that Willow was a normal teenager who needed space to grow, but it had been like talking to a brick wall. The whole time, Ava had been watching the clock and wishing she hadn't taken the painkillers out of her purse when she'd repacked it. But Roman hadn't come out to get her, so she figured the tasting was still delayed.

Finally, Olympia had said, "Oh, your father's back. I have to fill him in."

"Tell him I said hi," Ava mumbled tiredly.

"You're such a good listener, Ava. I wish Willow would be more like you were when you were her age."

Ava fervently hoped her sister was never burdened with the kind of responsibilities Ava had, but all she said was goodbye.

When Ava returned to the ballroom, Roman was the only one there. He sat on a padded folding chair with one ankle crossed over his knee, writing on his tablet with a stylus. He looked up when she walked in.

"Sorry about that," she muttered. "It was my stepmother."

He clicked the stylus onto the side of the tablet and closed the protective cover. "Everything okay?"

"The usual. She had a fight with my sister and needed me to reassure her that she's a good mother." Ava waved that away and plastered on a bright smile, ready to give him another chance. "Where's the food? Have you started yet?"

Roman got to his feet slowly. "It's over."

Her breath hitched. "What do you mean, *over*?"

He checked his watch. "The tasting was already running late, and we didn't want to delay further."

"Wait a second." Stunned, Ava looked around the empty ballroom, as if a platter of hors d'oeuvres might be hiding in a corner. "You did the entire tasting without me?"

He shrugged. "It wasn't a big deal. Belinda has organized hundreds of weddings, and I'm familiar with the resort's offerings. Come on. Let's get back to the house."

He reached for her arm, but she jerked away before he could touch her. Lack of sleep, a brewing migraine, and the fact that she hadn't had anything to eat or drink for hours spiraled into a perfect storm of frustration. Her tone came out clipped.

"You know, I really don't appreciate you making all these decisions without taking my thoughts into account."

Roman's brow creased, like he didn't understand why she was upset. "You were on the phone. I didn't want to bother you."

"Telling me the tasting had started wouldn't have been bothering me."

"If I'd known you were letting your stepmother badger you into doing emotional labor, I would have interrupted." For the first time, a hint of irritation threaded his words. "My apologies for thinking your call was *important*."

He was right, but the way he said it got her back up, and she wasn't going to let him steer this conversation toward her unhealthy relationship with her family. "I don't just mean now. You've been doing this the whole day."

He shrugged and glanced at his watch again, which infuriated her even more. "Well, we already settled everything, so don't worry about it. It's time for us to get going."

Ava had spent too much time around children not to know when mischief was afoot, and the way he kept checking the time made her teacher's Spidey sense tingle. "Why couldn't you wait for me? What's the rush?"

"The chefs had other things to do," he replied vaguely, with a quick look at his phone.

She narrowed her eyes. "*They* had other things to do or *you* have other things to do?"

He didn't answer immediately, which told her all she needed

to know. The pieces clicked together, leaving her with a growing sense of outrage. "This is about what you said on the plane."

His expression was carefully blank. "What did I say?"

She planted a hand on her hip. "You planned something for us. That's why you've been rushing through everything with Belinda. That's why you didn't wait for me to come back for the tasting."

As he chewed the corner of his mouth, she expected him to deny it, but he nodded. "You're right."

She exploded. "I knew it. What is it? Some kind of fancy dinner? A cooking class with the island's top chef?"

His sigh sounded annoyed. "A private sunset cruise."

She barked out a humorless laugh. "I don't believe this. I'm here to make sure my cousin's wedding is perfect, and you're here to get laid."

His dreamy brown eyes flashed, not with anger, but with hurt. "After all this time, you think that's all you are to me? You think I'd fly to Puerto Rico just for that?"

Even as she'd lobbed the accusation, she'd known she was being unfair, but she was too tired and irritable to feel bad about it, and the pounding in her head had increased in tempo. Besides, she was nursing her own hurt feelings, and she was too wound up to let him off the hook. "Well, I don't think you're here out of the goodness of your heart to help Ashton."

"Of course I'm not." He scoffed. "I wanted to spend time with you, and this is the only way you'd let me."

Her heart gave a little leap at the words, but the scornful delivery made her throat tight. "If I mean so much to you, why have you been talking over me all day, refusing to give me a second to think or ask questions?"

"I was *helping*. That's what I'm here to do. Help make decisions for the wedding."

"You weren't helping, Roman. You were *doing*. And you completely cut me out of it."

His brow creased in genuine confusion. "If you wanted to ask something, why didn't you?"

"Because you never gave me a chance!" The words burst out of her, and any other time she would have been embarrassed at her lack of control, but today, her emotions were too close to the surface, and she couldn't tamp them down if she'd wanted to.

And for once, she didn't fucking want to.

"Look," she barreled on. "I get that you're an expert at throwing galas or whatever, but I'm an expert on Jasmine. She's been looking forward to her wedding for practically her entire life. We can't just make all the decisions based on what's *logical*. It has to be *perfect*."

Deep down, a little voice whispered, *Are you sure you're not just trying to make up for your own imperfect wedding?* Ava smacked it down viciously.

She couldn't explain why she felt like this was a do-over for her. Why Jasmine's wedding had to be as perfect as she could make it.

Why she felt like just maybe, if she did this part right, Jasmine would have not just the perfect wedding, but the perfect *marriage* too. Ava might have blown it in the happily-ever-after department, but by god, she was going to ensure her cousin had the ultimate happy ending.

Even if the combination of fierce family loyalty and bitter jealousy kept her up at night.

"I'm getting us through these meetings quickly and efficiently." Roman gestured at the planner tucked in the crook of her arm. "You've told me you're trying not to overthink things anymore. I'm doing you a favor. Not everything requires extensive preparation."

This wasn't the first time someone—*like Hector*—had given her shit about her planner, and Ava hugged it to her chest, as if to protect it.

"There's nothing wrong with being prepared," she said defensively. "Not all of us can make snap decisions without thinking them through."

"I think things through, but I also trust myself. And my ability to trust my decisions has served me well."

"You think I don't trust myself?" She was verging on shrill, but the implication that she gave things a lot of thought because she didn't trust herself rankled.

His gaze shot heavenward, as if he were praying for patience. "You need more time to be comfortable making a decision. I need less. That's all. But if you need more, you have to *ask* for it."

"Except we're supposed to be working *together*," she shot back. "You didn't ask me what I thought. You just steamrolled over me like what I think doesn't matter. Like *I* don't matter."

That, she realized, was the heart of it. This argument wasn't just about Jasmine's wedding. And it wasn't about the ceremony or the table arrangements or even the catering menu.

It was about her and Roman.

His dismissive attitude hurt far more than it should have if they were just the maid of honor and best man helping the bride and groom, which meant she'd broken one of the original rules she'd set out for them that very first night.

No feelings.

She felt something for him, and that was why his disregard came as such a betrayal.

Not being asked for her thoughts made her feel like he didn't value her input.

Which made her feel like he didn't value *her*.

And that was, unfortunately, something she was all too familiar with.

Memories of planning her own wedding came to mind, and she couldn't shut them out. Hector's voice echoed through her throbbing head.

Just make a decision, Ava. We don't have all day. Stop making it more complicated than it needs to be.

She'd made extensive mood boards for her dream wedding, spent hours researching vendors and budgeting every cent—since Olympia would never let her forget that Miguel was footing the bill—only for Hector to come in at the eleventh hour and scrap everything.

It should've been a sign. But she'd been so focused on their future, she hadn't seen the red flags waving right in front of her face.

Now here she was, once again trying to plan a wedding while a man walked all over her.

Old Ava would have hidden the messy feelings behind her Resting Pleasant Face. But she was hangry. And headache-y. And so unbelievably tired of being made to feel like she didn't matter.

So New Ava said exactly what was on her mind.

"You know who treated me like that?" Her voice shook a little, but remained strong. "My ex. He talked over me, never listened, and said I took too long to do . . . well, *everything*. It made me feel worthless. And I will be damned if I let a man make me feel that way ever again."

As her words sank in, Roman's expression turned stricken. "God, Ava. I'm sorry. I was trying to help, and I didn't realize—"

"I don't care whether you realized it or not," she snapped. "You've seen all the big personalities in my family. I'm tired of fighting to be heard. I want someone to care enough to give me the space to think and speak without my having to beg for it."

If she'd had a mic, she would have dropped it. She turned to go.

He caught her wrist. "Please, Ava. Let's—"

"*Space*, Roman." She tugged her arm away. Her head felt like it was going to crack open, and she wasn't in the mood for his apologies. "I'm walking back. Don't follow me."

Clutching her beloved planner to her chest, she strode out of the room.

Chapter 25

Roman watched Ava go and wrestled down the urge to run after her. He'd been an absolute ass. She'd been right to call him out on steamrolling her. And what was worse, he hadn't even noticed he was doing it.

Yes, part of him had been hurrying through the tasks at hand so they could get to their evening activity—which it looked like he'd be canceling. But more than that, he'd been trying to help in the way he knew best.

She'd accused him of making snap decisions and excluding her, but this was what he did for the people he cared about—he anticipated their needs and saved them the trouble of sorting out the logistics. It was a philosophy rooted in service, and it was what made his hotels a success.

Through the lens of hindsight, Roman could also see he'd put on his CEO hat once Belinda had gotten involved. But what was appropriate in a boardroom full of men who still saw him as some upstart Latino kid from Brooklyn wasn't the right strategy when you were helping plan a wedding with the woman you were trying to court.

Especially when you knew that woman needed time to think things through.

A sinking feeling came over him as he thought back to that day months ago when Mikayla had stormed out, right before Camille had given him the toy dog. In his mind, the best way he could show the women in his life that he cared was to do things for them, but they weren't guests at one of his hotel properties, and maybe what they wanted from him wasn't top notch concierge service.

So what the hell did they want?

A text from his local travel agent came through on his watch, and he set about canceling the cruise and making arrangements to have their meal delivered to the house instead.

Instead of leaving right away, he strode out of the ballroom and went in search of the resort manager on duty. Since he was here, he'd meet with the staff, mostly to hear about the renovations and improvements they'd made over the past year, but also to listen to their suggestions and let them know they weren't just cogs in a machine. He wasn't supposed to be working, but he couldn't pass up the opportunity for face-to-face time with the staff before the wedding. Besides, it would keep him from running after Ava.

Two hours later, Roman was back at his house. Ava's door was closed, but he hesitated before knocking. She'd asked for space, so he'd respect that. The dinner he'd planned for them to eat on the boat would be arriving soon, so he grabbed his laptop and went to sit on the patio. Hopefully more work would help him take his mind off their argument until he could apologize properly.

He pulled up some reports to review, but found himself struggling to concentrate. Normally, slipping on his reading glasses gave him a mental cue that it was time to focus. But all he could think about was Ava.

Knowing that he'd reminded her of her ex and made her feel like she didn't matter tore him up inside. He needed to do better, to treat Ava with the respect she deserved, which meant making time for her way of thinking, even if it was different than his own.

It meant *apologizing*.

But how? Saying he was sorry wasn't enough. And all the ways he could think of to show her how he felt involved lavish gifts or solving problems for her. But right now, *he* was her problem.

So, what to do?

Well, there was one thing. He pulled out his phone and texted Belinda to hold off on finalizing the decisions they'd discussed that day. That was a start, but it wasn't enough.

Ava had said she didn't want gifts, but there was a Cartier store nearby. He couldn't resist pulling up the website to see about booking an appointment. However, after a few minutes of scrolling through the selection of watches, he set the laptop aside and picked up his phone to text Ashton.

> **Roman:** What do you do when you've fucked up? Is a watch better, or should I get her earrings?

The phone rang immediately.

Ashton started in before Roman could even say hello, speaking rapidly in Spanish. "Tell me you haven't messed up my wedding already."

Roman answered in Spanish as well. "It's not about the wedding."

"So it's about Ava. What did you fuck up?"

Roman switched to English to explain the argument they'd had. After he finished, Ashton sighed.

"I told you, their family is complicated. Especially for Ava."

"I get that, but how do I make this up to her?"

"Does she want you to? Or are you throwing money at the problem to make yourself feel better?"

Damn, direct hit. Was that what he was doing? "Maybe a little of both?"

"If you get her an expensive gift, it'll look like you're buying her affection. A Cartier watch is not an apology."

"I guess the same goes for an overnight trip to Vieques," Roman said.

"Yes, that's a great way to not show off your money."

"I scheduled it before we got here. It's supposed to be romantic."

"Keep thinking. Ava won't open up until you do."

"I'm not hiding anything."

Ashton made a sound like he didn't believe that, but before Roman could demand clarification, Ashton said, "Look, Jasmine has been a lot more relaxed about this whole thing knowing that Ava is there, so don't screw this up, okay?"

"Jasmine doesn't strike me as a Bridezilla," Roman mused. "I mean, she is letting us make most of the decisions."

Okay, maybe that wasn't true, since *he* was the one who'd made all the decisions today . . . which was why Ava was currently locked in her room.

Fuck, he really needed to apologize.

Ashton's tone was ominous. "You have no idea. Ciao."

The line went dead. Roman lowered the phone, thinking about what his friend had said.

He recalled Ava's reaction when he'd offered to get her a

new phone. She'd pulled out that stern teacher's voice he found so sexy and told him, in no uncertain terms, not to buy her things. A Cartier watch or a new car wouldn't make the kind of impression he was aiming for. Besides, he needed to show Ava that he was more than his bank account—even if he sometimes wasn't sure of that himself anymore. He had to show her more of *him* and make it clear that he was nothing like her ex-husband.

Moreover, he had to show her he was *sorry*.

They were in Puerto Rico, a place that held a deep connection to both of them. Sure, there were all kinds of romantic touristy things they could do, like visiting Viejo San Juan or Culebra. There were places of historical and cultural significance, like hiking in El Yunque, the rainforest, or a tour of El Morro, the Spanish fortress. But none of those were personal to him, and while Ava might enjoy them, he didn't think they'd mean much to her aside from a good time together. These places didn't hold the emotional revelation Ashton was talking about. And Ashton, who'd been closed off for years, had learned a thing or two about opening up, thanks to Jasmine.

The patio doors slid open and Roman greeted Oscar.

"Señor." Oscar leaned down. "Pardon the interruption. Dinner has arrived. Would you like a drink first?"

Roman glanced at his laptop, which was still open to the Cartier page and not the reports he'd planned to look at. A drink wouldn't hurt. He *was* supposed to be on vacation, after all. He asked for the Casa Donato Quince neat. Oscar returned with the aged rum, and when Roman caught a whiff of the familiar scent of caramel and oak, he knew exactly where to take Ava.

He just hoped she understood how much it meant to him.

After firing off a text to put his plans into effect, he went inside to tell Ava that it was time to eat. He knocked on the door of her room, but there was no answer.

"Ava?"

Nothing.

He knocked again, then eased the door open and peeked inside. The room was empty.

After a quick check of the rooms upstairs confirmed that she wasn't in the house, Roman called for Oscar, who appeared in an instant.

"¿Dónde está Ava?" Roman asked.

"No sé, señor. Ella no está aquí."

A tickle of fear spread through Roman's gut. Where the hell was she? He tamped down on his panic and thanked Oscar. "Si ella llega, dímelo."

"Claro."

If Oscar saw her, he'd notify Roman. But in the meantime, that didn't explain where she was now. Roman sent her a text, waiting a few seconds to see if there was an indication she was typing her reply, but there was nothing. Then he called.

Once.

Twice.

Three times.

It went straight to voicemail each time.

Ava was an adult, not a missing child. She was allowed to come and go as she pleased. Still, Roman's mind supplied an image of Ava lying face down in the water—likely his mother's fault for watching so many true crime shows at home.

A line of thinking that did nothing to calm him down.

Roman called to Oscar that he was going out to look for her, then grabbed his wallet and stuffed his feet into sneakers.

He yanked open the front door—and caught Ava when she fell into his arms.

Relief washed over him, and he tightened his grip on her. "Hold on, mi amor. I've got you."

"I'm fine," she mumbled. "Just hot."

She clearly wasn't fine. There were no signs of blood or injury that he could see, but her face was flushed, and tiny hairs stuck to her sweaty forehead. Her gaze seemed unfocused, and she could barely stand on her own feet. Pressing his fingers to the side of her neck, Roman noted that her pulse was racing.

He exchanged a glance with Oscar, who hovered in the kitchen doorway holding two glass bottles of cold water from the fridge.

"Find a thermometer," Roman whispered to Oscar, who handed him one of the bottles. Oscar nodded and hurried off, and Roman walked Ava to her room with a stabilizing arm around her waist. The fact that she leaned all her weight on him meant she was in a bad state, and he was alarmed when her head lolled to the side.

"You wanna tell me what happened?" he asked softly, ignoring the anxious pounding of his own heart.

"I went for a walk on the beach." Her voice was breathy and faint. "I guess I went farther than I meant to, and it was so hot . . ."

"Sounds like you had a little too much sun. Did you drink water?"

She shook her head, then whimpered like it pained her. "I have a migraine."

"We're going to cool you down, okay?" Roman sat Ava on the edge of her bed and uncapped the water. "Here, take a sip of this."

He held the bottle while she drank, and willed his nerves to settle. She was here, and she was safe. It didn't matter that seeing her like this scared the shit out of him, he would do whatever was necessary to care for her.

This was different than when he'd seen her after the EpiPen incident. Then, he'd been able to comfort her. Now, he just wanted to make her better immediately. He couldn't remember the last time he'd felt this powerless.

"Not too much," he murmured, shifting the water bottle away. Then he eased her into a reclining position and touched the back of his hand to her forehead and cheek. She was warm, but he couldn't tell if she had a fever or not.

"Ava, we have to get you into the tub. Is that all right?"

Her eyes were closed. "Take my dress off. But not, like, in a sexy way."

He bit back a laugh. "You have my word."

When she waved her hand at the halter ties on the back of her neck, he took that as an indication to carry on. After slipping off her sandals, he eased the dress from her body. She wasn't wearing a bra, and her chest and shoulders were clammy and flushed from the sun. He left her panties on and helped her stand again.

The bathroom had a padded bench, so he sat her there while he turned on the taps in the tub and adjusted the temperature.

There was a quiet knock on the bathroom door, and after making sure Ava wasn't in danger of falling off the bench, Roman slipped out.

Oscar was waiting with a digital thermometer and packets of electrolyte powder.

"I called the doctor," the butler said in a hushed voice as he passed the items to Roman. "If her temperature is over one hundred and three degrees, we must take her to the hospital. She might need an IV."

"Let's hope it isn't."

"I'll leave more water on the dresser. Let me know if you need anything else."

"I will. Thank you."

Roman ducked back into the bathroom and turned on the digital thermometer. "Put this in your mouth," he told Ava.

"You promised not to make this sexy," she grumbled, her eyes barely open, but she complied.

Roman smoothed the hair back from her forehead. Jokes were a good sign, right?

When the thermometer beeped, he checked it. One hundred point two degrees. Not hospital levels, but she had to be feeling awful.

"Looks like you've got yourself a touch of heat exhaustion, mi amor," he said, helping her to her feet.

She wobbled. "No shit."

Roman would have laughed if he weren't so worried about her. "I'm going to pick you up and put you in the tub, okay?"

"You're going to get your suit wet."

"I'm—" He looked down at his polo shirt and chinos, just to be sure. "Ava, I'm not wearing a suit."

She wound her arms around his neck and spoke into his shoulder. "You're always wearing a suit in my mind."

Not knowing what to make of that, he lifted her gently and carried her over to the tub. He lowered her into the water with great care, glad he'd been keeping up with the lower back exercises his physical therapist had assigned. Ava let out a sigh as the cool water lapped over her bare thighs and she relaxed into the tub with her head resting on the edge.

"Is that better?" he asked, unable to keep the roughness out of his voice. His only focus was on her wellness, but he couldn't ignore the way her nipples hardened into peaks as the cool water teased the edges of her breasts.

Or the relief he felt that she was letting him take care of her.

"Mmm. Yeah." Then she held her breath and slipped down, dunking her head under the water. When she resurfaced, she wiped her eyes and blinked at him sleepily.

"This is better, thanks." She sounded a bit more like herself. "Can I have another sip? And my migraine meds. They're on the counter."

He retrieved the water bottle and the pill and stayed while she soaked, watching her attentively and helping her bathe. When she seemed to have cooled down, he lifted her from the tub, even though she protested about getting him wet. He dried her off as she shivered and he bundled her into a robe before tucking her into the bed.

"Sleep." He stroked her wet curls, winding them around his finger one by one, as he'd seen her do. "I'll stay right here."

"My hair is going to be a mess tomorrow," she murmured into the satin pillowcase.

"And you'll still be beautiful," he whispered, but she was already asleep.

Oscar brought Roman a plate of food and another bottle of water for Ava, and Roman ate dinner on the bed next to her. He read over sales reports on his tablet, pausing frequently to check Ava's temperature and replacing the cold towel on her forehead every time Oscar brought a new one. Roman didn't relax until she'd dropped below ninety-nine degrees, and he finally sent Oscar home. It was clear the older man didn't want to leave, but Roman promised he'd stay by Ava's side all night.

The Wedding Flashers group text—which had a new name every week, thanks to Michelle—was lighting up with questions about the day's meetings, but Roman didn't have it in him to provide details yet. Ashton had texted him directly: Please tell me you didn't buy her a car. So Roman notified the group that Ava had taken a little too much sun and was resting. Jasmine asked him to send an update on Ava's health in the morning, and the messages calmed down.

Ava slept, and Roman watched over her. Until finally, around 1 a.m., he stretched out beside her and let himself sleep, too.

Chapter 26

The sunlight slanting in through the open curtains woke Ava early the next morning, and the first thing she saw when she opened her eyes was Roman.

The sight startled her, as she'd grown unaccustomed to having a man in her bed. And the few times she'd slept beside him, he'd risen before her. It took her a moment to even remember where they were, and why Roman was fully clothed on top of the covers while she was under a sheet and—she took a peek—naked.

A fluffy white robe was bunched up beneath her. She must have wriggled out of it during the night.

Memories of the previous day came flooding back, along with no small amount of embarrassment. She'd gone for a walk on the beach to work off her mad and process her argument with Roman. Apparently she could add, "New Ava is not afraid to express her feelings" to the list, because she still couldn't believe she'd said all of that to him. It never would've happened if she hadn't been feeling so shitty. Her cousins and Colleen, her old therapist, would probably commend her on letting him have it, but Ava prided herself on maintaining a placid façade, no matter the circumstances. Even when Hector had come home and told her he was leaving her, she had responded calmly. Somehow Roman had achieved what no one else ever had—he'd made her lose her cool.

Despite the heat and her splitting headache, the beach and the rolling turquoise surf had soothed her, so she'd taken her time walking back. By the time her anger had faded, she had a full-blown migraine. Dizzy and sweaty, she'd completely overshot the house and had to double back after realizing she'd passed the turnoff.

But Roman had been there the second she'd reached the door, taking care of her every need before she could voice it, and staying with her all night to make sure she was okay.

In the early morning quiet, she could admit there was something sexy about his decisive, take-charge nature. She hadn't liked him talking over her yesterday, but when she'd needed him, he'd been there.

Hector had always required instructions when she was sick. The last time she'd had the flu, she'd had to tell him where to find the thermometer—even though it was always in the medicine cabinet—and he'd only gone to the store for Gatorade and broth after she'd asked him to. It was like living with a child, and she'd often wished he would think of those things on his own without being told.

While she didn't want to compare Roman to Hector, it was hard not to sometimes. She'd been with her ex-husband for so long, and he was her only barometer for romantic relationships.

She wasn't in a relationship with Roman, though. She didn't know what they were, but it wasn't that.

Still, it didn't hurt anything to admire his profile while he slept. He was stretched out on his back, breathing deeply with his head turned toward her on the pillow. Her gaze traveled over his thick lashes fanning against the tops of his cheeks, the curve of his upper lip, his expressive brows—finally relaxed, as if they were asleep, too.

On the king-size mattress, there was still enough room between them for another person. Tempting as it was to close the distance and kiss him, it would go against the rules she'd laid out. She needed to remember why she'd implemented them in the first place.

Their situation was too complicated, too messy. This man wasn't for her.

Even if she wanted him to be.

So instead of kissing him, she shifted away and tried to get up quietly. The bed creaked and the sheet fell to her waist. When she glanced over at him, his eyes had opened a crack. They were trained on her breasts, and under his gaze, her nipples tightened into hard peaks, as if straining toward him.

"Good morning," she said, her voice husky with sleep and desire. Old Ava whispered that she should cover her nudity, but New Ava ignored the command. While it might be wrong to tease him this way, she loved the way he looked at her, like she was a priceless work of art he was privileged to lay eyes on. Her body soaked up his attention like parched earth during a rainstorm.

Roman cleared his throat. His gaze shifted away from her as he eased himself into a sitting position. "How are you feeling?"

"Much better. Thank you." That wasn't enough. This man had acted as her bedside nurse all night after she'd bitten his head off. "Roman, I—"

"Shh." Before she could continue, he popped a digital thermometer in her mouth. Beyond him, the bedside table was littered with empty water bottles, along with Roman's tablet, phone, and glasses. While they waited for the temperature reading, he touched the back of his hand to her forehead, his fingertips dragging gently along her hairline and teasing the sensitive baby hairs.

She did feel warm, but now it was because of him and not a lingering fever. She ached for him to trail his hand down the curve of her neck to her breasts. As she imagined him cupping their soft weight, his lips and tongue lavishing her nipples, her body tingled.

But when the thermometer beeped, all he did was pluck it from her mouth and squint at the tiny screen before setting it aside.

"No fever." Before she could open her mouth to respond, he added, "I want to apologize. I was a total ass yesterday."

Her eyebrows leaped in surprise. She hadn't expected him to broach the topic so soon. But when had Roman ever beat around the bush?

"You kind of were," she agreed, even though Old Ava wanted to brush it aside with a dismissive *It's okay.*

Despite her teasing tone, his expression was serious. "I'm used to being in scenarios where the final decision comes down to me, and other people rely on my ability to decide quickly and confidently. But you were right—you know your cousin better than I do. I should have asked for your input and listened to what you had to say. I'm deeply sorry, Ava."

His sincerity made her stomach drop out like she had crested the top of a roller coaster, not because she didn't believe him, but because she wasn't used to such open and honest communication. Had she and Hector ever spoken this clearly to each other?

If they had, would they still be married today?

Ava spoke slowly around her discomfort. "I can appreciate how that approach serves you well in your work. And it's not that I can't see the benefit in being decisive. But I operate differently. For one thing, I want to make sure I'm making the *right* choice. I also need time to process information, and make sure I've fully thought about it. That's what helps *me* move forward with confidence."

"I'm starting to see that. From now on, I promise to give you space to process. You don't have to ask for it."

"Thank you." And because it needed to be explicitly stated, she added, "For that, and for last night. Thank you for taking care of me."

"Ava." His brows creased, and his voice was pained. "You don't have to thank me."

"I do, though. You thought of everything. You stayed with me all night, even though we'd argued."

He made a small sound of distress. "I would never hold that against you, or punish you for telling me how you felt."

"Hector did." The words squeezed through a sudden tightness in her throat. "If I ever expressed any sort of negative emotion, he'd get defensive and withdraw. Then, regardless of what started it, I'd end up apologizing for having feelings. So it just got easier . . . not to."

"Not to . . . have feelings?"

She nodded, and because the look on his face said he wanted to hold her—and because she wanted to let him—she drew her knees, still covered by the sheet, up to her chest and wrapped her arms around them, holding herself. "It wasn't hard. When I was a kid, I'd get in trouble anytime I got upset about something. If the message you receive your whole life is 'be good,' the idea of being bad is untenable. So I just hold it all in."

His chest heaved like he was the one holding back, and his voice came out ragged. "I *always* want to know how you feel. Even if you're mad at me. *Especially* if you're mad at me. How can I fix it if I don't know?"

She gave a little shrug and toyed with her necklace, the only thing she was wearing. "Luckily you seem to be the only person I can't hold back around."

"*Good.*" His tone was savage, and his fists flexed on his thighs. "Fuck, Ava, I was so scared when I couldn't find you."

She saw lingering traces of his fear etched across his handsome face. "I'm sorry, I didn't—"

"Don't apologize," he murmured, and one of his hands slid toward her across the bed. "Just let me hold you. Please, for the love of god, let me hold you."

She didn't care what it said about her boundaries, but she couldn't deny an entreaty like that. She moved to him and he met her in the center of the bed. Her sheet tangled between them as she melted against his chest. With a soul-weary sigh, he pulled her into his arms and pressed his face to her hair. Enveloped in his warmth, in his scent, something settled within her, and she closed her eyes.

His lips touched her temple in a feather-light kiss. "I'm sorry for acting like your ex. That's the last thing I want."

"I'm sorry I said that."

"Don't be. You were right to call me out."

"I know. I'm just . . . not used to it yet."

"It'll get easier. You can practice on me all you want."

Her chest shook with a silent laugh, and because she couldn't ignore the role her own actions had played, she said, "You were right too. I missed the tasting because I can't say no to my stepmother."

He eased back to look at her face. "I could've phrased that better."

"Maybe, but it's true. I don't have good boundaries with my family."

"Can you explain that a little more for me? You told me about their reaction to your divorce, but I don't understand why your family meeting me meant we had to cut things off."

She sighed and leaned back on the pillows piled against the headboard.

"You have to understand, my ex and I met during our sophomore year in college and he was my first serious boyfriend. Our families didn't live that far from each other in the Bronx, and they were really involved in our lives. We'd babysit my little sister together, I'd go shopping with his mom, he'd help my grandfather fix things around the house, stuff like that.

"When we separated, nobody saw it coming and they didn't take it well. And since I never brought anyone else home, before or after, I think they're under the impression that he's still the love of my life or something, and that the divorce is just a speed bump. They mention him all the time, like we split up two weeks ago instead of two years. I can't get away from him."

"And you want to." At her severe look, he held up his hands. "Just making sure."

"Yes. Desperately. I want to move on but they never let me forget what I did."

"But what did you do wrong?"

She rolled her eyes. "In my family? Everything."

"Because you got divorced?"

"Nailed it in one."

"And now he's getting remarried."

She sighed. "You heard about that, huh?"

"Ashton might have mentioned it."

She swallowed hard. "You want to know the worst part?"

"Tell me."

"The worst part is that I was completely unprepared for my family's reaction. I was the perfect one, my grandmother's favorite. And suddenly, I wasn't anymore."

She told him about the night she'd broken the news to her grandmother, how it had turned into a massive family argument, with her cousins and aunts trying to run interference while her grandmother, great-aunt, and mother-in-law shouted at her.

The weight of their censure had crushed her. For a perfectionist, a people pleaser, someone who found their value by being part of the family unit, their reaction had torn her apart inside. At a time when she'd wanted to cry and rage and break down, she'd had to suck it up and take everything they gave her with a patient smile.

"It was the worst moment of my life," she said quietly as she finished. "And I had to comfort everyone else."

When he gave her a little tug, she moved closer, and before she knew it, he was folding her in his arms again. It wasn't sexual, it was . . . comforting. Like the night they'd watched movies in his bed and she'd fallen asleep in one of his T-shirts, with her head on his chest, listening to the sound of his heart beating.

"You shouldn't have had to do that," he said. "It wasn't fair to you."

His words and his embrace eased something inside her, but it didn't matter. "They're all I have, Roman. I can't go through that again."

His chest rose under her cheek as he took in a deep breath and let it out slowly. "I understand that my connection to Ashton complicates things. And I'm sorry my hidden agenda caused you stress yesterday, so I'll spell it out. I want to be with you, Ava. Nothing has changed for me."

Warmth suffused her limbs, even as she fought against it. She wanted to be with him too, but didn't have the courage to say so.

"It's too messy," she whispered, although the words lacked conviction.

"Life's messy," he said simply. He pulled back to look at her and stroked a thumb over her cheek. She knew he wanted to kiss her, and she waited for it, but all he said was, "I'll see you at breakfast."

Still, when he turned to get off the bed, she noticed the front of his shorts sticking out.

It seemed she wasn't the only one turned on this morning. Part of her wished he'd just push her onto the bed and ravish her, which was very unfair of her since *she* was the one who'd set the boundaries. She should be glad he was adhering to them.

Didn't stop her from wanting it, though.

Roman grabbed his devices from the bedside table, and because Ava was watching him closely, she caught the adjustment he made to his crotch. Then he gave her a quick nod and exited the room.

Leaving Ava a jumble of confused hormones.

It was for the best. Her body might miss his hands and mouth, but being with Roman was a bad idea. Ava didn't need to complicate things by asking him to stay and fuck her into next Tuesday.

The real question was why she couldn't control her reaction

to this man. Yes, Roman was sexy as hell. But it wasn't just that. She craved the way she felt when she was with him. And every time they were together, it wasn't enough. That was why she always resisted the urge to text him again right away, holding out for as long as she could, until something weakened her defenses and she could no longer deny her need for him.

She flopped back onto the pillows and let out a heavy sigh. It wasn't just the sex, it was the care Roman took with her. The way he paid attention to her like she was the most important person in the world, which was why his behavior the previous day had thrown her off. But she'd told him how she felt, and he'd apologized maturely and with sincerity. Was there anything hotter than that?

He said things hadn't changed, but she didn't know how to go back to the easiness they'd had prior to the engagement party. Before, there wouldn't have been any reason to hold back from kissing him, or asking him to touch her. She'd at least grown comfortable enough to ask for those things. But now? It would be a mistake.

Why the hell did he have to be Ashton's best friend?

Since part of her was still tempted to call him back, she slid from the bed and padded barefoot to her suitcase. Knowing she'd be spending a lot of time around Roman, she'd packed a little something to help take the edge off. Unzipping a discreet inner pocket, she grabbed the fully charged air vibe she'd stashed there and brought it into the shower.

She'd just have to take care of this one on her own.

Chapter 27

Five Minutes Later

The shower stall was bigger than Ava's entire bathroom back home. She stood with one leg braced on the wooden bench, an orgasm within arm's reach thanks to the vibrating suction on her clit. Steam swirled around her and the water pattered against the iridescent blue tiles like her own private rainstorm. She closed her eyes, recalling the way Roman had eaten her out against the door in that empty office, and shifted her foot on the bench. There was a clatter of tiny plastic bottles as she knocked her hair products to the floor, but she paid them no mind. A moan escaped her lips, and she raised her free hand to tweak her own nipple. She was close, so close—

The sound of the door hinge made her eyes fly open. Roman stood frozen in the bathroom doorway wearing an almost cartoonish expression of shock.

"Sorry," he stammered. "I—I forgot my glasses. I heard a noise, thought you were hurt—never mind. I'm leaving. Carry on."

He turned to go. Without pausing to consider the consequences, Ava called, "Wait."

In the back of her mind, she wondered if they should talk about this. Asking him to join her in the shower definitely counted as "hanky-panky." But New Ava was firmly in charge and she was so fucking tired of denying herself what she wanted.

Him.

She. Wanted. *Him.*

Roman stilled. Their eyes met through the foggy glass, and Ava knew she'd have to be the one to say it. He was too good of a man to overstep the line she'd drawn.

She extended a hand, reaching for him. "Come here."

She wasn't sure he'd heard her over the sound of the water, but a second later he was stripping off his clothes and joining her in the shower. Without a word, Roman dropped to his knees and pressed his face to her pussy. Ava shut off the vibrator and tossed it onto the bench as his tongue took over, and oh god, the real thing was *so much better.* The water beat down on his head, plastering his hair to his skull, but it did nothing to deter his efforts. He licked her just like she'd been imagining before he walked in. She sank her fingers into his wet hair as his mouth brought her to the peak once more.

What will your family say when they find out?

If only the rule-following part of her brain would *shut the fuck up* and let her enjoy this perfect man with his face between her legs. She wanted him. He wanted her. Why did it need to be more complicated than that?

Because it is, her brain warned.

"Shut up," she mumbled, and Roman lifted his head. "What?"

She pushed his face back down. "Not you. Keep going."

He did as she asked. Seconds later, an orgasm chased away all those pesky little thoughts, leaving only exhilaration in its wake. Panting and leaning against the cool tiles, she gave Roman's arm a weak tug. He stood and hitched her hip up on his thigh, nudging her opening with his dick. Then he paused and dropped his head to her shoulder.

"Fuck," he muttered. "I don't have any condoms. I'll have to go get one."

She draped her arms—heavy with the thudding pulse of her climax—around his neck. What she was about to admit had the potential to change everything between them, but she was feeling too good to care.

"I have an implant. And you're the only . . . well, the only other person . . ." She swallowed hard and couldn't go on. He had to know he was not just the only person she'd been with *since* Hector, but the only other person she'd been with *ever*.

His stare ran the gamut of emotions. She thought she saw surprise, arousal, and maybe even something deeper, something too scary to name.

Just as she was starting to rethink her impulsive suggestion, Roman cupped her cheek and kissed her. She tasted herself on him, which reminded her of how good he'd already made her feel this morning. Her body trembled with remembered aftershocks.

"You, as well." He rested his forehead on hers and voiced the admission into the scant space between them. "Since the moment we met, I have wanted no one but you."

Her heart pounded as steam billowed around them, forming a sort of cocoon where it was safe to say such things. It was a different sort of admission than the one she'd made, but she nodded in acknowledgment. Their no-strings fling had somehow been exclusive all along.

He rubbed the head of his cock through her folds, bringing her back to the present moment and banishing all thoughts other than anticipation for what was to come.

"Can I?" he asked, and when she nodded, his hips pushed forward. As he filled her, she gasped at the difference in friction, at the deliciousness of being skin to skin. He gripped her other leg and lifted her, pressing her back into the tiles. She hung on around his neck as he pumped into her, water streaming over his back.

"God, you feel good." He pressed kisses into the wet skin of her neck. "I've missed this. Missed *you*."

Me too, she thought. But she just hung on tighter.

"Touch yourself," he commanded, and changed the angle so she could reach between them to rub her clit. Her fingertips brushed his shaft, and she thrilled at feeling him both inside and out.

"Fuck, Ava." Roman scraped his teeth over the side of her neck, drawing a moan from her lips.

His hips moved faster, but it was like time slowed down, and Ava was aware of every thrust, of the water falling from the showerhead, of the cool tiles behind her shoulders, of Roman's warm hands gripping her thighs and ass, of the bunch of his back muscles under her hand, of his scent, his taste, his cock burrowing deep inside her. She collected every detail, committing them to memory, so she'd have them to hold when this thing between them was over.

"Keep touching yourself." He nipped her earlobe, and she

realized she'd been so consumed with the experience of being with him, she'd forgotten what she was doing. She resumed her efforts, and sensation swelled inside her, centering in her core and spreading outward like the precursor to an earthquake.

"Roman, I'm close," she said on a gasp, and he changed the angle once again, hitting her right where she wanted it. "Yes. Oh god, yes, there."

"Come, Ava. Come all over me."

The thought of it—of coming on him with no barrier—did the trick. Her thighs tightened around his hips, her back arched, and the climax bore down on her. She cried out, her toes curling against his ass as spiraling fissures of pleasure sparkled through her veins, making her see stars.

Roman let out a grunt and thrust hard into her. As he stiffened, his fingers dug into the backs of her thighs, and he groaned as he came inside her.

Ava could barely breathe through the pulse pounding in her throat, and her legs wobbled when Roman gently set her down.

He pulled out and once again fell to his knees before her. He held her steady with a hand on her hip, then slipped her other leg over his shoulder. Parting her with his thumbs, he gazed at her with open longing.

"Beautiful," he whispered, licking his lips.

"What do you see?" It was something she never would have dared ask in the past, but Roman's open adoration made her bold.

He dragged his fingertips through the stickiness between her legs, sending another sizzle down her limbs. "You and me. Mingled. Inseparable."

She swallowed hard. "I wish I could see."

"Next time."

Reality thudded into her thoughts like the Kool-Aid Man, and Ava let out a long sigh.

Roman's gaze flicked up to hers, doing an admirable impression of a guilty puppy. "Did I just break a rule?"

A laugh burbled out of her, but she sobered quickly. "I think we broke *all* the rules."

He leaned toward her, his expression devious. "Are you going to spank me with a ruler, profe?"

And then his tongue darted out to lick her clit.

The move gave her a full-body shiver. "I should. You've been very naughty."

A devious light sparked in his eyes. He rose to his feet and gripped her chin. "We'll save that for later."

All this talk of "later" and "next time" was too much for her. Ava turned, grabbing the soap to wash off again. As her system went back to normal, she couldn't block out the doubts any longer.

What the hell was she doing?

It didn't matter how much she enjoyed being with him. She didn't want to be involved with someone who had any ties to her family.

And Roman definitely fell into that category.

His hands landed on her hips and slid around her belly. He hugged her from behind and rested his chin on her shoulder.

"Are you having second thoughts?"

"No," she lied, then stuck her face in the spray. When she stepped back, he turned her to him. His brows drew together, and she was glad she couldn't see her expression. She probably looked like a cowering mouse, about to be eaten alive by the most frightening of monsters, *emotional intimacy.*

"Ava, is this because we didn't use protection? Because if it is—"

"No." She cut him off before he could issue an offer that would make them both uncomfortable. "I mean, yes, but not—not for the reason you think."

"Then what is it, if not that?"

Suddenly the enormous shower stall seemed claustrophobic. She tried to shrug him off, unable to explain how the lack of a physical barrier between them mirrored her emotional walls coming down. "It's fine."

"Ava." He let go of her and stood naked with his hands on his hips. With the water running down his chest and legs, he looked for all the world like some kind of wet, pissed off Greek god. Or, she supposed, a *Roman* one. "You're clearly not fine."

"You're right, I'm not," she snapped. "I'm pissed. I set those rules for a reason, and now I've broken them all."

His eyebrows twitched, his expression shutting down, and she could tell she'd hurt him. That hadn't been her intention but fuck, she had to get out of this shower and away from him. He was too overwhelming in the best ways, and being around him made her forget all the reasons why this was never going to work.

She scrubbed herself with quick, angry movements and rinsed off. "I'm getting out."

He caught her wrist before she could go, and the look on his face was devastating.

"Look, I understand that you're scared and you need time to process things," he said, and the steady patience in his voice nearly made her crack. "Let's table this for now, call a truce, and meet with Belinda again so you can give her your feedback on the things we discussed yesterday. Sound good?"

It sounded far more reasonable than she deserved. To deny would make her seem petulant. "Okay."

He kissed her forehead. "We're not done here, Ava."

She swallowed hard, dreading the conversation to come. He was going to make her own up to pushing him away again. "I know."

"Get dressed. I'll see you at breakfast." With that, he grabbed a towel and left the bathroom.

Chapter 28

For the next few hours, Roman did everything in his power to make up for how he'd treated Ava the day before. Instead of rushing around the resort, he and Ava sat with Belinda in her office and reviewed everything, along with Ava's notes from Jasmine. Belinda was impressed by Ava's thorough planning and said her job would be a lot easier if all her clients had such a clear vision of what they wanted.

"Jasmine is lucky to have you as her maid of honor," Belinda said before they left for the florist. "This is above and beyond."

Ava blushed and thanked her, but Roman felt a trickle of unease he couldn't quite decipher.

On the short drive from the resort to the florist's shop in Old San Juan, Ava received calls and texts from no fewer than four family members wanting a piece of her. After the last one, where she reminded someone named Ronnie that she was in Puerto Rico and could not, therefore, babysit that night, Roman took a chance.

"How about we turn our phones off for the rest of the trip?" he suggested. "It's the only way we're going to be able to focus."

She gave him a look of surprise. "Don't you have work to do?"

"Camille can handle whatever comes up." The thought of

being incommunicado should have terrified him more than it did. "Come on. I'll do it if you will."

After a glance at her phone screen—which had just lit up with another text from Olympia—Ava nodded. "All right."

Ava turned her phone off and stuffed it in her bag. Roman shot Camille a text letting her know what he was doing.

Roman: You're in charge.

Camille: Excellent.

She added the purple devil horns emoji and Roman couldn't help smiling.

The floral designer, Manu—chosen by Ava, after copious amounts of research—was tall and slender, with russet brown skin, intelligent dark eyes, and black hair cut short and choppy. Manu met them at an event planner showroom with a reception area Roman could only describe as ostentatious, with geometric chrome and black leather furniture, furry throw pillows that looked like they wanted to shed on his pants, and too many animal horns. The walls that didn't display enormous photos of Latin women with flowers in their hair were lined with vases of every size, shape, and material. Roman had his misgivings about this place, but Manu wore a simple dove gray silk top and straight black slacks, and they didn't seem to be responsible for the office décor. Besides, Belinda had confirmed that Manu knew their stuff when it came to modern floral arrangements.

Manu led them to a larger back room that held an assorted selection of chairs and tables. They assembled around a high-top table with three different bar stools pulled up to it. This time, Roman let Ava take the lead. Ava asked lots of questions and listened carefully to the answers, and she seemed to have a firm grasp of florist lingo. They discussed line and shape, negative space, and filler. Ava had extensive mood boards, which seemed to delight Manu, who showed a variety of options and even sketched directly on their tablet. When Ava showed Manu pictures of the centerpieces she'd created for her grandmother's eightieth birthday and the arrangement she'd made for her aunt's retirement party, the designer praised Ava's eye for form and texture.

Roman's unease deepened.

"Can I see your planner?" he asked. Ava handed him the binder absent-mindedly while continuing to deliberate over how large was too large when it came to bridal bouquets.

Roman flipped through the pages, taking note of Ava's precise, sloping cursive, as well as some sections that were written in a looping brush script.

He recognized that script, and not just because he'd looked through her planner on the plane.

While Manu was off selecting vases, Roman returned to Ava's side.

"Did you hand-letter the addresses on the envelopes for the wedding invitations?" he asked.

She glanced up from a catalog open to photos of monstera leaves. "Hmm? Oh, yes. I did."

"Did Jasmine pay you for it?"

Ava's eyes widened in indignation. "Of course not. She's family."

With his mouth set in a grim line, Roman handed back the planner and paced through the aisles formed by mismatched furniture.

It was becoming increasingly clear to him that this trip was yet another way Ava's family took her for granted. It wasn't just painting chairs and playing therapist for her stepmother, cooking and cleaning for her grandmother, checking her sister's homework, or babysitting for her cousins. Her commitment to being maid of honor and making this wedding "perfect," as she'd said the day before, was just another way she was failing to have anything resembling healthy boundaries with her loved ones. Yes, Ava had offered to be here in Jasmine's stead, but as Belinda had observed, this was above and beyond.

Except he couldn't bring that to her attention without betraying his own role as best man. Besides, he could just imagine how Ava would respond. And between his behavior yesterday and her emotional withdrawal after their impromptu shower interlude, he had pushed her enough for now.

God, that shower. He'd been trying not to think about it because whenever he recalled the way she'd reached out to him and said, "Come here," he got hard all over again. Being inside her, *coming* inside her, with nothing between them, had been the purest form of ecstasy he'd experienced in all his forty-one years. Despite the way she'd pulled back afterward, her actions revealed a level of trust that humbled him. She'd probably scared herself shitless, and he'd have to tread carefully to keep her from retreating further. It was his turn to reciprocate.

Ashton had said that Roman needed to show Ava who he really was instead of throwing his money around. She'd seen four of his hotel properties already. She'd been to his home. There was something else he could show her while they were here on the island, and while he wanted it to be a surprise, he'd learned his lesson about keeping things hidden from her.

As they climbed into the SUV parked at the curb, Ava sent him an apprehensive look.

"Our schedule says we're going to meet with a master mixologist to develop the wedding's signature cocktail, but it doesn't say where," she said. "I assume you know?"

"I do. I wanted it to be a surprise, but—"

"It's okay," she cut in, giving him a small smile. "It's all right if you surprise me."

He held her gaze across the seat, then nodded. He wanted to do more. He wanted to pull her across the bench and kiss her, but he understood this for what it was: she was forgiving him for yesterday.

Something in his chest eased, a tightness he hadn't realized was there until it was gone. It wasn't that he couldn't stand to have her mad at him—she was entitled to her emotions, and lord knew he deserved her ire—but he hated that he'd made her feel like anything less than the brilliant, beautiful woman she was. Today he'd set out to show her that he valued her thoughts and feelings, and while he still felt like he had some groveling to do, he'd take her peace offering. And since he didn't want to ruin it by saying, "I think your cousin and my best friend are taking advantage of you," he kept the revelation to himself. Instead, he vowed to make the rest of their trip as low-stress and vacation-like as possible.

The car wound its way west toward Bayamón, and as always, Roman was struck with the sense of coming home. This was where he'd spent his childhood and the summers of his youth. Surrounded by his grandparents, aunts, uncles, and cousins, he'd felt grounded, safe, part of something bigger, in a way he hadn't in Brooklyn. New York City would always be his home base, but this place called to the boy he'd once been, the boy who still lived inside him somewhere.

The car turned a corner and the buildings that housed Casa

Donato came into view. Next to him, Ava made a small gasp. Roman bit back a smile.

She peered out the window as the car rolled to a stop in front of a hundred-year-old white house with terra-cotta roof tiles and an outdoor walkway framed by arches and simple columns. On the other side of the property sprawled a low concrete building marked with the Casa Donato logo. Next to it, a newer wooden structure housed the museum, gift shop, bar, and mixology classroom. Overall, Casa Donato was a smaller operation, not on the scale of distilleries like Don Q on the southern end of the island or Bacardi to the north. But to Roman, it felt homey and inviting, like it had when he was a child.

The driver opened Ava's door and helped her out. Roman exited the car and rounded the hood to stand next to her, where she gaped at the Casa Donato sign.

"This is where your rum is made," she said, sounding a little awestruck. He wondered if, like him, she was remembering the night they'd met.

"It is." He looked toward the house, shielding his eyes from the sun. "They were going to shut this place down. Or sell it to a bigger company who would commercialize it."

"So you saved it."

"I *bought* it, under the condition that their master blender stayed on. I think you'll like her. She's a genius."

"And you didn't commercialize it?"

He shrugged, uncomfortable with the way she was trying to frame him as some sort of savior instead of a guy with too much money and the privilege of indulging his whims. "Introduced a few new products. Made some small upgrades. But for the most part, they're making rum the same way they did when my grandfather started working here in the fifties."

She paused mid-step. "Your grandfather? Did your family own it?"

He huffed out a laugh. "No, we didn't have that kind of money. It's been run by the Donato family for a hundred years."

"But this is where your family is from?"

"My mother's family, yes. I was born in Brooklyn, and after my dad left, my mom came back here and we lived with her parents until I was five. My grandfather brought me here sometimes. I grew up among these barrels."

Ava's stunning eyes searched his face, and after a moment, she reached for his hand and gave it a squeeze. "Show me."

Inside, they met up with Joaquín, one of the Donato sons who still worked there. He was around sixty now, with a ruddy complexion, stocky build, and close-cropped gray hair. He wore black jeans, sneakers, and a navy-blue polo shirt with the Casa Donato logo. Joaquín was the only remaining person who remembered seeing little Roman running around, and while Joaquín no longer led the tours, Roman had asked him to do this one as a special favor.

Joaquín began in the museum, where he recounted the history of Casa Donato. Then he brought them into the distillery, where he showed Ava the still and explained the process of making rum. He took them through the rows of stacked barrels, where the scents of oak and alcohol and molasses brought Roman back to his youth. Ava asked lots of questions and Roman could tell the older man was delighted by her interest in the subject. When she wasn't looking, Joaquín shot him an approving grin.

After the tour was over, Ava clapped and Joaquín gave a little bow.

"This is where I leave you," he said, and nodded to Roman.

"You know your way around. Estrella will meet you when you're ready."

Roman thanked him, then led Ava back through the rows of barrels. He gazed up to the high, shadowed ceiling and breathed in the familiar, comforting scents. "This was my favorite spot," he mused. "When I was a kid."

Her head tilted with curiosity. "Why?"

He shrugged. "It just felt so old. But it was also cool and quiet. They let me run up and down the rows, after making me promise not to knock anything over. I never did."

"It's sweet that your grandfather brought you to work with him. Do your grandparents still live around here?"

"They passed away two years ago. My grandfather first, and my grandmother within the year."

"I'm sorry. You must miss them."

"I do, but I'm grateful I had the time with them that I did. And that I was able to make their later years more comfortable."

"I'm sure they were proud of you."

Her words, uttered softly, hit him square in the chest. He had to swallow a lump in his throat as he remembered his grandparents' reaction to the house he'd built for them. His grandmother had cried, and his grandfather hadn't wanted to accept.

You took care of me when I was small, Roman had told him. *Please let me take care of you.* And then his grandmother had seen the size of the kitchen, and that was it for the objections.

"Yeah," he said, voice tight. "They were."

"This place is special." She ran her fingertips over the wooden staves forming the side of a barrel. "It's another piece of you."

"It's personal," he admitted. "More than the hotels."

She nodded, her expression serious. "I can see that."

"Everything I've done . . . it's all been for my family." Ashton had told him to let Ava see him, to open up. It was time to take the risk of revealing more. In doing so, he was letting her in. And then maybe she would let *him* in.

So he told her about his mother, about his family in Puerto Rico, about growing up in Brooklyn. He told her about his stepfather, about his sister, Through it all, Ava listened, her hazel eyes solemn.

"That's why," he finally said. "That's why I work so much. My family is my highest priority. I want to know that if I died tomorrow, they'd be taken care of for the rest of their lives."

"But the distillery," Ava said. "This is for you."

He nodded. It was amazing how clearly she saw him, and what this place meant to him. A connection to his family's home, to his childhood, to his past, but also preserving a piece of history while doing right for the future. Something he could preserve *and* put his mark on at the same time.

"Some of my associates have told me it's a waste of resources," he admitted, looking around. "But I don't care. It's valuable to *me*."

She took his hand. "Thank you for showing me."

He lifted her fingers to his lips and kissed them. "There's one more surprise. Come on."

Chapter 29

As Roman released her, it was on the tip of Ava's tongue to suggest they make out among the barrels like a couple of teenagers, but she swallowed the words and followed him outside and down a paved walkway that led to the museum.

The events of the day had her rethinking all her stupid rules, especially the *no sexual touching* one. But she had a sneaking suspicion Roman was going to make her talk first, and she still had a lot of thinking to do.

Yes, her body was very clear on what it wanted—him, in all the ways she could have him—but her mind and heart were another matter.

She'd hoped to keep her heart out of the equation altogether, but it hadn't gotten the memo, and the treacherous little organ had *opinions*.

For one, it found his behavior today unbearably romantic. He'd immediately made up for the way he'd acted the day before, and if that wasn't enough, he'd shown her something that was obviously very personal to him, then followed it up by telling her about his family.

How the hell was she supposed to resist a double punch of vulnerability like that?

Since her body and heart were in cahoots, it was up to her brain to reinforce all the reasons why the two of them could never be.

Starting with the biggest reason: he was best man in her cousin's wedding, and the two of them being involved would make things awkward for Jasmine.

Ava's Primas of Power had stood by her, defended her, and helped her put her self back together after Hector left. Being with Roman jeopardized one of the most important relationships in her life, and that should be the only reason Ava needed to stay away from him.

So why didn't it feel like enough?

Roman held the door to the museum open for her, and they passed through the gift shop, which sold bottles of rum, branded merchandise, and everything needed to make rum cocktails. At the other end, they entered a large space with soft lighting and half a dozen rectangular high top tables. The room smelled delicious, sweet and sugary, with a citrus tang, and looked like what you'd get if a science classroom and a pub had a baby. Each table held all the tools of the bartender's trade—shakers, stirrers, tongs, and other things Ava couldn't identify—along with bottles of Casa Donato rum.

At the front of the room, Roman introduced Ava to Estrella Martín, Casa Donato's master blender.

Estrella was a firecracker—short, bursting with energy, with solid arms that looked like they packed a punch. Her cloud of spiraling curls was a mix of gray and reddish brown, and her smooth brown face creased into a smile when she saw Ava. Dark eyes sparkled behind round red glasses, and she pulled Ava down to kiss her cheek.

"Qué linda," Estrella murmured, shooting a knowing look at Roman. "No me dijiste que tienes novia."

Ava waited for him to correct Estrella and say that Ava wasn't his girlfriend, but he just smiled, so Ava kept her mouth shut. It wasn't her place to correct the other woman. And if some part of her didn't mind being mistaken for Roman's girlfriend, well . . . she'd think about that later.

"So, how much do you know about rum?" Estrella asked in Spanish, getting down to business.

"More than I did this morning?" Ava replied, and the older woman laughed.

"Don't worry, I'll teach you some practical tricks, and then we'll work on the wedding cocktail. Let's begin."

Estrella started with a tasting, similar to the way Roman had introduced Ava to his rum the night they'd met. At Ava's insistence, Roman once again busted out his barback tricks. Estrella called him a show-off, but her teasing was good-natured.

"Roman is the reason I'm still here," Estrella told Ava. "I told them if they sold to some big company that was going to swoop in and change everything, I was out. But Roman has roots here, and more than that, he understands spirits. You know he was a bartender, right?"

"He might have mentioned it," Ava said, shooting Roman a private little smile.

"Bars trust him. He understands the industry better than most celebrity owners."

Roman absently spun a cocktail shaker on the back of his hand and snorted. "I'm not a celebrity."

"Yes, you are," Ava and Estrella said in unison, then laughed together at his exasperated sigh.

"I was on *one* telenovela," he protested. "Almost twenty years ago."

"Who cares about that?" Estrella said saucily. "Not me. I'm

talking about Pepito el cocodrilo, the character you voiced on that cartoon. What was it called? *El Zoo de Mateo.* My son loved that show when he was small."

"You played a crocodile?" Ava asked, delighted.

"A baby crocodile," Roman clarified. "You really haven't internet stalked me?"

She shook her head. "Have you searched me?"

"I tried, but your social media accounts are private."

"I'm a teacher. I can't have my students following me."

"Makes sense." He gave her a sly look. "What would happen if I sent you a friend request?"

She shrugged and continued squeezing lime juice for the Donato Mule they were making. "Try it and see."

"I think I will."

Ugh, why couldn't she stop flirting with him?

In their quest to develop a signature cocktail for the wedding, they made a mule, an old-fashioned, and a piña colada. After they tasted all three drinks, Roman turned to Ava. "What do you think?"

Ava held his gaze and couldn't smother the smile that curved her lips. "Thank you for asking," she said quietly. Despite the cool drink and the air conditioning working overtime, his answering smile warmed her to the tips of her toes.

Aware that Estrella was watching them intently, Ava took another sip from the glass in her hand, then smacked her lips lightly, savoring the spiciness of the ginger beer.

"Personally, the mule is my favorite," she said. "But I can tell you from years of experience, my family enjoys a piña colada that kicks you in the teeth."

"Let's make it shaken instead of blended," Roman said. At Ava's quizzical look, he explained. "Easier on the bartenders."

Ava consulted her notes. "Jasmine said it would be nice if the drink were a fun color, or at least looks good in photos."

"Guava," Estrella said decisively. "You want a pretty drink that doesn't taste overwhelming? Add guava. It's extremely versatile."

"Could we add guava to a shaken piña colada?" Ava asked.

"You can add any fruit nectar or puree to a piña colada," Estrella said. "It's just a matter of how much."

They got to work figuring out the perfect blend of ingredients. In addition to the guava, Estrella added some fresh-squeezed lime juice to the cream of coconut and pineapple juice. And instead of white rum, they used the Casa Donato Siete, a gold rum aged up to seven years. It was strong, but smoother than Ava had expected it to be, carrying a pleasant aroma of vanilla with a hint of smokiness. The slight taste of oak, almond, and warm spices balanced the guava and pineapple nicely, and kept the drink from being overwhelmingly fruity.

For presentation, they tested coconut flakes on the rim and a flower for garnish, but ultimately decided to keep it simple with a dehydrated lime wheel.

Once they agreed on the final recipe, Estrella made them each a fresh drink. They stood together around the table and clinked their glasses together.

"To the happy couple," Estrella said with a wink.

Ava met Roman's eyes over the rim of her glass, and the cold, refreshing drink did nothing to cool the heat in her cheeks.

Or elsewhere.

There was nothing untoward in his expression or posture. He seemed completely at ease, with one hand in his pocket and the other wrapped around the glass tumbler, projecting his specific brand of casual confidence. But Ava knew him well enough to see the barely leashed desire in his eyes.

Then, in a nonchalant gesture no one but her would have noticed, he slid his hand out of his pocket just enough to reveal a sliver of white lace.

Ava inhaled sharply, then took a quick sip to cover her response. The shameless man had her panties in his pocket!

"Ava, will you be all right for a few minutes?" he asked, cool as a fucking cucumber. "I want to speak to the staff before I leave."

"Of course." She gave a jerky nod. "I wanted to take a closer look at the museum exhibit."

And get her heart rate under control.

A few people had shown up for a scheduled tour, and Roman went to greet them. Ava pretended to look at framed black and white photos of Casa Donato in the 1950s while she wrestled her thoughts into some semblance of order.

At first, when they'd arrived at the distillery, she'd thought Roman was showing off a bit. Now she understood that this place was a part of Roman in a way the hotels weren't.

The Dulce Hotel Group was a brand, but through the distillery, he was conserving a piece of history and culture. It spoke to his values not just as a business owner, but as a person.

Still, Roman had put his mark on it. The vibe matched what she'd seen in his hotels. The rustic industrial décor was tasteful and appropriate for the setting. The combination museum and bar area invited visitors to take their time and mull over the historical display while slowly sipping rum . . . before purchasing a caseload to bring home.

Roman seemed more relaxed here than when they were in the public areas of his hotels, closer to the way he was at home.

Despite being the owner, Roman didn't throw his weight around. Not that she'd ever seen him do that, but he could have. This was a fairly small operation, and it was clear he was deeply knowledgeable about the rum distilling process and the business of artisanal spirits. Even so, he'd let Joaquín lead the tour, and he deferred to Estrella as the expert during their mixology lesson. Moreover, it was obvious to Ava that the people who worked here liked and respected him. He knew everyone's names and asked about their families, and he was respectful of the original Donato family who'd started the distillery.

The man was almost too good to be true. He'd taken the feedback she'd given and immediately put it into practice. He hadn't punished her for speaking up for herself—instead he'd cared for her all night, apologized, and done something special for her.

He made her feel . . . safe, she realized. There was safety in being able to voice her feelings and knowing she wouldn't be chastised or met with a defensive attitude.

And she'd be lying if she said she didn't enjoy being with him. He was funny, caring, and open. He was willing to hear critique and change. He took responsibility for himself and his actions in a way Hector never—

Shit. The difference finally hit her. Hector had been a *boy*, whereas Roman was a *man*.

Hector, as much as Ava had once loved him, had never grown up. He'd been a little boy who wanted a mommy to take care of him, and Ava had eagerly jumped into that role, thanks to the toxic and deeply imbalanced cultural gender roles that had been modeled for her throughout her life. No wonder their relationship had been unsustainable.

Roman didn't need a mommy. He was a grown-ass adult

who ran multiple businesses, provided for his mother and sister, and willingly opened up about his feelings. Not only that, he could listen to someone else talk about their feelings without pouting.

He was so mature it scared her, because it meant she'd have to rise to his level. She'd given into fear that morning, pulling back after letting him get too close. Instead of storming off or getting defensive, as Hector would have done, Roman had cut through her peevishness with patience and maturity.

Now he looked over from where he chatted with the gift shop attendant, sending Ava a smile so broad and full of life that it nearly broke her heart.

When this ended, it was going to *hurt*.

Once the tour group left, Roman strolled over to her.

"I've called for the car," he said. "Do you want to go to the beach when we get back? Before dinner?"

"Absolutely," she said without a second's hesitation.

Fuck her rules. Figuring out how to break things off after they got back to New York was a problem for Future Ava.

Present Ava was going to enjoy every single second they had together.

Chapter 30

Roman had initially suggested they visit the beach because he needed Ava out of the house so he could implement his next surprise, but once he saw her clad in nothing but a pink bikini, he forgot about everything else. The high-waisted bottoms laced up the sides and emphasized her rounded hips, and the top consisted of some string and two tiny scraps of spandex that highlighted her pert breasts. She'd braided her hair back in two neat plaits.

"You are a goddess," he breathed.

She ducked her head like she was hiding a blush. "Not looking too bad yourself."

"This old thing?" He glanced down at the black swim trunks he'd found in the dresser upstairs. They were a little big on him—apparently he'd slimmed down since he'd last been here, a result of the PT regimen he was actually sticking to these days—and he knew his abs were more defined than they'd been since . . . well, probably since he'd starred on a telenovela.

Thinking about Ava in that swimsuit was going to make it difficult for him to go out in public, so he cleared his throat and gestured toward the front door. "Your chariot awaits."

They left their phones behind, and Roman switched out

his smartwatch for a waterproof one that only told time. The car drove them to Bellísima, which had a pool deck that led right onto the beach. The deck had a bar, rows of white lounge chairs with golden yellow cushions and navy-blue umbrellas branded with the resort's logo, and an aquamarine pool shaped like a kidney bean. They claimed two lounge chairs far away from the other guests, and an attendant brought over mocktails made with coconut water, seltzer, mint, and lime.

"Drink this," Roman said, passing one to Ava. "I won't chance you getting dehydrated again."

"Yes, sir," she said with a cheeky grin that made his groin tighten. She accepted the drink and took a sip. His gaze zeroed in on her lips where they wrapped around the end of the straw, and he forced himself to look away.

He didn't think he was imagining the shift in her energy. She'd been cautious around him in the morning, like she expected him to talk over her again, but she'd gradually loosened up. During the distillery tour she'd been curious and attentive, taking in the information with genuine interest. They'd had fun during the mixology class, joking and inventing ridiculous names for the drink, like "Telenovela Foreva" and "Jashton in Love," and he hadn't been able to resist giving her a teasing glimpse of her panties in his pocket. Her face had flamed red but she didn't appear scandalized.

Estrella had pulled him aside afterward and whispered, "I like her."

"Me too," he'd answered truthfully.

Ava had been quiet on the ride back, and then she'd surprised him by strolling out in that sexy pink bikini. He couldn't have said exactly what he'd expected her to wear, but it wasn't that. He'd never been happier to be wrong.

Then she pulled a bottle of sunscreen from her tote and he stopped thinking altogether.

After pulling off the gauzy white cover-up she'd worn in the car, she squirted sunscreen onto her palm and began to smooth it over her arms.

Roman froze with the glass halfway to his mouth as he watched her work the lotion onto her shoulders. After a moment, he realized his jaw was hanging open, and he took a long pull on the paper straw.

Damn, he had to get a hold of himself. It wasn't even like she was applying the sunscreen in a sexy way. He just found everything she did appealing.

She moved to her legs, and when she saw him watching, her lips curved in a coy smile. Her movements slowed, becoming more like caresses. Roman swallowed hard and took another gulp of his drink.

Then her hands went to her breasts, slipping beneath the fabric of her bikini top. With her eyes on his, she worked her fingers over her skin, and Roman realized she was tweaking her own nipples under the pink spandex.

He groaned and tunneled his fingers through his hair, which was damp with sweat. From her or from the humidity, he wasn't sure. "Ava, what are you doing to me?"

"You're right, how selfish of me." Was it his imagination, or did he detect a breathy little purr? She drew her hands away from her breasts and held up the sunscreen. "Want me to do your back? We don't want you to burn."

He raised an eyebrow. "Are you saying I'm pale?"

"I don't need to say it."

He choked out a laugh and stretched out on his stomach. "Do your worst."

He'd been kidding, but there was nothing innocent about the way Ava buttered up his back. She slid her hands up and down his skin in slow strokes. Her thumbs and fingertips traced the contours of his muscles and the ridge of his spine. She tickled his sides and dug into the tension he perpetually carried in his traps. By the end, he was putty in her hands and his dick was hard as a fucking rock.

"There," she said, easing back. "You're ready."

"Fuck yeah I am," he muttered under his breath. "Give me a second, or I'm going to cause a scandal."

She let out a husky chuckle and stretched her long body out on her lounge chair. "But you have to do me next. My back, I mean."

God, was there anything sexier than flirty Ava? Roman didn't think so.

He sat up, and she laughed when he immediately tossed a towel over his lap.

"You feeling okay over there?" she asked. "You seem a little . . . flustered."

"Just fine," he grumbled.

They still had a lot to talk about—he wasn't letting her off the hook for the way she'd snapped at him after they'd made love in the shower—but this wasn't the time or place, and if she wanted to break some of her rules, he was game. He took the sunscreen from her, rubbed it between his hands, and began to smooth it onto her back. It was a pleasure just to touch her, and as he worked it over her shoulders, she let out a satisfied hum.

"You like that?" His voice came out gravelly with desire.

"Mmm. It's nice. I never splurge on massages."

Roman made a mental note to book spa services for them the next day.

He ran his hands all over her back, then down her legs, sliding the sunscreen over her thighs. When he got to the bikini bottoms, he dipped his fingers underneath, massaging her gorgeous butt. When her thighs parted, he was tempted to go further, to stroke her and see if she was as turned on as he was, but he stuck to the uncovered skin.

"You're very thorough," she murmured.

"You're not getting burned on my watch."

"I appreciate it." Then she sat up, drained her glass, and jumped to her feet. "See you in the water!"

She took off, jogging down to the beach and leaving Roman staring after her with a raging boner.

He laughed. Damn, she was fun.

Since he wasn't going anywhere for a few minutes, he sipped his drink and watched her stride into the water, her long, strong legs cutting through the breaking waves. And when she raised her arms over her head and dove in, he waited with bated breath until she resurfaced.

Roman was glad they'd left their phones behind but he wished he could take a picture of her as she was now, diving in and out of the water in her pink bikini, a smile on her face, as carefree as a frolicking seal. Since he couldn't take a picture, he committed every detail to memory, determined not to miss a thing.

Ava bobbed back up and wiped the water from her eyes. Her head turned, like she was scanning the shore, and when she spotted him, her face lit up and she waved. Roman could see her huge grin all the way from where he sat, and warmth suffused his chest. He waved back, and when she relaxed into the water to float, his pulse sped up and his skin prickled like he'd caught a chill. But how? It had to be almost a hundred degrees out.

Then it hit him. It wasn't a chill, it was *shock*. Shock, because his body had realized something before his brain could interpret the feeling. The goosebump-inducing warmth was . . . Fuck. It was *love*. He *loved* her.

He fucking loved Ava.

With something akin to terror, his mind raced to catalog the feelings she brought out in him. Excitement whenever her name appeared on his phone. Longing when she went months without contacting him. Fear when he thought she was in trouble. Delight at doing something nice for her. And determination to treat her like a queen.

There were more emotions to sort through, but this was a starting point, and when he factored in additional data—like how he dropped everything to see her, something he'd done for literally *no one* who wasn't a blood relation—all signs pointed to love.

He loved her hesitation because it made the moments when she was bold all the more electrifying. He loved her kindness, but he loved her sass and spark even more. He loved her generosity, even when she gave too much, and he especially loved when she let him swoop to her rescue like a knight in a fairytale. He loved the way she curled against him when she needed comfort, the way she read every item on a menu before making her decision, the way she crafted the most polite booty call texts ever. He loved her neat cursive, her perfect curls, and how magnificent she was when she finally let her hair get wet. He loved the way she wrapped her long legs around his hips like a snare he never wanted to escape from, the way her plush mouth sucked on his bottom lip when they kissed, the way her eyes revealed everything she was feeling, even when she thought she was hiding it. A blend of colors—brown and green, yellow and red, and deep enough to drown in—her eyes held galaxies and reflected his entire universe back to him. Everything he was and ever would be was tangled up with her.

He'd never been in love before, but he knew with soul-deep certainty that this was worlds beyond desire, and far different than what he felt for his family. When he thought of Ava, the unparalleled sense of connection stretched out far into the future, eternal and boundless. He wanted to be part of her life, and for her to be part of his, forever.

It wasn't what *she* wanted. He knew that. But feelings changed, didn't they? His had. When they'd met, he'd been content with one night of fun. And now here he was, head over fucking heels in love with her.

Wasn't it possible her feelings could change too?

From the water, Ava beckoned to him, and Roman rose to his feet. God, this woman had total control over him, and she didn't even realize it. More, he wanted to give her that control. He wanted to give her *everything*.

Setting down his glass, he walked toward the water as if there were an invisible cord pulling him to her. He didn't fight it, just let the feeling tug him forward, across the sand and into the breaking waves splashing over his feet. He charged into the surf as it battered his knees and threatened to knock him over. When he reached her, the water was calmer. The words *I love you* were on the tip of his tongue, but he resisted the urge to tell her what he'd discovered. He knew her well enough by now to know it would scare her. Roman wasn't used to holding back— when he had an idea, he *acted*. But Ava wasn't like that. She'd need time to think, to process. So he would wait, even though the feeling swelled inside him like a balloon until he thought he would burst with it.

"We have to stop meeting like this," she murmured when he approached.

"Like what?"

"In the water." With a saucy grin, she splashed him right in the face.

"Oh, it's like that?" He dove after her, and with a peal of laughter, she darted away like a nymph. They played for a few minutes, laughing and splashing each other in the turquoise blue sea while the sun beat thickly down overhead, and Roman couldn't remember the last time he'd had this much fun. Finally, after she'd tackled him into the waves, he grabbed the waistband of her swimsuit and yanked her over to him. She gave up the fight immediately and turned in his embrace, looping her arms over his shoulders and locking her legs around his hips like she had that first night in the pool.

Roman was instantly hard again. He gripped her ass, his fingertips teasing her skin under the edge of pink spandex.

Around them, on the sand and in the water, people talked and played music, kids laughed and screamed, and the waves crashed. But it felt like they were alone. Roman wanted to kiss her with every fiber of his being.

"You're killing me, profe," he rasped.

"Am I?" Her lips quirked in a teasing smile. "Let me check."

And then her hand dove under the water to untie his swim trunks.

He groaned and pressed his face into her neck as her fingers reached into the clingy fabric and netting to grip him. They were both soaking wet and her hand was cool, but where their skin touched, heat flared.

They weren't supposed to be doing this yet. Right? Wasn't there some reason why he'd been holding back? Oh yeah, they needed to talk first. And then he needed to tell her he loved her. But fuck, her hand felt so good caressing his cock, and her ass felt amazing in his hands.

His fingers flexed, sliding over her wet skin and inching closer to her center.

Fuck it. They'd talk later.

He trailed his mouth along her jaw. "Ava—"

A wave crashed down, knocking them sideways and sucking them under the water. Ava was pulled from his grip. Saltwater rushed into his mouth and nose, and he couldn't tell which way was up. Then Roman's feet touched sand and he propelled himself upward, his head breaking the surface. He came up coughing and spluttering, wiping water and snot off his face. When he looked around, he spotted Ava a few feet away, doing the same. He trudged through the water toward her, feeling a little less resistance than before . . .

Ava gasped. "You're naked!"

Roman glanced down at himself. Ah. That was why there was less drag. His swim trunks were completely gone.

"So I am," he said, sinking lower in the water. "Well, this is a predicament."

Ava burst into peals of laughter. "This," she said, choking out the words between giggles, "is your payback for stealing my pan—"

She was cut short when another wave smashed into her back and toppled her over. The current was pushing them into the breaker zone. Roman waited for her to come up, then took her arm to pull her into deeper waters.

Her hair was coming loose from its braids and she pushed it away from her face, rubbing seawater out of her eyes. When she lowered her hands, Roman's eyes nearly fell out of his head as he gazed at her bare breasts.

Without thinking, his hands shot out to cover them.

"Roman, what—" She let out a strangled screech when she saw why he was suddenly groping her. "My top!"

"You can't make this shit up," he mumbled, but she wasn't in the mood for jokes.

"Find it!" she hissed, covering her chest with her arms.

He made a helpless gesture toward his crotch. "Between the two of us, you're still more covered than I am. And the beach will respond a lot better if you go out there topless than if I come out with no pants."

"I can't believe this is happening," she muttered, searching the water around them.

"¡Mira esto!" a high-pitched voice called somewhere to Roman's left. He glanced over to where a trio of kids played in the water, just in time to see a boy around Yadi's age wave what looked like a wet pink flag.

Roman surged toward them as the boy threw Ava's bikini top to his friend. The other kid caught it and held the pink triangles in front of his own skinny chest, laughing. He raised his arm to throw the top to the third boy when Roman lunged through the water and snatched it from his hand.

"Gracias," he said, a little out of breath. "Eso es mio."

"¿Qué?" the boy asked. "¿Tuyo?"

"Es de mi novia," Roman explained with a wink, reveling

in calling Ava his girlfriend, even if it was only to a bunch of children. All three boys looked past him to where Ava waited, red-faced and crouching in the water up to her neck. Roman dove underwater and swam away before they noticed he was missing something too.

He returned the top to Ava, who struggled to get the wet spandex triangles back over her breasts under the water. "Do you think anyone saw?"

"If they did, they are very lucky."

"Roman!" Despite her indignant tone, she smothered a laugh as he helped her with the ties.

Once she was covered, Roman wiped his face again.

"Are you okay?" she asked.

He rubbed his nose. "Fine. I just have seawater leaking out of my brain."

"Pobrecito." She pushed his hair back from his forehead and gave him a look of utter fondness. "I was planning to tease you a whole lot more—turnabout is fair play, and all that—but I think we've beached enough for one day, don't you?"

"More than enough. I'm totally beached out." Roman glanced at his waterproof watch. His surprise was likely under-way. If he could get Ava to her room and keep her away from the kitchen and patio, there was a good chance it would stay a surprise. "Can you bring me a towel and a robe from the deck?"

She nodded, but before she left, she put her hand on his chest and gave him a soft, closed-mouth kiss. "This was fun. Thank you."

Mi sirena, he thought, as he watched her cut through the waves to the shore. When she was in the water, she was as care-free as a mermaid, shedding her reserve along with her clothes and leaving all her inhibitions on land.

He was so fucking lucky that she let him see this side of her.

If he hadn't already realized he was in love with her, this would have been the moment that did it. And as much as he wanted to announce it to the entire beach, he'd keep it to himself.

For now.

Chapter 31

After they returned to the house, Ava showered and washed her hair, then slipped into a white cotton dress. The dress had a halter top with a deep vee and skinny straps, an embroidered waist, and a floaty skirt that fell to her knees. She could get away with not wearing a bra, but when she opened the drawer where she'd put her underwear, she hesitated.

What if she forwent the panties, too?

No panties meant she expected something to happen tonight. That she *wanted* something to happen.

She thought about what she and Roman had done in the shower that morning. What they'd done at the beach before their epic wipeout.

It was time to face facts. Despite her best intentions, she couldn't keep her hands off him.

Damaris was right. Ava deserved to make the most of this romantic island getaway with Roman. Instead of denying herself what she wanted, she'd go after it. She still had her boundaries—two more days in Puerto Rico, two more days to revel in pleasure—and then she'd go back to real life. Back to Old Ava.

She shut the drawer with a decisive snap, leaving the panties neatly folded inside.

In front of the bathroom mirror, Ava worked product into her hair in silence. She usually listened to music or audiobooks while she did her hair, but her phone was still on the coffee table in the living room next to Roman's, where they'd left them before heading to the beach.

At first, the thought of having her phone off all day had rocketed up her anxiety levels. But in hindsight, it was nice to have long stretches of uninterrupted time to think.

Lord knew she had a lot to think about. Visiting the distillery and seeing how much it meant to him touched something in her. She was still mulling over everything he'd shared about himself and his family.

Their connection was deepening, which scared her. But maybe . . . that was okay?

"Stop overthinking it." She scolded herself in the mirror as she finger-curled a few locks of hair around her face. "You'll be home in two days. Worry about it then."

It was almost time for dinner, so she decided to let her hair air dry, something she almost never did. If she went swimming again tonight or tomorrow, she'd regret spending the time to dry it with a diffuser. Next, she glanced at her makeup bag, but as she had with the blow dryer, she hesitated.

Roman had seen her first thing in the morning. He'd cared for her while she was sick. If he didn't like her face the way it was, too bad for him. She swiped on some tinted lip balm and called it a day.

New Ava isn't afraid to be seen without makeup, she thought. It had taken years before she'd let Hector see—

No. No more thinking about Hector. No more comparing who she was then and now. That part of her life was over, and it was time to embrace who she was at this very moment and move on.

With Roman? a little voice in the back of her mind asked.

With myself, she replied fiercely.

After slipping on her chancletas, she went out to the patio, where Roman had told her to meet him for dinner.

Dusk was falling, and with it came the song of the coquí, the little tree frogs that were native to Puerto Rico. The temperature had dropped marginally, and the patio's ceiling fan worked overtime to cool the space. Soft yellow light came from sconces on the walls, and the pool water lapped lazily in the languid breeze.

In the middle of it all, Roman sat in one of the armchairs, reading a magazine. He wore a short-sleeved chambray shirt and tan shorts. With his reading glasses and his wet hair springing into loose curls, he was unbelievably adorable. And all hers, at least for the next two days.

As she approached, she saw their "dinner" and gave a surprised gasp. "What's all this?"

The low outdoor table was positively groaning under the weight of dishes. It was like their first night together, when Roman had ordered a little of everything, and it had amounted to a lot.

Smiling, he set his glasses and the magazine aside and rose to his feet.

"I felt bad that you missed the tasting yesterday," he explained, bringing her a glass of sparkling rosé. "I arranged for a few of the items to be served tonight, so you can give your opinion."

"A few?" Ava gaped at the table. "This must be everything!"
He shrugged. "Most of it."

Ava shook her head, unable to take it all in. "This is too much. It was my fault I missed the tasting. You were right, I'm too available to my family."

"That may be. But you're right that you know Jasmine better than I do, and you're here to have a hand in these decisions. Shall we sit?"

Ava let him lead her over to the round daybed and sat while he retrieved his own drink—amber liquid with a large cube of ice and an orange peel.

"Another Romy Negroni?" she asked.

"Of course. Every time I have one, it makes me think of you, and how glad I am that you ordered that horrendous lemon drink—which, by the way, has been removed from the menu." He sat beside her. Not across, but next to. Like he wanted to be close to her.

This absolutely charming man. How the hell was she supposed to guard her heart against him?

She couldn't. It was as simple as that.

Two more days, she told herself. She had two days to enjoy this, enjoy *him*.

So she cuddled against his side as he launched into an explanation of all the dishes, as knowledgeable as any head waiter. When Ava made to get up, saying she needed her planner to take notes, he put a hand over hers and shook his head.

"I'll remember for you," he said, and it was the sexiest thing she'd ever heard.

Dinner was a slow, sensuous affair. Roman fed her bits from each dish, watching her reaction carefully and asking for her thoughts. Such close scrutiny from anyone else would have made her nervous that she was being a nuisance, but with Roman, she understood the gift of his undivided attention. Under his gaze, she felt sexier, and more present, than she probably ever had in her whole life. Besides, if he wanted to be elsewhere, he would be. He'd gone out of his way to take this trip with her—to spend time with her, he'd said. She knew it wasn't only for Ashton. They were friends, but Roman wouldn't miss entire days of work, with his phone off, for just anyone.

And yet he'd done it for her.

What did it mean?

Don't worry about that, she told herself. *Just enjoy. Savor this moment.*

So she did.

Around them, the humidity in the air finally reached saturation point, and it began to rain. Softly at first, a gentle smattering against the roof of the patio, then harder, with a force and velocity specific only to a tropical rainstorm. The noise cocooned them, making their outdoor oasis feel even more secluded, and the temperature cooled to something bordering on pleasant.

By the time they reached the cupcake tray, Ava was in flavor overload. She'd never thought so much about the food she'd put in her mouth.

Then Roman dipped his index finger into the smear of lemon icing and held it out to her. "Ready to taste?"

She fought back a shiver. This man was going to incinerate her.

Leaning forward, she closed her lips around the end of his finger and sucked. The icing was sweet and tart, creamy with a slight sugary crunch, and underneath, the taste of his skin. Keeping her eyes on his, she swiped the pad of his finger with her tongue before easing back. Because she was watching, she caught the movement of his throat as he swallowed hard. His brown eyes filled with banked fire, and Ava was real freaking glad she hadn't bothered with panties.

"Ava," he whispered huskily.

For once, her mind, body, and heart were in agreement, all three screaming, *Yes, yes, take me now.*

His lips parted.

She leaned in, eager for his kiss . . .

"I love you."

Every single one of her cells *froze.*

Seconds ticked by as she stared at his face, uncomprehending. Finally, her tongue thawed enough to utter, "You—what?"

Roman took her hand and bent toward her, his gaze intense. "I know this is against your rules . . ."

Rules? What rules? She couldn't think straight. What the fuck was happening?

". . . but it's not in me to hide something like this."

Her heart pounded in her throat, making speech difficult. "What?" she choked out.

The center of his dark brows creased. "I love you."

So that *was* what he'd said.

"I wanted to give you time to process . . ." he went on, while Ava struggled to remember how to breathe.

Process. Yes, she needed to process this. But he was holding her hand, and he was right next to her, warm and good-smelling, and all she could see was the open and earnest expression on his face, and those dreamy eyes . . .

"Roman." Oh good, she could still say something other than "what."

He stopped talking. She hadn't the faintest idea what he'd been saying. She cleared her throat.

"I don't . . . I don't know what to say." The words came more easily now that the initial shock had worn off.

"You don't have to say or do anything," he said calmly. "I just want you to know where I stand."

"Oh." That sounded reasonable. "Thanks?"

The corner of his mouth twitched, like he was trying not to smile. "You're welcome."

And then her skin tingled and her heart started pounding like a snare drum as her brain reminded her *what the fuck he'd just said*.

"Holy shit," she whispered.

And then she bolted.

Chapter 32

Ava leapt to her feet and ran out into the pouring rain. She was drenched in seconds. This was no romantic drizzle; this was a torrential downpour, falling in sheets, soak-you-to-the-bone kind of rain.

It did nothing to clear her head.

She came to a halt at the edge of the pool, staring down at the violent patter of bullet-size raindrops on the surface of the water, illuminated from below by underwater lights.

Roman came up behind her, but didn't touch her. He waited a long moment before asking, "What are you thinking?"

"I'm thinking of jumping in."

He made a soft noise, muffled by the sound of the rain, that she was sure was a laugh.

"Does it scare you that much?" he asked lightly.

New Ava doesn't run away from emotional intimacy, she scolded herself, despite the fact that she'd literally done just that. Forcing her body to turn and face him, she looked into his eyes, their brown depths somehow still warm and steady despite the rain pounding his hair flat over his forehead and shrink-wrapping his shirt to his muscles.

"How are you always two steps ahead of me?" she asked. "I

just came to terms with having a torrid tropical affair with you for the rest of this trip, and here you go bringing love into the equation. What am I supposed to do with that, Roman?"

His lips quivered like he was fighting back a smile, and he put his warm hands on her shoulders. "Don't do anything with it. I'm only telling you so you have time to get used to the idea."

"How do you know?" she demanded. They should probably get out of the rain, but she couldn't bring herself to take a step toward the patio, to the place where *those words* had been uttered.

His smile was patient. "Where's my phone?"

"In the living roo—oh."

Understanding dawned, and with it, the acknowledgment that he was telling the truth—or at least, what felt true for him. Wasn't this what she'd just been thinking? His time was valuable, and the fact that he'd taken days away from work to spend with her was the biggest gift he could give someone. She knew he wasn't just here for the wedding, either. Yes, he was dutifully attending all the meetings, but he'd also planned romantic surprises for her—something she'd reprimanded him for. And even though he'd never said it, she knew it must have been a hardship for him to meet her every time she'd beckoned over the past ten months.

Is that why you do it? that annoying little voice in the back of her mind nagged. *To make him prove how much he wants you? You're the queen of planning. Why not schedule with him in advance?*

Because I'm trying not to want him, and our fling is spontaneous?

Wrong! God, why was her inner voice such a sarcastic little bitch? And it wasn't done with her yet. *It's because deep down, you've been waiting for him to tell you no, to prove he's just like every-*

one else who refuses to put you first. Well, guess what, sucker? He's put you first since the moment you met. Now what are you going to do about it?

I don't know, she thought back. I don't know what to do about it.

But she did know he'd admitted something big, and even though it terrified her, she couldn't leave him hanging.

"Roman, I—"

But he'd started to speak at the same time. "I know I'm just a coping mechanism for you—"

"Wait, what?" She grabbed his arms in surprise and forgot whatever she'd been about to say. "No, you're not."

His smile was pained. "Ava, you've been up front about what this was from the beginning."

Was this really what he thought? "Roman, you're not just a coping mechanism for me. Okay, maybe at first there was some element of that, but it hasn't been that way for a while."

The night was dark all around them. She could see in the light cast from the patio that his expression was patient, even as water streamed down his face, but his eyes revealed his uncertainty. "What am I then? To you."

No going back now. She couldn't let this sweet man think she was only using him to get over Hector. Especially since he'd just said he loved her. Taking a deep breath, she blinked the raindrops out of her eyes and told him the truth.

And it was surprisingly easy.

"Roman, when I'm with you, it's the only time I can fully be myself. The only time I feel free. You're not a coping mechanism, you're . . ."

Everything I was too scared to want, she thought, but she couldn't say that.

"You're my safe space when the stress of being perfect

threatens to break me. You're my reminder that I'm allowed to want things, just for me, regardless of what anyone else thinks. You show me what it's like to live boldly, to have fun, to let myself take up space." She flicked the ends of her sodden curls where they dripped cool rainwater down her shoulders and back. "With you, I can literally get my hair wet. I can't think of a more fitting metaphor than that."

He wound a lock of her hair around his index finger. "Explain it to me, profe. What does this metaphor mean?"

"It means I trust you." She took a step closer, pressing their wet bodies and clammy clothes together. "It means you're not helping me cope—you're giving me room to *heal*."

Not just from the divorce, she realized. He was helping her heal damage that had been part of her makeup well before Hector had ever entered the picture. But that was too much to face right now, so she filed it away to think about later.

Roman's expression was heartbreakingly tender as he lifted a hand and stroked her cheek. "Then why are you so adamant about ending this?"

She closed her eyes and leaned into his touch. "I don't want my family to ruin it."

"Is that what happened before?"

She sighed. "In my family, everyone is all up in your business. Nobody gets to have secrets." Opening her eyes, she met his gaze with a silent entreaty. "With you, I wanted something, *someone*, who was mine. Who didn't belong to all of them. Do you understand?"

"I do."

She let out a shaky breath. "Good."

And then she threw her arms around his neck and kissed him.

Chapter 33

Roman filled his hands with Ava as she captured his mouth in a hot, soul-twisting kiss. Their tongues moved together in a perfect rhythm, sliding and tangling in fierce caresses. She tasted crisp and sweet, a heady combination of fruity wine and raindrops. He couldn't get enough.

She was his mermaid, his sirena, a watery seductress who'd stolen his heart.

While Roman hadn't started dinner with the intention of professing his love for her, the setting had been too romantic to resist. He'd never imagined feeding someone could be so fucking sexy and so intimate at the same time. The moment had seemed right, and like he'd told her, he wasn't the type to hide how he felt. For what? Fear that she wouldn't return the words to him? That wasn't why he'd said them. From the beginning, he'd put all his cards on the table where Ava was concerned. He wouldn't hide this realization from her either.

He hadn't expected her to reciprocate—he knew it was too soon for her, that she'd need to examine her feelings from twelve different angles before coming to any sort of conclusion—but at least there would be no doubt in her mind regarding how he felt about her. He wouldn't give her any more reasons to put space between them than she already had.

What she'd given him instead was more than he could have dared hope for.

I trust you.

Her trust, a fragile, precious thing, given cautiously by someone who'd been hurt in the past. He'd wanted to drop to his knees and vow to prove himself worthy of this gift, but not every moment needed a grand gesture. He was learning the value in simply being present.

"I'm tired of fighting this," Ava murmured against his lips. "I want you. All of you. All to myself."

His voice came out rough with desire. "*Then take me.*"

She nipped his lower lip and gave him a seductive smile. "Oh, I will. But like you said, we're too old to fuck on concrete, so get that sweet ass of yours over to that bed."

She punctuated the words by pinching his butt through his wet shorts.

"Sí, señora." A hot spike of arousal zipped through him at hearing her paraphrase what he'd said to her that first night, and he let her hustle him back under the patio overhang. Once again, they fell onto a bed together soaking wet, but this time, Ava was the aggressor.

And he was more than happy to let her take the lead.

She shoved him down into the cushions and climbed on top of him, continuing the kiss they'd started in the rain. Pressed together, her thighs were warm on his lap, and he needed to feel more of her heat. Thrusting his hands under her dress, he pushed the skirt up, running his palms up her thick, gorgeous thighs. When he reached her butt and nothing impeded the slide of bare, wet skin, he rounded his hands over her cheeks, searching.

Nothing there.

He pulled back to find her gazing at him with a soft, knowing expression.

"You're not wearing any fucking panties," he ground out. Her kiss-ripened lips curved as she shook her head. His fingers dug into the flesh of her bare bottom as he growled. "*Fuck*."

With something like a laugh, she reared back and wrangled the dress upward. The wet fabric clung, so he helped her pull it over her head. The garment landed on the patio floor with a splat and then she was completely, gloriously naked, save for the necklace with her name on it. Soft yellow light gilded the curves of her body, sparkled in her dripping hair, and caressed the outline of her cheekbone.

His chest swelled with love. Around them, the rain fell in sheets, sending a cooler breeze through the patio and making a heavy pattering sound on the roof and the pool. Thunder rumbled in the distance. The muffled noise and the thick foliage surrounding the yard made it feel like they were the last two people on earth, completely alone, free to enjoy each other's bodies without judgment or shame. His hands slid up her torso to thumb her small, tight brown nipples.

"Mi sirena." Awe made his throat tight. "Mi diosa."

But she shook her head at the endearments. "Just Ava," she breathed. "And just Roman."

He nodded, massaging the warm weight of her breasts as she undid all the buttons on his shirt. He sat up so she could peel it off him, and it landed on the floor next to her dress. When he reached for her, she surprised him by shaking her head again and circling his wrists with her fingers.

"My turn," she said, stretching his arms over his head and guiding his hands to the wicker rim of the daybed. "Hold on and don't let go until I tell you."

His pulse beat thickly in his throat and he didn't ask for explanation. He understood—this was her showing that she trusted him. For someone else, trust might look like giving up control. But for Ava, being the one to initiate, to unleash her desire without hesitation, was the deepest form of trust she could give him. She wasn't holding back. She was letting him see her as the strong, beautiful, sensuous woman she was, and trusting him not to judge her, laugh at her, or make her feel ashamed for what she wanted.

As if he ever would.

He gripped the wicker bar so tight it creaked. "Anything you want, mi amor."

She gently pinched his lower lip between her thumb and forefinger. "I want . . . this mouth."

Her kiss was deep and thorough, sucking his tongue and nipping his lips. He groaned into the cavern of her mouth and thrust his hips up to grind against her, but she was already moving away.

"And I want this skin," she said next, trailing her teeth down the taut line of his neck to suck at the base of his throat. She dragged her mouth downward to lick and tease his nipples, making him gasp. In the center of his chest, she pressed a kiss over his sternum, her lips lingering long enough that he imagined the accompanying words: *I want this heart*. This soft, simple kiss seemed to acknowledge that she knew it was already hers. Something inside him melted at the thought, but then she was continuing down his abdomen, kissing his skin until she was stopped by the waistband of his shorts. His muscles quivered but he didn't move his hands.

She wrestled the fastenings open and he lifted his hips to help her push his sodden shorts and boxers down. And just like that, they were both naked.

Ava sat astride his thighs and gazed down at him like he was good enough to eat.

"And . . ." she breathed, "I want . . . this cock."

He groaned as she wrapped her hand around the base of him and gave a few idle pumps.

"You know," she said conversationally, "I've been wanting to do this since I first saw you climb out of that pool."

Words were hard. *He* was hard. He gritted his teeth and held on to the edge of the bed for all he was worth. "You have?"

"Mmm." She trailed her fingers up and down his length and he swallowed back a shout. "But you're always too busy going down on me, so I never get to."

"Fuck." He slammed his head back into the cushions when her lips closed over the head of his dick. "I won't apologize. I fucking love eating your pussy."

"You're so good at it too," she purred, nuzzling his groin. Slowly, she lowered her mouth onto him, taking him deep.

Roman bit back a curse and slid his fingers into the damp hair at the nape of her neck. "Sí, mi vida. Just like that."

She lifted her head and gave him a stern glare. "Hands."

"Oh, shit. Sorry." He grabbed the bar behind his head. "Don't stop."

"Say please."

Fuck, why was that so hot? "*Por favor,*" he begged.

Her glare melted and she looked like she was trying not to smile. "Very good. Now let me focus."

Roman lost track of time, place, everything but Ava's hot mouth moving up and down his length. He threw his head back and closed his eyes, reveling in the pull of her lips and the slide of her tongue. But he needed to imprint every sensory detail of this moment in his memory, so he opened his eyes, but the visual combined with the slick caress of her mouth threatened to overwhelm him.

"That's enough, mi amor," he whispered, his voice hoarse. "I'm too close. Ava—god. Fuck. Esperate."

He was bucking his hips and thrusting into her throat when she finally lifted her head. Her full lips were shiny and slick, swollen from her ministrations, and she looked eminently pleased with herself.

His lungs heaved like a bellows as he struggled to catch his breath. "That was incredible," he said, panting.

"And you'll let me do it whenever I want?"

"Anytime. Anywhere."

Her mouth curved. "All right, since you've been such a good boy . . ."

She climbed up his body while he muttered filthy things about how good he'd be if she would just *sit on his fucking face*, and then she was clasping the edge of the bed on either side of his hands and lowering herself to his mouth. He inhaled the scent of her and stretched his neck, licking and sucking until she came, shuddering, and his face was drenched again, this time with a combination of his saliva and her juices.

When she eased back, her breath was ragged, her cheeks and neck flushed, and her gaze bleary. She'd never looked more beautiful to him.

"Good boy," she said unevenly, patting his cheek, and he turned his head into her touch. He'd never thought he'd be into this kink, but it was really fucking doing it for him.

Ava slid back down his body, kissing him as she settled onto his lap. He delved his tongue between her lips, fucking her mouth like he wanted to fuck her with his body, before pulling back.

"You taste yourself on me?" he rasped. When she nodded, he said, "One of these days, I'm going to taste myself on you."

He could tell that surprised her, but from the way her lips parted and her eyelids lowered, she liked the idea.

Good. For all her talk of barriers, she'd soon find out he had not a single one where she was concerned.

With a rough exhale, she slid her wet folds over his cock, making them both groan. He muttered obscenities in English and Spanish as she reached between them, angling his dick upward, but he didn't release his grip on the wicker rim. Not even when she notched him against her slit and sank down.

As her slick warmth enveloped him, he stuttered out an oath that came from the depths of his being. Even though she was wet, it was a tight fit, and she had to work herself onto him. By the time she was fully seated, he was beside himself, nearly mindless with need, sweating and panting and cursing a blue streak.

But his hands remained firmly fixed where she'd placed them, and he did not let go.

In that moment, Roman's life was complete. There was not a single other thing he wanted in this world other than this woman, this connection, for the rest of his days.

I love you, he thought, gazing into her eyes. *I love you so fucking much, it's killing me not to say it.*

Her hands stroked over his hair, his shoulders, his chest in soothing movements, almost like she was petting him, almost like she *knew* he wanted to tell her.

And then she planted her hands on his stomach and began to move.

She rocked on top of him, first keeping a slow and steady rhythm, then faster and more frantic as Roman rolled his hips to fuck upward into her. With a sobbing gasp, her nails dug into his skin, and then she reared back. Her hand snaked up his chest and she slid her fingertips into his mouth. He moaned as he sucked them, scraping the sensitive pads with his teeth, swirling his tongue over the edges of her neatly manicured nails. Her eyes were dazed with lust as she brought her hand, now wet with his saliva, to her clit. Praise fell from her lips—he was such a good boy, he fucked her so good, just like that, *perfect*—and he responded with his own endearments—his goddess, his life, his love, his *Ava*.

She touched herself as she rode him, and with her other hand, she pinched and twisted her own nipples. Desire suffused her features and flushed her cheeks red, and he thought she'd never looked more magnificent, more powerful, than she was like this, taking her pleasure and trusting him to let her.

When her inner walls fluttered around him, he clenched his jaw to hold back his own orgasm and thrust into her—harder, faster, *now*—and then she was crying out, shuddering on top of him, her lashes falling to cover her clouded hazel gaze.

Her hips slowed and she braced her wobbly arms on his chest, holding herself up. Her curls fell over her shoulders and around her face as she hung her head, trying to catch her breath.

He felt her pulsing around him and though he didn't touch her, he begged.

"Ava, *por favor*," he pleaded. "Let me touch you. Please, my love, I need to, I need . . ."

He trailed off when she raised her head. She always looked a little disoriented after she came hard, and while the sight of her blank, blinking eyes filled him with pride, he was wound too tight to wait any longer.

She stroked her fingers—the ones that had just been rubbing her clit—down his cheek. "You'll be good?"

"So fucking good," he promised.

She touched his hands where they were white-knuckled on the bed. "All right," she said softly. "You can let go."

And he fucking did.

Grabbing her ass, he rolled them into the mountain of cushions. Her strong thighs locked around his hips as he rose up over her. This time, when he gripped the back of the bed, it was for leverage. Gazing down at her, he thought, *I love you.* And then he began to pound.

There was no finesse, no rhythm, no checking in. There was just heat and sweat and grunting—him—and cries of pleasure—her. There was the bite of her nails digging into the flesh of his ass, the bruising press of her heels on the backs of his thighs, the sweet friction of her channel clenching around him.

Through it all, her gaze remained locked on his.

He was lost, utterly fucking lost over this woman. Love for her overwhelmed him, spiraling with the fierce arousal pumping through his veins, magnifying this experience to something he'd never imagined.

But he couldn't do this alone. Not without her. Never again without her.

He stuck his hand between them, working it between their damp, heated bodies, and found her clit with his thumb. Her mouth fell open and her lashes fluttered as he stroked her, inside and out.

"Come with me, mi amor," he panted, begged, demanded. "Don't leave me alone."

The words didn't make sense but she nodded anyway. Her hands dove into his hair, clutching it in fistfuls, as she brought their mouths together. She moaned into their kiss with each of his thrusts. He knew her sounds as surely as the familiar rhythm of his own heartbeat, and he knew when she was close. He sped up his touch, deepened his strokes, and let go of the reins on his own control.

When she shattered, so did he.

The orgasm shot through him, leaving him as devastated and wrecked as if it had been a lightning bolt from the storm raging around them.

Harsh breaths sawed in and out of his lungs. He dropped his head onto her shoulder and her arms wound around his back. Seconds ticked by, and she held him while his heart rate returned to something closer to normal.

"I meant what I said earlier," he said into her neck. It was perhaps slightly unfair to bring this up when he was literally still inside her, but he needed her to know.

Her breasts pressed against him as she inhaled. "I know you did."

He rolled her on top of him so he wasn't crushing her, and so he could see her face. "I don't want this to end, Ava."

Her expression was soft, and she brushed his hair back from his forehead. "I need to think about it, but . . . you mean a lot to me, Roman. More than I wanted you to, if I'm being honest."

He thought back to their first encounter. "I didn't expect this either."

She placed a hand flat on his chest, as if seeking his heartbeat. "You feel safe. It's my own feelings that don't."

His heart squeezed, thinking of how much she'd been hurt. She felt safe with him. She trusted him. It was enough, for now. But, greedy bastard that he was, he always wanted more.

"Sleep in my room tonight," he said.

There was a fifty-fifty chance she'd say no, but she nodded. "Okay."

But then she lifted her head and looked around, as if noticing their surroundings for the first time. "How do we—"

"Oscar's gone," he told her. "The house is empty. And there are towels in that chest in the corner."

She ducked her head, hiding a smile. "You know me so well."

Not as much as I want to, he thought. But what they'd shared tonight was a start. The start of the rest of everything.

Assuming she didn't hightail it to the airport in the middle of the night.

Chapter 34

Ava did not, in fact, run away in the middle of the night, but she couldn't blame Roman for being worried. Instead, she slept with him in his room upstairs, and the next morning, she woke him with a kiss, which led to more.

By the time they left to finish the last of the wedding tasks, she was floating on a cloud of bliss. And now that they'd figured out each other's patterns, they got through the meetings with minimal fuss.

From there, they spent the rest of the day at the resort spa, getting massages and facials. After dinner and a quick swim in the pool, Roman shuttled her off for another "surprise," which turned out to be the bioluminescent bay in Fajardo.

Ava had been kayaking exactly once in her life and wasn't a fan, and she was even less excited about the possibility of large aquatic animals swallowing her whole out of a dark, neon-accented abyss. But New Ava embraced new experiences, right? So she'd gone. Then, when she'd been very close to a panic attack, Roman had sidled his kayak as close to hers as he could and whispered the filthiest dirty talk she'd ever heard. Miraculously, it calmed her down to the point where she could actually enjoy herself. After they returned, exhausted but exhilarated, Ava was more than happy to curl up in Roman's arms.

"This was the best day ever," he whispered to her before he fell asleep.

"For me too," she murmured into the darkness. She expected the admission to scare her, and it did, but only a little.

She slept like a rock, but the next day, she woke up with a ball of dread sitting low in her gut. Their private island getaway was coming to an end and they were returning to New York in a few short hours.

Ava didn't want to leave. Once they got home, she'd have to go back to being Old Ava, the pathologically helpful middle-school teacher who wasn't involved with a handsome hotelier who was sweet, thoughtful, charming, and sexy as hell.

She'd have to go back to a world where Roman wasn't hers and hers alone.

With a deep sigh, she shoved down her worry. She refused to spend her last few hours of vacation feeling depressed. Besides, something smelled really good, so she sat up in bed to investigate. Blinking in the muted sunlight filtering through the filmy curtains, she rubbed her eyes and peered around the room.

"What's all this?"

A massive floral arrangement took up the nightstand on her side. Red gingers, orange lobster claws, and yellow orchids exploded from a base of palm, monstera, and philodendron leaves. At the foot of the bed sat a tray laden with food. Ava breathed in the mouth-watering trifecta of bacon, maple syrup, and orange juice.

At the sound of her voice, Roman looked up from where he sat in a plush armchair. Their eyes met, and his face broke into a wide smile. Setting down his tablet, he padded over to her in nothing but his boxers.

"Buenos días, mi amor." He dropped a kiss to her forehead, then handed her a hot cup of coffee.

She accepted it and took a small sip. "Mmm, thanks. Good morning to you too. Did you do all this while I was asleep?"

"I wanted to surprise you." He gestured at the table. "Help yourself to breakfast. I'm checking in with Camille. If I re-arrange a few things, we can stay an extra couple of days."

Ava hadn't met Roman's assistant, but Roman spoke highly of her organizational skills, something Ava could appreciate. He'd said Camille was handling things in his absence, but when he'd briefly turned his phone on the day before, he'd been in-undated with missed texts, emails, and voicemails. Rearranging "a few things" would mean a logistical nightmare for Camille, so Ava put a hand on Roman's arm before he could continue.

"We should head back," she said. "You're busy, and I didn't clear out my fridge."

It was the best she could come up with before the caffeine kicked in. As much as Ava didn't want this to end, she knew Roman had more important things to do than get massages and go swimming with her.

That sarcastic little voice in the back of her head whispered, *You just can't let yourself have too much of a good thing, can you?*

Ava kindly told that little voice to mind its own business.

Roman studied her face for a moment, like he knew the fridge thing was an excuse. But all he said was, "All right."

Ava set aside the coffee and resolved to make the time they had left memorable. She gave Roman's arm a tug, catching him off guard and toppling him onto the bed with her.

"We still have a few hours before we have to leave," she said, climbing on top of him to straddle his thighs. The sheet fell away, leaving her naked, the only thing between them the silk of his boxers.

The way he smiled up at her made her heart squeeze. His sweet brown eyes filled with tenderness, and . . . shit, maybe that was love. It had been so long since she'd seen it. She hoped she was reflecting something similar back at him. Not love yet, but . . . something.

He cupped the back of her head and pulled her down for a kiss, sending her thoughts scattering. She made no attempts to reel them back.

By the time they sat down to eat, the food was cold, but neither of them cared.

On the plane, while Roman was on the phone with a senator explaining Puerto Rico's real estate crisis and the political corruption surrounding the electrical grid system, Ava listened with one ear and tried to lose herself in the crochet project she'd brought. But making a blanket for a coworker's baby shower just wasn't holding her attention. Even as her fingers worked the hook, guilt ate at her.

Why did the thought of returning home, back into her family's orbit, fill her with trepidation? She loved them. She would do anything for them.

Except tell them about Roman.

Setting aside the yarn, she pulled out her personal planner and flipped to a section in the back that she used for journaling. Riffling through her pencil case, she selected a fountain pen with purple ink and began to write.

At the top of a clean page, she wrote, *What will happen if I tell my family about Roman?*

And then she made a bullet list.

The "What Will Happen?" game was a tool Colleen had given Ava for when her anxiety threatened to get the better of her. Instead of spiraling out, her therapist had directed Ava to actually ask and answer the question that plagued her.

For the first point, Ava wrote, *They'll tease me.*

Teasing was a fact of life in the Rodriguez family. At first it would start with a wink wink nudge nudge *Ava tienes un novio* level of teasing, like she was sixteen. But after that, the helpful "reminders" would start.

Remember what happened with Hector, they'd warn. *Do you really want to go through that again?*

She knew, because they'd done it to her mother when Patricia had dared to go on dates after breaking up with Ava's father, even though it had been an amicable split and years had passed. *Remember what happened with Miguel,* they'd said.

Of course, no one said anything to Ava's father when he started bringing Olympia to family gatherings. And when Tio Luisito divorced his wife and married a man, everyone fell over themselves to congratulate him, and not a single person had said *Remember what happened with Helen.*

None of the women were allowed to forget their mistakes, and god forbid they moved on from the wrong man. Internalized misogyny was a real beast.

On the next line, she wrote, *When it's over, they'll make my life hell.*

If she'd learned anything from her experiences, it was that true love wasn't forever, at least not for her.

Hector had loved her. Hector had made promises, spoken vows. And then he'd changed his mind.

Things were great with Roman now, but they hadn't yet been

subjected to any of the stressors of real life. Something would inevitably come along and burst the bubble. It might happen tomorrow, it might happen in two months, it might happen in two years. But it *would* happen.

And when it was over, her family would trot out, *Remember what happened with Hector?* Like she was a fool for daring to believe she could be happy again.

Something startlingly close to anger simmered in her veins. All of this would have been fine if Roman weren't in the wedding. But because he was, her whole family knew him now, and by the time the ceremony and reception were over, they'd feel a claim on him.

Her family and Hector's had been so entwined in their lives, disentangling those threads had been as hard on her as the separation itself.

Roman was everything she could ever ask for in a man, and she wanted him all to herself. But he wasn't just hers. He was Ashton's, too.

Which brought up the question of what this would do to her relationship with Jasmine.

Fighting the sudden tension in her limbs, she forced herself to write, *It'll make things awkward with Jasmine.*

She could just picture it. When this thing between them had run its course, Jasmine and Ashton would have to decide which of them to invite to events. Or worse, Ava and Roman would have to pretend everything was fine. And maybe he would be fine. He probably had a lot more experience with this sort of thing. But Ava knew she wouldn't be. God, just look how she'd reacted to running into Hector. Something told her it would be even worse with Roman.

Ava knew she should tell Jasmine about Roman, but she couldn't suppress the anxiety that cropped up every time she thought about telling anyone but Damaris.

Oh, shit. *Damaris.*

Ava turned her phone on and gasped at the number of text messages. Nowhere near as many as Roman had been inundated with the day before, but damn. There were messages from the Primas of Power and the Wedding Flashers group texts, from her mother, her grandparents, her stepmother, her sister, from the group text she had with a bunch of Alliance teachers, and even one from Hector's sister. And of course, a series of texts from Damaris, spanning the past couple days. Ava opened those first.

Damaris: How's Puerto Rico?

Do you have phone service?

I hope you're not dead.

Text me if you're dead.

Fuck, please don't be dead.

If you don't reply by this afternoon, I'm filing a missing persons report.

I'm serious, by the way.

The last text had been sent two hours earlier. Ava scrambled to reply.

Ava: I'm here! Not dead.
Sorry to worry you.

Damaris: Well, shit. What happened to checking in when you're with Roman? I know he's your cousin's fiancé's best friend but I'm the only one who knows you two are 🐍🍑

Ava: Ew. And I'm sorry. I'll explain later. We had our phones off. I'm on the plane back to New York now.

Damaris: You can buy me brunch tomorrow to make up for the near heart attack.

Ava: Absolutely. See you then.

Ava shot off a quick text to her mom letting Patricia know she would be home soon, then because her strong sense of responsibility wouldn't let her ignore them, Ava began to skim through the other messages.

Willow: HELP Mom is driving me CRAZY

Olympia: This child will be the end of me. Can you talk to her?

Dad: look i got a new grill

Abuela: Ayúdame a cocinar pernil este fin de semana OK   ?

Ronnie: Hi A! Can you babysit Friday night? 7pm. Thanks!

Michelle: Don't you dare babysit for Ronnie. She never pays you!

"Pretty handy that you already have your travel size bottles with you," Roman said, breaking into her thoughts before she'd managed to catch up on all the texts she'd missed.

"What?" Ava glanced over and saw he was done with his call.

"All your hair stuff," he said. "You can leave it at my place."

She blinked, not following. "What do you mean?"

"When we get home," he said, throwing around the word like it was the most natural thing in the world. "Feel free to put things anywhere in the bedroom and bathroom."

Home. He was talking about *his* home, about making space for her there.

Ava's heart rate sped up. This was going way too fast. Even as one small part of her thrilled at the idea—she had loved sharing a room with him—most of her was terrified.

She had a flash of moving into the "guest room" at her father's new house, because even though she'd spent every weekend with him, she'd never had her own room. Not even when she lived there full time at the end of high school to help with Willow.

"Don't your mother and sister live with you?" she asked,

trying to bring him back down to earth with the reminder that they didn't exist in a bubble like they had in Puerto Rico.

He sent her an indulgent smile. "I'm forty-one, not fourteen. You can be there. I don't need to sneak you in."

Ava thought about Michelle, who had been sneaking Gabe in and out of Titi Val and Uncle Dom's house the year before. *And they got caught.*

"Still, we should keep this quiet for now," she said. "We shouldn't tell anyone else yet."

His smile dimmed, and his eyes cut away from hers for a second. "About that . . ."

Her pulse thumped even harder. "Yes?"

"Um, Ashton knows."

Ava stopped breathing. "He knows what?"

Roman gave an apologetic shrug. "I had already told him about you, and then at the engagement party . . . Long story short, he figured it out."

Ava covered her face. "Oh my god."

This was her nightmare. Already, this whole thing was unraveling. How the hell had her simple fling become so damned *complicated*? Because if Ashton knew, it was only a matter of time until Jasmine did. And if Jasmine found out before Ava could tell her herself . . .

It would be Michelle and Gabe all over again, and Jas would be *furious.*

Fuck. She had to tell her primas. But when?

"Don't you have a friend who knows about us?" Roman asked.

"One." She held up a finger. "I have *one* friend who knows about you, and that was only in the event you turned out to be a serial killer. She has no connection to my family. *Unlike Ashton.*"

Roman's lips quirked.

"Do not laugh," she growled.

"Sorry." He coughed, probably to hide a chuckle. "Aren't you glad I'm not a serial killer?"

"This isn't funny!"

"You're right. It's not." He schooled his features into a mock frown.

"I'm serious. No one in my family can know."

No one else, she thought, since Ashton was technically one month away from becoming her cousin-in-law, if that was even a real thing.

Roman moved to the seat closer to her so he could take her hand. "Will it make you feel better if we don't tell anyone until after the wedding?"

Ava took a deep breath and let it out slowly. "Yes. I think so."

"Then that's what we'll do." He paused. "Except for my mother and sister. I want you to meet them. I would've introduced you to my aunt and cousins while we were in Bayamón, but my mother would've killed me if her sister got to meet you first."

Compromise. This was a compromise. She could do that. Even if, in the back of her mind, a little voice whispered, *This is how it starts.*

Memories flashed through her mind, of helping Hector's mom pick out a new sofa, of being a bridesmaid in his sister's wedding, of reading picture books to his niece.

Why did romantic relationships have to involve other people?

It would be okay. She could meet Roman's family. There

was a big gap between saying hello and helping his mom reno-vate her house.

"All right," she said, because Roman was clearly waiting for an answer. "But not today. I'm really tired, and I'd just like to go home."

He studied her face for a moment, then leaned in to press a soft kiss to her lips. "Anything you want, mi vida."

My life, he called her. God, what was she getting herself into?

Chapter 35

One Month Until the Wedding

All right." Ashton gestured with his hand. "Díme. What happened while you were in Puerto Rico with Ava?"

They were in Roman's living room sipping rum negronis. Ashton had come back to New York from Vancouver before Jasmine because Yadiel was going to spend a week attending a computer camp in Westchester. At the moment, Yadiel was in the TV room playing video games with Mikayla.

Roman opened his mouth to answer, then broke into a wide smile.

Ashton narrowed his eyes. "What does that smile mean?"

Roman touched his cheek. Yup, he was grinning like a fool. "It means . . . I love her."

Ashton dragged a hand down his face. "Ay Diós mío."

"I really do, man."

"Didn't you two just meet a few months ago?"

"We met in October."

Ashton blinked in surprise. "I didn't realize it had been that long."

"I only told you about it once it . . . progressed."

"Progressed to what?"

"Feelings?"

Ashton reached for his drink. "Jasmine is going to murder me."

Roman grimaced. "It gets worse."

"How could it?"

"Ava knows that you know."

"Coño. How did she react?"

"Let's just say she's not thrilled about it."

Ashton grunted. "I bet."

"She doesn't want anyone else to know about us until after your wedding."

"Of course she doesn't." Ashton leaned forward, his expression serious. "Let me explain something. It was a *thing* when Jasmine moved to Los Angeles. It was a *thing* when Michelle quit her job. But it was the biggest *thing* of all when Ava got divorced from that pendejo. Now, I've heard about all this secondhand, but you need to understand where she's coming from."

Roman mulled that over. "She told me about her family's reaction to the divorce."

"Then you know why she wouldn't want to introduce anyone to them again. And now that they already know you . . ."

"I mean, I get it, but . . ."

But he wanted to tell everyone. He wanted to buy a fucking billboard in Times Square.

"Mira. Jasmine moved across the country to escape. Michelle, she's like a cactus or . . . ¿Cómo se dice *puercoespín* en ingles?"

"Porcupine," came Yadiel's voice from behind them.

They both turned to see the boy rounding the sofa.

Ashton sighed. "What have I told you about eavesdropping?" To Roman, he added in an undertone, "It's been a problem lately."

"I heard that." Yadiel grabbed a handful of cashews from the tray in front of them. "And I wasn't. I just *overheard*."

"A technicality," Ashton muttered. "¿Qué pasó?"

"Nothing, I'm just hungry."

"Don't you and Mikayla have a ton of snacks?" Ashton asked.

Yadiel shrugged. "I don't want those snacks."

"Help yourself to anything in the kitchen," Roman told him.

Yadiel's dark eyes lit up. "*Anything?*"

"Sure," Roman said, missing Ashton's look of alarm until it was too late.

Yadiel whooped and raced toward the kitchen, clearly excited by the thought of unfettered access to Roman's pantry and fridge.

"No alcohol and no caffeine!" Ashton called after him. When Roman sent him a quizzical stare, the other man shrugged. "We're in a boundary-pushing phase."

Roman made a noncommittal hum and sipped his drink. There was that word that Ava liked so much: *boundaries*. Maybe Roman was in a boundary-pushing phase too, because he didn't want any barriers between them.

Their time in Puerto Rico had been perfect. Okay, maybe not the first day, but afterward. He didn't see why they couldn't have that at home.

And yet, he could already feel her putting distance between them. It had started during the flight back, and while she was responsive when he called and texted, he hadn't seen her as often as he'd wanted. Granted, he'd been extra busy making up for the time he'd been away, but he couldn't help wishing she were here waiting for him when he dragged himself home in the evenings.

She was finally coming over tonight to meet his mother and sister, after weeks of making excuses.

"Anyway," Ashton said. "My point was, Ava's family is very important to her. She always puts them first, even over herself."

Which meant she wouldn't put Roman over her family. "Got it."

Ashton's expression was still troubled. "I'm just saying, if she won't even tell las primas poderosas . . ."

"Then she's never going to tell the rest of them," Roman finished.

"I don't like being in the middle of this," Ashton went on. "You're the closest thing I have to a brother, and Ava has become like a sister to me. And you both have me *keeping secrets from my wife*."

"You kept that kid in my kitchen a secret from everyone—including me, I might add—for years. This should be easy for you."

"It's not the same." Ashton sent him a dark look. "And it's not a matter of *if* Jasmine finds out, it's when. And *when* she finds out that I knew about you two, estoy jodido."

They would all be fucked if Jasmine found out. Roman had known her long enough to understand that, at least.

"I just don't get why Ava won't tell her cousins. Her parents and everyone else, sure. But why not Jasmine and Michelle? They seem supportive."

Ashton shrugged. "The three of them are weird about relationships. When Jasmine and I got together, Jasmine didn't tell Ava. And when Michelle started seeing Gabe, she didn't tell Jasmine. I don't try to understand it."

"Ava seems to believe that her family will mess things up with us if they know."

"Maybe. They're very . . ." Ashton frowned as he searched for the word. "*Involved*. And they treat Ava like she's Cenicienta."

Roman searched his brain for the English translation. "Cinderella?"

"Sí, ella." He gestured with his glass. "She's always in the kitchen at parties. She gets there early to help and leaves late because she stays to clean up. I was going to tell Jasmine not to let Ava go to Puerto Rico for us, but then you jumped in and I didn't want to cockblock you, even though I have a sneaking suspicion you're going to ruin my wedding."

"I agree that Ava's taking the maid of honor role too seriously. And I'm not going to ruin your wedding."

"So you say." Ashton's tone clearly conveyed his skepticism. "But if you or Ava don't tell Jasmine what's going on with you two, I'm telling her. You have until the wedding ceremony. I'm not going to speak my vows knowing I'm hiding something from my wife."

"That's fair," Roman grunted. It was at odds with the promise he'd made Ava about waiting until after the wedding, but Ashton had a point, and Roman was anxious for Ava to stop treating their relationship like a dirty little secret.

Ashton gave Roman's knee a swat then rose to his feet. "Vámanos. We need to make sure my son isn't lying on your kitchen floor in a sugar coma."

Roman set down his glass and followed Ashton to the kitchen, reviewing everything his friend had told him.

Ava's fears weren't unfounded, and the likelihood of her deciding to tell her family about their relationship was slim. So what did that mean for their future together? Did they even have one? She couldn't keep him a secret forever, could she?

He was afraid the answer was yes.

Chapter 36

Was it normal to hope your boyfriend's family *didn't* like you? Because that was Ava's mindset on her way to meet Roman's mother and sister.

She'd put it off as long as she could, and had gone so far as letting Roman come to her apartment in order to avoid going to his. They'd spent an amazing weekend together, ensconced in their own little slice of paradise, but it was unexpectedly shattered when Ava got a text from Willow that she and Olympia were driving through Ava's neighborhood and would be stopping by momentarily. Ava had leapt out of bed and hustled Roman out the door. She'd barely finished putting the apartment to rights by the time they showed up. Roman hadn't been thrilled about being kicked out, and in the chaos he'd extracted a promise: Ava would have dinner with his family before the week was out.

And here she was. The car Roman had sent dropped her off at his building, and the doorman sent her right up in the elevator, since Roman had already given her the code.

The elevator doors opened, but instead of Roman standing there waiting for her, it was Ashton.

Ava's blood turned to ice at the sight of him. Ashton clearly wasn't expecting her either, since his eyes widened and he backed up a step. He recovered first and moved forward to greet her.

"Ava. ¿Cómo estás?" He leaned in to kiss her cheek, and Ava did the same.

"Hi Ashton. Welcome back." Her heart pounded in her throat. *Ashton knew.* And if he hadn't before, he certainly did now, because why else would Ava be showing up at Roman's home with an overnight bag?

Roman strode toward them with a big smile on his face. "You're early," he said, sounding delighted.

Of all the days not to run into traffic. Ava gave a little shrug. "So I am."

Ashton held up a phone with a cracked screen and a navy-blue Yankees case. "Yadi left his phone so I came back up to get it."

"Ah." Ava gave a little nod. "Can't forget that."

Ashton sighed. "He's obsessed with playing games on it. I'm worried about his thumbs."

"We should all be worried about our thumbs." Roman gave Ashton a one-armed hug and patted his back. "See you."

"Ciao."

Ava stepped out of the elevator so Ashton could take her place. She didn't miss the loaded glance he sent Roman's way, but Roman seemed immune or oblivious. The second the doors closed, Roman slipped an arm around Ava's waist and pulled her in for a toe-curling kiss.

One part of Ava worried that someone might see. But the rest of her responded enthusiastically, clinging to his shirt and opening her mouth for his tongue.

When Roman finally broke the kiss, Ava was lightheaded.

"Hi," she said, breathless.

"Hi yourself." Roman released her, but only to grab her hand and lead her farther into the apartment. "Mikayla can't wait to meet you. You don't even want to know what I had to bribe her with to keep her from ambushing you in the lobby."

"Oh?" Ava's throat dried up, and all the endorphins brought on by his kiss shriveled and died.

Roman paused, and after a look at her face, he squeezed her hand. "Don't worry. They're going to love you."

That's what I'm afraid of, Ava thought.

She'd spent so much of her life trying to make sure everyone *did* like her, it was strange to think about how to ensure someone *didn't.*

Just be cool, she told herself. *Aloof. Don't get in any deeper.*

But of course, the second she saw Mikayla, Ava broke into a wide grin. Who was she kidding? She couldn't stay aloof around a kid. Her teacher persona was too ingrained.

Ava knew the girl was eighteen, but Mikayla looked a few years younger, like she was going into her freshman year of high school instead of college.

"Ava!" Mikayla bounded over from the kitchen counter and threw her arms around Ava in a hug, like they were reuniting after many years apart instead of meeting for the first time.

Unable to stop herself, Ava hugged her back.

Roman's mother Dulce looked up from where she stirred something in a large sauté pan. Upon seeing Ava, Dulce set down the spoon.

"Hola, Ava. Es un placer." Dulce cupped Ava's shoulder and leaned in to kiss her cheek. "I'm so happy to finally meet you."

"Igualmente," Ava murmured, kissing the older woman's cheek. Dulce's skin was lighter than her daughter's but more tanned than her son's, and while neither of her children favored her much in coloring, looks, or build, they all had the same long-lashed brown eyes.

"It smells wonderful in here. Can I help with anything?" Ava asked Dulce. Roman had told her not to, but standing still while his mother cooked didn't sit right with her.

"You know how to make tostones?" the older woman asked.

Ava grinned. "Of course I know how to make tostones."

While Ava sliced, smashed, and fried the plantains in oil, she chatted easily with Dulce and Mikayla. It was clear they were close, and Ava was charmed by their easy manner.

"Do you like reading?" Ava asked Mikayla. As an English teacher, this was always her first question when meeting a younger person.

"Are you kidding?" Mikayla crunched on a tortilla chip from the bowl on the counter. "I'm a total bookworm."

Dulce handed Ava a glass of wine. "Mikayla makes costume plays of the characters too."

"It's called *cosplay*, Mom." Mikayla hoisted herself onto one of the bar stools lining the counter. "And yes, while the word technically comes from 'costume play,' that makes it sound like a weird sex thing."

Roman almost choked on his wine, but Dulce just laughed.

"No kink-shaming, ¿verdad?" Dulce smiled as she returned to the stove. "Besides, I don't know what you do on that phone of yours all day."

"Yes, you do," Mikayla grumbled. "You like and comment on *all* of my posts."

"I'm being supportive." Dulce sent Ava a wink.

Ava couldn't help it. She loved them already.

As they cooked, Ava chatted with Mikayla about books and

Broadway musicals. Mikayla, consulting a list on her phone, asked Ava approximately a million questions about herself, because, as she put it, "Ro's never brought a woman home before, and I can tell he really likes you."

"I *love* her," Roman said easily from where he whisked salad dressing.

Ava felt her face heat and she braced herself for his family's reaction to his declaration, but nobody acted like he'd said anything strange. Nobody laughed or teased them or made inappropriate jokes.

Eventually . . . Ava relaxed.

Roman listened, for the most part, interjecting comments here and there, enduring light teasing from his sister, and helping his mother when she asked him.

It was . . . normal, Ava thought. Just like her family. If anything, Ava felt more comfortable here because there wasn't years' worth of emotional baggage to trip over. She'd thought his family might be haughty, based on the luxury in which they lived. But they were warm and welcoming.

When Roman and Mikayla stepped away to set the dining table, Dulce sidled up next to Ava.

"¿Y tu familia?" she asked. She pursed her lips and jerked her chin to gesture toward Roman. "They've met him?"

Ava's hands stilled on the tomato she was chopping for the salad. "Ah . . . well, he knows Ashton and Jasmine, of course. And everyone else saw him at the engagement party."

Dulce's gaze turned shrewd. "They don't know you two are . . . dating?"

Dating. *Were* they dating? Shit, what else was this, if not dating?

Ava's back hunched. "Um . . . no."

"I see."

Dulce's knowing nod made Ava feel the need to explain herself. "They'll make it a big deal. That's just what they do. And I don't want . . . I'm not ashamed of him. He's amazing. You know that. But my family . . ."

She trailed off, not knowing how to describe them without sounding like she was complaining. But Dulce nodded like she understood.

"Yo entiendo. Family pressure can be hard on a new relationship."

Ava's shoulders slumped in relief. "Yes. Exactly."

"You'll know when you're ready. And don't let that one"— she gestured at Roman with the wooden spoon—"rush you. He jumps into things. It's worked very well for him in business, because he's always a million miles ahead of everyone else. But you? This is new for him."

Ava swallowed hard. "Okay."

But inside, she wasn't sure she'd ever be ready. As easy as it felt being with Roman's mother and sister, when she tried to imagine bringing him to dinner at her father's house, or worse, to a giant family gathering, just the thought made her feel sick.

When the food was done, they carried everything to the dining table. In addition to the tostones, there was juicy roast chicken, rosemary garlic potatoes, and ratatouille con chorizo. Roman sat across from Ava, and Mikayla sat next to her. Dulce took the seat across from her daughter.

"We don't usually eat here," Mikayla explained. "But tonight's special, since you're here."

"Now who has no chill?" Roman said mildly, raising his eyebrows at his sister.

Mikayla shrugged. "Seemed like you needed a wingwoman."

Roman met Ava's eyes and his held a spark of humor. "For the record, I did not ask her to do this."

Ava smiled down at her plate and had the sudden urge to introduce Roman to Willow. Would he get along with Willow as easily as Mikayla seemed to be getting on with her? Was there a universe where Mikayla and Willow could meet without involving anyone else? Willow could keep a secret better than most of the Rodriguezes, but it was unethical for Ava to ask her teenage sister to do that.

For the first time, Ava began to consider what she might be missing by keeping Roman hidden.

Conversation turned to Mikayla's impending freshman year at Yale, which led to the topic of Dulce's move to a new apartment.

"It's not too late to change your mind," Roman was saying. "You can stay here, either indefinitely or until you find something more suited to your needs."

"My needs?" Dulce gave him an indulgent smile. "It's a four-bedroom duplex with natural light in a doorman building. What more could I need?"

"The bedrooms are small. I'm sure we could find something better."

"We used to live in the projects. Trust me, the apartment is *fine*."

"You deserve better than fine," Roman insisted. "I'm just worried. That's all."

"Because I'm such a viejita?" Dulce's eyes, so like her children's, twinkled at Roman over the rim of her wine glass. "Is that it? You think I'm too old to live on my own?"

Roman's lips curved. "I know better than to answer that."

"Then what are you scared of?"

Roman raised his hands, then let them fall. "I just want to protect you."

"And you feel like you can't do that if I'm not here."

He nodded, and the compassion in Dulce's gaze made Ava's heart squeeze.

Dulce reached over and clasped Roman's hand. "You can't control everything. When is it going to be enough?"

One corner of his mouth lifted. "Never?"

Ava watched their body language. Roman sat with his forearms resting on the table. Dulce leaned back in her seat, her posture relaxed, sipping from her wine glass. They were looking at each other intently, but neither was angry. No one was yelling or issuing ultimatums. Mikayla had her bare feet on the chair with her phone balanced on her knees as she scrolled through a webcomic. She wasn't looking at anyone, but neither did she seem anxious.

This, Ava realized, was what healthy communication among family members looked like.

Ava had a flash of memory, from when her parents were still together. Patricia had called the money Miguel spent fixing his old car—which lived in his parents' front yard—a waste. His offhand response, that Patricia mind her own damn business, had led to a stony silence between the two of them for the rest of the night.

Another flash, from when Ava had lived with her grandparents. Willie had complained that Esperanza cooked the same thing too often, and Esperanza had yelled back that if he didn't like it, he could eat garbage. Then she'd tossed his dinner, plate and all, into the trashcan.

On the heels of that, another memory, of Ava begging Hector to *please* leave his shoes by the door where they belonged instead of in the hallway where she could trip on them, and him snapping at her that it would take less time for her to move them than it took to nag him.

Shit. No wonder she was scared of being in a relationship. She hadn't the faintest idea what a healthy one looked like. What would it be like for two people to discuss their thoughts and emotions in a rational and calm manner? To actually be heard by the other person, instead of dismissed? To have an argument where no one lashed out or got defensive?

This was what she wanted. Instead of holding back with everyone in her life for fear that they'd get angry with her for having feelings, for not being good, for being difficult.

She recalled her argument with Roman in Puerto Rico. He'd listened. Apologized. And corrected the behavior. He told her he always wanted to know what she was thinking and feeling.

Did he really mean that? Would that change as time went on?

You were never that open with Hector, that annoying little voice inside her piped up.

It was true, she realized. They'd been young when they got together, and she'd been trying so hard to be perfect that by the time she felt comfortable enough to speak up, there was no foundation for them to have a healthy disagreement. They just didn't know how. They'd been two little kids playing house, subject to the whims of their families and lacking the emotional skill set to have a real adult relationship.

Roman knew how to do that. He acted like an adult, which forced Ava to act like one too.

And that was . . . a little bit scary. But also exciting?

God, Colleen would have a field day with this. Maybe it was

worth it to schedule a session with her, even if it meant paying out of pocket.

Just as Ava was starting to wonder if she should change the subject, Mikayla jumped to her feet.

"We forgot about dessert," she exclaimed. "I'll go get it."

While Dulce went to help Mikayla, Ava and Roman collected the dirty dishes to bring them back to the kitchen.

"I'm sorry if you didn't want me to hear that," Ava said quietly as she stacked plates.

Roman's brow furrowed and he paused in gathering the silverware. "Hear what?"

"Your argument with your mother. About her moving out."

Roman stared at her blankly. "Why wouldn't I want you to hear it? We were just talking."

She shrugged, worried he'd see too much. "Never mind. I guess it made me think about my own family, that's all."

He only nodded, but his watchful gaze said they'd come back to this later. "Are you having fun tonight?"

"I am." She couldn't stop the smile that spread across her face. "They're great, Roman. Really great."

"I know." He gave a huff of laughter. "It's probably weird that I don't want them to leave, but you can see why, right?"

She could. This was the core of who he was. He took care of the people he loved, in every way he knew how.

That includes you now, that little voice whispered. But instead of scaring her, it made her feel warm inside.

Chapter 37

Roman leaned back in his chair, a slice of chocolate torte sitting ignored on the plate in front of him as he watched Ava chat with his mom and sister.

He was so fucking happy.

These three women meant more to him than anything else in the world, and seeing them together in his home made him feel settled in a way nothing ever had before. They were getting along well—not that he'd expected otherwise. Ava fit here. As seamlessly as if she'd been coming over for years. It was like he was being given a glimpse into the rest of his life, if he could only convince Ava to give them a real chance.

He was tired of hiding and sneaking around. He understood that she was uncomfortable opening up with her family, but she wasn't alone anymore. Didn't she know he'd protect her from anything that caused her distress? Even her own relatives.

After dessert, Dulce insisted on showing Ava photos from Roman's childhood. Mikayla took that as her cue to go watch her friend's video game livestream.

Roman had told Ava that his wealth was new, but it seemed like, while perusing photos of him as a little boy in the 1980s in different neighborhoods in Brooklyn, she looked at him with deeper understanding in her eyes.

"This is why you work so hard," she said, coming up next to him after Dulce had excused herself for the night.

He stuck his hands in his pockets and surveyed the apartment around him, as he did so often, still unable to believe it was his, and that it wouldn't be going away.

"I had to learn all this," he said. "How to be a wealthy person in this city. How to manage money and business. I did my MBA as quickly as I could while bartending at night. I had to learn how the people with generational wealth do it, so I didn't screw up, so I could secure Mickey's future the right way. I was terrified that I'd blow all my money on stupid shit, or that a corrupt financial adviser would clean me out because they saw me for what I was—a poor Puerto Rican kid from Brooklyn who didn't know what the fuck he was doing."

"You've done so much." Ava took his face in her hands. "When do you get to rest?"

He cupped his hands around hers where they pressed his cheeks. "I'm still that kid, Ava. He's still with me, in me, every second of the day. He doesn't rest."

He needed her to know this. To *see* him. He wasn't just Mr. Roman Vázquez, CEO of VQZ Ltd and the owner of Dulce Hotel Group and Casa Donato Rum. He was Ro, that kid who would do your homework for five bucks, the guy who worked at the pizza place around the corner, the bartender who never lost his grin, even after the most chaotic closing shift. He was Román, the college grad who'd stumbled his way into a short-lived but surprisingly lucrative television career. Every version lived within him, along with the *him* he'd always felt himself to be at his core, no matter his age, what he wore, or how much money was in his pocket.

"I admire you," she said softly, her sparkling hazel eyes drawing him in. "You know that? The more I learn about you, the more I like what I see."

"It's one of the things I love about you," he told her. "A lot of people only see me as I am now. But I think you would have liked me, even back then."

She pursed her lips and pretended to think. "The teacher in me isn't thrilled about your homework smuggling ring, but you were just a kid, and your intentions were noble. Otherwise, yeah. I think I would have liked you then, too."

He barked out a laugh and moved in to press a lingering kiss to her lips. It started slow, a gentle slide, then deepened into something more luxurious, with a simmering undercurrent of passion.

"Come to bed," he whispered against her mouth. Her lips trembled like she was inhaling his words.

"Okay," she said, sounding almost shy.

He understood. Something about this night felt different. It wasn't just the two of them anymore, existing in a little pocket of pleasure and romance, contained by the shifting boundaries Ava set for them. His family was involved now, and he knew that scared her, but she was *here*, and she wasn't running away.

He should be happy with that. Anything she gave him was enough.

But he wouldn't be him if he didn't push for a little more.

He waited until they were in his room and she'd changed into a silky periwinkle nightie before he broached the topic. "I'd like you to consider leaving some things here."

Her expression turned wary. "What kind of things?"

"Overnight things." He sat next to her on the edge of the bed and took her hands so she couldn't get up to pace. "I know I've been traveling a lot, but when I'm home, I want you to sleep over."

She fidgeted the way she did whenever their conversation verged into emotionally intimate territory. He didn't think she knew she did it, but it was adorable, and a really useful tell.

"Are you sure?"

"Of course I'm sure."

"I don't know. I feel a little strange staying over when your family is here."

"We're adults, and this is *my* apartment. Besides, they like you. What are you afraid of?"

She squirmed like she was sitting on hot coals. "I don't want it to seem like I'm getting too comfortable."

"Ava, I *want* you to be comfortable in my home."

She let out a strangled laugh. "I don't even feel comfortable in my *own* home."

His brows drew together. "Why not?"

"I've just . . . never had a space that was completely mine before. Where I didn't have to worry about upsetting other people."

Now they were getting somewhere. "Upsetting who?"

"My mom, my grandmother, and my stepmother, to start with. And the day my parents split up, they'd told me to clean up all my toys, and I didn't do it. For a long time, those two things were connected in my head, like I was sent away to live with my grandparents because I was messy. Even though I know now that it's irrational, and their divorce wasn't my fault, I still can't go to bed with dirty dishes in the sink, no matter how tired I am."

Roman cupped her face in his hands. "I promise you, I will never care if you leave dishes in the sink or panties on the floor or—"

"Oh, I'm sure you'd like it if I left my panties around." Her expression was playful, and he pulled her closer, softening his tone as he leaned his forehead to hers.

"I'd love it, because it would be a sign that you were *here*. I want you to feel at home here, Ava."

She shut her eyes. "I'm scared of how normal this is starting to feel."

He leaned back and raised an eyebrow. "Would you rather it feel abnormal? I'm sure I can think of ways to make it really weird."

She sputtered out a laugh. "No, but I appreciate the offer."

"Then what's the problem?"

"I don't know. It just doesn't feel like a hook-up anymore."

"Because it's not. I love you." Maybe if he took every chance he could to say it, she'd get used to it.

She made a frustrated sound. "This is happening very fast for me."

"I'll try to slow down."

Her lips quirked. "I don't think you know how."

"That's true. But for you, I'll try."

"Thank you. I think it's that when we're alone, anything seems possible. But the more people who are involved, the riskier it feels."

"You said you trust me."

"I know. And I do. I just want to make sure you're not rushing things with us to distract you from what's happening with your family."

He gave her a direct stare. "You think I've fallen in love

with you because my mother and sister are moving out. Do I have that right?"

She refused to look at him. "Something like that."

He suspected it was exactly like that.

"What else?" he pressed. "Maybe I'm asking you to leave a toothbrush here because I'm afraid of being alone?"

She expelled a breath. "The thought did occur to me, yes."

"I won't be alone. I have Sinvergüenza."

Her eyebrows pinched in confusion. "¿Quién?"

"That mangy beast." He gestured to the robotic dog Camille had given him. It sat on his nightstand next to his reading glasses, looking deceptively innocent. "See? I told you I could make this weird."

Ava sputtered out a laugh. "You named it Sinvergüenza?"

"It fits. Go touch it."

Ava patted the dog's head. With a grinding whine, it threw itself on its back.

"See?" Roman said. "Shameless. Rolls over for everyone except me."

When Ava petted the dog's tummy, it waved its legs in the air and let out a mechanical yip. "I see."

"Ava." He waited until she met his gaze. "Both things can be true. I love you *and* I'm worried about my family. Not *because*."

It seemed to be the right thing to say. The stiffness in her shoulders eased, and she leaned into him. Her arms wound around his waist and he pulled them down into the mattress until she was lying beside him with her cheek resting on his chest.

"I should make you negotiate for every item I leave in your bathroom," she mused. "It's what you'd do to me."

"Let's start with a toothbrush," he said. "What do you want? Diamond earrings?"

"Don't you dare!" she said with a laugh. "If that's what my toothbrush is worth, I can't imagine what a pair of underwear would net me."

"A new car," he said solemnly.

She shook her head and tightened her hold on him. "You can talk to me about it, you know."

"About what?"

She tilted her chin up to look at him. "Your family moving out."

He sighed. "They're going to be fine. My mother's right. I know she is, but . . ."

"You're going to miss them," Ava said simply.

He opened his mouth to argue, to say that it had more to do with protecting them, or ensuring their needs were met, but . . . "Yeah," he said. "I am."

Ava kissed his collarbone. It was a sweet, comforting little peck, but Roman wanted more. He rolled on top of her, and soon he was trailing his mouth in a leisurely path down her neck to her sternum, pulling aside the fabric of her nightgown and kissing every inch of skin he exposed.

Her breathing became shallow, her chest rising and falling against his lips with increasing speed. When he wrapped his mouth around her nipple, she let out a soft moan and tunneled her fingers into his hair. Her thighs parted to cradle his hips and she bucked against his erection.

"Slow, mi amor," he whispered against her breast, sliding his hands down the length of her body in soothing strokes. "We have all night."

This might be the first time they were making love in his bed, but it wouldn't be the last. Still, he wanted to make it memorable.

With steadfast patience, he worshiped her body from the top of her head to her soles of her feet, treasuring each gasp, each moan, each sigh. When she was quivering and all but sobbing with need, he filled her in a gradual slide before setting a languid and leisurely pace. Through it all, he pestered her with soft, tender kisses, refusing to hurry even when she clenched her inner muscles around him in an effort to snap his control.

"Relax," he breathed into her hair. "I have you."

Finally, she calmed, her body going loose and pliant under him as he coaxed orgasm after orgasm from her with the precision of a master cellist playing a concerto. When she'd whispered, "It's your turn to let go," he'd done just that, his climax overtaking him as profoundly as hers had.

When it was over, Roman lay on his back with Ava's head on his shoulder, her long legs twined with his. He stroked her hip as he stared at the ceiling in the dark.

This was what he wanted. No barriers, no boundaries, no rules. Just Ava in his home, in his bed. Every single night, for the rest of their lives.

Except he was leaving again in two days. The hotel group had a number of deals in the works, acquisitions and expansions and licensing agreements. Many of them relied on him being physically in the room. And then, of course, there was Casa Donato, a side project that had previously taken up every second of his already limited free time.

Maybe he could shift some of his responsibilities. Promote some people, so he didn't have to travel as often, or for as long.

When do you get to rest?

He didn't know. Up until now, he'd operated under the *I'll rest when I'm dead* work ethic. But to spend more time with Ava, he'd have to figure it out.

He fell asleep with his mind full of personnel lists and logistics. When he woke up, he was no closer to an answer than he'd been the night before.

But Ava was still curled against him, warm and real, and that was more than enough.

Chapter 38

Jasmine's bridal shower was held in a suite at the Dulce Flor. Ava never would've had the guts to ask Roman for such a favor, for fear that he'd think she was using him for free event space or something like that. Luckily, Ashton had no such qualms, and Ava was saved from trying to host the shower in her grandmother's living room.

It was half an hour before the party was officially set to begin and the suite was in chaos. All the tías had shown up early bearing trays of food, and now, after decimating the first pitcher of mimosas Ava had made, they were standing around gossiping amid spontaneous bursts of salsa dancing. Marc Anthony blasted from the speakers in the seating area, where Abuela Esperanza and Titi Nereida were engaged in an argument about seasoning with Jasmine's other grandmother, Lola Sofia, and Jasmine's aunt, Tita Myra, who had both flown in from San Diego. Ava and Michelle were setting out warming pans.

"More food." Jasmine plopped a large aluminum foil tray labeled "bacalaitos" on the dining table and knocked over a stack of pink "Here Comes the Bride!" napkins in the process. She cursed under her breath as she righted them. "I should've had this thing catered."

Michelle ripped open a package of matching bridal plates. "Bad enough you're not holding the shower at Abuela's house. If you didn't let them bring food, you'd be hearing about how you're too good for Abuela's arroz or Titi Nereida's pastelillos for the rest of your life."

"And Ronnie's still pissed you didn't let her plan the engagement party," Ava added. "Giving her full rein over the shower decorations was the compromise."

Jasmine eyed the giant balloon arch Ronnie was erecting in the seating area. "That looks like it belongs at a baby shower."

It did, but Ava tried to look on the bright side. "At least Ronnie went with blush pink instead of mint green. She told me that was her other color option."

Jasmine pinched the bridge of her nose and groaned.

"Where do you want these?" Jillian asked, clomping over with a box of forty goody bags, which Ava knew contained bracelets made by Titi Val, coffee-scented candles made by Willow, and rustic handmade soaps from Ronnie's mom, Titi Nita. The bags themselves had been decorated by Ronnie's stepdaughter.

Ava took the box. "I'll set them up near the gifts."

Jasmine sniffed one of the bags. "When did our family get so crafty?"

"Everyone needs a hobby," Jillian said with a shrug.

Their grandmother hurried over to them. "Muchachas, tengo mas goodies for the bags."

"That's my cue to leave," Jillian muttered, ducking away.

Esperanza reached into her purse and pulled out a fistful of square white packets. "My friend at the makeup store gave me some extra skincare samples."

Michelle took one and read the label. "Nighttime eye cream? What are you trying to say, Abuela?"

"No necesito decir nada. The shopping bags under your eyes say it all." Esperanza dumped the samples into Jasmine's hands. Half of them fell on the floor.

Jasmine opened her mouth, closed it, then just said, "Thanks, Abuela."

After Esperanza sailed away to greet Olympia and Willow, Jasmine sighed. "It hasn't been announced, but I have a sponsorship deal with a skincare line. I have to call and make sure this doesn't violate that agreement."

"No rest for the rich and famous," Michelle teased, and Jasmine groaned.

"You wouldn't believe the number of brands who've reached out about *swag bags* for the wedding guests."

"Ooh, you're having swag bags?" Michelle asked.

"No! This isn't the Oscars. Although we've had a surprising number of offers from publications who want to cover the wedding as an exclusive," Jasmine admitted.

"Are you going to do it?" Ava asked.

Jasmine shook her head. "It's tempting. They're offering a lot of money—and I mean *a lot*—but this is private. Letting the press into our personal lives is a slippery slope."

"Good choice," Ava said. Considering the spotlight had nearly torn Jasmine and Ashton's relationship apart before it had the chance to begin, the decision made sense.

Jasmine pulled out her phone. "I'd better call and check on this brand thing."

"Don't bother." Without a second's hesitation, Ava scooped

up the eye cream samples and dumped them into the trash. "We'll say they got misplaced."

Michelle raised her eyebrows. "Who are you and what have you done with my cousin?"

Ava fought a smile. Was this New Ava rearing her head, without any prompting? "I'm going to make another pitcher of mimosas before the tías stage a riot."

She rounded the counter into the suite's kitchen and pulled champagne and orange juice from the fridge. She mixed two pitchers and was carrying them to the beverage table when she caught sight of Esperanza and Willow. Abuela was plucking at the sleeve of Willow's shirt and wearing a critical expression Ava was all too familiar with.

"You know I don't understand Spanish, Grandma," Willow said, pulling away. "Isn't one colonizer language enough? Why do I need to speak two?"

"Colonizer?" Esperanza repeated, then she rounded on Ava, her dark eyes flashing. "¿De qué está hablando?"

"Teenage slang," Ava muttered, not wanting to get into an explanation of the colonial history of the United States *or* the Caribbean. "What's going on?"

Esperanza gestured broadly toward Willow's clothes. "I said she looks like she's going to a clown's funeral."

Ava glanced at her sister. Willow wore an oversize black-and-white-checked sweater vest and wide-legged black trousers rolled up to reveal chunky Doc Martens on her feet. The outfit was very much in line with Willow's aesthetic, which she called "weekend Wednesday Addams."

Willow's chin trembled as she met Ava's gaze, and she looked to be seconds away from ruining the smoky eye Ava had taught her to do.

Ava quickly set down the mimosas and did something she almost never did around her grandmother.

She drew herself up to her full height.

"Abuela," Ava said, in a voice that was quiet but firm. "Willow is seventeen. She is allowed to make her own choices about what she wants to wear. Just because her personal style is different from yours doesn't give you the right to make her feel bad about it."

"Pero she's such a pretty girl, if she'd only—"

"This is her body," Ava interrupted. "No one gets to dictate what she does with it. Not even you."

Esperanza, perhaps realizing that she had a new opponent, switched to Spanish and let loose a barrage of tried and true Latina grandma jabs.

Who do you think you are to talk to me like that?

I can say whatever I want to anybody.

I'm just telling the truth—

In the middle of it, Willow mouthed a teary "thank you" to Ava and slipped away.

Ava stood her ground, Esperanza's angry words crashing against her like waves battering a cliff in a storm. Ava didn't argue, she didn't talk back, but nor did she back down.

And for once, her grandmother's criticism didn't touch her.

Instead, she recalled her high school graduation party.

Her grandmother had pressed a hundred dollar bill into her hands and given her a tight hug.

We were so worried you were going to do something foolish, like major in drama, Abuela had said.

It had been a dig at Jasmine, who'd been standing right next to Ava. Everyone had known Jasmine's dream school was Juilliard.

Ava had accepted the money and murmured, *That wouldn't have been practical*, but the words had pricked like daggers on her tongue, because deep down, she'd *wished* she had Jasmine's courage.

Her whole life, this was what Ava had been trying to protect herself from. She'd twisted herself into knots to avoid her grandmother's ire.

And where the fuck had it gotten her?

Nowhere. Her grandma was an angry old woman, and no amount of outward perfection would change that.

"Bwela." Ava broke into the tirade and leaned down to kiss Esperanza's cheek. "Do you want me to make you a cup of coffee?"

Esperanza blinked, and her face cleared. Maybe she sensed this for the olive branch it was, or maybe she was just winding down, because she nodded and returned Ava's kiss. "Sí, nena. Pero not too sweet, tú sabes? My blood sugar."

"I know." Ava carried the pitchers she'd abandoned over to the beverage table and began to fix a cup of coffee when Titi Val joined her.

"Hi mamita." Titi Val rubbed Ava's back between her shoulder blades. "What was the old lady lambasting you for this time?"

Ava huffed out a laugh and felt some of the tension in her body ease. "You saw that, huh?"

"Sure did."

Of all of Ava's aunts, Titi Val was the one Ava had always felt closest to. Maybe it was because Val was Ava's godmother and best friends with Patricia, or maybe it was because Ava had slept over at her and Uncle Dom's house countless times. Ava still had a set of keys, which was how she'd discovered that Michelle and Gabe were hooking up last year. Make no mistake, Valentina Rodriguez Amato was as big a gossip as they came, but Ava would never forget the way Titi Val had stood up to Esperanza after the announcement of Ava's divorce.

"She said something mean to Willow about her outfit," Ava explained. "I told her not to do that."

"Ah. That went over well, I see." Val's eyebrow quirked. "Mami can be a bitch, but we all love her anyway."

Ava's hands slowed as she stirred sugar substitute into her grandmother's coffee. Her aunt was right. Esperanza was controlling and difficult at times, but they still loved her.

What if—

"You've been doing a lot to help with this wedding," Val observed. "Don't overdo it, okay? Ask for help."

"I will," Ava replied automatically.

But her aunt's smile was knowing. "No, you won't. Here, I'll bring the vieja her coffee. Why don't you pour yourself a mimosa and take a minute to yourself before this shindig really gets going?"

Ava gave her aunt a grateful smile and took her advice. She was just finishing her drink when the door to the suite opened and a raucous cry went up—the sound of half a dozen Puerto Rican women exclaiming over the real life telenovela actor in their midst.

Michelle came up to Ava and rolled her eyes. "You'd think they'd be used to him by now."

Ava glanced over to see Ashton strolling into the suite, his arms laden with shopping bags. As usual, the family he was marrying into pelted him with questions about his various TV roles over the past two decades.

"When's the *Victor in Charge* spinoff?" Titi Nita called out, referencing *Carmen in Charge*, the telenovela remake that Jasmine and Ashton had starred in together.

"Never," Ashton quipped, treating them to a dazzling smile. "We all know that Jasmine, I mean, *Carmen*, is in charge."

As if it were a movie, the crowd around Ashton parted for Jasmine to approach. He leaned down to plant a kiss on his fiancée's waiting lips, much to the delight of the assembled relatives. They clapped and oohed like it was the final frame of a romantic comedy.

Michelle sipped her mimosa. "They really have no shame."

"Jasmine and Ashton?" Ava asked, and Michelle snorted.

"No, our family."

Just then, the door opened again and Gabe, Michelle's boyfriend, walked in carrying a tray of conchas covered in plastic wrap. The Mexican pastry was his mother's specialty, and Michelle had asked her to make them for the shower.

"Here we go," Michelle said with a sigh, and she tipped back her glass to drain it.

On cue, the women shifted their attention from Ashton to Gabe. He wore a tight tank top that showed off his powerfully built upper body and arms.

Ava shot Michelle a smirk. "Did you tell him to wear that?"

Michelle's light brown eyes gleamed with mischief, and she ran her tongue along her bottom lip as she gazed at her boyfriend. "I sure the hell did. And I told him to flex a lot while carrying those conchas, just to whip them into a frenzy."

"You better go rescue him before Titi Nita grabs his butt again. She's already at least two mimosas deep."

"If anyone's going to grab his butt, it should be me." Michelle set aside her empty glass, then strode forward to claim her man.

Ava watched her go and realized that the feeling she usually had when she saw her cousins with their partners was absent. She dug a little further and no, the jealousy that was at times nearly painful in its intensity wasn't there. Or at least, nowhere near as strong as it had been during other recent family events.

Before she could examine that thought further, the door opened again, and this time, Ava's heart lurched.

It was Roman.

He wore a charcoal gray suit and a wide grin, and he carried a bucket of expensive champagne bottles.

At the sight of him, Ava's chest heaved, and she struggled to take a deep breath. God, she'd missed him so much. He'd been traveling for work, and it had been two weeks since she'd last seen him. Every single cell in her body wanted to run to him, to throw her arms around his neck and press herself to him, to breathe in his scent and sink into the steady strength of his embrace. Resisting the urge was a physical ache, the sense of longing settling over her like a cold fog.

"On behalf of the Dulce, para mis dulces," he announced.

The ladies ate it up, fluttering and tittering around him. Jasmine and Ashton greeted him, then went about introducing him to everyone, many of whom recognized him from the engagement party. Roman passed the champagne to Gabe and moved through the crowd with ease and charm, fitting in among Ava's family like he belonged there.

Ava's fingers tightened around the stem of her glass as she took him in.

Yes, Ashton was movie star handsome and Gabe was built like a superhero, but Roman shone with an inner light that called to her like nothing and no one ever had. He radiated genuine goodness and a real interest in people, and when he met her eyes across the room, what she saw there speared into her, as sudden and breathtaking as a lightning strike.

The breath backed up in her lungs. No. Oh god, no.

Damn it, she hadn't wanted this again. Hadn't wanted this all-consuming wealth of feeling.

But here it was.

She . . .

Fuck.

She *loved* him.

Loved him back, more accurately, because the truth was written all over his face, as plain as day to anyone paying attention.

Luckily, no one except Ava was looking at him. Everyone was too busy laughing at something Ashton had said. They didn't see the quiet, adoring look Roman sent her, one she was probably reflecting back to him. Unless her face was revealing the shock of her revelation.

But even as she thought it, the shock melted away, leaving only gentle acceptance. She'd felt this coming. It was different than before—steadier, more mature. Maybe because *she* was steadier and more mature. And it wasn't a surprise—how could it be? Roman was everything she could ever hope to find in another person—playful, caring, honest, open. And he was *hers*.

Except she couldn't claim him. Couldn't walk right up to him and plant a big, smacking kiss right on that soft, agile mouth. Not in front of her family.

Cold despair filled her, along with—ah. The familiar prick of jealousy. Her cousins could go to their men without fear, but Ava couldn't.

Her eyes fell on her grandmother, on Titi Nereida, on Titi Nita, on Olympia. The echoes of their past words, ranging from censorious to accusatory to passive aggressive, rang in her head, holding her rooted to the spot.

She's not even pregnant!

Just apologize for whatever you did.

Not everything is meant to last, you know.

Let's not talk about unpleasant things like divorce.

Ava shook their voices away.

Maybe she wasn't brave enough to go over there and grab him, but nor could she stay away from the man she loved a second longer.

As he made his way farther into the suite, she moved to intercept him.

"Roman, can you help me with something?" she asked nonchalantly.

He smiled. "Of course."

She led him down a short hall to the bedroom and shut the door behind them.

"What did you need help wi—"

Ava cupped his face and pulled him in for a kiss.

Roman—beautifully sharp, quick-witted Roman—didn't miss a beat. His hands gripped her waist and drew her closer. His mouth slanted, deepening the kiss. As his tongue slid against hers, Ava felt it from her lips down to the tips of her toes and back up, desire twisting low in her belly and making her whimper. Her hands trailed down his neck to grip his lapels.

"I missed you," she said breathlessly against his lips. "I missed you so much."

The words *I love you* welled up, but they were too new, too scary, too private. She needed to turn them over in her head and examine them more closely.

Even as her heart whispered, *There's nothing to think about.*

"I'm sorry," he rasped. His hands molded over her hips and around to grab her ass. "Come with me next time. I can't be away from you this long again."

"Where?" She let out a little laugh as he dragged his mouth down her neck, licking and nipping and biting. Her toes curled in her sandals.

"Wherever." His voice was muffled against her collarbones. "Anywhere I go. Come with me."

The idea was too exciting, too tempting. "I'll think about it," she said, and pulled his face back to hers.

"I know you will."

Her mouth swallowed the rest of his dark chuckle and they were kissing again, deep and hungry, the only sounds in the room the soft little moans in the back of her throat and the groan rumbling in his chest.

And then the door opened behind them with a sharp squeak.

Gasping, Ava tore herself away from Roman and stared.

Gabe stood in the doorway in his too-small tank top, one hand on the doorknob, his dark eyes quickly sweeping them, from their wet, swollen lips to their rumpled clothes to—

Shit. Instead of letting go, Roman's hands had tightened on her ass, the fabric of her skirt bunching to the tops of her thighs. There was absolutely no misreading the situation.

Gabe's face went blank. Without a word, he backed out of the room and started to shut the door again.

With a speed that was nearly superhuman, Ava leapt forward and grabbed his arm.

"Don't tell Michelle," she ordered, still breathless from the kiss. "Do you hear me? *Don't* tell her."

Gabe was strong enough that he could have torn himself from her grip if he'd wanted to, but he froze. His features twisted and he made a pained noise in the back of his throat, something close to a whine. "Why are you doing this to me, Ava? That woman can sniff out secrets like a bloodhound. She'll know I'm hiding something."

"You owe me for staying quiet about you sneaking in and out of Titi Val's house last year," Ava hissed.

Gabe squeezed his eyes shut and grimaced. "Fuck. All right."

When he opened his eyes, he shot Roman a warning look. Then he left and closed the door behind him.

"Drinks with the guys just got more interesting," Roman said in a mild tone.

Ava pressed her hands to her face as horror doused her libido like a bucket of ice water. "This is a disaster. Now Ashton *and* Gabe know."

Taking her in his arms, Roman stroked a thumb over the curve of her cheek and looked deep into her eyes. "Would it really be the end of the world if everyone knew?"

Yes, she thought, but all she said was, "Just give me until after the wedding. Please? You said we could hold off until then."

Something flickered across his face and she expected him to argue, but after a short nod, he dropped a gentle kiss to her forehead. "Anything you want, mi amor." Then he stepped back and gestured to the door. "After you."

She paused with her hand on the doorknob and turned back to him. "Wait a few minutes before you—"

"I know," he said, and waved her on. His smile looked tired, sort of frayed around the edges, and she remembered that he'd just arrived that morning after a long flight. He worked too damn hard. They should've been lounging in his bed, watching movies and playing with Sinvergüenza, instead of sneaking kisses behind her relatives' backs at a bridal shower. She wanted to hold him in her arms, to insist he take a nap, and then, when he was sound asleep, whisper to him that she loved him. Instead, she opened the door and slipped into the hallway.

She stopped in the bathroom first to make sure she didn't look too mussed. While she was there, she stared at her reflection and whispered, "You dummy."

This is your fault, that nasty little voice whispered.

A month ago, she would have freaked out and broken up with him. But New Ava or whomever the hell she was now didn't want that. She *loved* Roman. And she wanted some kind of relationship with him, along with the time and space to figure it out without other people's opinions or expectations.

Roman's words came back to her.

Would it really be the end of the world if everyone knew?

Maybe not, but her family's interference would put stress onto something that felt as fragile as the first blooms of spring, and, despite the fact that she'd been in love before, unfamiliar. Didn't she deserve this? Something that was just hers, at least for a while longer? Didn't she and Roman deserve the chance to find their way in this new and budding relationship without input from everyone else?

Except now Ashton *and* Gabe knew, while Jasmine and Michelle *didn't*.

Ava covered her face with her hands, unable to look at herself any longer. God, what a fucking mess.

She knew she should tell Jasmine. She absolutely should *tell* Jasmine.

But the wedding was just two short weeks away. Jasmine had more than enough on her plate without worrying about the possibility of her maid of honor ruining her big day.

Ava loved Roman. There was no denying it. And he said

he loved her. While she did trust him, a teeny, tiny part of her still didn't believe it. And that part could just imagine a world where in the next couple weeks, this thing between them turned bitter and sour and dramatic and *messy*. It would put Jasmine and Ashton into an awkward position. It would turn attention away from the main focus—their wedding—and put it on Ava and her fucked up love life.

Be good, Ava.

She couldn't cause a problem for her cousin. Which meant she couldn't tell Jasmine about Roman. Not yet, anyway. Someday. *Soon*, she told herself.

They just needed to be careful. No more slip-ups before the wedding. After that, they'd figure it out.

Ava slapped on her Resting Pleasant Face and left the bathroom.

Text Exchange with Damaris Fuentes

Ava: Something terrible happened.

Damaris: OMG what??

Ava: I'm in love with him.

Damaris: You are such a fucking drama queen. Don't scare me like that.

Ava: But it's terrifying! Also, my cousin Michelle's boyfriend caught us kissing.

Damaris: Tell me EVERYTHING.

Chapter 39

As much as Roman hated to leave without saying goodbye to Ava, he exited the suite with Ashton and Gabriel and brought them up to the Dulce Flor's private lounge for VIP guests.

Being away from her for two weeks had sucked. He'd dreamed about her almost every night, and despite the exhaustion of a long trip and an overnight transatlantic flight, the thought of reuniting with Ava had energized him more than a triple shot of espresso. Walking into the suite and seeing her had been like entering one of his dreams. She was right there, almost within reach, but a crowd of women had stood in the way and he hadn't been able to go to her, for reasons that seemed nebulous and only made sense in the depths of the subconscious.

It was getting more and more difficult to hide his feelings for her, and he just didn't want to fucking do it anymore. So while Ava was probably freaking out about Gabe walking in on them, for Roman, it was actually a relief. He needed to talk to Ashton about Ava, and this meant they could do it in front of Gabe. Hell, Gabe was also dating one of the Primas of Power, maybe he'd have some additional insights to offer. Roman would welcome all the suggestions he could get.

They took seats at a circular booth set lower into the floor and placed their drink orders—a sidecar for Roman, a gin and tonic for Ashton, and a seltzer with lime for Gabe.

Once the waiter was gone, Gabe wasted no time in broaching the topic of Ava. "Gotta say, man, I'm not thrilled about hiding this secret romance thing from Michelle."

Ashton grunted. "Join the club."

Roman spread his hands. "I don't like it either. If it were up to me, I'd take out a full page ad in the *New York Times*."

Gabe propped his elbows on his knees. "Let me guess—Ava doesn't want her family to know?"

Roman scowled. "Is this a common occurrence?"

Ashton nodded. "Por las primas poderosas, sí."

Roman leaned back, sensing he was in for a story. "So all three of them have done it?"

Ashton rubbed his jaw. "Jasmine and I—well, you know the tabloids were an issue for both of us. Plus, she had something called a Leading Lady Plan."

"What the hell is that?"

"I'm still not sure, but the primas bring it up every so often. Something about making jefa moves."

"Huh." Roman turned to Gabe. "And you?"

"Michelle and I used to be best friends," Gabe said. "There was some past baggage we had to work through. And our parents are next door neighbors."

"Why does that matter?" Roman asked.

Gabe and Ashton exchanged a look, and Gabe launched into an explanation about his history with Michelle. How they'd reconnected after more than a decade of silence and Michelle tricked him into staying with her at her parents' house—right next to his own family, whom he'd been estranged from at the time. Gabe made a point to emphasize how their attempts at sneaking around had completely backfired.

While they were talking, the drinks arrived, along with a selection from the tapas menu. Someone must have noticed that he was there.

At the end, Roman tried to put it all together. "You and Michelle were pretending to be dating to keep everyone from finding out you were actually dating?"

"We weren't dating yet, we were—you know what, never mind, that's a good way of putting it."

Ashton spoke in a mock whisper. "They were fucking."

Roman laughed. "Yeah, I got that."

"And you and Ava are pretending *not* to be dating, but you are," Gabe summed up. "So what's the deal? No, wait, let me guess—you're her boss."

Roman shook his head.

"You're already married?"

Roman flipped Gabe off with his bare left hand.

"Secret baby? No, wait, that was you." Gabe sent Ashton a shit-eating grin, and Ashton threw a balled-up bar napkin at him.

"You weren't even around for that."

"No, but I've heard all about it. Many times."

Ashton jabbed a finger in Gabe's direction and gave Roman a pointed look. "¡Verás! Es por eso que ella no quiere que nadie lo sepa."

"Exactly," Gabe went on, picking up the thread of Ashton's words. "She doesn't want anyone to know because she'll never hear the end of it."

"From her relatives," Roman clarified, and the other two men nodded.

"It's not an irrational fear," Gabe pointed out. "Right now you have an excuse to be around her, but if you even look at her too long at the wedding, the Boricua bochinche circuit will be on that shit faster than any paparazzo. Before you know it, they'll be throwing you an engagement party masquerading as a barbecue and forcing you to sleep with her in her brother's childhood bedroom."

Roman eyed him across the low table. "That is . . . oddly specific."

"I still have nightmares about it," Gabe said with a shudder.

"How do I help her get past this fear she has of her family?"

Ashton shrugged and drained the last of his G&T. "You don't. Stop trying."

Roman scowled. "It's stressing her out. I want to fix it."

"You can't protect her from her family, Ro. Only she can do that."

The sense of powerlessness made Roman feel like his custom-made suit jacket was suddenly three sizes too tight. "So then what *can* I do?"

"Just be there." This was from Gabe. He said it like it was so simple.

Roman blew out a breath. "Come on. That's not enough."

"It is," Ashton insisted. "Look who *isn't* there."

"You mean her ex?"

"Sí. You want to prove you're better than that asshole who left her? Be there. Every day. That's it."

"You know me," Roman said. "I need a more proactive plan than that. Something concrete."

"Mira, cabrón, *no* le compres un carro." Ashton's voice was severe.

Gabe sent Roman a bewildered look. "That's your plan? To buy her a car?"

"It crossed my mind," Roman grumbled. "What did you guys do?"

"I introduced Jasmine to the most important people in my life," Ashton said.

"I already did that." Roman turned to Gabe. "Next."

Now it was Ashton's turn to give Gabe a smug smile. "Go ahead. Tell him what you did."

Gabe coughed and mumbled something about fanfiction.

Roman stared at him blankly for a long moment. "That doesn't help me."

Ashton pinned Roman with a direct look. "¿Y qué quieres con ella?"

Roman spread his hands. "What do I want with her? I want everything."

Ashton shook his head. "See, that's your problem. You always want more than what you have. You have to learn to be satisfied with what she's willing to give, until she wants to give more."

Roman sighed. "I'm trying to take it slow. I asked her to leave stuff at my place and she got all squirrely."

"Ava doesn't rush into things," Ashton said. "Take it a day at a time. And for fuck's sake, make her tell Jasmine. Hide it from the rest of them if you have to, but Jasmine needs to know before we walk down that aisle."

"I'm trying." Roman's voice was strained.

"Try harder."

Chapter 40

The bridal shower was going about as well as could be expected. There were nearly forty people on the guest list, mostly family, with a few of Jasmine's industry colleagues and a handful of the friends she'd stayed in touch with from high school and college.

The younger guests—Ava's sister, Michelle's niece, Ronnie's stepdaughter, and Sammy's oldest daughter—teamed up with Lily Benitez and Nino Colón, Jasmine and Ashton's costars from *Carmen in Charge*, to trounce the cousins and tías in games of Bridal Taboo and Wedding Family Feud. The older generations got them back by kicking ass in Name that Disney Love Song.

"What even is *The Rescuers*?" Michelle's twelve-year-old niece Phoebe asked scornfully, to which Jillian replied, "It's a classic, you infant."

Titi Nereida surprised them all by writing the dirtiest version of Fill in the Blank Wedding Vows imaginable.

"¿Qué?" the old woman said, looking around innocently. "Penis is a noun, ¿verdad?"

"I'm going to be hearing that in my nightmares for the rest of my life," Michelle muttered, draining another mimosa. Abuela declared that she'd peed herself laughing, and Titi Lisa agreed that her pelvic floor had never been the same since having Jasmine.

"How many times do you want me to say I'm sorry?" Jasmine grumbled.

Even with Ronnie and Michelle moderating the games, Ava had more than enough to keep her mind off Roman.

She was stacking champagne-glazed donut holes—pink with sugary sparkles—into a pyramid on a tray when Michelle strolled over. Her tank top read "Bisexual & Bicoastal."

"I haven't seen you since you got back from PR," Michelle said, popping a donut hole in her mouth. "How was your sexcation with Roman?"

Panic jolted through Ava's body. Four donut holes fell to the floor as she whirled around and grabbed her cousin's arm. "Gabe wasn't supposed to tell you!"

Michelle's eyebrows flew up to her hairline and she almost choked. "Relax, I was *kidding.*" Then her eyes narrowed in suspicion. "What wasn't Gabe supposed to tell me?"

Ava pressed her hands to her face. Michelle had been joking, her particular brand of irreverent and slightly raunchy humor. But Ava had overreacted and given the game away.

Everything was falling apart.

Before Ava could deflect, Michelle gave a dramatic gasp. "Oh my god, are you and Roman fucking?"

"Lower your voice, and *yes*," Ava hissed. There was clearly no getting out of this conversation.

Michelle flicked Ava's arm. "How come Gabe knew before I did?"

"He only found out today. *By accident.*"

Michelle crossed her arms and leaned a hip against the counter. "I think you'd better start at the beginning."

Resigned, Ava told Michelle about meeting Roman ten months earlier, and everything that had happened since, ending with Gabe walking in on them kissing.

By the time the full story was out, Michelle was pressing her fingers to her temples like she had a headache.

"Let me get this straight," she said. "Ashton knows, but Jasmine doesn't. Do I have that right?"

Trust Michelle to zero in on that part.

"Um . . . yes."

"Ava, Ava, *Ava*," Michelle moaned. "What the hell are you doing? Did you not learn anything from my mistakes? Jas is gonna be *so* pissed."

"She'll be more pissed if Roman and I break up and ruin her wedding." Ava returned to the donut hole pyramid. With her luck, Titi Nereida would burst in to ask why the sweets weren't out yet.

Michelle gave a knowing nod. "I see. This is about Hector."

Ava slapped a hand on the counter, nearly upending the box of donut holes. "*It is not about Hector.*"

"Bullshit." Michelle pointed a finger at her. "That fucker did a number on you and now you think every relationship is doomed to fail. So if you and Roman break up before the wedding, you think it's going to make things weird for Jasmine."

"Exactly," Ava snapped, irritated at being so thoroughly dragged. "Jasmine has enough to worry about."

Michelle stuck her hands on her hips. "What happened to that 'a burden shared is a burden halved' nonsense you told me last year?"

"Did I say that?"

"You sure the hell did."

"Well, this is different."

"Really? Because it sounds to me like you're trying to have your wedding cake and eat it too. And you know what? That cake is going to blow up in your face."

Michelle mimed an explosion with both of her hands and made a sound effect to go with it.

Ava knew her cousin was right, but the thought of anyone else finding out made her lungs seize up. "Just keep it to yourself for now, okay? And make sure Gabe doesn't say anything either. Let's get through this wedding, and then I'll figure out how to tell Jasmine."

Michelle huffed. "Only because it should really come from you, but let the record show that I think this is a disaster waiting to happen, and I will one hundred percent be saying 'I told you so' when the time comes."

"Fine," Ava ground out. She placed the last donut hole on the pyramid. It was flat on top, thanks to the four that had fallen and the one Michelle had eaten. *Not perfect.*

You are five donut holes short of a pyramid if you think you can keep kicking this can down the road, that sarcastic little inner voice taunted.

"We'll see about that," Ava muttered to herself, and then she hefted the tray and carried it out to the party.

Chapter 41

After Jasmine texted the group chat to say the shower was winding down, the guys finished their second round of drinks. As they were leaving to go help clean up, Roman's phone rang.

"It's my lawyer," he said, glancing at the screen.

Ashton waved him off. "Take the call. We've got this. See you at rehearsal, sí?"

Roman said goodbye to Ashton and Gabe and accepted the call. While he listened, he wound his way around the edges of the lounge, where it was less populated. Most people were by the bar, or in the cozy seating areas.

"You'll be there, right?" his lawyer asked. "I don't think we can push this deal through without you."

"Of course," Roman said, even as his gut sank. He'd been hoping to cut back on his travel commitments before the wedding, but it looked like that wouldn't be happening.

After they hung up, Roman stuck his hands in his pockets and continued to pace the perimeter of the room, turning over everything Ashton and Gabe had shared.

They'd spent a lot more time around Ava's family than Roman had, and they'd seen firsthand how Ava was treated. Like Cinderella, Ashton had said. Like love was conditional.

But the problem was twofold—she wasn't just afraid of her family's reaction to finding out about him, she was afraid of their reaction to her relationship with him *ending*. On some level, despite what she said about trust, she was still afraid he was going to leave her.

Like her ex. Like her parents.

How was he supposed to prove he wanted forever with her when she wouldn't let him? He'd propose tomorrow if he thought she'd say yes, but he knew it would just scare her away. Look how she'd reacted to the idea of leaving a toothbrush by his sink.

Be there. Every day.

Ashton's directive stuck with him. It sounded simple, *too* simple, except . . . Roman couldn't actually do it. He was gone too often. What was he going to do, ask Ava to quit her job to go on business trips with him? That wasn't fair to her. She had a career, even if it sounded like she was dissatisfied with her current position. And it wasn't like he had tons of free time while he was away. He was still working nonstop.

He recalled how Ashton responded to Roman's desire to help Ava with her family. *You don't. Stop trying.*

Yeah, like it was that easy.

Mikayla's voice, yelling at him. *I don't want you to do anything!*

Who the hell was he if he wasn't trying to solve problems for the people he loved? If he wasn't trying to make their lives easier and save them from hardship?

The idea flummoxed him, making him feel tense and out of control.

His mother's words came back to him then. *You can't control everything. When is it going to be enough?*

It was never going to be enough. Therefore, he'd never be

able to *be there* for Ava the way he wanted to, the way she deserved.

A hollow pit opened in his gut, and before he could question the impulse, he called his mother. Dulce picked up on the third ring.

"Hi, Ro."

"Is this what I do?" he blurted out. "Fix things, instead of being there?"

"Hold on." The sound of the K-drama in the background went off. "What do you mean?"

"For you and Mickey." He shoved a hand through his hair and paced the corner of the lounge, walking a tight loop. "Is this my MO? Rushing to fix, instead of, I don't know, just *being there* for you."

He heard his mother sigh. "If you're asking, you already know the answer."

"But fixing things isn't *bad*." He sounded childish, but somehow, talking to his mom made him feel like he was ten years old again. "Why would I let the people I love suffer if I can do something about it?"

"Listen to me, Roman." Her voice was quiet and firm. "You cannot change the fact that your father left."

Her words landed like a direct hit to his solar plexus. He wanted to deny it, to say that this *absolutely wasn't about his fucking father*, but now that she'd said it, put those words—"your father"—into the air, the subject coalesced into something tangible and distracting and real.

Yes, he realized. This was, at least in part, about his fucking father.

"Maybe not. But if we'd had more money, more security,

our lives would have gone differently." And the part he didn't say: *Maybe he wouldn't have left.*

As usual, his mother read his mind. "Your father was always going to leave, whether we had one dollar or one million. He couldn't handle responsibility, and no amount of money would've fixed that."

On an intellectual level, Roman knew she was right. But some part of him had always wondered, *What if?*

"I don't remember him," Roman admitted in a hushed tone. "But I knew you were struggling. And there wasn't a goddamn thing I could do about it. Except work."

He'd felt powerless as a child, watching his mother bust her ass to pay the bills and take care of him. When he'd handed her money for the first time, something had shifted in him, a growing sense of purpose.

Money had given him control over his situation. The more money, the more control. And the feeling of helplessness had diminished.

Yet it had never entirely gone away.

"Ay mijo." There was pain in his mother's voice. "That wasn't your responsibility. It never has been."

"Someone had to take care of you."

"I'm an adult, Roman." She let out a heavy sigh. "I knew I shouldn't have let you contribute at such a young age, and I can see now, I never should have let you take care of us after Keith died either."

"Mami, I *wanted* to. I promised him that I'd take care of you and Mickey."

"And you have, but Roman, it's too much. I think you used that fear to drive you, and maybe, it's driven you too far. Money will not protect you from pain. It wouldn't have stopped your father from leaving, and it didn't stop Keith from dying."

"Mami—"

"No, please listen to me. You threw as much money at his illness as you could. But you're not God. He was sick, and he died. You made his last year as comfortable as you could. But you can't prevent people from experiencing pain or heartache. No one can."

"I can do everything in my power to try to protect you from it. And Mikayla." *And Ava*, he thought. If only she'd let him.

"That's no way to live your life, just avoiding pain. Life is risk. *Love* is risk. And it's worth it."

"Do you still believe that?" he asked softly. "After everything that's happened?"

"Of course I do. Did it hurt when your father left? Absolutely. Was it hard? Yes. But if I'd tried to avoid that pain, I wouldn't have had you. I wouldn't have met Keith and had Mikayla. Did it hurt when Keith died? More than you can possibly imagine. It still hurts, every single day, and I hope you *never* have to go through that kind of pain. But I won't tell you to avoid love to spare you from that. Love is worth the possibility of pain."

Her words rang in his ears, but he had a point to make. "You can't tell me that having money doesn't help."

"Well, of course it helps!" She let out a chuckle. "Money solves a lot, and I'd rather have it than not. But it doesn't protect you from suffering. I've had a wonderful life. Yes, I've experienced heartbreak, but I healed. I don't want you to have a life without joy. I want you to be happy."

"Taking care of you and Mickey *does* make me happy. It's literally all I want."

"Don't you see? This is why I have to move out. You deserve to have your own life, and as long as Mickey and I are here, you're too focused on working and taking care of us to let yourself live. *Really* live."

"I don't want you to go." His throat felt thick with emotion.

"I understand." Her voice was kind. "And that means more to me than you'll ever know. But I have to do it. For you, and for me. It's time I start living again, too."

With something almost like defeat, but more like release, he said, "All right. I'll stop trying to convince you otherwise."

"I love you so much. And I'm so proud of you. My smart, loving, hardworking boy."

Roman let out a deep breath. "I love you too."

She hung up, and Roman slowly returned his phone to his pocket.

And then he just sat there, staring into the distance, facing things he would've preferred never to think about.

If he slowed down, he'd have to see what he didn't want to see.

He'd never wanted to believe that his father had any kind of effect on him. But in this quiet space, he could admit that was foolish. It didn't matter that he couldn't remember the guy, or that he'd left when Roman was just a baby. The man's very absence had been a constant presence in Roman's life, shaping who he'd become, whether he liked it or not.

He loved his mother and his sister, but he never got to spend time with them in the way he claimed to want. Having them in his home was the compromise he made with himself—he wasn't *there*, but he at least knew where they were, and that they were safe.

But that safety was an illusion. As Dulce had said, he couldn't protect them from everything.

Even if Ava decided to stop hiding their relationship, what would it matter? His work would always drag him away from her. Ava deserved someone who would *be there*, like Ashton and Gabe had said. It was the only way Roman could show her how much she meant to him.

Without it, the relationship would fail.

He propped his elbows on his knees, then rested his head in his hands. He was *so fucking tired* of being *busy*.

He tunneled his fingers into his hair, gripping it like a lifeline, as the truth he didn't want to acknowledge raised its hand, slow and hesitant, afraid of rebuke.

The truth looked like a skinny little boy with brown hair and big, hungry eyes, clothes that were clean but definitely not cool, and a constant knot of anxiety in the pit of his stomach.

A poor, powerless little kid who had nothing. No means, no security, no faith in his future.

Roman's eyes squeezed tight as he faced this kid, the kid who was *him*, the one who'd been steering his life, operating out of helplessness and fear.

This is why you work so hard, Ava had said, after seeing Roman's baby pictures.

Yes, the boy who was Roman said. *This is why*.

Making money had given him a sense of purpose and power. But now, the thought of opening another hotel or buying another business didn't excite him like it once had.

He'd made a different choice the night he'd met Ava. He'd stepped off his excessively scheduled path and gone down the road of spontaneity with her. Making her a drink and taking his time with it. Canceling his car and asking her to have dinner with him. The pool. The *bed*.

And the freedom that came with it. The *joy*.

If he stayed on the path before him, the path of Mr. Roman Vázquez, CEO, he was never going to have room in his life for the things that made it worth living.

He wouldn't have room for *Ava*.

He loved her. The soul-deep kind of love that required taking a risk. He wanted to *be* with her, like the guys had said.

Something had to change.

Who was he if he wasn't putting every ounce of his energy into protecting his family?

Instead of running away from the question, he let the boy inside him answer it.

Just Roman.

It was enough.

You're safe now, he told the boy. *I've got you.*

The boy nodded. Turned. Disappeared.

Not gone, just . . . resting. Finally.

Roman took a deep, cleansing breath.

The future he wanted was within reach. Freedom. Flexibility. Spontaneity. Connection. *Love.*

And Ava. All of it with Ava.

When do you get to rest? she had asked.

Now, he thought.

He pulled out his phone and called Camille.

When she picked up, he said, "I know what I have to do."

Chapter 42

Two Days Until the Wedding

How's your hot billionaire?" Michelle asked Ava as the two of them left their waxing appointment at the Bellísima spa. The Primas of Power had flown to Puerto Rico early to make sure everything was going according to plan.

Ava huffed out a breath. "He's not a billionaire."

Michelle smirked. "Oh, just a lowly millionaire? My bad."

Between Roman's work and travel schedule, Ava's back to school prep, and last minute pre-wedding tasks, they hadn't seen each other in person since the bridal shower. Missing him was a constant ache, but the distance made it easier to pretend she wasn't hiding a big secret from Jasmine.

"Shit or get off the pot, Ava," Michelle muttered.

"I'll tell Jas eventually," Ava hissed back. "She has enough going on."

There had been a mistake with the wedding favors Jasmine and Ashton had chosen—cutting boards shaped like the island of Puerto Rico with their names carved into them. Somehow, two-thirds of the boards read "Jashmine," and no one had caught it until Jasmine opened all the boxes, which had been delivered to the resort. As a last minute replacement, Roman had offered flask-size bottles of a Casa Donato small-batch rum blend, and Jasmine was currently working with Belinda "De Bellísima" Barrios and Joaquín Donato to design custom labels that commemorated the wedding.

The bachelor and bachelorette parties were happening that night, the rehearsal would take place tomorrow, and the day after that, Ashton and Jasmine would walk down the aisle as husband and wife.

Ava and her mother were taking a quick trip to Barbados after the wedding to visit Patricia's relatives. Ava hadn't seen her other grandparents or cousins in a few years, and as Patricia had said, "It'll be good for you to remember you have another family."

Ava knew Roman was arriving in a few hours, too, and he would be staying at the resort instead of his house. Her heart twisted when she remembered the wonderful nights they'd spent there, cut off from the world and completely absorbed in each other. Waking up in bed next to him, sharing meals, swimming in the evenings, and doing the *New York Times* crossword puzzle in the mornings.

She wanted that back, the no-phones unfettered access to Roman without a care for what anyone else in their lives did or didn't want.

They'd called and texted over the last couple weeks, but it hadn't been the same. She missed kissing him, touching him, falling asleep with her head on his shoulder. She missed the way he asked her what she wanted and listened intently, as if filing away the answer in his permanent memory banks. She missed hearing about the fascinating trajectory his work life had taken, and brainstorming ideas with him for chapters of his book. She even missed the flirty way he negotiated with her, ever the businessman.

She missed everything about him.

It was only going to get worse once the school year started. Then she'd be working all day and grading or lesson planning at night and on the weekends. Just the thought of it made her cringe.

As if reading her mind, Michelle asked, "Ready for the upcoming school year?"

Ava groaned. "I don't want to talk about it."

Michelle lowered her voice to an ominous tone. "*September is coming.*"

That drew out a huff of laughter. "My students aren't a horde of ice zombies," Ava said, then sighed. "But Mr. Gunderson might as well be."

Michelle's expression turned serious. "Still no answer?"

Ava shook her head. She'd been emailing the principal for weeks about implementing her proposed drama program, hoping this year would finally be the one where he made good on his promise, but he had yet to reply.

That in itself was an answer, she supposed.

"Alliance isn't the only school in the city," Michelle offered, and Ava shrugged. Thanks to recent budget cuts to the Board of Education, she didn't have much hope of teaching drama anywhere else.

All she wanted to do was introduce New York City kids to the magic of theater. Why was it so freaking hard?

Her phone rang, and Ava glanced at the screen with a sigh. "It's Abuela."

"Don't answer."

"I have to." Ava picked up. Her grandmother immediately launched into a tirade about something Titi Nereida had done, and Ava struggled to keep up. Not because Esperanza was speaking rapid-fire Spanish, but because she was referencing something that seemed to have happened sixty years ago.

Michelle backed away and mouthed, "I'll see you later."

Ava waved to her, then attempted to interrupt her grandmother. "All right, Bwela. I'll be right there."

She hung up and headed to her grandparents' room to do damage control.

By the time she returned to her own room later that evening—a suite she was sharing with her mother, thanks to an unexpected upgrade from Roman—Ava had helped put out fires for Esperanza, Olympia, Tío Luisito, and Ronnie's stepdaughter.

After a quick shower and a refresh of her curls, Ava got ready for the bachelorette party in record time.

"You look beautiful, honey," her mom said when Ava walked into the living room area to meet her.

Ava felt her cheeks heat, but she accepted the compliment with a smile. "Thanks."

She *felt* beautiful. Her "New Ava" edict to feel more confident in her own skin had taken hold, and she'd chosen a sleeveless emerald green sequined dress that came up to her neck but left her back bare. The skirt was tight and ended mid-thigh. She usually wore flared skirts to camouflage her hips, but tonight, she was embracing her curves.

Her makeup was light, save for a velvety plum lipstick, and she'd twisted her hair into an updo that left a riot of spirals cascading over the top of her head, with a few meticulously chosen tendrils trailing down around her face. Since a party bus would be transporting the guests, she wore black stilettos that put her at six feet tall.

It had been a long time since she'd felt this pretty. And it felt *good*.

While Patricia retrieved her purse, Ava snapped a selfie in the long mirror by the suite's door and texted it to Roman.

> **Ava:** Maybe I'll see you tonight after the parties?

He replied thirty seconds later. First the heart-eyes emoji, then one word:

> **Roman:** Maybe.

Followed by a winky-face.

Slipping her phone back into her slim black clutch, Ava indulged in a dreamy smile before her mother returned. The guys were going to a bar in Old San Juan for Ashton's bachelor party, and she hoped they'd be back early enough for her to sneak away to see Roman. Otherwise, it was going to be hell not being able to touch him for the next two days because her family was around.

Patricia joined her, and they left the room and headed for the buses parked out front.

Michelle had organized the bachelorette party. All Ava knew was that they'd rented out a small venue at one of the neighboring resorts, and that a group called "The Adonis Experience" would be performing.

Not wanting to leave anything to chance, Ava had looked

them up. The Adonis Experience was a highly-rated male stripper revue with a female emcee. For her own bachelorette party, Ava had chosen to do a wine tour of the Hudson Valley, which Jasmine had organized. It had poured for part of the day, she remembered. But by the time they reached the third vineyard, the sun had come out and everyone had danced drunkenly the whole bus ride home. It was probably the only thing that Hector or Olympia hadn't ruined.

For some reason, finding a nice memory related to her own wedding experience eased an ache she hadn't known she carried.

Huh. Something to examine more closely later.

"You sure about this?" Michelle asked Jasmine as the Primas of Power stood in front of the resort's main entrance, supervising the loading of the buses. Jasmine had decided at the last minute to invite not just her friends and cousins, but her aunts, mother, and grandmothers. They'd had to order a second bus.

"Why not?" Jasmine said. "It'll be fun."

She wore a white strapless jumpsuit with loose pants that laced up the back. Her dark hair fell in perfectly styled waves around her bare shoulders, and a twinkly little tiara with a short veil sat on top of her head.

Michelle shrugged. "If you say so."

Michelle was wearing black high-waisted short shorts with a black bralette covered only by a sparkly mesh crop top. Her black hair was pulled into a high ponytail. A tattoo featuring a stylized black cat sitting in a crescent moon made of flowers was visible on her forearm.

"We look like we're going to three different parties," Ava observed.

"Maybe, but we also look extremely hot," Michelle replied.

Jasmine turned to Ava. "I wanted to ask you—"

Before she could finish, Titi Lisa came running over with her phone. "Smile, girls!"

Ava and Michelle posed on either side of Jasmine, mugging for the camera until Jasmine's mom was satisfied. Then Michelle grabbed Jasmine's arm and hustled her onto the first bus. "Time to go!"

Jasmine looked over her shoulder but Ava waved her off.

"Don't worry, I'll make sure the latecomers get on the other bus."

Ava was in charge of the second party bus, which contained most of their older relatives. Two long padded benches lined both sides of the bus, with coolers tucked under the windows, a bathroom at the back, and, interestingly enough, a pole.

It was a short ride, but the women had found the chilled champagne bottles before Ava had gotten on, and they were all drinking expensive bubbly through penis-shaped straws in neon colors, courtesy of Ronnie. Abuela and Titi Nereida were giggling about "plátanos," an obvious euphemism. Titi Val and Ava's mom were reminiscing about the last time they had gone to a strip club, and Ava decided that there were some things she didn't need to know. She carefully made her way toward the back of the bus to chat with Jasmine's Filipina cousins from California, and counted her blessings that Olympia wasn't arriving until tomorrow.

The venue was located in the lower level of the other resort. The air conditioner pumped out cool air, and the room smelled like liquor and citrus. A low, square stage jutted out from one end of the room, and a long bar lined the other end. Rows of chairs faced three sides of the stage, with the one front and center decorated with white and gold balloons and a banner that read, "Bride's Last Ride."

Jasmine walked in, saw the sign, and covered her face. "Oh my god, Ronnie."

Behind her, Ronnie wagged a finger in the air. "Don't blame it on me! That was all Michelle."

"Only because I thought 'last hoedown' was tacky," Michelle said breezily. "Come on, Sister Bachelorette, time to take a seat."

Jasmine followed her, then came to a halt when she saw the other side of the chair. She let out a laughing groan.

Ava came around her to see what was so funny. A pillow waited on Jasmine's chair, embroidered with the words, "Bach That Ass Up."

"You would not believe how many terrible bachelorette puns there are," Michelle said gleefully.

The partygoers got drinks, either from the open bar or the wait staff rotating around the room. When the lights dimmed, they took their seats. Jasmine sat in her decorated chair, with Ava and Michelle on either side of her. Patricia sat on Ava's other side, and various family members filed around them.

Music continued to play in the background, and everyone chatted until the spotlight came on. The room fell quiet as a short, curvy woman entered stage right. She was pale, with brown hair held back in a low ponytail and tastefully done stage makeup. She was dressed all in black—blazer, slacks, heels—except for a sparkling silver bustier top. She carried a glittery silver microphone.

"Hello, my lovelies!" The emcee's voice was rich and resonant, with a playful lilt. "How are we tonight?"

In response, there were whoops and cheers and a "Wepa!" or three.

"I'm your host, Taylor Tirado." Taylor ambled around the stage as she spoke conversationally into the mic. "My boys and

I have come all the way to the enchanting island of Puerto Rico to celebrate our beautiful bride-to-be. Let's make some noise for Jasmine!"

The crowd, already well on their way to getting drunk, cheered raucously.

"Jasmine and Ashton had a bit of a storybook romance, am I right? The classic tale of girl meets boy, boy films TV show with girl, and girl and boy become Hollywood's latest power couple."

Everyone laughed, and when Ava glanced over at Jasmine, she saw her cousin was smiling. There were a lot of ways that sentence could have gone—boy hides secret child, girl becomes media scapegoat—but Ava guessed Michelle had signed off on the script, so there wouldn't be anything offensive.

Unless this was a roast. You never knew with Michelle.

Oh well, it was too late to worry about that now.

On stage, Taylor continued giving a humorous account of Jasmine's romance with Ashton, along with references to their acting roles. The crowd seemed entertained, and Jasmine took it well. After a couple minutes, Taylor came to a stop at the center of the stage.

"Now, Jasmine," she said. "I know you love Ashton and you're ready to make the 'same dick every day' commitment. But before you ride off into the sunset for your happily-ever-after, we want to ensure you've made the *right* choice. To help you out, I've brought along a selection of extremely eligible bachelors. Come on out, boys!"

The music rose, Adam Lambert's cover of "Holding Out for a Hero." The lights went dark, save for a single spotlight on Taylor, standing in the center.

"Tonight, The Adonis Experience brings you . . . The Bachelorette Experience," Taylor said over the music. Around her, several men ran out and took their places around the edge of the stage, standing with their backs to the audience. There were three men lining the front of the stage, and two on each of the sides. "Each one is a romantic fantasy come to life. Jasmine, are you ready to meet your bachelors?"

"Yes!" Jasmine yelled, and all the guests *woo*-ed.

"Let's meet our first Adonis!" Taylor waved her arm in a flourish and a spotlight fell on one of the men standing downstage stage right. The angle of the lighting made it hard to decipher any details other than his physique and attire. He had broad shoulders and a trim waist, and he was dressed like a cowboy, complete with hat, boots, and chaps.

Taylor provided the introduction with a tongue-in-cheek tone. "This rough and tumble rancher is looking for a little filly to ride *all night long.*"

Her words were met with catcalls and cheers. The man mimed galloping on a horse and spinning a lasso.

"Save a horse, ride a cowboy!" Titi Val called out from behind Ava.

Michelle turned around with wide eyes and a delighted expression. "Mom! Show some decorum."

Valentina stuck her tongue out at her youngest daughter.

The spotlight over the cowboy fell dark and one on the other side of the stage lit up, highlighting a slender blond man in a long black coat with dark sunglasses. He executed a series of fluid dance moves like he was at a rave.

"This creature of the night is a perfect gentleman," Taylor said, then waited a beat. "He'll ask for permission before he *comes inside.*"

Howls of laughter from the audience. The vampire turned his head and snapped his teeth.

Jasmine bounced in her seat. "This is so fucking corny, I *love* it!"

Now the spotlight was on a tall, burly man with long hair, dressed in a blousy white shirt and a green tartan kilt with a matching sash.

"This Highland warrior will let you see what's under his kilt . . . *if* you can *sheath his sword*!"

The man in the kilt held the sword at his waist in a two-handed grip. He mimicked stabbing with a thrust of his hips.

Now the light fell on a man in a sports jersey and a helmet.

"This athletic beefcake is raring to get his stick in there and *score a goal*."

The guy pretended to hump his hockey stick. The crowd ate it up.

Someone grabbed Ava's shoulder and she jumped, half-expecting to see a hunky hockey player behind her, but it was her grandmother.

"He's cute," Esperanza yelled over the music and cheers. "I'll get his number for you!"

"No, thank you!" Ava yelled back.

The spotlight landed on the man standing closest to Ava, gilding the edges of his sharp gray suit. His build was similar to Roman's, and between that and his costume, Ava was hit with a pang of longing.

Taylor supplied the intro. "This X-rated executive will show you who's the boss . . . *in the bedroom*."

The man shot his cuffs in an exaggerated fashion before turning the motion into a pop and lock sequence.

Opening her clutch, Ava pulled out her phone to see if Roman had texted again, but Taylor's next words made her pause.

"This adorable boy next door is all grown up and ready to take your friendship to the *next level*."

Ava's eyes flew to the stage, where a spotlight shone on a brawny guy in casual attire—a Yankees jersey, jeans, Tims, and a fitted cap pulled low over his face.

Boy next . . . ? Wait a second.

Ava squinted, first at the guy flexing in the spotlight, then back at the one in a suit, standing motionless in the shadows.

Her hand flew to her mouth, but before she could fully make sense of what she was thinking, the spotlight switched to the man standing directly in front of Jasmine. He wore a tuxedo and carried a single red rose in his hand.

"This red-carpet ready thespian likes to do it *on camera*," Taylor said with a wink-wink nudge-nudge.

To Ava's left, Jasmine let out an audible gasp.

"He'll read your body like a script and cast you as the lead in *all* his fantasies."

The man turned around to face the audience, revealing what Ava had already suspected. Jasmine let out an ear-splitting shriek.

It was Ashton.

The stage lights went up, and sure enough, Ashton was flanked by Boy-Next-Door Gabe and Roman the "X-rated Executive." In addition to the gray suit, Roman wore a pair of fake glasses without lenses.

Ava's pulse beat thickly in her veins as their eyes met. Roman gave her the quickest little wink, and then he was looking away, casting that confident smile over the audience like he hung out on a stage with male strippers every day.

Jasmine turned to Michelle with tears streaming down her face. "Did you know?"

Michelle's grin was smug. "Whose brilliant idea do you think this was?"

Jasmine sobbed as she stared up at her fiancé. "This is the best night of my life!"

Michelle gave a triumphant fist pump. Around them, the bachelorette party guests hollered. Someone—it sounded like Ronnie's mom, Titi Nita—yelled, "Take it off, Ashton!" His head whipped around and he broke character for a second as his eyes landed on the row of people sitting behind his fiancée—namely her mother, grandmothers, and all her aunts.

Ava stifled a laugh at the look of abject horror on his face, and suddenly Michelle's dubiousness from earlier made sense. Ava would bet her meager savings that no one had told him about the expanded bachelorette party guest list.

But Ashton was a professional, and his smile snapped back into place after only the barest lapse.

"All right, Jasmine," Taylor called from the stage. "Are you ready to see what these guys can do?"

Jasmine screamed her assent. A remix of "Gasolina" by Daddy Yankee came on and the guys flew into motion. They bopped around in a choreographed dance routine that combined breakdancing, hip hop, and nineties boy band moves with hip thrusts, body rolls, and subtle crotch grabs. It was clear the men of The Adonis Experience were all dancers or gymnasts, as they incorporated impressive spins, backflips, and surprisingly balletic leaps, with hip gyrations and dropping down to hump the floor. But Roman, Ashton, and Gabe kept up with them, never missing a beat.

Ava was *mesmerized*. She couldn't take her eyes off Roman. And if anyone had spared her a look, they would have noticed, but luckily, they were all just as enthralled by the performance.

He's mine! she wanted to shout. *That's my man!*

The secret that had once felt so special and exhilarating now sat in her gut like a lead weight. She'd wanted Roman all to herself, had done things she wasn't proud of to hide their torrid affair behind the boundaries she'd set. Now? Those very walls she'd diligently erected to keep her safe were threatening to crush her.

She glanced to the left at Jasmine, who was clapping and cheering for all she was worth. To the right at Patricia, who was doing the same, but slightly more subdued.

What would they say if they knew? What would they say when it was over?

She remembered their responses when Hector left. They'd both been supportive, of course, but also concerned. Pitying. Anxious, as if waiting for Ava to break.

Which, of course, had made her feel like she couldn't. Like she had to hold everything together, even as her life was falling apart.

Can't disappoint or inconvenience anyone, that sarcastic little voice sing-songed. *How dare you burden anyone else with your mess?*

Exactly. Haven't I done that enough? Ava couldn't go through it again. She just couldn't.

You're being ridiculous, the voice urged. *Just tell them.*

No.

God, she was losing it. New Ava, Old Ava, Sarcastic Ava—all of the conflicting impulses were mixed up in her head, in her soul, and she didn't know who was in charge anymore.

Scared Ava, came a little whisper, and she quashed it down.

The music changed to something with a slower tempo and a more pulsing beat, and Taylor pushed through the crowd of guys, drawing Ava's attention away from her own heavy thoughts.

"Now wait just a second." Taylor's expression was comically distressed. "I heard this was a bachelorette party!"

She waited for the audience reaction before gesturing at the men's costumes. "These boys are wearing far too much clothing. Jasmine, are you ready to see some skin?"

Jasmine screamed so loud, she'd probably be hoarse the next day.

Taylor pointed the mic toward the crowd. "How about the rest of you?"

More screams.

"All right, guys." Taylor spun her arm like she was throwing a pitch. "Let 'er rip!"

At Taylor's command, all seven men began a coordinated striptease, pulling at their respective costume tops. Ava's eyes were glued to Roman as he loosened his tie with slow, seductive movements. The suit jacket was next, sliding down each bulky shoulder before he pulled the blazer off and flicked it in quick arcs like a whip. He tossed it to Ava with a wink, then his hands went to the buttons on his shirt, which turned out to be snaps. He undid the first two slowly, then yanked the rest of the shirt open, revealing the muscular expanse of his torso. The smile he sent her was pure sin.

Ava's cheeks flushed. She'd gone commando tonight in the hopes of stealing a moment with him, but now, as she rubbed her thighs together and fidgeted in her seat, she wondered if that had been the best idea.

The choreography moved him out of her line of sight and

Gabe took his place. Gabe's jersey was open and he shrugged it off, revealing multiple tattoos.

Jasmine grabbed Ava's arm and leaned forward, narrowing her eyes. "Are Gabe's nipples pierced?"

Michelle gave her a surprised look. "You didn't know?"

"Why would I know that?"

"You've never seen him without a shirt?" Ava asked, sparing Gabe a glance. The lights glinted off the silver bars in his nipples as he dragged a hand down his abs toward his jeans-clad crotch.

Jasmine dropped her hands in her lap. "When would I have seen him topless?"

Michelle's smirk was wicked. "He might have inspired me to do mine too."

Jasmine's mouth fell open and she snapped it shut. "We are absolutely discussing this in more detail later."

Michelle gazed up at Gabe fondly. "This isn't the first time he's stripped for me either. You wouldn't *believe* what I had to promise to get him to agree to this."

"I see we have a *lot* to talk about." Jasmine sent Ava a meaningful look. Before Ava could decipher it, Ashton reappeared on the stage in front of them, and Jasmine's attention returned to him.

Once all the men were bare to the waist, Taylor strode forward with her sparkly microphone. "Jasmine, have you chosen which bachelor to give your rose to for the rest of your life?"

Jasmine's reply was immediate. "Ashton! I choose Ashton!" She was already reaching for him when Gabe and Roman came down to get her. Roman's eyes passed over Ava, and she didn't miss the way they heated as they trailed up her bare legs.

Her skin felt tight and she squirmed in her seat as she watched him guide her cousin onto the stage, where a single chair had appeared.

The other dancers melted away, including Roman and Gabe, leaving only Ashton, Jasmine, and Taylor. The music and lighting took on a dreamy quality, a whimsical tune playing while mini spotlights swirled around them, cycling through soft colors—white, pink, and yellow.

Ashton took Jasmine's hands and brought them to his lips. He whispered something to her, and there were tears in Jasmine's eyes as she nodded, even though her mouth was stretched into a brilliant smile.

"Ashton, is there something you wanted to say to Jasmine?" Taylor held the mic up to him.

As Ashton spoke into the mic, he gazed into Jasmine's eyes with such undisguised adoration, it made Ava's heart hurt.

"Jasmine. Mi corazón." His voice was husky with emotion and exertion, and his hands trailed languidly down her body. "You have the sweetest soul. The biggest heart. And the most amazing . . . ass."

Jasmine giggled as he gave her butt a quick squeeze. Her hands were doing some exploring of their own, sliding up his chest.

"I love your smile. Your laugh." He gripped her wrists and draped her arms around his neck, bringing their bodies closer together. "And the way you leave wet towels on the bathroom floor?" He let out a contented sigh, like he could think of nothing better. "It's incredibly sexy."

The guests laughed, and from behind Ava, Titi Lisa yelled, "Really, Jasmine? *Still?*"

"Before I met you," Ashton continued, "I was living in the

dark. You healed me and showed me that it was safe to trust. You are my light. My guiding star."

Now the audience was swooning and making "aww" noises. Ava's throat tightened, thinking of all the years Jasmine had searched for this kind of love, only to be hurt again and again. But she'd still put herself out there, still believed that the love she wanted and deserved could be hers. It had taken additional work—validating herself and demanding to be seen as her own person, separate from a relationship—but Jasmine had done it, and she and Ashton had built a solid foundation for their future together.

There was a lesson here, but Ava wasn't sure she wanted to see it yet.

"My heart . . ." Ashton went on, then lowered his voice suggestively, ". . . and every other part of me . . . is yours. Forever. Para siempre."

Tears leaked from Jasmine's eyes as Ashton leaned in and kissed her, deep and passionate, right in front of their friends and family. When he pulled back, his eyes cut away from Jasmine's and he muttered, "To my future mother-in-law, I am truly sorry for what you're about to see."

The lights flickered off, leaving only a red spotlight focused on the chair. The music changed abruptly, and in a forceful move, Ashton hoisted Jasmine up with an arm under each of her thighs. Taylor melted away as Ashton carried Jasmine to the chair, setting her down carefully and dropping to his knees in front of her. "Jeans" by Jessie Reyez and Miguel played while he proceeded to give Jasmine a lap dance that could have set the stage on fire.

It was more than a little awkward to watch your cousin's soon-to-be husband mime having sex on stage. Worse, it just made Ava wish Roman were there, climbing on top of her own chair and undulating his pelvis in her face.

Ava had never in her life hoped to receive a lap dance, but now, she wanted it with every fiber of her being.

From Roman, though. Only from Roman.

No offense to Ashton. He was doing a great job. A+ work, really. Jasmine was a lucky woman.

But so was Ava. *And no one knew it.*

All told, the lap dance lasted maybe thirty seconds, forty-five tops. By the time the song ended and the lights went down, Jasmine was on the floor with Ashton slithering around on top of her like a sexy alligator. Then the music changed to a party anthem by Pitbull with flashing colored lights. All the men, including Roman and Gabe, came running back onstage.

"Let's hear it for Jasmine and Ashton!" Taylor called out. "The hottest couple in creation!"

Amid claps and cheers, Taylor joined the guys for a high energy dance with lots of gyrations. Ava screamed along with everyone else, but she couldn't look away from Roman. The lights reflected off his muscular form as he moved, and if she hadn't known better, she would have thought he was a member of the troupe. He hit his moves with rhythm and precision, a fuck-me grin spread across his handsome face.

Ava wriggled in her seat and concocted an elaborate fantasy about dragging him offstage to fuck in the bathroom.

Suddenly, the guys streamed into the audience.

"Now that Jasmine's made her choice," Taylor said into the mic, "we've got a slew of romantic fantasies come to life just waiting to shower you with . . . attention!"

Ava's heart galloped as she saw Roman and Gabe rounding the corner of the stage to head straight for her row. Gabe immediately grabbed Michelle's chair, lifting himself up with just the strength of his massive arms, and began grinding on her.

But Roman . . .

Ava's eyes went wide. Roman was reaching for *her*.

The breath backed up in her throat even as her skin called out for him.

Yes, her dream was coming true!

But wait, no—what was he doing? No one was supposed to know they were together.

Fuck it. She was going to enjoy the hell out of this.

These thoughts passed through her mind in an instant, her body swaying toward him as he came closer.

But he passed her and instead came to a stop . . .

In front of her *mother*.

What the fuck?

Roman took Patricia's hands and lifted them to his chest. Ava's mom giggled—*giggled*, for fuck's sake—as Roman straddled her lap.

Ava stared, uncomprehending. If it had been awkward to watch her cousin receiving a lap dance, it was even weirder to watch *her own boyfriend* give one to her *mom*.

Not just her boyfriend. Her *secret* boyfriend.

She was thirty-three years old with a secret boyfriend. What was she *doing*?

Roman had done the right thing. Hadn't he? She was relieved he hadn't chosen her. It would have been too obvious, and she would've had to answer too many uncomfortable questions about it later.

But fuck, did he have to choose her mom instead? Jesus.

Objectively, Ava could admit that Roman's lap dance was fairly tame. A few undulations with lots of space between his body and her mom's, before he drew her to her feet for some easy salsa moves. Patricia was grinning ear to ear by the time Roman kissed her hand and returned to the stage. Suddenly, Ava was no longer upset—Roman had made her mom feel special, and if she hadn't already loved him, she would have fallen for him hard and fast right then.

Ava watched the rest of the dance—which involved all the men shucking their pants to reveal tiny briefs patterned like the Puerto Rican flag—and had to admit that in addition to feeling relieved, she was also disappointed. Not only because Roman hadn't chosen her, but because a very small, immature part of her wished he'd taken the choice out of her hands.

It wasn't fair of her, and she would have been angry if he'd done that, but this secret was getting harder to hold on to, and it would've made everything so much easier if she could just . . . let it go.

Two more days.

After that, she'd figure out how to tell Jasmine, at least. And then her mom. From there, well, she'd play it by ear.

For now, Roman was still hers. Only hers.

Even if her heart begged her to come clean and claim him in front of everyone.

Chapter 43

Dancing on stage with a group of male strippers had never been on Roman's bucket list, but now that it was over, it ranked as one of the top five most fun and empowering things he'd ever done in his life.

Making time for rehearsals had involved twisting himself into a pretzel, and there had been moments where he'd felt positively ancient compared to the other guys, but learning the moves and choreography had invigorated him. The experience reminded him of acting opposite Ashton back when they were young, and it had also brought him closer to Gabe, whom Roman now considered a friend. Not only that, it had given him a taste of the freedom and spontaneity he had so far only attributed to his liaisons with Ava.

Roman hadn't felt this alive in ages.

Getting to do it all in front of Ava had been the icing on the stripper cake. The way she'd looked at him, her eyes shining with a mixture of admiration, arousal, and something he didn't dare name, had made him feel ten feet tall. Every rescheduled meeting and the nights he'd spent babying his lower back had been worth it.

She'd looked absolutely gorgeous in that sparkly green dress that showed off her long legs and curves, with her curls falling in seductive little spirals around her beautiful face. He'd wanted to pull her up on stage and kiss that dark, sexy lipstick right off her lush mouth. Limiting himself to a few winks and heated glances had used every ounce of his restraint, and he didn't know how he was going to get through the rest of this wedding pretending he wasn't completely captivated by her.

Not only that, he was bursting at the seams to tell her what else he'd been working on. But it wasn't the kind of thing one said via text or even video call. He had to get her alone. Somehow.

After giving Ava's mom a lap dance—he'd recognized her from photos—and finishing the group number, Roman went backstage with Ashton and Gabe. Three actual members of The Adonis Experience replaced them, and the show continued.

"Good work, viejos," Gabe said, shooting a grin at Roman and Ashton as they trooped into the dressing room. "Didn't think you old guys would be able to keep up."

Ashton threw a towel at him, the one he'd just used to mop the sweat from his face. "You're talking to two professional actors. We weren't the ones whining about being embarrassed."

"And that was before you knew their mothers would be there," Roman teased.

"Why didn't Michelle warn us?" Ashton groaned.

"Because she's a chaos demon." Gabe passed them cartons of water from the dressing room's mini fridge.

Ashton pulled a change of clothes out of his locker. "I'm never going to be able to look my mother-in-law in the face again."

Roman counted his blessings that his own mom and sister weren't arriving until the next day.

"Speaking of mothers," Gabe said, turning to Roman. "I thought for sure you were going to dance for Ava. Did you know that was her mom you were grinding on?"

"Yes, and I barely touched her."

"But why not just dance with Ava?"

Roman's jaw tightened as he retrieved his stuff from his own locker. "Don't get me wrong, I wanted to." He'd *really fucking wanted to.* "But I didn't want to upset her."

"She still wants to keep the relationship a secret?" Gabe asked, and Roman nodded.

Ashton had fallen unusually quiet, so Roman added, "Don't worry, I'm going to remind her tonight to tell Jasmine before the wedding."

"Mm-hmm." Ashton didn't look at him. "You'd better."

They cleaned up and changed, then went to meet the rest of the bachelor party guests in the resort's night club. The plan was for Michelle to bring everyone to join them when the show was over.

Roman was sipping a rum and Coke while chatting with Ashton's father, Ignacio, when the bachelorette contingent arrived. The volume skyrocketed as the boisterous group filed in, led by Jasmine's grandmother and aunts. Roman automatically looked for Ava. She wasn't difficult to spot, since she towered above all her relatives and most of Jasmine's friends. Their eyes met, and he had the surreal experience of everything else falling away. He was dimly aware of Ignacio talking to him, of the Bad Bunny song playing overhead, of the press of the crowd and the lingering sweetness of cola on his tongue. But the only real, true thing for him in that instant was Ava.

He loved her with his entire heart. And he was so fucking tired of hiding it.

Excusing himself from Ignacio, Roman drifted toward her. She saw him, and her eyes took on a knowing expression. She parted from the crowd and tilted her head toward the hallway that led to the restrooms. When he nodded, she made her way back.

Roman waited a few seconds, then followed her. There were several individual stalls and a communal sink area. The row of hanging Edison bulbs cast a low, warm light over the space, and despite the grunge industrial décor, everything was clean. They locked themselves in the largest stall and were on each other in seconds.

"That was so fucking hot." Her words were muffled against his lips.

Roman licked into her mouth. "You liked it?"

A throaty sigh. "I *loved* it."

"All for you, mi vida." And then he kissed her soundly, soaking in the feel of her body, warm against his, and the taste of rosé on her tongue.

Two weeks was too long to be away from this woman. Hell, two *days* was too long.

Never again, he vowed. His plans had been set in motion, and once all was said and done, he wouldn't be separated from her for that long ever again.

"I can't believe you gave my mom a lap dance and not me," she said when she came up for air. Her voice carried a breathless, pouting tone, and he chuckled against the sensitive skin below her ear.

"You don't want anyone to know about us." He dragged his lips down her neck, sucking and biting. Not hard enough to leave a mark, although the thought did occur to him.

"I know, but . . ." It came out like a whine.

"Trust me, Ava." His voice was husky as he pulled the neck of her dress aside to taste her. "If I'd given you a lap dance, *everyone* would know how I feel about you. I wouldn't have been able to hide it."

The hand pressed to his chest trailed downward, her fingers tracing each shirt button, his belt buckle, and lower. Her nails scraped lightly over the bulge in his slacks, eliciting an intense wave of desire that made him shudder.

"You mean this?" The words were nearly a purr as she cupped him, molding the fabric over his thickening length.

He caught her chin and angled her head so he could search her eyes. "What are we doing, Ava? Are we going to fuck in this bathroom?" It came out rough, propelled by his quickening pulse.

"I was imagining it," she admitted, her tone almost shy even as she continued to fondle him through his pants. "While I was watching you on stage. I was picturing us just like this . . ."

"Like this, huh?" There were things they had to talk about, important things that were on the tip of his tongue, but it had been weeks since he'd seen her, and even longer since he'd touched her intimately.

Fuck it. Everything else could wait. He needed to make her come, needed to feel her warmth and hear her gasps of pleasure.

"Or maybe like this?" He skimmed his hands along her thighs, pushing the short dress up her luscious hips. One thumb slid toward her heat and he was hit with a jolt of lust when he found her completely bare.

And soaked.

He glanced down at his fingers, slick with her arousal. "Look at you, all wet and ready for me."

"I missed you." There was more than lust in her tone, something deep and complex that had his heart stuttering in his chest. Reading her emotions was like teasing out the flavor notes in an exquisitely aged rum, more of an art than a science, but one that became second nature with time.

But he wouldn't push her on it now. Instead, he kissed her, slow and thorough, while he plied her sensitive flesh. She clung to his shoulders and whimpered into his mouth, her hips rocking in a rhythm known only to the two of them.

His dick was so hard he thought it was going to burst through his pants, but this was for her, and as much as he wanted to, he wasn't going to fuck her standing up during another wedding event.

There would be time later to lay her out and cherish her the way she deserved. Or to let her take the reins.

After all, he was aiming for forever.

Soon, her kisses became bruising. Taking that as his cue, Roman sped up his ministrations, dipping his fingers into her wet heat just enough to tease before focusing his attention back on her clit. His other arm wound around her waist, holding her up.

Ava came with a sharp gasp, throwing her head back. Roman plunged a finger into her channel, grunting when she clenched around him in rhythmic pulses. It was a dim echo of how she felt coming around his dick, but still enough to have him nearly spilling in his pants.

When she sagged against him, he slipped his hand from between her legs and held her close.

"I missed you too," he whispered into her ear, and her arms tightened around his neck.

They stayed like that, just hugging, until the squeak of another stall door broke into the haze that had surrounded him since Ava had walked into the club.

Reality came crashing back, and Roman heaved a deep sigh. A bathroom stall wasn't the place for important conversations.

"Sorry," Ava whispered, drawing back once they heard the person use the sink and leave. Her hand drifted to his pants again. "Do you want me to—"

He shook his head, cutting her off. "No, mi amor. It's not that." God, she thought he was sighing because he hadn't gotten his rocks off. It made him want to show her again how much giving her pleasure brought him pleasure too.

"I just wish we were alone, so we could catch up properly," he said. "We have a lot to talk about."

She pulled her skirt back down. "Maybe at the hotel?" she said softly. "I could sneak over to your room—"

"Ava." He pitched his voice low, aware that someone else might enter the bathroom area at any moment. "I'm tired of sneaking around."

She froze, a wary look entering her eyes, and he forged on before she could misunderstand.

"Ashton knows. Gabe and Michelle know." He let that sink in. He'd found out about Michelle during rehearsals with Gabe, and he'd been sort of annoyed, sort of hurt that Ava hadn't told him herself. When she didn't say anything, he went on. "It's time to tell Jasmine."

She was already shaking her head before he finished. "No. We said after the wedding."

"*You* said," he pointed out. "But when? At the reception? Before she leaves for her honeymoon? After she gets back?"

She was shutting down before his eyes, her mouth pinching, her shoulders drawing inward. He cupped her arms and kept his tone gentle, willing her to stay with him.

"Ava, I understand that you're worried, but keeping this secret is hurting you. For your own peace of mind, I think you should tell her. Tonight."

"Tonight?" The word held a note of panic. "Why tonight?"

He should tell her that Ashton had issued an ultimatum, but he wanted her to do this on her own, not because there was suddenly an external deadline.

Somehow, telling Jasmine about their relationship had become synonymous with Ava accepting Roman into her heart. He couldn't have explained why he thought that, but there it was.

"She'll want to know sooner rather than later," he reasoned. "And this has the potential to affect your relationship. Especially since the others know."

That got through to her. Her eyebrows drew together and her expression turned thoughtful. After a moment, she closed her eyes and let out a heavy sigh.

"I should have told her after the engagement party, instead of dragging this out."

He pressed a kiss to her forehead. "Don't worry about the past. Just talk to her. She loves you."

When she opened her eyes, there was a wealth of pain in their depths, but she nodded. "I'll try."

Roman wanted to believe her. He really did.

But just in case, he mentally prepared himself for the fallout when Ashton broke the news to Jasmine himself.

As for his own update, he'd get Ava alone tomorrow so he could tell her somewhere that *wasn't* a public bathroom.

Chapter 44

After sneaking out of the bathroom, Ava headed for the bar. The men of The Adonis Experience had joined the party in their street clothes, and the crowd was louder and more rowdy than when she'd arrived. Esperanza was dancing salsa with the cowboy, a handsome Black man with broad shoulders, and Titi Nita was grinding on the tall, red-haired Highlander.

Ava considered getting sloppy drunk, the better to spill her secret to Jasmine before the night was over, but that was the coward's way out, and besides, she didn't need to add "nursing a hangover" to her already full to-do list. So instead of another glass of rosé, she asked for a ginger ale.

Several of Ashton's telenovela friends had placed their drink orders before her, so she settled in to wait and considered how to tell Jasmine.

Should she do a slow reveal?

Hey, remember when I went to that teaching conference last October? Well, I met someone . . .

Or just blurt it out?

Surprise! I'm fucking Roman. And I've fallen in love with him. Believe me, no one is more shocked than I am.

Ava rubbed her temples, which throbbed in time with the

Cardi B song blasting overhead. The main thing she had to figure out was how to explain why she hadn't come clean after seeing Roman at the engagement party. Before that, it had just been a fling, and she hadn't been aware of his connection to Ashton. But since then, not only had she known Roman was in Jasmine's wedding, their relationship had gotten more serious. It was absolutely the sort of thing she should have told her best cousins.

How was Jasmine going to take the news?

She'd probably be pissed that Ava hadn't told her sooner, but after that, Ava could just see Jasmine getting excited by the prospect. Assuring Ava that her fears about the future were unfounded. That Roman was a great guy, that he wasn't Hector, that he wouldn't hurt her.

Hell, she'd probably be over the moon. After all, Roman was Ashton's best friend. There would most certainly be double dates in their future.

For a brief moment, Ava let herself imagine what it might be like. Dinners. Events. Holidays. Joint vacations.

But Ava, who was trying to temper her expectations, couldn't chance getting her hopes up.

Which meant she didn't want her cousins getting their hopes up, either. No matter what, she didn't want to be blindsided again. She'd enjoy the time she had with Roman, but she was keeping her eyes open.

This time, when it ended, she would see it coming.

But then what? How would it affect her relationship with Jasmine?

She could see it now. *Sorry, Ava, we're inviting Roman to this one. You'll come to the next, okay?* Or worse, making them choose sides. Ashton would obviously take Roman's side. Would Jasmine side with Ashton, her husband? Or Ava, her cousin?

This was what had happened with Hector. Their lives and families had become so entwined, it had been hell to untangle them. She already feared that losing Roman would destroy her, but if it meant losing Jasmine too . . .

How could she bear it? It was the thing that had terrified her from the beginning. Not just losing romantic love, but her family as well.

She turned to the dance floor, easily finding her cousins where they danced with their men. Under the flashing club lights, Jasmine all but glowed in her white outfit and veil as she shimmied and twirled in Ashton's arms. Michelle and Gabe were full on making out in the middle of the dance floor, heedless of all the Rodriguez relatives surrounding them.

Jealousy licked Ava's insides like fire, not because of her cousin's partners, but at their freedom in showing them off to the world. Jasmine and Michelle had both been unlucky in love before, and now they were incandescently happy, like Lizzie and Darcy at the end of *Pride & Prejudice*. Ava knew how that felt, and she dreaded the possibility of making them support her through *another* breakup.

Poor Ava, their eyes would say, even if their mouths didn't. While they waited for her to shatter so they could pick up the pieces.

Jasmine and Michelle had done enough, helping her get rid of Hector's stuff and holding her hand while she initiated the divorce proceedings. They had their own lives, their own loves, and Ava vowed never to burden them like that ever again.

Her ginger ale appeared on the bar in front of her, garnished with a lime wedge and a sprig of mint, and Ava dug a bill out of her purse for the tip. But when she lifted the glass and put the straw to her lips, her throat felt too tight to swallow. She set the soda back down, untouched.

She couldn't tell Jasmine now. Not with the wedding bearing down on them. This was Jasmine's special time. Ava wouldn't detract focus from that, not even a little bit.

Because, and this was the part that scared her the most, what if Jasmine *didn't* react well? What if Jasmine saw, just as Ava did, the clear possibility for mess?

Why, Ava? Why couldn't you fall in love with literally anyone else other than my husband's best friend?

Just the thought of it made Ava's head pound with renewed vigor. The revelation had the potential to cast a pall over the whole wedding. Every time Jasmine looked at the photos, she'd remember Ava's utter selfishness, usurping Jasmine's special time and making it about *her*.

And if there was one thing Ava *would not do*, it was ruin Jasmine's wedding.

I'll try, she'd told Roman. But she couldn't do it. Not now. She'd wait until after Jasmine returned from the honeymoon, when it was just the two of them, and she could tell her the whole story. Somehow, she'd assure Jasmine that this wouldn't cause problems for her,

And hopefully, her prima would forgive her.

Just then Ronnie appeared next to her, breathing hard with exertion. She grabbed a bar napkin and attempted to fan herself with it.

"I haven't danced like this since the quinceañera last year," she said breathlessly, referring to her stepdaughter's fifteenth birthday. "Are you going to dance?"

Ava shook her head. She didn't feel like it, not if she couldn't dance with Roman the way she really wanted to.

"Headache," she murmured.

Ronnie's eyebrows dipped. "You still get migraines?"

Ava nodded, thinking of the last big one she'd had, the day she and Roman had arrived in Puerto Rico and had an argument. He'd taken such good care of her. The man really deserved more than being hidden like an illicit affair.

Ronnie placed her drink order—Malibu and pineapple juice, the same thing she'd been ordering since they were in college—then turned back to Ava. "I've been meaning to tell you. You've been an amazing maid of honor."

"Even though I vetoed most of your decoration ideas?"

Ronnie laughed. "Even so. Jasmine is lucky. I wish I'd asked you to be mine."

"Your sorority sister did a great job."

"She did, but damn, Ava, you go above and beyond for this family."

Ava expected the praise to feel good. Didn't she want the validation? But it just made her tired. "You know Michelle planned this party, right?"

"Obviously. I don't know how she got the groomsmen to join the strippers, but that was genius." Ronnie's drink appeared on the bar, topped with a Maraschino cherry. She picked it up and turned to face the rest of the club. "Speaking of, is that Ashton's friend?"

Ava had already spotted Roman making his way onto the dance floor, probably looking for her. She didn't say anything.

Ronnie sent her a sly look. "He's pretty cute. And I heard he's single."

A chill went down Ava's spine. The dramatic irony was going to kill her.

"Oh yeah?" she heard herself say. She tried to summon her Resting Pleasant Face but didn't have the energy.

"Just saying, you don't need to be alone forever. And you could do a lot worse than a guy like that."

Sarcastic Ava wanted to say, *If I were in a relationship, who would be your last minute babysitter?* But she didn't. Ronnie meant well. Even if she did sound exactly like their grandmother.

And then, Ava surprised herself by saying just that. "You sound like Abuela."

Ronnie blanched. "Damn, you're right. It's wild how their limiting beliefs sink into us, even if we want to believe we're more evolved and shit. Sorry."

"Don't worry about it." Ava picked up her ginger ale, just to have something to do with her hands. Ronnie had unknowingly said something extremely wise.

It's wild how their limiting beliefs sink into us . . .

But Ava was too tired to fully examine it.

"I'm going to get back out there," Ronnie said. "Feel better, Ava."

"You too."

The reply had been automatic, and luckily, Ronnie hadn't heard her over the music. It was a sign that Ava was too much in her head. She needed to get out of here.

Except . . .

She pressed her fingers to her eyes, which had started to feel dry and achy—a sure sign that she needed to take something if she wanted to stave off a migraine. Roman was going to be so disappointed that she hadn't told Jasmine. No matter what she did, she was hurting someone.

Be good, Ava.

She tried. She really did. But it was never enough.

It was never going to be enough.

After texting her mother that she had a headache, Ava slipped from the party without saying goodbye to anyone.

Scared Ava was firmly in control. And it sucked.

Chapter 45

One Day Until the Wedding

The next day, Roman texted Ava multiple times, but she either didn't respond or said she was "busy."

He had a feeling he knew why.

But she couldn't avoid him forever. They both had to attend the rehearsal. And after a call with Camille that morning, he was going to explode if he didn't tell Ava his news soon.

Belinda gathered everyone on the beach. It was late afternoon, and as hot and humid as one would expect from late August in Puerto Rico. A few markers were set in the sand to show where the chairs, aisle, and arch would be. The crashing surf provided the soundtrack, reminding Roman of the last time he'd been here, when he'd lost his swim trunks. The groomsmen and bridesmaids were all there, along with Jasmine's parents and brother. Yadiel was present in his capacity as ring bearer and Michelle's ten-year-old niece, Danica, was the flower girl.

Jasmine had decided to walk herself down the aisle, but her parents would be waiting for her. When she reached the arch, they would take their seats. Jasmine's brother was going to read a poem, chosen by the bride and groom. Then, the officiant would perform a short ceremony.

Ashton had told Roman there had been some drama over the officiant. Jasmine had asked Miriam Perez, who'd played her onscreen mother in *Carmen in Charge*, to perform the ceremony. Miriam, in addition to being a renowned improv actress, had also officiated dozens of weddings. But Jasmine's grandmother had booked a priest without clearing it with anyone first. A huge argument had ensued, and Esperanza hadn't let it go until Ashton played the machísmo card and intervened.

Roman spotted Ava talking in hushed tones with Michelle. When he approached, Michelle took one look at him, said, "See ya!" and darted off to where Gabe chatted with Jasmine's brother, Jeremy.

Dark sunglasses shielded Ava's eyes, and her smile was polite, but cool. Ah, the Resting Pleasant Face was back. Was it because her family was around, or was it for him? He guessed she hadn't told Jasmine and feared his reaction.

He wanted to slide the sunglasses off her face and kiss her, to tell her that he wasn't going to scold her. Instead, he stuffed his hands in the pockets of his linen slacks.

"How was the spa?" he asked. He knew she and several of her relatives had gone for mani-pedis earlier in the afternoon.

"Fine."

"Relaxing?"

Ava huffed out a humorless laugh. "With my grandma and aunts? How could it be?"

"Silly question." He moved closer and lowered his voice "Did you . . . ?"

She was already shaking her head before he could finish the question.

"No," she said quietly. "I'm sorry."

"I see." He said it slowly, trying to unpack the myriad emotions tightening her voice. God, he *wished* he could see her eyes. "Are you okay?"

She shook her head again. "I've had a headache since last night."

Shit. And she was standing out here in the glaring sunshine. "What do you need? I can bring you a chair. Get you some water. An umbrella. A fan."

"It's all right. I have a water bottle." She pulled a metal cannister out of her shoulder bag and took a long drink.

"Ava . . ." He gave in to the urge to run his fingers through his hair. "I gotta tell you, it's killing me to stand here with my thumb up my ass, acting like I don't love you more than life itself."

Her lower lip trembled, breaking his heart. "I'm sorry," she whispered.

"I don't need you to apologize." He fought to keep the frustration out of his tone. "I just need you to *talk* to me."

"I will. I promise." She started to turn away from him.

"When?" He said it quickly, because he wanted to grab her wrist and pull her back, like they were the leads in one of the Korean dramas his mother loved.

Ava bit her lip. "Before the rehearsal dinner."

And then she plastered her Resting Pleasant Face back on and went to speak to Jasmine's mom.

Roman watched her go, a hole opening in his stomach as he resisted the impulse to go after her and kiss that fake-ass smile right off her face.

Miriam, the officiant, was the last to arrive. "Sorry," she called out, as she hurried across the sand. "I was getting a massage and fell asleep on the table. Ten out of ten, highly recommend."

Belinda clapped her hands to draw everyone's attention. In her usual domineering manner, she reiterated all their roles and took them through the timeline of the ceremony.

"Why does the wedding planner remind me of your mother?" Roman overheard Jillian whispering to Michelle.

"Same Latina ringmaster energy," Michelle replied, stifling a laugh. "Necessary for wrangling a bunch of clowns like us."

Finally, it was time to practice, and no one dared deviate from Belinda's meticulous plan.

When Michelle's niece Danica went forward as flower girl, she flounced down the aisle and mimed the act of dropping petals with exaggerated flourishes.

"Is she going to do it that way tomorrow?" Ashton asked Jasmine.

Jasmine grinned. "I sure the hell hope so. It's exactly how I would have done it at her age."

Roman took his place next to Ava at the little orange flag that marked the start of the aisle. She'd finally removed the sunglasses and he desperately wanted to talk to her, but her serene smile was firmly in place and he knew there was no reaching her now. So he held his tongue and offered her his elbow.

Walking down the aisle with her was bittersweet. One of her hands was on his arm, and she pretended to hold a bouquet in the other. Her eyes remained straight ahead and it was a wonder Roman didn't trip because he couldn't look away from her. For the briefest moment, they stood in the spot where the arch would go, and in his imagination, they weren't maid of honor and best man, but bride and groom. Then the moment was over and they parted to stand on either side of the imaginary arch, waiting for Gabe and Michelle to join them next.

Once everyone was assembled in the proper order, Belinda called, "And now it's Jasmine's turn!" She began to hum a slightly off-key rendition of "Here Comes the Bride."

As Jasmine started down the aisle, it was clear why she was an award-winning actress. She moved with gravitas and grace, like she was clad in a diamond-encrusted gown with an eight-foot-long train instead of a white tank top and denim shorts. Roman glanced over at Ashton, who watched Jasmine walk toward him with his heart in his eyes. Then Roman looked to Ava. She still wore the same placid expression, but he knew her well enough now to know the truth: this experience was breaking her. It was there in the tightness around her eyes, the pinch of her mouth, the set of her shoulders. She was holding herself very still, as if the slightest breeze would shatter her into a million pieces.

He wanted to hold her, to comfort her, to fix whatever was hurting her. But he couldn't. She wouldn't *let* him. And it was tearing him apart inside.

This ends today, he thought. No more hiding. No more secrets. Come hell or high water, they were getting to the bottom of whatever was still holding her back, and he would convince her to *let him fucking help.*

Somehow, he got through the rest of the rehearsal. Most of it was a blur. He couldn't have said what poem Jasmine's brother read, or what the officiant said, even though it had everyone laughing. All of his attention was on Ava.

When it was over and they all filed off in pairs, he stayed close to her and spoke out of the corner of his mouth. "Let's go inside and talk before everyone else gets to the dinner."

She gave him a brief nod and slipped her sunglasses back on. They made their way over the sand and across the pool deck, where they had once flirted and lathered each other in sunscreen.

The exact spot where Roman had realized he was in love with her.

As they passed the rows of lounge chairs, his steps slowed and he fondly remembered that day. A few people sat sipping drinks, their faces shielded from the sun by beach umbrellas tilted low. Two women were chatting loudly in Spanish, their voices clearly audible over the music drifting from the bar inside.

"Where's Gloria?" one of the women said. "I thought you were bringing her as your guest."

Ava froze, and Roman nearly ran into her. Alarmed, he turned her to face him. Was it her headache? Was she going to faint? He opened his mouth to ask, but she pressed a finger to her lips to shush him. He played back the question he had overheard. The name "Gloria" sounded familiar but he couldn't say why.

An older woman's voice responded in Spanish. "Jasmine said no." The words were punctuated with an offended sniff.

Ava grabbed Roman's arm, whether to stop him from interrupting or for emotional support, he wasn't sure. He stood still and listened.

"Why?" the first speaker asked.

"Because of Ava."

"Oh, that's right. Gloria was her mother-in-law."

Ah. *That* was why the name sounded familiar. He kept his gaze on Ava, who fairly vibrated with tension. He suspected she knew exactly who the women were.

The second speaker went on. "After everything Gloria did for her, Ava won't even answer her calls." A *tsk*. "So selfish."

Next to Roman, Ava sucked in a sharp breath. He wanted to hold her, but her grip on his arm was like iron. His blood started to boil.

"Is Ava still upset over the divorce?"

"You know how she is. Always too sensitive."

"I heard Hector is getting married again." The first speaker's tone held the hush of hot chisme.

"Yes. To some girl from the neighborhood."

"Is she pretty?"

Another sniff. "Not as pretty as Ava."

"Well, who is?" The woman's tone turned thoughtful. "With that face, you'd think she'd be able to find another man."

"She's not trying. I told her to apologize. You don't have to mean it, I said. But men like to think they're right."

"Did she do it?"

"Clearly not, since Hector is marrying someone else!"

"And they didn't even have any kids." Roman could practically hear the head shake that went along with those words. His skin broke out in goosebumps from the stress of holding his tongue.

"Such a shame." The second speaker let out a deep sigh. "My sister is so disappointed."

"Let's hope Jasmine doesn't make a mess of her marriage too."

"She probably will." There was a pause, followed by a speculative, "How much do you think they spent on this wedding?"

"More than Miguelito spent on Ava's wedding, that's for sure."

"Well, that was a waste of money."

What. The. Fuck.

Roman had heard enough. Red flashed across his vision as he started toward the chismosas, but Ava hissed and yanked on his arm.

"Don't!" she said in a desperate whisper. "You'll make it worse!"

He let her drag him inside, then gave in to the urge to snatch the sunglasses off her face.

Her hazel eyes were wet and devastated. Helplessness slashed at him, warring with the impulse to fight for her.

"*Now*," he said, his tone fierce. "We are discussing this *right the fuck now.*"

She let out a trembling breath and nodded. "Okay." Her voice shook, and he wanted to go out there and toss all the lounge chairs into the pool, along with their occupants. Instead, he grabbed her hand and pulled her toward the ballroom where the rehearsal dinner was being held.

And he didn't give a damn who saw them.

Chapter 46

Hot, angry tears pushed their way up Ava's throat as the words "selfish" and "sensitive" rang through her pounding head.

Never mind that she'd gone out of her way to squash down all her emotions so as not to inconvenience anyone else with them, or that she gave and gave and gave, until she had nothing left for herself.

It wasn't good enough. Nothing she did would ever be good enough.

Be good, Ava.

She was going to put it on her tombstone. *Here lies Ava. She tried to be good, and eventually, it killed her.*

When they reached the ballroom, she let Roman propel her into the backstage area, past the AV team setting up equipment for speeches and karaoke. To the right, there was a large supply closet, its door propped open by a box filled with wires and cords. Roman kicked the box aside on their way in. The second the door shut behind them, Ava began to tremble with rage.

"Do you see now?" She stabbed a finger toward the door, indicating what they'd just overheard. "That right there is why I don't want anyone in my family to know about you."

Roman pushed both his hands into his hair and let out a long, slow breath. "Jesus. I've never wanted to fight an old lady before. Relatives of yours, I presume?"

"My great-aunt Nereida and her daughter, Marta." Ava crossed her arms, hugging herself. "That was mild. They can be a lot worse."

He dropped his hands. "Look, I get it. You're not exaggerating about your family. But we're too old to be sneaking around like teenagers, worried about what our parents are going to say."

She released a strangled laugh. "If only it were just my parents. They're a lot more reasonable than everyone else."

"Great, let's tell them about us. Introduce me to your dad tonight."

She blanched. "No! He'll tell Olympia."

"Your mom then."

"She'll tell Michelle's mom, who will tell Jasmine's mom, who will—"

He held up a hand to cut her off. "Ava, I'm not entertaining this line of thinking anymore. We've gone at your pace, and it isn't working, so now we're going to try mine. You like lists, so let me make this simple." He held up a finger for each point. "One: I love you. Two: I want to spend the rest of my life with you. And three: I'm stepping down as CEO so I can do just that."

Ava stopped breathing. Her heart was stuck on the second point, but her brain was working overtime to make sense of the third, and coming up with nothing.

"You're doing what?" she croaked.

His expression was placid as he repeated himself. "I'm stepping down as CEO. It's been in the works for two weeks, and the transition should be complete by the end of the year. I wanted to tell you sooner, but it's been impossible to get you alone for any length of time in a place that isn't a closet or a bathroom." He gave the shelf of industrial-size rolls of toilet paper a pointed look.

She took a shuddering breath, and against her wishes, fresh tears sprang to her eyes. "Roman, you can't."

"Why not?" He stuck his hands in his pockets, the pose deceptively relaxed.

"This is a huge decision, and someday, whether it's tomorrow or ten years from now, you're going to look back and realize that I'm . . ." She stopped. The next part wasn't going to go over well.

"You're what?" His words carried a dare, like he was already prepared to pick apart her reasoning.

She swallowed hard and said it anyway. "I'm not worth it."

His eyebrows rose slightly. "No? I have an entire spreadsheet that says you are."

That both thrilled and terrified her. "Please tell me you're joking."

The corner of his mouth quirked. "I never joke about spreadsheets."

"Roman." She rubbed her temples. "I can't ask you to do something like this for me."

"You didn't. I *want* to do this. For us, yes, but also . . . for me." He took her hands in his, his expression open, reminding Ava of the first time she'd seen him all those months ago, showing off his tricks behind a bar.

"I'm tired of working every second of every day," he went on. "Of not having time for my family, for my friends, for *myself*. In the past year, the only times I've felt like I was truly living were those stolen moments when we were together. I

want to stop hustling and finally enjoy the fruits of my labor."
His fingers tightened on hers, and his tone deepened. "I want
to *live*, Ava. With *you*."

Her heart melted at the earnestness in his voice, at the love
shining in his eyes.

Believe him, a little voice inside her begged. *Trust him.*

"I'm scared." It came out thin and ragged, drawn from
somewhere deep and dark. Even that small admission felt too
vulnerable, but he deserved that much, at least.

There was an unlimited depth of kindness in his gaze. "Of
what, mi amor?"

"Of how much I want this to work . . ." She forced herself to
voice the fear. "And how sure I am that it won't."

His eyebrows drew together and something like pain flit-
tered over his face. "You don't trust me not to leave you."

She shook her head. "I don't trust *me* to keep you here. My
own parents didn't even want me. Why should you?"

"Ah," he said gently. "Now we're getting somewhere."

And they were. It wasn't just the divorce, Ava was starting
to understand. Yes, Hector's departure had hurt, but hadn't it
also confirmed what she'd already known about herself? It was
why she tried so hard to be the perfect wife, daughter, sister,
granddaughter, niece, cousin, friend—everything. Because she
knew that underneath the façade, she was just a huge inconvenience for everyone around her. And it was only a matter of
time before they all realized it.

"Ava, I know you think you're difficult to love." The tenderness in his expression made her want to weep. "But for me,
falling in love with you was the easiest thing in the world."

The words cracked her open and healed something inside
her, all at the same time.

"See?" she said, her voice raw. "You say things like that, and if I weren't already completely in love with you, that would have done it."

A rueful smile twisted his lips. "I knew you loved me."

The tears she'd been holding at bay finally spilled over. "How?"

He gave a little shrug. "We wouldn't even be having this conversation if you didn't. You'd have run away a long time ago."

Her laugh sounded waterlogged, even to her. "You're probably right." And then she sighed. "I'll tell Jasmine about us after her honeymoon. I promise. After that . . . I just need time before I tell anyone else."

His jaw worked, like he was thinking about something, and then he shook his head. "Ashton is going to tell Jasmine tonight."

Panic sliced through her. "No!"

"They're about to be married," he pointed out, not unkindly. "It's not fair to ask him to hide this from her."

He was right, but anxiety had her in its grip. "Why didn't you tell me sooner?"

He sighed. "I probably should have, but I didn't want an ultimatum to be the only reason you opened up to your cousin."

Ava pulled her hands away so she could pace. "What if this ruins her wedding? What if she hates me?"

"She's not going to hate you."

"You don't know that." She was verging on shrill. "When this ends, it could destroy my relationship with her."

He shook his head slowly, never taking his eyes off hers, and his tone contained barely concealed exasperation. "Ava, why do you still think we have an expiration date?"

"Because . . ." She bit her lip. Because all of the relationships in her life did. It was something she knew in the core of her being, but she couldn't figure out how to explain it in a way he'd understand. She just hugged herself tighter and didn't finish the thought.

"Let me guess," he said conversationally. "Your ex left, so you think I will too."

That's exactly right seemed like the wrong answer, so she kept her mouth shut.

"And if you tell Jasmine about us . . . what? She's also going to abandon you? Is that it?"

Ava glared at him. He'd hit the nail right on the head, but he didn't need to sound so smug about it.

"Is this why you work your ass off like you're Cinderella?" he continued. "Because if you don't, your family will cast you out?"

Okay, now he was making her sound ridiculous.

"Yes, goddamn it," she snapped. "You're right. About all of it. Happy now? You heard my great-aunt. All I have ever done is put everyone else's needs and feelings first, but what am I? *Selfish* and *too sensitive.* My parents didn't want me, my stepmother treats me like a servant, and according to my grandmother, I'm difficult and spoiled because I won't get myself knocked up. No matter how hard I try, nothing I do will ever be good enough for any of them."

He stuck his hands in his pockets. "So stop trying."

She gave a cynical laugh. "You say that like it's so simple."

"It's not. But you have to start somewhere. Trust me, I understand the guilt of being a first-generation immigrant kid. But you *are* allowed to live your own life. You don't have to keep doing what your family expects in order to earn their love."

"I do."

"Why?" When she didn't answer, he pressed on. "Because if you don't, they punish you for it?"

He was right, but she didn't want to admit it. "I wouldn't exactly call it that."

"No?" Roman raised a sardonic eyebrow. "What else do you call the snide comments and histrionics? Maybe it's not intentional, but the messaging is clear: do what's expected, or they'll make you regret it."

"Fine!" She threw her hands up. "Yes, I am trying to earn their love. But they're my *family*. What do you want me to do?"

"Marry me."

The words, stated so casually, stole the breath from her lungs. Ava stared at him, absolutely sure she'd misheard. Because it sounded like he'd *proposed to her* in the middle of a fight.

She had to clear her throat twice before she could respond. "Are you serious?"

He stood there with his hands in his pockets, cool as could be . . . and shrugged.

He fucking *shrugged*.

Ava's face grew hot, and her body went numb. Everything inside her screamed, *Yes*, but Scared Ava was not to be deterred. "I tried being married," she said. "It didn't work."

"You haven't tried being married to *me*."

He said it like it was the most reasonable thing in the world, and she sputtered out a reply.

"Marriage isn't something you keep trying until you acquire a taste for it. It's not *olives*."

"I don't know what you have against olives, but fine, we'll table the topic of marriage for now." His voice had taken on that bargaining lilt that made her wary. "Counteroffer. Let me kiss you, tonight, in the middle of the dance floor."

"In front of my family? No way!"

His tone softened. "Then walk out of here, right now, holding my hand."

She swallowed hard as her pulse throbbed in her throat.

"Ava." He held out a hand toward her, palm up. "What would you do if you didn't have to be perfect?"

Warmth spread through her as she remembered the first time he'd asked her that question. The roof. The pool. And everything that had followed, all leading up to this sweet, charming, handsome man offering her everything.

All she had to do was let herself take it.

Her fingers twitched. Her hand started to rise.

The door burst open behind her. They both jumped, and Ava spun around to see Gabe standing there with a wild-eyed expression on his face, taking up the whole doorway. Gabe's gaze bounced around the closet and finally landed on the box Roman had kicked aside earlier. Lunging, Gabe reached a hand inside, rummaged around, and came up holding a microphone.

A microphone . . . with a green light.

Ava sucked in a breath.

No.

Gabe flicked a switch on the mic, and the light turned from green to red. He shot Ava a look full of sympathy. "Sorry. No one knew where it was."

Roman strode forward, his expression grim. "Did everyone out there hear our conversation?"

Gabe grimaced. "Yeah."

Ava mentally replayed the things they'd said. God. How

much had they all heard? Panic swelled within her like a balloon about to burst.

Roman turned to her. Slowly, he extended his hand.

"They already know," he said quietly. "You have nothing to lose."

Didn't he see? She'd already lost everything.

She stepped back and saw the moment Roman realized she wasn't going to take his hand. His shoulders slumped slightly. His arm fell to his side, moving as if through molasses. Like he'd still been hoping . . .

Chest tight, she turned and ran for the door.

Gabe, who was built like a linebacker, danced out of the way as if Ava's hair were on fire, giving her a wide berth as she charged into the hallway.

She heard the men talking behind her, but she didn't care what they were saying.

Why should she? Her life was over.

Her family would never forgive her for this. There weren't enough dishes she could wash or diapers she could change to make up for a disaster of these proportions.

She'd committed the biggest sin of all: she had *embarrassed* them.

Now she really was going to lose their love, just as she'd always feared.

There was no way out except through the ballroom. With dread pooling in her belly, Ava pushed the door open.

And stepped out into chaos.

Chapter 47

When Roman realized Ava wasn't going to take his hand, his stomach had dropped with the heat and velocity of a meteor burning through Earth's atmosphere. He still felt like he was falling. But before he could try to fix the situation, he needed information.

"What the hell happened?" he asked Gabe, who quickly filled him in.

The rehearsal dinner technically hadn't started yet, but a number of family members had shown up early. The mic began broadcasting during Ava's revelation about her parents, a detail that made Roman wince. Jasmine had wanted to shut the sound off immediately, but the system required a password and a reboot, and the AV guys had disappeared. Ashton had gone to look for them, while Michelle sent Gabe off in search of the rogue mic.

Roman pinched the bridge of his nose. Everything in his body screamed at him to run after Ava, to make sure she was okay, that *they* were okay.

But this was his best friend's wedding, and not only was Roman the best man, he was the boss of this particular establishment. He'd get the fucking sound system sorted, and then he'd find Ava.

And then what?

He didn't know.

The emotions that had flitted across her face when he'd told her to *marry him*—fuck, he hadn't even phrased it as a question!—had made his insides quake. Stunned shock, followed by what he thought was hope, before landing on fearful disbelief. It had taken every ounce of acting ability he possessed to keep his composure and follow through with the negotiation.

He'd thought he had her. It was such a benign request. Just hold his hand. He was sure she was going to accept his terms, accept *him.*

And then the world had come crashing in on them in the form of Gabriel Aguilar and a missing microphone, along with all the reminders Ava had piled up around herself for why she didn't deserve to be loved.

Roman would spend the rest of his life showing her that she did, if only she'd let him.

He was terrified she wouldn't. What if this was the last straw? What if her fears were stronger than his devotion?

Ashton appeared with the AV techs in tow. One of them winced when he recognized Roman, and he muttered something about "el jefe" to the others.

Roman followed them to where the sound system was set up. He didn't say anything, just stood with one hand in his pocket, the other holding the microphone that had potentially ruined his life. The techs got to work, sweating and darting nervous looks over their shoulder at Roman.

Once it seemed like they were sufficiently afraid, Roman

joined Ashton and Gabe where they waited off to the side. Since he didn't want to dwell on his own thoughts any longer, he asked, "Was Jasmine upset when she found out?"

Ashton scratched his cheek and wouldn't meet Roman's eyes. "Ah . . . no. I told her two weeks ago."

"Good," Roman said, then added, "I'm sorry. We never meant for it to get this complicated."

Ashton waved Roman's apology away. "It wouldn't be a Latine wedding without at least one escandalo. Ask Gabe to tell you what happened at his sister's wedding."

Gabe's laugh was strained. "Trust me, this was nothing."

Roman was too distraught to care about other people's scandals. "Another time."

Ashton clapped a hand on Roman's back. "If you could forgive me for not telling you about Yadi, I can get over you broadcasting a marriage proposal during my wedding rehearsal dinner."

Gabe sent Roman an incredulous look. "Did you really propose to Ava in a supply closet?"

Roman groaned. "Don't remind me."

"Do you even have a ring?" Ashton asked.

"Of course I have a ring."

"Where is it?"

"This happens to be the one time I don't have it on my person." Roman scrubbed a hand over his face. "I'm an idiot."

"You're in love." Ashton's words were tinged with schadenfreude. "Welcome to the club, muchacho."

"Did you mean it?" Gabe asked. "The proposal?"

Roman sighed. "Yeah. But I didn't expect her to accept. Not yet, anyway."

Gabe frowned. "Then why bring it up?"

"Ava needs time to get used to things. Besides, I was only trying to get her to hold my hand."

Gabe's dark brows rose, impressed. "That's genius."

No, it was stupid. Roman had planned to lay the groundwork slowly, not spring the idea of marriage on Ava like a flippant command, and in the least romantic setting possible. But now the question was out there. He couldn't take it back, couldn't create the perfect moment to bring it up. Goddamn his impulsive tendencies.

He groaned again. "I need to find her. To explain."

Ashton rubbed the back of his neck. "I think she's a little busy right now."

Roman's gaze narrowed. "What do you mean?"

Once again, Ashton wouldn't look at him. "If you think her family let her leave this party without comment, you haven't been paying attention."

Roman's eyes went wide.

"Now," Ashton said sharply.

Before Roman could take a single step toward the ballroom, Gabe grabbed him in a headlock.

Chapter 48

Ten Minutes Earlier

Ava's eyes darted around the ballroom, taking note of her relatives like an antelope trying to maneuver through a grassland scattered with lions.

There, by the bar, her mother and Titi Val spoke quickly with their heads together.

Next to the buffet table, Willow and Olympia yelled at each other, tears streaming down their faces.

Behind them, Ava's father rubbed his temples the way Ava did when she was getting a migraine.

At the edge of the dance floor, Abuela and Michelle argued animatedly, while Titi Nereida prayed the rosary in Spanish at the top of her lungs.

Santa María, Madre de Dios, ruega por nosotros pecadores . . .

For one brief, shining moment, Ava thought she'd be able to sneak out unnoticed.

Until Olympia spotted her.

Her stepmother turned her tear-stained face to Ava and wailed, "How could you say that about me?"

Willow's face pinched in anger. "Because you're the evil stepmother, Mom!"

The commotion drew Abuela's attention and she barreled toward Ava like an oncoming express train, wagging her finger in the air. "Mira, I never said I wanted you to get knocked around."

"It's knocked *up*, Abuela." Michelle was hot on Esperanza's heels. "It means pregnant."

"Embarazada, sí," Abuela answered, like Michelle had just suggested a wonderful idea. The old woman turned back to Ava with an expression that somehow melded glee and reproach. "¿Por qué no nos dijiste que tienes novio?"

This, Ava thought dully. *This is why I didn't tell you I have a boyfriend.*

Ronnie hurried over, a sleepy three-year-old balanced on her hip. "So I was right?" she asked, breathless. "Roman *is* your boyfriend?"

"He's her fiancé," Titi Nita amended, joining the growing crowd around Ava.

"I *knew* it." Ronnie shot a smug grin over her shoulder. "Pay up, Sammy!"

"Is this because Hector's getting remarried?" Titi Nereida's daughter, Marta, asked from somewhere in the background.

Sammy began to sing an off-key rendition of "We Don't Talk About Hector" with gusto.

"Shut *up*," Michelle shouted. "Everybody, give her some space—"

"Really, Ava, we're happy for you, but your timing could have been better," Titi Lisa chided.

"Don't mess this one up, too." Titi Nereida shook a finger in Ava's face. "That man is very, very rich."

"*Are* you pregnant?" Esperanza pulled the fabric of Ava's dress taut over her stomach, searching for a baby bump.

Nereida leaned in and adjusted her glasses. "No, just gordita."

It was too much. Too fucking much. Ava could feel herself slipping away, numbing out. Her Resting Pleasant Face morphed over her features, glazing her eyes, curving the corners of her lips, her jaw so tight it felt like it would crack.

Someone pinched her arm. "*Stop it.*"

Startled, Ava glanced to her right, where Michelle gazed up at her with a fierce expression.

"Don't do that," Mich said in an undertone. "Don't let them do this to you."

Michelle was right. Keeping things hidden was what had gotten Ava into this mess in the first place. Hadn't she often fantasized about telling her family exactly how she felt? This was her chance.

New Ava is not afraid to express her feelings.

Right?

Right.

Fuck. She was really doing this.

With a deep breath, Ava straightened to her full height and pulled away from her grandmother.

"Abuela, *stop.*"

The sharp tone barely registered, and Esperanza was distracted as she asked, "Stop what?"

Ava swallowed hard. *Now or never.* "Stop it with the invasive questions."

Esperanza's penciled-in brows drew together. "¿El qué?"

"Las preguntas invasivas," Ava translated. "No more."

Her grandmother shared an incredulous glance with Titi Nereida. "Pero why can't I ask?"

"Because it's none of your business, Grandma!" This came from Willow, whose baby goth mascara had smeared around her eyes. Ava felt a swell of gratitude and pride for her sister, along with shame that Willow felt she had to defend her. Ava should have been modeling this backbone for her sister well before now.

It's not too late.

Esperanza threw her hands up. "How is my granddaughter's life not my business?" She rounded on Ava again. "That man just asked you to marry him. What are you so upset about?"

"What am I upset about?" Ava repeated the question with an edge bordering on hysterical. "I'll tell you. I'll tell you what I'm upset about."

She ticked it off on her fingers. "I'm upset about being asked if I'm pregnant and then being called *fat*."

Nereida clutched her rosary to her chest.

"I'm upset about wagers being made regarding my relationship status."

Ronnie looked away guiltily.

"I'm upset about the way everyone *still talks about Hector.*"

Sammy had the grace to look abashed, while Marta studied her nails.

Esperanza, who had evidently had enough of Ava's feelings, waved a hand dismissively. "Families always talk about each other. Es normal."

"No." Ava's heart pounded from the stress of outright disagreeing with her grandmother. "It went beyond typical bochinche. And while I do *not* regret my divorce, I *am* upset by the way everyone reacted. It was the most painful time of my life, and instead of being supported, I was judged and blamed me and treated like a failure. It was extremely hurtful, and still is." Ava addressed the rest of the group. "After all that, can you understand why I'd be scared to introduce someone new?"

There were some nods, a few shrugs. Titi Val had joined the group, and she sent Ava a sympathetic smile.

Someone else moved into Ava's line of vision—Jasmine, approaching from the back. Ava sucked in a breath as she turned to her cousin. "Jas, I'm so sorry you found out this way."

Jasmine's expression turned sheepish. "I kinda already knew. Ashton told me after the bridal shower."

"Of course." Ava's shoulders slumped, the weight she'd been carrying replaced by the shame of her actions. "I should've told you sooner."

Jasmine's glance darted around the group surrounding them, and when their gazes met again, Ava saw deep understanding in her cousin's dark eyes.

Esperanza, who'd been conducting a rapid-fire conversation in Spanish with Nereida, rounded on Ava again. "Mira, nena. What do you want me to say? I'm sorry?"

Despite speaking the words out loud, it was clearly not an apology. Still, Ava murmured, "Thank you."

Shaking that off, Abuela pressed her cool hands to Ava's cheeks. "I just don't want you to be alone."

"I don't want to be alone either." A note of pleading entered Ava's voice "But I needed time to heal, to figure out who I am now and what I want from the rest of my life. I needed my family, I needed *you*, and instead, it felt like . . . like you didn't love me anymore."

Ava's voice cracked at the end, the words forced out through a throat jammed with tears. The vulnerability of her admission left her feeling raw and exposed.

Esperanza's eyes went wide and she sputtered, as if such a thing had never occurred to her. As if such a thing were impossible.

"Muchacha, of course I love you!" She stepped forward and pulled Ava into a hug. "Ay, mi bebé. You could have *murdered* Hector and I would still love you. Not only that, I would tell everyone you were innocent."

Ava leaned into the embrace, tears and laughter clogging her throat. "Why didn't you say that at the time?"

Abuela shrugged as she pulled away. "Porque I thought it was obvious."

"It still helps to hear it," Ava said, because it definitely hadn't been obvious.

Esperanza's brow creased in thought, and she turned to her sister. "¿Sabes qué? I remember having a similar conversation with our mother, a long time ago."

Nereida's eyes narrowed on a point in the distance. "I remember that. Ay Diós, she was so angry that anyone dared to question her."

Esperanza blinked. "Aha. I see now that this is the problem." But then her expression turned coy. "Y este hombre," she began.

Ava suppressed an eye-roll at the immediate shift away from self-examination. Before her grandmother could continue interrogating her about Roman, Ava blurted out, "I'm quitting my job."

Esperanza's thin brows leaped. "¿Qué dijiste?"

Ava braced herself, but at that moment, Cardi B and Megan Thee Stallion's ode to wet ass pussies blasted through the ballroom at top volume.

Everyone jumped at the sudden noise. Jasmine snarled and stormed off, no doubt to throttle the AV techs. Michelle doubled over laughing.

The music was, luckily, too loud for anyone to ask follow-up questions. Abuelo Willie appeared to draw Esperanza toward the open bar. Over his shoulder, he sent Ava a wink and mouthed, "Te quiero, nena."

As the crowd began to disperse, a soft hand landed on her arm. Ava turned to see her mother. Wearing a pained smile, Patricia wordlessly enfolded Ava in a hug.

Ava breathed in the familiar floral scent of Patricia's perfume. Tears pricked the corners of her eyes yet again, and she remembered that everyone had overheard more than just Roman proposing to her. "Mommy, I'm sorry. I didn't mean—"

"Baby, don't apologize." Patricia shifted back, her eyes filled with sadness. "I'm the one who should be saying sorry. When we sent you to live with your grandparents, I never imagined you would think it was because we didn't want you. It seemed like the best option at the time, but . . . maybe we should have tried harder to find another solution."

"It—thank you." Ava cut herself off before she could brush it aside with an *it's okay*. "That means a lot."

She'd never meant for her mother to hear those things, but she had, and now Patricia had apologized. That was a start, wasn't it? Ava couldn't change the past, but she could determine how her interactions went from this point on.

Patricia's next words came as a surprise. "For what it's worth, I understand why you kept Roman to yourself."

Ava squinted at her mother. "Is this because of the lap dance?"

Patricia's face registered shock, and she burst into embarrassed laughter. "Oh my goodness. I won't go into detail, but . . . *whew.*" She fanned herself. "No, I meant that I understand how your father's family can sometimes feel like . . . well, like being on a stage. Everyone is watching, and while they're cheering for you, they're also waiting for you to make a mistake."

Ava blinked. She hadn't known her mother understood so deeply. Why hadn't they ever talked about this before?

Patricia grasped Ava's hands. Her light brown eyes bored into Ava's hazel green ones.

"Listen to me, baby. I will always be on your side. No matter what happens, or who says what. Okay?"

"Thanks, Mommy." And then Ava really *looked* at her mother, seeing Patricia not as her mom, but as a woman who had lived a life, who'd gone through many of the same things Ava had. Patricia likely had her own wisdom to share, if only Ava had the courage to ask.

But before she could even consider what to say next, her father appeared on Patricia's other side, a look of contrition on his face.

"Lo siento, mija."

Ava nearly swallowed her tongue. Another apology? And from her *father*?

He rubbed the back of his head, his salt-and-pepper hair more salt these days. "Willow always says you help us too much, but I didn't realize it was so bad. I'll talk to Olympia."

"I'd appreciate that." These were bigger conversations that shouldn't occur in the middle of a ballroom. But still, to receive apologies from both of her parents, after what they'd heard her say . . . it was mind-boggling.

Jasmine and Michelle drifted over, each carrying two glasses of champagne. The music—now a slightly more family-friendly playlist, starting with Beyoncé—had been lowered to an appropriate volume, and the dance floor was filling up. Waitstaff rotated around the room with platters of finger food. The party had officially begun.

Patricia kissed Ava on the cheek. "We'll talk more later. I love you, baby." She accepted the glass Michelle handed her with a smile, then went off to join Titi Val.

"Love you, kid." Miguel pulled Ava into a one-armed hug and pressed a kiss to her forehead, like he used to when she was little. "Just for being you."

Ava's heart twisted. It was what she'd needed to hear for so long, but the words didn't provide the immediate sense of healing she'd once thought they would. Instead, the wound they touched simply felt a little less sore. For so many years, Ava had been trying to meet other people's expectations of who she should be. But over the past few months she'd discovered that just being herself was, well . . . it was enough.

"Thanks, Daddy." Ava let herself lean against him for a moment. She wasn't quite ready to let her father off the hook, but this was a start. She was grateful for Willow, and while she knew things with Olympia would take work, maybe, with time and communication, they could find some semblance of balance.

Before her father walked away, he murmured, "Hola, mis

sobrinas," to Jasmine and Michelle, who responded with, "Hi, Tío," in unison.

The second he was out of earshot, Jasmine and Michelle turned as one to stare at Ava.

It was time to face the music.

Chapter 49

Out with it." Jasmine handed Ava a champagne flute. "What nonsense reason did you have for not telling me?"

"Isn't this for the toast?" Ava raised the glass and gave it a sniff.

Rolling her eyes, Michelle lifted her champagne and muttered, "*To Jasmine.* Now quit stalling and answer the question."

Ava knocked back a long gulp, savoring the tart, crisp flavor. As the bubbles danced over her tongue and tickled her nose, she cast around for where to begin.

"I'm sorry," she said to Jasmine. "I should have told you about Roman after the engagement party."

"Why didn't you?" Jasmine asked.

So Ava explained how her relationship with Roman had started as an occasional fling, something she hadn't been ready to share with them yet. And even though she'd broken it off after discovering Roman's connection to Ashton, her feelings for him had only deepened after they went to Puerto Rico together. Finally, Ava confessed her fears about putting Jasmine in the position of having to choose between her cousin and her husband's best friend.

Jasmine listened, and gnawed her lower lip before she spoke.

"I get the concern. But Ava, you're always going to be my family. Nothing will ever change that. We're not just cousins, we're friends. And we're not just friends, we're blood. Primas of Power forever."

"Primas poderosas para siempre," Michelle repeated, raising her champagne. "Put it on a T-shirt."

"I was going to tell you after your honeymoon," Ava insisted. "Your wedding should be perfect, and I didn't want to ruin it . . . like I just did."

"Ava, listen to me. The *only* way you could ruin my wedding is by not being here." Jasmine grabbed Ava's hand and gripped it tight. "I also should've considered how hard all this would be for you. Ashton said I relied on your help too much. I'm sorry for that."

The validation was nice, but Ava had trouble accepting it. "I still feel terrible about causing problems for you again."

Jasmine's forehead creased in confusion. "When have you ever been a problem for me?"

"Other than tonight?" When her cousins continued to stare at her, waiting for an answer, Ava shrugged. "Last year. With the move and everything. I know it was a huge inconvenience for both of you—"

"Do you think we begrudge you for that?" Jasmine interrupted. "Ava, we love you. We were *glad* to help."

"Except you're both in happy, committed relationships, and I—"

"What? You're Debbie Downer?" Michelle rolled her eyes. "Ava, we're big girls. We're capable of holding space for your emotions, even if they're different from what we're going through."

"That's what we're here for," Jasmine added. "As you've been there for us, many times over."

Ava shook her head. "I just didn't want to burden either of you with—"

"*Bullshit.*"

Ava and Jasmine both stared at Michelle.

"What makes you so special?" Michelle's tone was relentless. "What makes your problems so fucking special that no one can help you carry them?"

Ava's mouth opened but nothing came out. It was harsh, but that was Michelle.

And she was . . . right.

"Nothing, I guess." Ava's voice was quiet with the impact of this revelation.

"It's us, Ava." Michelle sounded almost exasperated, while Jasmine's eyes pleaded for Ava to trust them. "What are you so afraid of?"

Throat tight, Ava spoke her deepest fear aloud. "Losing you. Losing everyone."

"The only way you lose us is by not letting us in," Jasmine said, butting Ava gently with her shoulder. "We'll always be as close as you'll let us be."

Ava let that sink in, reassessing everything she'd once believed. What if accepting someone else's help wasn't an act of selfishness, but rather, an opportunity for deeper connection? Like with Roman. By allowing him to care for her, she'd soothed something in him, too. Each experience had brought them closer together, even when Ava had been adamant about keeping him at arm's length. Refusing to let her mother or cousins comfort her during her times of need had only broadened the emotional distance between herself and them. But relationships were give and take. Insisting on being the one who gave all the time would only make her a martyr, and Ava didn't want that. Not anymore.

Martyrs died. Maybe it was time to let the part of her that needed to be seen as helpful, useful—*good*—die as well.

In her quest to be perfect, Ava had hidden herself. She'd locked away her messy feelings, sure that no one would love her if she revealed them. On some level, she'd thought she was sparing the people around her. But really, she was only protecting herself, and she hadn't trusted anyone enough to see the real her.

Until Roman. She'd let him see her, mess and all. Partly because she'd felt safe enough to be vulnerable with him, but partly because she'd felt *strong* enough to be.

It wasn't only her family getting in the way of her happiness. *She* was denying herself what she wanted because she thought she was fundamentally lacking in some way.

But what if she wasn't?

What if she was good enough as she was?

"I guess it all sounds silly when I say it out loud," she said finally.

"It's not silly." Jasmine put an arm around her. "Your feelings are valid."

"Even when they're silly," Michelle said in a stage whisper.

Ava glanced to her left and her right, at her two beautiful, smart, loving primas. "What's wrong with us? Why did we all feel like we needed to hide it when we fell in love?"

Michelle snorted. "Where do we start?"

"The toxic chisme cycle," Jasmine blurted out.

"Outdated gender roles," Michelle added.

"Intergenerational family trauma," Ava said, and the other two nodded in agreement.

"Cheers to unpacking emotional baggage." Michelle raised her champagne. Ava and Jasmine clinked their glasses to hers and drank.

"I know I need better boundaries," Ava admitted. "I have a hard time saying no."

"You don't say?" Michelle shot her a wry grin.

"Boundaries can help someone feel safe," Jasmine agreed. "But having problems with boundaries isn't just saying 'yes' to everything and putting the needs of others before your own. It can also look like saying 'no' to the *good* things in your life."

Ava mulled that over. Her need to make others happy because she was worried their love would be withdrawn if she didn't live up to their expectations had started with her parents, was reinforced by her grandmother, and then continued to play out in her marriage and all her other relationships.

Except with Roman. From the beginning, he'd allowed her to call the shots while maintaining a steady, supportive presence. He had respected her boundaries, even when they were silly, which showed her that she could trust him. That trust had allowed her to expand the parameters at her own pace, letting him in little by little, until they'd forged a solid bond.

The behaviors she used as shields—always being helpful, not rocking the boat, forgoing her own desires—were trauma responses to a childhood where she'd felt unwanted and alone.

But now those protective shields were suffocating her. She wasn't just letting fear control her happiness. She was letting the past affect her future.

She'd been piecing together New Ava one positive affirmation at a time, wearing her like a suit of armor, while her true self was waiting to be set free.

If she could let go of the need to be perfect, the need to please other people . . . if she could live authentically as herself . . . what would that look like?

Not Old Ava, not New Ava, not Scared or Sarcastic or *Good* Ava.

Just Ava, and all the parts that made her *her*.

With Roman, she felt safe. She felt whole. It wasn't that he completed her, or supplied a missing piece. It was that he gave her the space to complete *herself*. Why else would she have turned to him, instead of anyone else she knew, whenever she was in distress?

Speaking of . . .

Ava sucked in a breath. "I need to find Roman."

Michelle gave her an affectionate shoulder bump. "To accept his marriage proposal?"

"Oh my god." Ava took a quick sip of champagne to cover her blush. "I don't think he was really asking."

Jasmine pursed her lips. "Roman Vázquez is not someone who tosses around marriage proposals lightly. If he asked, he meant it."

Ava shook her head. "The negotiation thing is just a game we play."

"I want to hear more about this game." Michelle gave a lewd wink.

But Ava didn't reply. She was reflecting on what Jasmine had said, and remembering what else Roman had revealed.

His decision to step down as CEO wouldn't have been made

lightly either. If he was doing that, it was because he saw it as a solution to a problem . . .

The problem, in this case, was that he worked too much, and also . . . that he wanted more room in his life for *her*.

It still terrified her. But now that she'd calmed down and thought it over, she was unbelievably touched. This was how much he cared about her, that he was willing to change his entire life to fit her into it.

How could she do any less?

She loved him. That much was crystal clear to her. But she needed to make it clear to Roman, as well. He'd put his heart on the line for her time and again, and he'd been more than patient with her shenanigans. He deserved to hear the full extent of her feelings. Right the fuck now. But as she scanned the ballroom, she didn't see Roman.

Or Ashton.

Or Gabe.

Her eyebrows drew together. "Where the hell are the guys?"

Michelle blinked innocently. "What guys?"

Chapter 50

I can't *believe* you did that." Roman rubbed his neck and shot Gabe a dirty look.

Gabe's grin was utterly unrepentant. "It was Ashton's idea."

"Michelle tasked us with keeping you occupied," Ashton said, effortlessly dispersing the blame. "And I told Gabe to use force, if necessary."

Roman's mind raced as he pictured Ava having an emotionally confronting altercation with her family. "I can't just hang back while she's in trouble."

"You have to," Ashton said severely. "Because this is what she needs. That woman is used to people leaving her. The best thing you can do is be here when she's ready for you."

"You can't fix this for her." Gabe's tone was more gentle than Roman would have expected. "No matter how much you want to."

The guys were right. Roman would slay dragons for Ava, but she had to fight her own inner demons—and that meant having a long overdue heart to heart with her relatives. Besides, he trusted that her cousins wouldn't abandon her afterward, even if Ava herself didn't believe it.

All he could do was give her space, manage his own feelings

so they didn't spill over onto her, and be available when she needed him.

Even if sitting still made him want to gnash his teeth.

"I'm stepping down as CEO," Roman said, needing to change the subject before he did something that made Gabe tackle him.

Ashton's brows shot up. "You're selling the company?"

"Hell no. It's still mine. I'm just taking a backseat from the day-to-day operations."

"I did wonder why you were so involved in the minutiae," Gabe commented. "I've worked with some CEOs, and they always seemed to have a lot more free time for golf and shit."

"Should I take up golf?" Roman mused.

"Before you do, let me give you some different exercises for your lower back."

"Golf?" Ashton snorted. "You're kidding yourself if you think you're not going to find some other project to throw yourself into."

"I want to have more time to spend with Ava, and my family."

"Except Ava has a job, your sister will be in college, and your mother is moving out," Ashton said pointedly. "So what are you going to do all day?"

"Well, there's Casa Donato," Roman admitted. "I have a lot of ideas for expanding distribution."

Ashton spread his hands. "Así es."

"I also want you to be a celebrity spokesperson."

Ashton looked thoughtful. "Will I get free rum?"

"Obviously."

"I'm in."

Roman sighed. "I also have to finish writing the book."

Gabe perked up. "What book?"

Roman explained how he'd been contracted to write a combo business manual and memoir—and how he wasn't making much progress.

Ashton rubbed his chin. "Gabe's a bit of a writer himself."

Roman raised his eyebrows. "Any chance you want to help me?"

"Sure. Send me what you got."

Ashton glanced between the two of them. "I think we have some things other than las primas poderosas to discuss."

Gabe glanced at his phone, then snapped to attention. "They're done."

As one, the three men turned to the door. Roman pushed into the ballroom first and immediately spotted Ava barreling toward him. He sped up to meet her halfway and they crashed together. Her arms locked around his shoulders and his banded around her waist. She was warm and smelled like sun and beach and orange blossoms. And despite the tight hold she had on him, there was a distinct lack of tension in her body. Whatever had happened tonight, she'd finally set down a weight she'd been carrying for as long as he'd known her.

He pulled back just enough to look at her face. "Good chat?"

Her eyes were red but she smiled. "I'm ready."

His heart rate sped up. "For?"

"To respond to the things you said in the closet."

"Ava, I didn't mean to pressure—"

She touched her fingertips to his lips. He was barely aware of Jasmine and Michelle pulling Ashton and Gabe onto the dance floor.

"Not just that part," Ava said softly, her expression warm. "Although we'll get to it."

"Whatever you want, mi vida."

She pressed her cheek to his. "Have I ever told you I love all the terms of endearment you use?"

"Not yet."

Her mouth quirked. "Well, I do. Come on."

She took his hand and pulled him out of the ballroom, across the main lobby, and through the front doors to the tiered stone fountain that stood outside the resort. Roman had considered removing or replacing it, but it had stood in the center of the main walkway since the resort had first opened, well before he'd bought it, and it was iconic to the look of the entrance. And so the fountain had stayed.

Ava drew him over to sit on the ledge surrounding it. The front of the resort rested in the shade as the sun set, and the water tinkled prettily, creating a buzz of white noise to afford them a semblance of privacy.

"In an ideal world, I'd take more time to think about what I want to say." She grasped his hands in hers, her face earnest, even as her cheeks flushed. "I'd have a color-coded list in my planner, to make sure I say everything in the right order and don't leave anything out."

"It's not too late to make a spreadsheet," he teased gently, but she shook her head.

"I don't want to waste any more time." She gave him a small smile. "And anyway, I have a mental list with three bullet points."

"Only three?"

"The last one has a lot of points under it."

"Let's start with the first," he said gently.

Her expression turned serious, her full mouth tightening at the corners. Before he could give in to the urge to kiss her until she softened, she said, "Roman, I'm sorry."

Shit, this was it. She'd brought him out here to let him down easy.

He took a moment to get his voice under control. "You don't have anything to be sorry for, mi amor."

"But I do." Her tone was brittle, and her eyes took on a glassy sheen. "I'm so sorry for hiding you, and for treating you like you were something to hide. It was only ever because of my own fears and not because of you or anything you did. Please know that."

He exhaled slowly. His chest cavity felt like it was full of shattered glass. "I know, Ava. I know."

"I love you, Roman."

Suddenly, all he could see was her face. The serious slant of her brows, the sweet curve of her lips, and her eyes—yes, that was love shining in them, even as tears glittered on her lower lashes.

She was still talking, unaware of the spell her words had cast upon him. "I want to be with you," she said earnestly. "And I don't care who knows it."

"You—" Relief made him dizzy. And then he couldn't keep away from her for another second. He tugged her closer, sliding his arms around her, and her fingers gripped the front of his shirt.

"I'm so sorry—"

"Shh." He rubbed her back in slow, gentle strokes. "I understand."

"I know you do." She tilted her head to look at him. "You understand *me*. I don't know if I'll ever be able to convey how big of a gift that is."

His breath hitched. "See what happens when you let me give you gifts?"

She laughed, and her fingers flexed on his chest, right over his heart. "From the very beginning, you've given me the biggest gift of all."

His lips twisted into a suggestive smirk, and she gave a surprised giggle. "Okay, yes, but I didn't mean *that*."

He couldn't resist teasing her. "If not *that*, then what?"

"Your *time*, Roman. You're the man who has everything, except for free time. But from the moment we met, you gave the gift of your time whenever I asked. And I know it wasn't easy. I know you had important things to do. Whenever I reached out, I expected you to say no, that you were too busy, thus proving what I believed about myself, that no one would ever put me first." She swallowed hard and took a deep breath. "But you never said no. You have always, *always* been here when I need you."

He lifted a hand to cup her cheek, his thumb stroking over her soft skin. "And I always will. For as much and as long as I'm able, I'll be here."

"I . . . actually believe that." She leaned into his touch. "You said that when we're together, you feel like you're truly living."

He nodded. "You've given me a gift too, Ava."

She liked that, he saw. Her lips curved, and she pressed a kiss to his palm. "You deserve to rest," she said. "You've worked so hard, for so long. It's time to rest, Roman. Or to play. Whatever you want."

"Only if I get to do it with you," he said.

"Who else is going to make sure you don't revert back to your workaholic tendencies?"

"I might have discussed some potential business ventures with Ashton and Gabe."

Her laugh was indulgent. "This is why you need me to keep an eye on you."

"I can't think of anyone better." He leaned in to kiss her, but she pulled away.

"I'm not done with my list yet," she said playfully.

"Where are we on the bullet points?"

"The last one."

"The one with multiple parts?"

She nodded, gazing into his eyes, and what he saw there made his breath catch. "This is where I tell you all the things I love about you."

"Oh yeah?" He couldn't stop the goofy grin from spreading across his face. "What's the first item on that list?"

"Your eyes." She brushed a fingertip under his left one. "These dreamy, trustworthy eyes. They were one of the first things I noticed about you."

"Were they?" He'd been teased as a kid for having "pretty" eyes, but they'd landed him a job on TV and the trust of this woman, so he couldn't complain. "What else did you notice?"

"Your smile." Her own lips pulled into a grin as she stroked her fingers over his mouth. "It's so genuine and friendly."

"So in summary, you like my face," he said.

"I *love* your face," she corrected. "But that's not all."

"No?"

"I also love your confidence."

He let out a soft chuckle. "Some would call it ego."

She shook her head. "Ego is unearned, or else delusional. You believe in yourself, and it's an extremely sexy quality."

That gave him a weird, warm feeling in his chest. "Go on."

"I love the way you listen and pay attention. The fierce way you protect the people you love. The way you *see* me. I can be messy around you without worrying that you'll love me any less. I trust you with my whole being, in a way I've never trusted anyone, not even myself. You ask me what I want and genuinely care about the answer. You make me feel treasured. You're considerate of my feelings, and you understand that I need time and space to think. You're emotionally open, and you make it safe for me to feel all my emotions around you." Her voice grew stronger, nearly gutting him with the depth of her regard. "You take responsibility for your actions, and you receive feedback like an adult. You *apologize*. And you never, ever withdraw or withhold yourself from me. You're shaking your head, and maybe these are small things to you, but to me, Roman? They're *everything*."

"Ava, that's . . ." Even for someone who had a pretty high opinion of himself, the thoroughness of her observations made his cheeks heat.

A delighted smile lit her face. "Are you blushing?"

"I think I am." He definitely was.

She took his hands again. "When I went to the bar that night, I was looking for something different. Something new. I decided to trust the Universe . . . and it led me to you."

"I'm really glad you ordered that shitty drink," he murmured, and she laughed.

"God, me too." She stroked his knuckles with her thumb. "Do you remember what you said that night? On the roof?"

"I said a lot of things. Which part?"

"You made a toast. I remember, because I wrote it down."

"Of course you did." His lips curved. "What did I say?"

"You made a toast to me, and to imperfection, dreaming, and welcoming whatever comes next—"

"With or without a plan," he finished, remembering.

She shifted closer to him. "At the time, it seemed like the future I wanted was no longer available to me. I was scared to dream. Scared to *want*. And then you showed up. And suddenly . . . wanting was easy."

He twined one of her curls around his index finger, needing to touch her, needing the connection. "And dreaming?"

"I don't need to," she said simply. "You are more than I ever could've dreamed of, more than I would have dared to wish for. You've always urged me to tell you what I want. Roman, what I want is *you*."

His throat went tight as he whispered, "I want you, too, Ava. You're all I want. It's why I'm stepping down as CEO. I can't stand the thought of you alone in our home, waiting for me to come back from a business trip or a long day at the office. I want to *be there* with you."

"I love your home," she confessed.

"Then why haven't you moved in with me already?"

Her chuckle was breathless. "Because until now, I've told myself I can't have what I love."

"You can," he said simply. "Me, my home, anything I have—it's yours, Ava." Then his tone turned serious. "I know you've been hurt before. And while I can't predict the future, what I can promise is that I'll always be open with you and tell you how I'm feeling, so we can deal with it together."

"That's enough for me," she said, her eyes shining. "I promise to do the same."

"And planning for the future?" he asked.

"All I know is that I plan to be with you. Wherever this life takes us." She smiled. "Love is worth the risk. *You're* worth it."

"And so are you." He cleared his throat. "Now, can we discuss the other thing I said in that closet?"

Her face flushed, but she nodded.

"I didn't mean to bring it up that way," he began. "I was . . . well, I was upset by what we overheard, and pissed off that I couldn't stand up for you the way I wanted. But I meant it, Ava. I want to spend the rest of my life with you. I want to marry you."

Her beautiful hazel eyes locked on him. He saw a little bit of fear lurking there, but he also saw . . . well, he *hoped* he saw acceptance.

He lowered his voice and stroked her fingers. "Consider this me giving you time to get used to the idea. We'll go at your pace, but if, at some point, you do decide you want to get married again, I'm ready."

"What if I'm never ready?" The words came out hushed, and she blinked rapidly.

"I'll love you anyway." He raised their joined hands and kissed her knuckles. "Do you believe me?"

A tear spilled down her cheek, but her smile was radiant. "Yes. I believe you."

It was all he needed to hear. He finally brought his mouth to hers, pouring everything he felt into the kiss, knowing it would take an infinite number of kisses to fully convey how much he loved her. She melted into him, stroking her tongue against his and making tiny sounds in her throat.

His spirit soared. He didn't care that they were outside and it was a hundred degrees. He didn't care that the lobby staff was probably watching through the front windows. Ava loved him and he loved her. Everything else? They'd figure it out together.

After what seemed like a second or a lifetime, he pulled back, breathless. "Now can I buy you gifts?"

Her full-throated laugh was the most beautiful sound he'd ever heard.

Text Exchange with Damaris Fuentes

Damaris: I'm on my way from the airport. How's it going?

Ava: Holy shit. I have so much to tell you.

Damaris: I'll be there soon!

Ava: By the way, I decided to quit Alliance.

Damaris: OMG me too! Gunderson is the fucking worst. I can't suffer through another semester.

Ava: What are you going to do instead?

Damaris: I don't know yet. Trusting the Universe. Manifesting my best life. You know how I roll. But in case that doesn't work out, you know anyone who wants to hire a math teacher who can read astrological charts and lead group meditations?

Ava: Actually . . . I might.

Damaris: Who??

Ava: Me. I'm starting a nonprofit for my theater program. Want in?

Damaris: Um, YES!

Chapter 51

Wedding Day

Ava knew there was a lot of speculation about her and Roman as they walked down the aisle together and took their places on opposite sides of the floral arch. Titi Nereida had hissed, "Are you next?" as they'd passed her, and Sammy made a comment that started with, "If this were a movie . . ." but Ronnie smacked his arm before he could finish.

For once, Ava didn't care what anyone thought. She had never felt more loved, or more confident in her ability to speak up for herself. Sure, it would take practice before it came easily, but she knew Roman and her primas would encourage her.

The bride was absolutely radiant in her boho style wedding dress and white sandals, with the enormous bouquet of tropical flowers Ava had helped design. Jasmine wore her hair loose, opting for diamond encrusted clips instead of a veil to keep the wind from blowing her hair into her face. Ashton waited for her with love shining from his every pore. He wore a beige linen suit with a white shirt and no tie, and he looked every inch the telenovela heartthrob. Behind him, the sun setting over the water provided a gorgeous backdrop.

The groomsmen sported long-sleeved white guayabera shirts, and the bridesmaids were clad in magenta cocktail-length halter dresses. In deference to the sand, everyone wore flat sandals.

As Ava stood holding her smaller bouquet, she checked in with herself. But there were no lingering feelings of jealousy, of wishing she had what Jasmine had. Jasmine was on her path, and Ava was on her own.

As Ava looked to Roman, who sent her a grin, she thought that right now, the path ahead looked pretty damn good.

The ceremony was beautiful and blessedly short. By the time it was over and Jasmine had yelled, "Let's party!" from the end of the aisle, the viejitos were drooping from the heat and Ava had sweated through her makeup.

Instead of taking Roman's elbow to walk down the aisle, Ava held his hand and laced their fingers together. He raised their joined hands to his lips and kissed her left ring finger, right in front of all the assembled guests.

It felt like a promise.

Endless photos were taken, and at the reception, everyone made a beeline for the open bar to try the guava piña colada Ava and Roman had created together at Casa Donato.

Michelle appeared at Ava's side and held up her glass. "You know all the tías are going to get drunk on these, right?"

"Oh yeah. Willow's planning to record videos for blackmail purposes."

Mich smirked. "Smart kid."

The DJ played all the Latin party hits, and Jasmine and Ashton performed a duet of "(I've Had) The Time of My Life" from *Dirty Dancing* that included the famous lift.

Ava and Roman gave their speeches, keeping the content firmly focused on Jasmine and Ashton. However, when Roman was nearing the end of his, someone called out, "Were you on *Recuerdos Peligrosos*?"

Roman paused. "Yes. Yes, I was."

Another voice yelled, "I knew it!"

After a slight hesitation, Roman bowed, and the attendees clapped.

Many piña coladas later, Jasmine dragged Ava and Michelle onto the dais with her to sing "Wannabe" by the Spice Girls.

"But we haven't practiced!" Ava protested.

Jasmine shoved a microphone into Ava's hand. "We sang this a million times in Michelle's bedroom."

"When we were ten!"

But Ava went along with it, bopping around with her cousins, laughing through the lyrics as she sang Emma and Mel C's lines. Ava couldn't remember the last time she'd done something so silly, or so fun.

Ava and Roman were spinning around the dance floor to a Marc Anthony song when Ashton grabbed Roman's shoulder.

"*Mira*," he commanded, turning Roman to the left.

They all looked, and Ava's mouth dropped open. Roman's mother and Ashton's father were dancing a few feet away, but that wasn't all they were doing.

They were also *kissing*.

Ignacio caught the guys watching and smirked. "What, you two are the only ones allowed to have a secret romance?"

Ashton looked shell-shocked, and Roman appeared to be hiding a grin. He elbowed Ashton in the side.

"Guess we'll be brothers in real life too."

Ashton sent Roman and Ava a wounded look. "That makes you two related," he retorted, and stalked off.

"No it doesn't," Roman called after him, then turned to Ava. "It doesn't, right?"

She laughed and shook her head. "Ashton is only my cousin by marriage. We're in the clear."

"Whew." He wiped his forehead in mock-relief.

The reception was a blast. Ava danced with her dad, her grandparents, Willow, Michelle, Titi Val, Gabe, and Damaris. Damaris flirted with Lily Benitez, one of Jasmine's former costars, and Mikayla chatted excitedly with Willow, who was recounting the drama from the night before. The food was delicious, and the cake—vanilla with lemon and raspberry—was divine. Every time Ava looked at Jasmine, there was a huge smile on her cousin's face.

And every time Ava looked at Roman, her own face broke into a grin.

She was fanning herself after an energetic salsa with Tío Luisito when Roman approached, holding two glasses of the guava colada. He passed one to her, and they stood and sipped, surveying the party in full swing around them.

"We did it," he said, gesturing toward Ashton and Jasmine. "They're married. Mission accomplished."

"Good work, best man," she said, nudging him with her shoulder.

He put his arm around her and held her snug against his side. "Back at you, maid of honor."

Ava cleared her throat. "You know . . . I'm still not sure if I want to get married again. And if I do, I don't want all this."

He met her gaze. "Ava, it's okay if—"

"But I don't think I'd be opposed to eloping."

His eyebrows shot up, and his expression of shock morphed into glee. "Right now?"

She laughed and leaned into him. "Not this very minute, but . . . maybe someday."

He hugged her tighter. "That's good enough for me. And whenever *someday* comes . . ." He reached into his pocket and pulled out a small velvet box. "I'm ready."

Ava's eyes went wide and her hand flew to her mouth. "Is that a—"

He nodded.

"When did you—"

"A month ago. Of course, the one time I didn't have it on me, I accidentally proposed." He grimaced.

When she reached for the box, he tsked and held it away, fighting back a grin. "You get it when you say yes. Not *maybe*."

Ava sputtered out a laugh. "I don't even get to see it?"

"No."

"How do I know there's a ring in there? It could be empty."

He appeared to be considering her question, then, quick as a wink, he opened and shut the box. Too fast for her to see any details, but enough for her to note the flash of gold and sparkle inside.

There *was* a ring. He wasn't bluffing.

Holy shit.

"Don't feel pressured," he warned. "Just because I always want more doesn't mean I'm not happy or that you aren't giving enough. You'll never be too much or too little for me, Ava."

Her eyes stung. She'd never realized just how much she'd needed to hear that from someone. To *feel* that. To rest easy in the knowledge that she didn't have to be perfect to be loved.

"I love you," she whispered.

His smile softened and he set their drinks aside on a high table, taking her in his arms. "Say it again."

"I love you."

"One more time."

She melted against him. "I love you."

He kissed her, long, slow, and all-consuming. Just the way she liked. He shifted back just enough to breathe, "I love you, too," against her lips.

Behind them, someone muttered, "They're next."

Ava turned her head to grin at Titi Nereida. "Maybe."

But she knew, deep down, that the answer was *yes*.

Epilogue

Next Year

How's the drama program coming along?" Jasmine asked.

"Really well," Ava replied, shaking the ice in her lemonade. She and Roman had spent the past two months in Europe, and Ava had a lot to catch up on with her cousins. While away, they'd worked remotely—Roman on Casa Donato, and Ava on building a nonprofit to pair public schools in the outer boroughs with Broadway actors for in-class drama workshops. "We're about to start a four-week summer camp and we're all set to launch in the new school year."

"That's fantastic," Jasmine said, as Michelle came over to join them. They all winced at Yadiel's ear-splitting scream as Gabe tossed him into the pool.

They were gathered in the backyard of Roman's house in Los Angeles—or rather, Ava's house. For someone who'd struggled to feel at home anywhere, it was taking some time for her to get used to the idea that all of Roman's homes were now hers, too.

Jasmine opened her mouth to speak, then her eyes went round. "Is that a *ring*?"

"Oh my god, you did it." Michelle snatched up Ava's left hand. "You eloped!"

"While we were in Europe," Ava said, blushing, as she told her cousins how it happened.

One night, when she and Roman were in Paris, Ava had turned to him as they were walking back to their hotel from dinner, and said, "I'm ready."

Roman dropped to one knee then and there, to the delight of the patrons at the sidewalk cafe beside them.

"Is that a yes?" he'd asked.

Tears sprang to her eyes as she'd nodded. "It's a yes."

As promised, he finally showed her the ring, but only as he was sliding it on her finger. Except Ava couldn't look away from his face, at the open vulnerability that had drawn her in from the moment they'd first met.

"I love you so much," she whispered as tears spilled down her cheeks. "I'll never be able to say it enough."

She'd pulled him to his feet and kissed him, and the by-standers broke into applause. Getting engaged on a street in Paris was horribly cliché and, hopeless romantic that she was, Ava loved every bit.

Alas, it was impossible for them to elope in France, so they'd flown to Italy, where Roman went to the embassy to initiate the necessary documentation for a civil ceremony. The man's ability to handle paperwork was a real turn-on.

Their witnesses were the older Italian couple who owned the florist where Ava bought her bouquet. The wife, impressed by Ava's creative vision and knowledge of flower arranging, had invited them to dinner. Roman hit it off with the husband, who'd grown up on a vineyard.

Ava donned the same white dress she'd worn the night Roman declared his love for her on the patio in Puerto Rico. Roman wore a plain black suit. He got a haircut and shave for the occasion and looked unbearably dashing.

For the ceremony, they used the typical vows—Ava knew better than anyone that actions were what really mattered, and Roman showed her every day that he loved and cherished her.

Their wedding had been simple and spontaneous.

In a word, *perfect.*

"I'm shocked Roman didn't go for something humongous and flashy." Michelle turned Ava's hand side to side and admired the classically beautiful but ethically sourced brilliant-cut diamond rings.

Ava gave a short laugh. "Believe me, he wanted to."

"This is much more you," Jasmine said, smiling.

"Are you upset that you weren't there?" Once upon a time, Ava would've been too scared to voice the question. Now, she just asked. And god, it was *so* much easier.

Jasmine shook her head. "Ashton still says we should've eloped. And while I loved our wedding—thanks, in large part, to you and Roman—sometimes I wonder if he was right."

"This was the only way you could do it on your own terms," Michelle said. "You know how our family gets about weddings."

"Do I ever," Ava muttered. But any bitterness that might have once accompanied the words was gone. She could look back and recognize how each step she'd taken had led her to this point. Without those experiences, she wouldn't have the context to appreciate her life as it currently was.

Perfectly imperfect. Or imperfectly perfect. Whichever one.

Michelle glanced at Ava's midsection. "Not to be a chismosa, but . . . any other news you'd like to share with the class?"

Not yet, Ava thought.

All she said was, "We'll see."

Next Year

"You did it," Roman whispered to Ava, leaning down to kiss her forehead where she rested against the pillow.

She beamed at the baby nestled in Roman's arms, love shining in her eyes. "*We* did it."

He shook his head. "I didn't do anything. You're the superhero."

"You were here," she said simply, and the impact of those words sank into his very bones.

Roman gazed down at his daughter's beautiful, precious, extremely squished little face. Then he looked to his strong, stunning, and compassionate wife. In his heart, he recited a promise.

I'll be here. For as much and as long as I'm able, I'll be here.

When the concept had first been introduced to him, it had seemed *too simple* and *not enough*. Now he knew better. His own father hadn't done it, but he'd learned from others, like Keith and Ashton, that nothing was certain, and being *there* for your family, in all senses of the word, was more valuable than gold.

Once, he'd been driven by the urge for *more more more*. And while he didn't regret it, he was so fucking glad he'd gotten his priorities in order before it was too late.

When the baby shifted in her blanket, Roman settled her back on her mother's chest and marveled at the way his entire world sat right here in front of him. He stroked his wife's curls away from her face and joined her in staring at this perfect little being they'd created. His ribs felt like they would burst, unable to contain all the love and happiness welling up inside.

"Welcome to the world, Isabella Benita Vázquez," Ava whispered. "We love you so much."

Next Year

"It's a good script," Roman said. These days he held meetings in his living room instead of a boardroom, but he still got right to the point.

"Yeah?" Gabe rubbed the back of his neck. He looked pleased, but also slightly embarrassed. "I mean, I took a couple classes, but screenplays are a whole different—"

"You're a writer, Gabe. Get used to it." Ashton set down their drinks and moved a stuffed rabbit off the armchair before he sat.

"Still feels weird," Gabe muttered, grabbing his seltzer and settling back on the sofa.

"Not just a writer." Roman flashed Gabe a teasing grin. "The *New York Times* bestselling author of *Destiny's Downfall*."

Gabe dipped his fingertips into his glass and flicked the droplets at Roman.

"We're really doing this?" Ashton directed the question to Roman.

"It's a bit late to be asking that now."

Ashton snorted. "I've been in this industry long enough to know nothing is set in stone."

"Look, I didn't create a whole ass production company for you to treat this like some rich man's whim."

Ashton smirked. "Isn't it?"

Roman sighed. His friend had him there. After stepping back from the hotels, Roman had thrown himself into expanding Casa Donato's profile while maintaining the small business vibe that made it special. Easier said than done, but it was now one of the premiere rums in the world, with a number of lucrative partnerships and distribution deals. The company's worth had skyrocketed from where it was when he'd bought it. But instead of getting caught up in the minutiae like he had with the hotels, he'd promoted a strong team to manage the continued growth and devoted all his attention to fatherhood.

He fucking loved being a dad. Even the hard parts. And he absolutely adored watching Ava be a mom. She was incredible, as he'd known she would be, and he did everything he could to make his girls' lives as effortless as possible.

But Isa was a year old now and she had five grandparent figures—Dulce, Ignacio, Patricia, Miguel, and Olympia—who all wanted to spend time with her. Ava was expanding her theater program to more schools, and as much as she told him to relax, Roman didn't like sitting still.

Then Ashton and Gabe had come to him with a business proposition, and Roman's instincts for a good deal had sparked. Now the three of them were the owners of Los Primos production company. Ashton had proven his worth as a celebrity spokesperson for Casa Donato—especially after his Oscar win. And without Gabe, Roman never would have finished writing his own book—*Building an Empire: Roman's Rules for Success*. Roman secretly hated the title, but the book had been an instant nonfiction bestseller, so what the hell did he know. Gabe's fantasy series was the first project optioned by Los Primos, and Michelle, whose marketing and consulting company was highly sought after by film studios, had already agreed to help craft the pitch—for a fee, of course.

Bottom line, the production company wasn't a whim to Roman. He loved these guys like they were his brothers, and what was more, he liked working with them.

"Let's make it happen," he said, rubbing his hands together. "Who do I need to schmooze?"

Next Year

The Primas held their annual holiday celebration a week before Christmas at Ava and Roman's house in the Hamptons. Snow glittered over the lawn, and inside, a gas fire flickered in the baby-proofed fireplace. The aromas of coconut, cinnamon, and Casa Donato rum competed with the scents of pine and gingerbread. Ava watched the proceedings as she made coquito at the kitchen counter.

Ashton sat on the rug with Isabella, building what looked like a gothic cathedral with her colorful magnetic tiles. Sinvergüenza the stuffed dog sat beside them, never far from Isa. Michelle, Gabe, and Yadiel were playing Super Smash Bros., which seemed to involve a lot of trash talking. Roman was cuddling Renee Rodriguez Suarez against his chest and singing a Spanish nursery rhyme. Jasmine and Ashton's infant daughter rewarded him with a sweet, gummy smile.

Jasmine joined Ava at the counter and snagged a gingerbread cookie from the festive plate.

"Oh, come on!" Yadi exclaimed, his jaw hanging open as he glared at Michelle. "How do you keep winning? You're *old*."

"Not older than Nintendo," she quipped. Spotting Jasmine and Ava, Michelle got up from the sofa. "I'm out. Have fun kicking Gabe's ass for a while."

Gabe rolled his eyes, but gamely started another round.

"Yadi, Isa, and Renee," Michelle said, coming to stand next to her cousins. "The next generation of the Primas of Power?"

Ava unplugged the immersion blender. "They'll have to come up with their own name. That one's taken."

Jasmine sighed as she polished off her cookie. "How do you manage the fear?" she asked, her eyes on Roman and Renee.

"Of what?" Ava asked. "Dropping her?"

Jasmine scoffed. "No, I'm over that. Renee's pretty sturdy by now. I meant the fear of . . . fucking up?"

"You're afraid of the kids turning out like us?" Michelle asked wryly.

"Exactly!" Jasmine sounded anguished.

Ava considered the question seriously. "Well, that's partly why we're in therapy, right? We'll probably mess them up in other ways, but god willing, they won't make our same mistakes."

"They'll make their own." Michelle's voice was uncharacteristically gentle. "And when they do, they'll tell you about it, because they know you'll love them anyway."

Ava's heart twisted at Michelle's astute observation. It had been difficult, but learning to love herself through her own mistakes was the only way Ava could teach her daughter that it was okay to be flawed, to be imperfect, to be *human*. To show her that letting people in led to growth, and that having healthy boundaries could be empowering.

And most importantly, that opening yourself to love in its myriad forms was worth the risk.

Ava glanced at the framed photos on the living room wall. This past Halloween, she, Jasmine, and Michelle had re-created their Primas of Power picture. The new photo, matted next to the original, showed the three of them sitting on the steps of the deck just beyond the kitchen sliding door.

Jasmine stood on the middle step, dressed as Wonder Woman with her fists planted on her hips. Michelle was Supergirl, balanced on one leg on the top step. And Ava, in a Batgirl costume at the bottom of the steps, had her mouth open in a battle cry and her leg extended, high-kicking the air. It was what she'd wanted to do when she was five, but "Smile for the camera!" had already been deeply ingrained, and she hadn't been able to do otherwise.

Now, she only smiled when she wanted to—which was still a lot, thanks to sheer happiness, but it was genuine. No more Resting Pleasant Face.

With the coquito done, Ava poured three tumblers and sprinkled freshly ground cinnamon on top. She kept one for herself and passed the other two to Jasmine and Michelle. They met each other's eyes as they clinked glasses and whispered, "Primas of Power forever!" in unison.

After the first sip, Michelle closed her eyes in appreciation. "Sorry, Abuela, but Ava still makes the best coquito in the Rodriguez family."

Smiling, Ava inhaled the comforting scents of coconut and

holiday spices before taking another sip. "I had a solid foundation to build on."

Like Isa forming towers with her magnetic tiles, Ava had been given the building blocks of family and tradition, but it had been up to her to expand on it, crafting a life that was all her own.

She looked to her cousins on either side of her. So much had changed in the last few years, but as they'd navigated the shifts with open communication, their bond had remained a constant, and was stronger than ever. They were creating their own traditions now.

On the sofa, Yadi cheered and Gabe grumbled. Michelle strolled over to listen to the teenager gloat. Renee started to fuss, so Roman passed her to Ashton. Spotting her father, Isa held out her hands and said, "Up, Papi." Roman scooped her into his arms and carried her over to Ava while Jasmine went to prep Renee's bottle.

Ava handed Roman the glass of coquito to try.

He took a sip and grinned. "I knew you'd make a killer coquito."

She shook her head at him. "You say that every Christmas."

"It's a tradition."

"Me too?" Isa reached for the glass.

"This one is yours, sweetheart." Ava handed the toddler a sippy cup of milk and Isa sucked it down happily.

Holding their daughter in one arm, Roman slipped the other around Ava's waist and dropped a soft kiss on her lips. He tasted like cinnamon and rum.

Here was her other constant. Not just his love, but his patience and his presence. The best kind of happily-ever-after.

"Are you happy, mi amor?" he asked, and she smiled.

"Incandescently."

He grinned at the reference to their shared comfort movie and kissed her again.

Their life wasn't perfect. But it didn't need to be. It was *theirs*.

And that was more than enough.

Acknowledgments

And with that, the Primas of Power have reached their conclusion.

This moment is bittersweet; I am so thrilled to have completed the trilogy and brought Ava, Michelle, and Jasmine their happily-ever-afters, but I'm also sad to say goodbye to them and to the Rodriguez family.

To my readers, I thank you for your patience as you waited for Ava's story to arrive. I hope you agree that she got the happy ending she deserved. And if you just found me and the Primas with this book, I hope you'll check out Jasmine's and Michelle's stories as well.

As always, I have a number of people to thank for helping me bring *Along Came Amor* into the world . . .

First and foremost, Elle Keck, who held my hand through the process of developing this story, when I started from the beginning not once, not twice, but three times. Thank you for your kindness and for being such an incredible champion of this series.

Next, Erika Tsang, who took the reins on this project during one of the most difficult times of my life and guided me with compassion and care.

And finally, Ariana Sinclair, whose editorial insight and management ushered this book over the finish line and into readers' hands.

As well as the rest of my team at Avon/HarperCollins—thank you all!

Then there's Sarah E. Younger, the best and most supportive agent anyone could hope for. I appreciate you more than I could ever fit into the acknowledgments page of any book!

Bo-Feng Lin, who provided the beautiful cover illustrations for this series. Having your art grace these books has literally been a dream come true, and I can't thank you enough for agreeing to be part of this journey.

Elsie Lyons, cover designer extraordinaire, who created a stunning and cohesive visual design for the series. I couldn't be happier with how they all turned out.

Joel Holland, whose stylish hand-written typography has completed the look of all three covers!

My LEO PR publicity team, Kristin Dwyer, Molly Mitchell, and Jessica Brock, who keep the promo machine (and me!) running smoothly.

Adriana and Zoraida, there would be no book without you two. Tracey, Mia, and Priscilla, my cheerleaders and sounding boards.

Ana Canino Fluit and Jen Prokop, who saw Ava so clearly in the early stages and who helped me see her more clearly too.

Kate Brauning, the most incredible writing coach an author could ask for, who has supported me throughout the series and without whom this book would not exist. Truly.

My friends on Rebelle Island, for the accountability, encouragement, and love.

The doctors and nurses at Mount Sinai West, who cared for me during an extremely harrowing experience.

My family—my child, my partner, my parents, and my in-laws. There is not enough I can say here to convey how much I love and appreciate you all. Thank you for everything.

The series might be over, but you can keep in touch with me via my author newsletter. I send monthly updates and exclusive subscribers-only content: alexisdaria.com/newsletter.

ALEXIS DARIA is the award-winning and internationally bestselling author of *You Had Me at Hola*, *A Lot Like Adiós*, *Take the Lead*, and more. Her books have been featured on several "Best of" lists and have received starred reviews from multiple trade publications. A former visual artist, Alexis is a lifelong New Yorker who loves Broadway musicals and pizza.